AIR DUEL!

The solution called for a short match. Hawk Hunter watched the Flanker reach its take-off point, and as soon as its wheels left the runway, he gunned the Mirage. The Flanker was bigger than his French flying outhouse. The only advantage Hunter had was his quicker take-off speed.

But now the Flanker had done a quick twist and was heading back toward him. The pirate was intent on shooting Hunter even before the Mirage could take off.

"OK, jerk," Hunter said. "You've just solved my problem for me."

Hunter wasn't even airborne when he launched the missile — he had simply raised the nose of the Mirage and fired the damn thing. It came off his wing with surprising smoothness, and impacted on the Flanker's nose cone. An instant later the Soviet jet's filled-to-capacity fuel load ignited and obliterated the airplane.

End of duel.

WINGMAN

HE IS THE LAST HOPE OF A RAVAGED AMERICA!
THUNDER IN THE EAST
BY MACK MALONEY

ZEBRA BOOKS
KENSINGTON PUBLISHING CORP.

ZEBRA BOOKS

are published by

Kensington Publishing Corp.
475 Park Avenue South
New York, NY 10016

First printing: September, 1988

Printed in the United States of America

PROLOGUE

Three years had passed since the United States lost World War III . . .

Although the Americans were the victors in the great battles of the War, they ended up the losers in the deception that followed the ceasefire. After arranging for the assassination of the President and his Cabinet, the traitorous US vice president allowed the country's defenses to drop long enough to permit a flood of Soviet missiles to obliterate the American ICBM force while it was still in the ground. This sneak attack left the center of the country—from the Dakotas down to Oklahoma—completely devastated. Now a nightmare swath of neutron radiation, these Badlands effectively cut the once-great country in two.

The "peace" that followed was dictated from Moscow. Called "The New Order," it mandated that America be divided into dozens of small countries and free territories. All references to the "old days" were prohibited. Now it was against the law to carry an American flag or even utter the words "United States of America."

Still reeling from their battlefield defeats during the war, the Soviets had a great interest in keeping this New Order America fractionalized and unstable. Through their agents and terrorist allies—and sometimes by direct intervention—their devious plans guaranteed that America would be constantly at war with itself. Early conflicts involved the leaders of the murderous Mid-Atlantic States—the hated Mid-Aks—trying to wrest control of the entire East Coast. Later battles involved the criminal elements now operating in New Chicago in an attempt to take over the free-wheeling but democratic independent state of Football City, formerly known as St. Louis.

In both cases, Hawk Hunter, the fighter pilot hero know as The Wingman, rallied the democratic forces and directed the defeat of the Soviet-sponsored aggressors.

But these victories for the forces of Freedom only led to an even greater conflict, known as The Circle War. A deranged Soviet KGB agent named Viktor Robotov managed to invade America from within—arming himself with thousands of Russian surface-to-air missiles. Only through much cunning and bloodletting did Hunter and the democratic forces defeat Viktor's Soviet-led Circle Army at the Battle of Platte River.

When Viktor escaped to the Middle East, Hunter followed, determined to bring him back to America to stand trial for his crimes. Yet soon after arriving in the Mediterranean, Hunter found that another war—actually a continuation of World War III—was about to erupt in the area, ignited by a lunatic named Lucifer. As it turned out, Viktor and Lucifer were one and the same. Hunter helped a valiant group of British RAF pilots and mercenaries salvage the abandoned nuclear aircraft carrier the *USS Saratoga,* tow it through the Med and preempt the war by stopping Lucifer's Soviet-controlled force at the Suez Canal. This adventure, known to all as The Lucifer Crusade, ended with a confrontation in the Arabian desert between Hunter and Lucifer/Viktor. Squared off in this man-to-man battle between Good and Evil, an assassin's bullet, fired by a mysterious character dressed in Nazi garb, took Viktor's life and robbed Hunter of the chance of bringing the madman back to pay for his crimes.

But while Hunter was pursuing Viktor across the Mideast, and in the months that followed, another great war was brewing in America . . .

PART ONE

CHAPTER 1

"They say the perfect football game is when neither team moves from the fifty-yard line," General Dave Jones, commander of the Western Forces, told the room full of military officers. "The offense perfectly offsets the defense and vice versa.

"That's the position we are still in today . . ."

A winter had passed since the Western Forces defeated the Soviet-backed Circle Army at the battle of the Platte River. The battered enemy had withdrawn back across the radioactive no man's land called the Badlands and into the only city they controlled on the western side of the Mississippi. This was Football City, formerly known as St. Louis.

Now the Western Forces—an alliance of democratic armies and militias joined together to rid the American continent of the Circle Army—were preparing to take the offensive.

Jones walked to the front of the Planning Room and unveiled a huge map. At its center was Football City. Blue flags to the north, west and south indicated the positions of Western Forces deployed around the Circle stronghold.

"I'm happy to report that we've solidified our positions to the north," Jones said. "We're now anchored here at Spanish Lake, thanks to the arrival three days ago of the Free Canadian volunteers.

"Now to the south, the Fourth Texas Armored Brigade has dug in here at Tesson Ferry. And of course, our major deployment—the Pacific Americans and the Football City Army—hold the strong line between them in the west.

"So you can see, we've got them sewn in on three sides, with our line roughly paralleling the old Route Two-seventy . . ."

"So when do we attack?" one of the newly-arrived Republic of Texas Army officers asked.

"Not any time soon," Jones answered.

"But why not?" the Texan followed up. "We've got them outnumbered at least two-to-one in manpower—and a lot of their guys are just hired hands, mercenaries or whatever. We've got more airlift than they have. Also we have four squadrons of fighters to their one and a half."

Jones shook his head. The Texan's unit had just arrived and the man wasn't totally up to date on the situation within Football City.

"All of this is true," Jones replied. "And I'm glad to see that nothing has diminished the fighting spirit of Texas. But any military training course will tell you that an offensive force attacking set defensive positions needs at least a four-to-one advantage for a successful outcome.

"We don't have those kinds of numbers and I can't risk the heavy loss of life that would result if we

12

jumped off any time soon."

Jones looked around the room. All of the Western Forces' top representatives were there: Louie St. Louie, the man who transformed the moribund post-war city of St. Louis into the fabulously hedonistic Football City, only to see it nearly destroyed in two successive wars. Mike Fitzgerald, the former Air Force pilot who transformed the municipal airport at Syracuse, New York, into the wild and wooly aircraft repair stop known as the Aerodrome. His territory too was still under Circle control.

Also on hand was Marine Captain "Bull" Dozer, the commanding officer of the famous 7th Cavalry, a near-legendary group of free-lance democratic fighters. Seated next to him was Major Frost, the Free Canadian Air Force pilot who was the unofficial go-between for the large "neutral" free nation to the north. Ben Wa and J.T. Twomey, who like Jones were former US Air Force Thunderbird pilots, were also there, as were a host of other commanders of the many free-lance armies and militias who had joined forces with the Westerners.

"As you know, we spent the entire winter planning for this campaign," Jones told them. "We agreed that the only way we'll be able to accomplish our objective is to play it smart. Up to now The Circle has been the one always on the attack. They're an offensive-minded army. Now, we've got to trick them into playing defense, something they don't do very well.

"But this doesn't mean we ignore the fundamental strategies of war. It gets back to that perfect football game. If the offense and defense exactly complement each other, no one is going anywhere. We have to wait to build up our forces."

13

A silence descended upon the room. Jones knew they were all anxious to take their measure of the Circle Army. But there was one more reason that demanded they move cautiously.

"We have to remember another thing," Jones continued. "The enemy is holding nearly ten thousand POWs, both military and civilian, inside Football City. We have to consider these people as hostages. We have good reason to believe that if we attacked The Circle now, they would start slaughtering those prisoners. And I won't allow that to happen . . ."

Yet the Texan persisted.

"But General," he said in a thick drawl. "Taking Football City is just one of many things we have to do, if we are going to solve our larger . . . problem."

Even the feisty Texan couldn't bring himself to say it. Yet everyone in the room knew what he was talking about.

"The Problem" was that the Westerners had information that a large invasion force was being put together in Scandinavia by the Soviets. Once assembled, this force—which was made up of terrorist armies and mercenary forces—was to be put on ships and sent to invade the east coast of the American continent, linking up with the weakened Circle Army and cementing the Soviet hold on the eastern half of America. Thus the overall and very ambitious goal of the Western Forces was to gain control of certain key cities and strategic positions in the east, thereby hoping that the invaders-for-hire would reconsider before attempting a landing.

It was a desperate campaign for the Westerners, one that already had all the earmarks of a noble failure. Yet Jones knew that did not deter anyone

14

sitting in the Planning Room.

They are brave Americans, one and all, he thought.

"True, we cannot solve the Big Problem until we deal with a host of smaller ones," Jones said. "But we also cannot let ourselves become over-anxious. Our overall war plan is risky as it is. We can't let our impatience hinder it.

"So we will continue our present strategy of siege against Football City. That includes our daily surgical air strikes and our regular shelling. Only when the rest of our reserves come in from the west coast and our further 'volunteers' from Free Canada arrive, will we start planning an all-out attack on Football City."

"And when will that be?" the Texan asked.

"Possibly another month," Jones answered. "In the meantime we are working on things inside the city. There is a small but effective underground that is helping us. As you all know, we also have a large group of fifth columnists working within the city even now as we speak."

The big Texan shook his head.

"But what good are these people doing, working inside?" he asked. "You said it yourself, General. The only way is to hit The Circle head-on. Attack 'em. Bomb the the living crap out of them. Open up all our big guns, then go in. Invade the city and get it the hell over with . . ."

Jones tried to stay calm, but he was quickly losing patience with the man.

"I said we have to stay smart," Jones replied sternly. "And I repeat that we have ten thousand prisoners being held inside that city. Those people will be massacred if we act harshly."

15

the Texan was up on his feet. "But by that line of reasoning, they're going to get killed no matter when we invade, so I say do it now!"

Once again, Jones took a deep breath and fought the temptation to lash out at the man. The Texans were good friends and superior soldiers. He didn't want to open up a rift with them now.

"My hope is," the small wiry general said in measured tones, "that by the time the rest of our troops arrive, our efforts inside the city will force the crackpot in charge of the Circle garrison there to see the light. Who knows? He may even pull out of the city altogether . . ."

"But that's no better for us," The Texan shouted. "If we don't fight them here, we'll have to fight them somewhere along the way to the east coast."

That was it—the breaking point for Jones. "Don't you think I know that?" he angrily shouted back at the man. "But there are brave men of ours risking their lives right now in that city, while we sit back here and discuss the finer points of warfare. They're doing everything from organizing the underground to directing our air strikes . . .

"We have to give these men time. Time to reconnoiter and identify strong points we'll have to destroy when we do invade. Time to come up with an escape route for the POWs when we do attack. These things are important to our larger goal. We just cannot risk being hasty at this very important juncture."

The Texan fell silent. A murmur went around the room. The majority of those assembled knew that these were tough decisions and that the burden of making them fell entirely on the shoulders of General Dave Jones.

But for his part, Jones just hoped that his fifth columnists were still alive and safe within the city . . .

CHAPTER 2

The two A-4 Skyhawks roared in without warning . . .

They passed low over the downtown section of Football City, their engines unleashing an unearthly scream, which shook buildings and people alike. The sun had just set and the devil-may-care activity of the the city was just starting to warm up. But now the bright lights and music of the gambling casinos and whorehouses were replaced by an immediate blackout and the wail of air raid sirens.

A scattering of anti-aircraft fire followed the A-4s as they pulled up and turned east, away from the heart of downtown. Major Tomm, the man in charge of the Circle's AA battalion, watched the two jets from the top of the circle headquarters, the former Federal Building just blocks from downtown.

"Goddamn Skyhawks are loaded with ECM," he cursed to his lieutenant as they watched two SA-7 surface-to-air missiles rise up from the city limits only to career away from the streaking jets and fall harmlessly into the Mississippi. "It's like those bastards know where every one of our SAMs is located."

He would never know just how close he was to the truth . . .

Tomm put his NightScope spyglasses back up to his eyes and zeroed in on the lead Skyhawk. Underneath its belly he could see a single bomb—a laser-guided AGM-65 Maverick air-to-surface missile. On the front of the airplane was the unmistakable nub of a AAS-35 laser tracking pod, the electronic brains which would direct the Maverick to its target.

As Tomm watched, the first Skyhawk banked, then roared in on a gasoline truck farm down near the river dock works. When the airplane was about a mile away from the target, he saw a puff of smoke spit out from under its fuselage. The Maverick had launched.

"Damn, he's got a lock on the gas trucks," he said.

The missile uncannily went through a set of gyrations before finally slamming into the first of six gas trucks parked in a line. All the while AA fire and SAMs were being launched at the attackers, but to utterly no effect.

The gasoline trucks exploded in a frenzy of blue and green flames. Then the second Skyhawk swooped in, and mimicking its flight leader, unleashed another precision-guided Maverick, which impacted on the control house for the truck farm.

"Jesus, another direct hit!" Tomm's lieutenant cried out in dismay. "How the hell do these guys *always* hit their targets? I know they're good, but no one is that *fucking* good!"

"They are if they've got a laser target designator working somewhere in the city," Tomm said in disgust. He knew the enemy's Maverick strikes were so accurate because the missile was capable of following a laser beam being bounced off the prescribed target. This meant the pilots were getting inside help—someone within Football City, probably atop one of its highest buildings, was shooting the laser beam at the targets, allowing the Mavericks to home in exactly every time. The Circle Army had been searching for the "trigger man" for weeks, but whoever it was, was simply too smart for them and had evaded capture every time.

"Just one more of our problems . . ." Tomm said to his subordinate as the Skyhawks streaked off to the west and disappeared unscathed over the horizon.

CHAPTER 3

Navy Lieutenant Stan Yastrewski—known as "Yaz" to his friends—stopped shoveling just long enough to clean the dirt out of his bleeding hand calluses.

His back was aching and he was filthy from head to toe. His neck was stiff, he was thirsty and the last thing he had had to eat was a small bowl of soup the night before. Now, his hands were bleeding so badly the shovel was sticking to his fingers.

Suddenly, a Circle Army guard came up behind him and poked his ribs with the barrel of his AK-47 assault rifle.

"Get back to work," the soldier told him gruffly, jabbing him again with the snout of the Soviet-made weapon.

How the hell did I get here? Yaz asked himself for the umpteenth time. In an instant he replayed the series of rather incredible events that took him from a hospital on the Mediterranean island of

21

Malta to digging in the goddamn "Hole" in the middle of Football City. Shit, the last time he had been in the states, this place was called St. Louis.

During the first battles of World War III, Yaz was an officer aboard the U.S. nuclear submarine, *USS Albany.* The boat went down off Ireland, but many of the hands were able to make it to shore. Eventually, he and some of the survivors got organized and went over to Britain after the war cooled down, finding work as technicians. Later on, they moved to Algiers where they were hired by some British RAF officers to help tow an aircraft carrier across the Mediterranean to the Suez Canal in order to thwart an attempt by the infamous world terrorist Viktor to invade the area and revive the World War.

The valiant adventure succeeded in delaying Viktor's armies at the Suez chokepoint long enough for the European democratic forces, known as the Modern Knights, to engage and destroy most of the enemy force. In the course of the early fighting, the carrier was sunk and Yaz, blown off its deck in an explosion, was later found by friendly forces and eventually taken to Malta where he spent three months recovering from his wounds.

Mixed up in all this was an American fighter pilot named Hawk Hunter. He was well-known, both in America and around the globe, as being the best fighter pilot in the post-war world. He had been convinced by the Brits to coordinate air operations off the carrier and he had led the air battle in the canal until taking off in pursuit of Viktor. While recovering in Malta, Yaz heard that

22

Hunter had caught up with the super-terrorist shortly after the battle in the canal and that the terrorist wound up dead. Exactly what happened to Hunter was unclear. Many people in the Med claimed that he too was killed along with Viktor. Others said Hunter had returned to America, where it was rumored that another great war was brewing between the democratic Western Forces and the Soviet-backed Circle Army of the east.

Those rumors proved correct—much to Yaz's dismay . . .

As soon as he recovered from his wounds, Yaz caught a flight from Malta to the near-abandoned airport at Casablanca. From there, he was given a seat on a free-lance Swedish C-130 gunship that was flying to America to look for work. But the gunship was jumped by MiGs near the coast of Cuba, and crash-landed off the beach at Guantanamo Bay. Captured by the communist Cubans, Yaz spent some time in jail and then was sold as a slave laborer to the Circle Army, who now had a tenuous hold on Football City.

It was a long, crazy story, unbelievable to him even though he had lived it. Ever since the end of the Big War, Yaz had dreamed of returning to America. Now that he was here, he longed for the hot, smelly days of Algiers . . .

Now he was part of a work crew—some 2000 strong—that was digging The Hole. Nearby were the handful of bridges that had all but been destroyed in a massive war between Football City and the Soviet-backed Family Army, out of New Chicago. These spans had suddenly become very important to the Circle troops occupying the city and their engineers were in the process of rebuilding most of them. Some said the Circle wanted the bridges rebuilt in order to reenforce the city against attack from the Western Forces to the west. Others said the Circle needed the bridges intact so as to insure their own escape route out of the city.

As for "The Hole," no one had yet explained to the prisoners why they were digging it. In fact, it wasn't a hole at all. It was more like a cave, with a large wooden door at one end. But it had become more than their home—it was their universe. They worked in The Hole during the day and slept there at night. The Circle guards simply locked them in every sunset and opened it up at sunrise for another full day of endless digging. All the while the cave got bigger. But at quite a cost. Many of the POWs were ill and every night a few would die, exhausted from the 16 hours of hard labor. It all seemed so futile, pointless and useless. What was even odder, Yaz had heard that The Circle was making four other POW groups dig similar holes around the city.

The Circle soldier shoved him once again, and Yaz had no choice but to resume digging.

His line of about two hundred slave laborers, chained at the feet, stretched out of the tunnel and up to the huge wooden door. The soldier routinely walked along poking every third or fourth man in the ribs. It was only about nine in the morning, yet Yaz and the others had been at it for three hours already. There had been no breakfast, no water.

Just then Yaz heard a commotion down the line a way. The guard had grabbed one of the laborers by the scruff of his neck and was questioning him intensely.

"Where the hell did you get this?" the soldier shouted at the man, poking him in his stomach with the butt of his AK-47.

"I found it, over there," the prisoner answered, terrified. "I was just going to use it . . . to sleep on."

The object in contention was a simple, uninflated inner tube.

Three more guards showed up. "Show me where you found it," the soldier ordered the man.

As the rest of the work gang watched, the prisoner was unhooked from his chains and led the guards to a spot off to the side of the huge cavern.

"In there," the man said, pointing to a hole in the dirt floor. "There's a bunch of them."

One of the guards jumped into the cavity and soon was passing up dozens of neatly-folded inner tubes.

The first guard inspected several of the tubes. "Where the hell could these have come from?" he asked.

"Left over from before the war I guess," one of his companions answered. "But the captain will go apeshit if he knew these scumheads were using them to sleep on."

The last of the tubes were recovered. "Take them all up to the end of the tunnel and burn them," the first guard said.

His companions did as told and Yaz went back to his shoveling. Compared to the dirty blanket he now slept on, he thought sleeping on an inflated inner tube would be like heaven . . .

Several hours passed, when Yaz felt another poke in his ribs.

"You . . . Go up to the entrance way," the guard told him. "Help the others carry down the chow."

"Yah, sir, massah . . ." Yaz said under his breath as the man unhooked his leg irons. Actually, he was thankful for the opportunity to get away from the monotonous shoveling, even for a short while.

He slowly made his way past the work gang and up to the front end of The Hole. Ten other laborers were waiting there.

"Ah, fresh oxygen . . ." he whispered as he breathed in his first taste of outside air in two weeks. The sun was out but it wasn't too hot. A quarter mile away was the Mississippi and even its muddy water looked inviting.

An old Ryder Rent-A-Truck pulled up to the mouth of the tunnel and two men, both of them wearing sunglasses and white coveralls, got out. They were POW trusties, prisoners allowed to perform more than menial tasks.

"You guys here for the food?" one asked.

Yaz and the others nodded. They went around to the side of the vehicle, opened its folding door to reveal ten pots filled with steaming soup. The drivers climbed up into the truck.

But the pots were hot and they needed help.

"Climb up here and give us a hand," one of the drivers told Yaz.

He climbed up into the truck and the three of them grabbed the first steaming pot and painfully lowered it to the ground.

"This is ridiculous," one trusty said. "We need a winch."

The second and third pots were worse.

Just then Yaz spotted a crowbar at the back of the truck sitting on top of a pile of cardboard boxes.

"Here, use this," he said, walking to retrieve the tool. But as he did so, he noticed that the top of one of the cardboard boxes was open. He glanced inside.

It was filled with neatly-folded inner tubes . . .

Suddenly, one of the drivers came up from behind and had his hands around Yaz's throat.

"That was a big mistake, mister," the man said. "You just looked somewhere you shouldn't have . . ."

Yaz was just about gagging from the man's stranglehold. The driver spun him around, and for the first time, Yaz got a good look at the other trusty without his sunglasses.

Oddly, the man looked familiar . . .

"I . . . know . . . you," Yaz was able to say, his words a gurgle.

The man stared at him, as if he'd seen Yaz before, too.

"Let him go," he told his partner.

Released from the chokehold, Yaz and the man stared at each other for a moment, trying to figure out where they had seen each other before.

"You're a pilot," Yaz said suddenly, as if the thought had magically appeared in his brain. "Back at Suez . . . you helped pull me from the water . . ."

The man looked at him closely and started shaking his head.

"Your name . . ." Yaz continued. "It's . . . Elvis."

The man shook his head and put his sunglasses back on.

"You're nuts, mac," he said briskly. "Now get your ass in gear and get that goddamn soup out of here."

With that the man climbed out of the truck, fiddled around at the back of the truck, then disappeared.

Using the crowbar, the other driver and Yaz lowered the rest of the pots to the ground.

The job done, the truck quickly pulled away, the man who Yaz had recognized behind the wheel.

Yaz shook his head. Maybe he was mistaken, but the driver looked exactly like one of the pilots who had come to the rescue of the survivors of the aircraft carrier that had sunk during the battle of the Suez Canal. Yaz had only seen the man briefly at the time, yet his wavy, jelly-roll haircut

28

and rock star looks were unmistakable.

He shrugged it off and went to pick up his gang's soup pot. That's when he saw that something had been scribbled in the loose dirt next to where the truck had been parked.

It was a single letter and Yaz had to stare at it for a few moments before its meaning started to sink in. When it did, he immediately knew that he was right in identifying the driver.

Using the heel of his boot, the man had scratched out a large "W" in the dirt . . .

CHAPTER 4

The RF-4 Phantom reconnaissance airplane set down to a bumpy landing on Football City's cratered and only working runway.

A service crew meandered out to the jet's parking area, as the free-lance pilot climbed out and retrieved four loads of exposed film from the RF-4's nose. He carefully placed them alongside another four rolls inside a lead-lined strongbox, then jumped into a waiting jeep, which whisked him to the airport's control center.

A major of the Circle Army was waiting for the pilot as the jeep pulled up to the control center.

"How'd it look out there today?" the officer asked the flyer.

"If anything, it's worse than yesterday . . ." the pilot answered. "Let me develop the still photographs first and I'll show you."

"Hurry it up," the major told him. "The colonel

has to be in the Viceroy's chamber in exactly one hour."

The pilot went into the control center and disappeared into the photo-developing darkroom. Meanwhile, the major climbed the stairs up to his colonel's office, gulping at the thought that he had to deliver more bad news.

The free-lance photo-recon plane had just overflown the Western Forces positions that surrounded the city on three sides. In previous flights of this, the only recon airplane available to the Circle troops, its cameras had photographed as many as 10 divisions of enemy troops, apparently preparing for an all-out attack on the city.

"Almost *two hundred thousand troops*," the major grumbled to himself. "How the hell were they able to raise that many men?"

It was a question that had been nagging him—and everyone else near the top of the Circle command. It seemed that every time the RF-4 came back from a photo recon run, its film contained more and more evidence that the Western Forces were growing stronger by the day.

"More bad news, I'm afraid," the major told his superior—a colonel named Muss. "The pilot said the Westerners have increased their troop strength."

"Jesus Christ!" Muss said, standing up to consult the map of Missouri which hung on his office wall. "Where the hell are they getting the men?"

"They've got to be hiring mercenaries?" the major offered.

"*Mercenaries*, be damned!" Muss shouted. "There isn't a division of honest mercenaries around these parts that they could recruit, never mind fifty thousand of them."

"Free Canadians, maybe," the major said.

"Maybe," Muss replied. "But the Canucks know full well what would happen to them if they intervened in large numbers. They know our Soviet allies would nuke their asses if they came down in a big way."

The major shrugged. "That's if the Russians have any workable ICBMs left," he said.

Muss gave the man a cold look. "I'd avoid that kind of talk, Major," he told him.

Muss was getting nervous himself though. The Westerners had been steadily backing the Circle into a corner while at the same time building up their strength. Every day it got worse. The problem was, it was up to Muss to tell all this to the Viceroy.

And he was not a man who liked to receive bad news . . .

Viceroy Richard St. Laurant was better known, though not to his face, as "Viceroy Dick." He was the Commander-in-Chief of the Circle Troops in Football City and, in effect, governor of the city. He was of undetermined European origin, and installed by the Soviets just after the battle at the Platte River. Once again, the Sovs had picked an unusual puppet. The Viceroy was neurotic, quirky, possibly even psychotic. He had a propensity for cocaine, young girls and on-the-spot public executions of friends and foes alike. He carried on with such a regal air that he had been known to ride the streets of Football City wearing a king's robe

32

and a small gold crown and partake of the city's still burgeoning night life, followed around by an entourage of teenage girls and tough, South Afrikaner bodyguards.

Several minutes later the recon pilot came into the room, holding a half dozen still-wet photographs.

"Quick, let's see them," Muss said.

The pilot laid out the photos on the colonel's desk. Right away, Muss felt his mouth go dry.

"These vehicles you see here are elements of an armored division," the pilot said. "It moved in just overnight. I count forty-five tanks and APCs. About three dozen support trucks, and a lot of ground troops. I figure about seventy-five hundred guys in all."

"Damn . . ." Muss said under his breath.

"Saw a lot of anti-aircraft capability in place too," the pilot went on, leafing through the photographs. "Look right here. They've moved in some SA-twos and some SA-sixes."

"They must have got them in the Badlands," the major said. "Left over from the Soviet Expeditionary Force."

The major was referring to the massive Soviet infiltration that had led up to The Circle War. Over the course of many months, the Russians had placed a wall of surface-to-air missile batteries along the western edge of the Badlands, effectively ending the cross-country airborne convoys which had been the only linking factor between the east and west coasts of the continent.

"If they got mobile SAM batteries, then they're really getting serious," Muss said. "They must know we've got all of eighteen airplanes here . . ."

"And I figure they've got at least ten squadrons in the immediate area," the RF-4 pilot said. "That's not counting what the Texas Air Force looks like these days."

Muss studied each photo once again. Each one of them was worse than the one before. Encampments of Western Forces infantrymen, Football City troops, Free Canadians, along with those of the Texas Army. Convoys of fuel and provision trucks. Ammo dumps. Helicopters. Surface-to-surface rockets. And now tanks and APCs . . .

"When will the movie film be ready?" Muss asked the pilot as he gathered up the still photos.

"Give it another hour," the pilot replied. "But I'll tell you, it ain't pretty."

"Just get it developed as soon as possible," Muss barked at him. "And get ready to go up again late this afternoon."

With that, Muss quickly put on his uniform jacket and cap and left.

The major waited until Muss was out of earshot before he asked the next question.

"Any sign of, you know, an F-16 out there?" the officer asked, nearly choking with anticipation.

"You mean The Wingman?" the pilot asked.

The major hastily shook his head. "Do you think he's out there somewhere?" he asked nervously.

The recon pilot laughed. "Let me tell you something, Major," he said. "If he was out *there*, I wouldn't be *here*, talking to you. I'd be scattered on a hillside somewhere, pieces of a Sidewinder sticking out of my ass . . ."

A look of relief came over the major. At least they didn't have Hawk Hunter to worry about. Maybe the rumors that he had died over in the Middle East were true.

"But while we're on the subject, can we settle up now?" the pilot asked the major. "You guys owe me for three runs and with those SAMs showing up, it's going to be dangerous from now on."

The officer shook his head. "This afternoon," he said. "We'll pay you then."

The pilot shrugged, left the office and went back down to the photo darkroom.

After locking the door behind him, the pilot carefully took the room's wastebasket and poured a small amount of developing fluid into it. Then he took the four rolls of film he'd retrieved from his cameras that day, put them in the basket, and added another chemical, this one an industrial acid agent. The developing fluid and the acid quickly ignited and, in a smokeless flash, destroyed the never-exposed film.

After he washed the very little residue left over down the sink, he opened his lead-lined box and took out the previously exposed rolls of film, the ones he had doctored weeks ago to make it look like a massive army was waiting just over the hill. The RF-4 pilot was one of the very few people in the city who knew that the Westerners' force was much smaller than what the Circle thought it was.

It was a chess game, the pilot thought. The Westerners kept The Circle off-balance with the intentionally misleading recon photos, daily air strikes and soon, other diversions, while the Circle kept the Westerners at bay by threatening to massacre the POWs they were holding.

"No one has made a move in a while," the pilot, an undercover agent named Captain "Crunch" O'Malley, thought aloud. "That can only mean something will blow sky high soon . . ."

CHAPTER 5

Yaz wrapped himself up in his dirty blanket and tried to sleep.

It was cold, dark and damp in the vast underground cavern, The Circle guards having locked up the POWs for the night inside the dimly-lit chamber several hours before. Using the Hole as a prison was one of the few things that made some sense — by shutting the POWs up like animals, there was no need to waste Circle manpower watching over them at night.

Yaz had retreated to his own corner of cave, preferring to sleep alone, thereby assuring himself that he wouldn't wake up next to a corpse in the morning. But there were disturbing thoughts spinning around in his head that were preventing him from dropping off to sleep: The pilot named Elvis, the load of inner tubes and the big W in the dirt. *What the hell was the connection?*

Suddenly, someone kicked his feet. He opened his eyes but found it hard to adjust them in the dim light of the cave.

"Is your name 'Yaz?' " the person standing over him asked in an urgent whisper.

"Yeah," Yaz answered, trying to get a good look at the man. "Who wants to know?"

Just then, the man lit a cigarette lighter and only for a second. But it was long enough for Yaz to recognize the man's face.

It was the guy named Elvis . . .

It had never occurred to Yaz—or anyone else in his immediate chain gang—to actually go wandering around in the darkened Hole after it was sealed off. Where would one go if they did? The large door at the cavern's entrance was the only means of getting in and out.

At least, Yaz had assumed it was the only way . . .

He was wrong. Ten minutes after being roused by Elvis, he was shimmying through a narrow pipe that had been dug into an isolated corner off to the side of the cavern. It led into an even larger underground chamber, that looked like it had once been used as a pumping station of some kind. It was lined with concrete and one wall was covered with dials and switches, that were pre-World War II. The other three walls were adorned with maps of the city when it was still called St. Louis.

A group of twelve men, rifles in plain sight, were off in one corner, going over some more maps. The room also contained several big boxes of ammunition, cans of food, bottled water and a radio. It was apparent that Elvis and the other men had been living in the chamber for at least several weeks.

"It's a good thing you didn't recognize me right away today," Elvis told him after they were both inside the chamber. "The other trusty is not in on . . .

all this." He spread his arms out to show the chamber.

"Well, the last time I saw you I was out on my feet with a stomach full of Suez Canal water." Yaz said, quickly telling him about his ill-fated flight from Casablanca, his capture by the Cubans and his subsequent sale to the slave market.

"Now, what the hell are you doing here?" Yaz asked him. "You're certainly not prisoners. Yet I saw you up top today . . ."

"Well, I'm a prisoner of design only," Elvis told him. But there's a lot to explain. And frankly, I'm not the one who can do that. So let me make a phone call . . ."

A phone call?

Elvis walked over to the chamber's control panel and sure enough produced an old rotary-style telephone from a desk drawer. He plugged it in and carefully dialed a seven-digit number.

He waited a few moments, then said: "Hello? Is he there?"

He motioned for Yaz to take the phone. He did, and then he heard the voice on the other end say: "Hey Yaz, this is Hawk."

Yaz had to take a few moments for it to sink in. *"Hawk?"* he finally said. "You got to be kidding me, how the hell are you?"

"Still seasick," came the reply. "Sorry to hear that you're toting the ball and chain . . . How'd it happen?"

For the second time in five minutes, Yaz told the story of how he came to be digging ditches underneath Football City. He wasn't totally surprised to be talking to the famous pilot—the letter that Elvis had scratched into the dirt earlier that day could only have meant one thing: W for Wingman.

"I'm not surprised that you're mixed up in this," Yaz told him. "What happened to you after Suez? And where the hell are you anyway? This has got to be the only working telephone in the country . . ."

"It would take too long to go into the first question right now," Hunter answered. "And I can't tell you where I am right now. But I *will* explain the situation to you, and then I hope you'll be able to help us. Interested?"

"Of course I am," Yaz said. "Being a slave gets tiresome very quickly."

"OK," Hunter replied. "Here it is in a nutshell:

"We're working inside the city in preparation for an invasion by the good guys, the Western Forces."

Yaz felt a jolt of excitement run through him. "You mean we're busting out?" he asked.

"Eventually," Hunter told him. "But we've got some problems. We have reason to believe that once the invasion begins, The Circle might decide to do something drastic to all the POWs."

"How drastic?" Yaz asked with a gulp.

"Well, let's put it this way," Hunter said. "We're working on a plan that will give everyone a chance to escape before our guys start the attack. And that means all of the POWs, including the wounded ones, and also the few hundred civilians that are left within the city."

Yaz knew right away that was an enormous task — even for someone like Hunter.

"How the hell are you going to do that?" Yaz asked him.

"I'll let Elvis explain the details and give you a tour," Hunter replied. "Let me just tell you that we've discovered a vast network of tunnels under the city. They are actually caves — catacombs — left over from the booze-running days of the 1930s. The gangsters used to move a lot of gin through St. Louis. They did it underground. The catacombs are all over the place, and they all lead right down to the river. We're trying to find out which ones are near the POW camps so we can provide an escape route for everyone on the inside."

"Jesus, how did you guys even get down here?" Yaz asked.

"Again, it's a long story," Hunter replied. "But believe me, it wasn't easy. By the time I got back on this side of the Atlantic, the Western Forces were already laying siege to the city. We knew there would be a heavy loss of life among the civvies but also among the POWs. So we used some radar imaging high flights over the city because we had heard rumors about the catacombs. Well, we found them. Then it was a question of getting our people into the city where they could pose as prisoners during the day . . ."

"So what you are saying," Yaz said, "is that you broke *into* prison?"

"Yeah, we did," Hunter told him. "But believe me, it's a lot easier breaking *out* of prison than breaking *in* . . .

"But now there's still a hundred things to do. The bottom line is that we have to get as many POWs out as possible. Every last one of them will be needed to continue the war."

"What war?"

"The war to regain control of the whole country," Hunter answered with no small amount of determination. "We've got a plan to knock The Circle right back into the Atlantic."

Yaz shook his head. "Jesus, Hawk, that will be a

tall order. I hear The Circle has about fifty thousand men in this area alone. And more of them the further east you go."

"We know all that," Hunter said. "But we have no choice but to carry the battle to them. And do it now . . ."

"But why?" Yaz asked. "I can see trying take over this city, but why the whole eastern half? Wouldn't it make more sense to do it a piece at a time?"

"Yes, it would," Hunter answered. "But there's a problem . . ." He then told Yaz about the Soviet-sponsored seaborne invasion force that was heading for the American east coast.

The Navy man listened with open-mouthed amazement. "So the plan is to recover the territory as quickly as possible and hope they don't land?" he asked.

"Sort of," Hunter replied. "Actually we've targeted some key areas that we'll have to win back—important cities mostly—that will give the *illusion* that we're in control. It's our only hope of preventing that army from landing."

"And I thought lugging an aircraft carrier across the Med was a chore!" Yaz said.

"That was a piece of cake, compared to this," Hunter replied, his tone taking on a somber pitch.

They talked for ten more minutes, then Yaz bid him goodbye and hung up. He turned and said to Elvis: "Hawk says to give me the tour."

Elvis nodded and told him to follow. The pilot walked over to the group of men studying the map, then led Yaz to a huge metal door on the far side of the pump chamber. This led to another pipe-tunnel, one large enough to walk upright in. Yaz stepped through this passageway, and less than a minute later, he was in the catacombs.

"Jesus, where are we?" he asked Elvis, looking at the moss-covered but somewhat elaborate walls and tunnels.

"We're right below the center of the city," the pilot replied. "You know the guy who's in charge here? The Viceroy? We're right under his headquarters right now."

They walked even deeper into the catacombs, occasionally passing an armed guard or two.

Finally they reached a junction in the catacombs that opened up to a wide tunnel.

"Here's where our plan will either go good or bust," Elvis said. "When I saw you today, checking out the truck filled with inner tubes, I knew we'd have to get in touch with you before the breakout."

"Well, I'm glad you did," Yaz said. "But what's with all these inner tubes. How do they fit in?"

"Sounds nuts," Elvis said. "But that's how we're going to get a lot of the wounded guys out of the city."

He pointed toward one end of the tunnel. "There's a water lock up there about a quarter mile holding back a couple million gallons of Mississippi," he said. "Once it's opened, the water flows down here, around to selected tunnels and back out to the river. These tunnels will fill up to about the three foot level. That's shallow enough for healthy people to move in, but too deep for wounded ones.

"So, with the help of some civvies who are in on all this — the Football City Underground — we've been gathering inner tubes from all over the city. When the time comes, we're going to flood the right tunnels, inflate all the inner tubes, bring the wounded down here, and float 'em out to the river, where we hope to have barges waiting."

"Wow . . ." was Yaz's first reaction to the outlandish plan. "But what's to prevent The Circle from waiting for the people at the end of the tunnel?"

"They should be busy," Elvis replied. "As it stands now, the night we break out will be the same night that the Western Forces attack the city."

CHAPTER 6

Colonel Muss was shown into the Viceroy's chambers, after waiting nearly ten hours in an adjacent office.

Muss had gotten used to putting up with lengthy delays in seeing the Viceroy, but never one that lasted from early afternoon until almost midnight. One would think the man who was in charge of the Circle's last city on the western side of the Mississippi would be spending all that time trying to defend it.

But it soon became obvious that the Viceroy was more concerned about other things. . . .

Muss was led in and was instantly shocked by what he saw. The Viceroy—a young, thin man who had perfected a kind of Sir Walter Raleigh look—was stretched out on an aircraft carrier-sized, elevated water bed. The man was surrounded by a half dozen naked girls—none any older than sixteen. A brass bowl nearby was filled with a powdery substance that Muss knew was cocaine. More than a dozen straws were protruding from it. Loud, irritating music was blaring from four large quadrophonic speakers.

"Colonel Muss!" the Viceroy called out as the officer walked in. "You're just in time for the oil wrestling."

"We have some disturbing news, sir," Muss said, holding up the photographs given to him by the RF-4 pilot. "Can I talk openly here?"

The Viceroy looked around at the bevy of young girls. "Why yes, Colonel," he replied. "I doubt if there are any spies in amongst these rather edible wenches."

Muss walked over to the side of the bed which was suspended about waist-high off the floor. He handed the photos to the Viceroy.

The man, clad only in a skimpy pair of designer underwear, sat up and studied the photos.

"Tanks," he said calmly. "And SAMs . . . Where in hell are they getting all this equipment? They suffered just as we did during The Circle War. They have to deal with the same arms dealers that we do—and ours are better. Yet they seem to be building a land army twice the size of ours here in the city. This is all a mystery to me . . ."

As he was saying this, the Viceroy was nonchalantly fondling one girl's breast with his toes.

"Their strength has been growing every day for the past two weeks," Muss said, trying to avert his eyes. "The recon pilot has a movie film that shows these new additions. We estimate the Westerners now have nearly two hundred ten thousand men under arms. That's four times more than we ever thought possible. And they're no more than thirty miles from here."

The Viceroy shook his head, routinely leaned over to the coke bowl and took a long, noisy sniff.

"Don't sweat it, Muss," he said. "Just continue the recon flights, and stay cool."

Muss took note of the sketchy orders, shaking his head as he did so.

"Problems with that, Colonel?" the Viceroy asked.

Muss immediately straightened up. "No, sir . . . It's just that it seems we should be doing more to counter the Westerners," he told him. "They have us practically surrounded."

The Viceroy retrieved a bottle of champagne from above his bed and quickly opened it.

"Colonel, I'm afraid to say, you are beginning to sound like the rest of my officers," Viceroy Dick replied, taking a swig from the bottle and passing it to the young girl nearest to him. "What we are engaged in here is called 'Tactical Defense.' Those cowboys aren't going to invade any time soon. Even if they do have us by four-to-one, they know we'll kill their prisoners in a minute if they make a move. What do you think we have them digging those holes for? We've got plenty of time, Muss. And suffice to say that when the time comes, and the Westerners do try to attack in force, we'll be ready."

"If you say so, sir," Muss mumbled.

The Viceroy reached over and snuggled the cute

little blonde nearest him, his hand roughly fondling her budding breasts.

"But let me ask you an important question, Colonel," he said as he continued to rub the young girl's body. "When will your men be finished rebuilding the bridges?"

Muss closed his eyes in thought, then answered. "Two of the spans can carry traffic right now," he said. "Three more will be open within the week. The further two, maybe two or three weeks from now."

The Viceroy thought this over and took another long sniff of cocaine.

"All right, Colonel," he said. "Here are some further orders:

"First, take all your workers on the sixth and seventh bridges and put them to work on bridges three, four and five. By your calculations, will this mean those bridges will be open in a matter of days?"

"Possibly," Muss answered.

"Very good," the Viceroy said. "Remember, in a tactical defense, *efficiency* is the key . . ."

Muss shrugged. He even imagined that he was beginning to get the Viceroy's drift . . .

"Now, Colonel," he said as the bottle of champagne made its way back to him. "Sit down and relax and enjoy the oil wrestling."

Muss did as he was told. Viceroy Dick clapped his hands once and instantly four more young girls were led in by a squad of tough-looking women guards.

"They're all dykes," the Viceroy leaned over and

whispered to Muss, pointing to the women guards. "I find they prime the ladies for me . . ."

A bucket of oil—scented cooking oil—was brought in.

"Colonel, you can have the first honors," the Viceroy said.

Muss wasn't quite sure what the man wanted him to do.

"You're supposed to rub the first one down, Colonel," the Viceroy told him, realizing the man's plight.

The bucket was brought up to Muss as was the first young girl. Like the other three girls, she was dressed in a tuxedo-negligee combination, all-black, wearing a low-cut silk blouse, with black stockings and short black boots. Muss noticed that each girl, like the naked ones frolicking on the Viceroy's huge bed, was blond, either natural or dyed, and wearing her hair in the same long, shaggy cut.

The girl who stood before him was a beauty. Muss swallowed and hoped, for his own soul, that the girl was at least seventeen. But he knew that was unlikely . . .

"OK, Colonel," Viceroy Dick said. "Take her clothes off."

Muss hesitated at first. But unwilling to balk at the order, he started to undo the buttons on the girl's tuxedo jacket.

"For Christ's sake, Colonel," the leader laughed as he he saw the man's timid approach. "We'll be here all night . . ."

The Viceroy signaled for two of the women

guards to step forward and help Muss, a duty which they gladly accepted. The women came up behind the girl and proceeded to rip the clothes from her back. The girl, who appeared to be heavily drugged, didn't know whether to laugh or cry, so she simply stood there while the older women stripped her, their hands roaming freely over her privates as they did so.

Now completely naked, the girl looked at Muss, waiting for him to make the next move. He put his hands into the bowl of slightly heated oil, then slowly began rubbing the lubricant on the girl's chest and stomach, then her thighs and backside. She giggled as he did this; he felt the bulge rise between his legs.

The women guards took care of the three other girls, delightfully stripping them and covering them in oil.

Meanwhile Viceroy Dick was having his way with two naked girls on the bed.

"OK, let the festivities begin!" he announced, sitting up and taking another long snort of cocaine.

The women guards spread a large rubber mat down in front of the bed and covered it too with oil. Then the girls were placed at each corner and told to go at it.

Muss found his pants bursting at the in-seam as he watched the teens grapple with each other, their lovely young bodies glistening in the slippery hot oil.

"What are the stakes, sir?" he asked, not being able to take his eyes off the wrestling match.

"The two winners get to sleep here with me," the Viceroy told him. "The two losers go with the dykes. If they survive forty-eight hours with those girls and their modalities, they get a chance to come back in here and try it again."

Muss could only numbly nod his head. The story of Sodom and Gomorrah came to him.

"You know we used to sacrifice them," the Viceroy said. "We were up to a virgin a night. Mabel, the big blond guard over there, used to love to do them in.

"But, just like everything else, there's a shortage of young attractive girls in this city. So, we have to conserve our supply. Again, *efficiency* is the key . . ."

Muss felt the urges in his body reach a breaking point. But just as he was about to ask the Viceroy to let him have one of the girls, Dick turned to him and said: "You're dismissed, Colonel . . ."

CHAPTER 7

Three hours later, Viceroy Dick knew he had had enough.

The oil wrestling match had lasted an hour—the two victors were now curled up unconscious at the foot of the huge bed. He had tired of them quickly, snapped on his TV screen instead to watch, via closed circuit, as Mabel and the other female guards took their measure of the two losers. This had amused him for another hour, after which he fell asleep.

Now, awake after his brief nap, he took a half dozen long snorts from his bowl of cocaine, then arose to go back upstairs to his private living quarters, where he knew another pair of young beauties waited. They would rub him down with warm towels then simply massage him back to sleep.

He rode the elevator alone, arriving at his 23rd story suite to be greeted by his major of the guard.

The man looked very nervous . . .

"You have visitors, sir," the major told him. "They've been waiting for some time . . ."

Viceroy Dick checked his watch. "It's nearly four in the morning," he grumbled. "Who the hell has the balls to be here disturbing me at this hour?"

The major shifted uneasily. "They're Soviet officers, sir," he said. "Two of them, with two bodyguards."

The Viceroy immediately stiffened up. "Did they say what their business was?"

"Not to me, sir," the major replied, reaching over to open the door to the Viceroy's quarters for him.

Before entering, Viceroy Dick whispered to the major: "Get a squad of your guys up here right now. If you hear any trouble, get your asses in there and protect me. *Comprende?*"

The major nodded. "Yes, sir," he said quietly, "May I suggest I order two squads . . ." He immediately turned to the phone in order to call up the first floor security office.

Viceroy Dick took a deep breath and strolled into his living quarters. Two Russian officers were waiting for him in the office section of the suite. Both were dressed in a Soviet style uniform that was not familiar to the Viceroy. It was all black-leather, with red epaulets. Their two bodyguards, both lieutenants wearing similar outfits, waited off in a corner, their Uzis in plain sight.

"Gentlemen," Dick said, walking in and sitting down behind his desk. "It's an early hour for you to be calling."

"We have been here for three hours," one officer,

a completely bald man of 50 or so told him.

"I was taking care of business," Dick replied. "Down in my recreation room. You two should have come down there, taken care of some business too . . ."

"Screwing little girls is not what we consider 'business,' " the other officer, a young, taller man with blond-red hair told him. Just like his companion, he spoke excellent English.

"OK, let's cut the bullshit," the Viceroy said. "What do you guys want?"

"Our superiors at the Ministry of State Security have asked us to travel here to review your defenses," the bald one said. "We understand that the enemy forces waiting nearby have increased their size substantially . . ."

"And they'll keep on waiting," the Viceroy said. "You guys must know the gig: I've got ten thousand of their prisoners and I have made it quite clear to them that those POWs will be history if they attack."

"And you view this as a successful strategy?" the younger man asked. "Even though the Westerners carry on at least two air strikes a day against you?"

The Viceroy shrugged and smiled. "It's called Tactical Defense. And it's working perfectly. I'm still here, aren't I? Football City is still under Circle control. They're harassing me, that's all. What's the beef?"

"The 'beef' is that the 'valuables' have not been moved as yet," the hairless one said. "This is correct, is it not?"

"The bridges are still down," Dick said quickly. "We're working like crazy on them, and when they're ready to handle substantial loads, we move the stuff. What's your hurry?"

Both Soviet officers were suddenly angry.

"You are talking about materials that the Ministry regards as critical to the continued success of our operations in America," the young officer said sternly. "A lot of time and effort went into gathering these valuables and I suggest that you concern yourself more with their welfare. Should the Westerners attack, there'd be no way to move the materials in° time."

Viceroy Dick hated the Soviets, even though, technically, they were his bosses. But he wasn't going to let them push him around.

"Look, boys," he said. "The situation is under control here. I'm sitting on top of ten thousand of their guys and the Westerners know better than to try and pop me. Look at it this way: I'm tying up thousands of their guys, without firing a shot. We could hold this status quo for years."

"They are gathering their forces, waiting until they have the clear advantage, then they will surely attack you," the bald officer told him sternly.

"Well, that ain't going to happen anytime soon," Viceroy Dick shot right back. "If you guys are so concerned, why don't you throw me a couple diversions? I'm short-handed as it is and you should be grateful I'm keeping these cowboys at bay."

The Soviet officers both looked stung, as if Viceroy Dick's mention of reenforcements had hit a raw nerve.

"You know we are reorganizing," the bald one said finally. "No reenforcements can be spared for you."

Viceroy Dick just smiled. "Then why the hell are you here bothering me?" he asked. "The bridges are being built. Your precious stuff will be moved as soon as possible. What else do you want me to do?"

It was a rhetorical question to which he hadn't expected an answer. But he got one nevertheless . . .

"We want you to start executing the prisoners," the bald Soviet told him. "Immediately . . ."

Viceroy Dick was taken aback. "Execute them?" he asked incredulously. "What the hell for? That would be giving up my advantage . . ."

"No!" the younger man shouted. "Because when you start killing them, you will send a message to the Westerners telling them the executions will continue unless they start to withdraw . . ."

"Withdraw?" Dick said with angry astonishment. "They ain't going to *withdraw.*"

"Ah, probably not . . ." Baldy said. "But when you start the executions, they definitely won't attack you either. This way, you turn your threat into action."

"That's nuts," Viceroy Dick said loudly. "I'm working with a fine balance here. If I start knocking off their POWs, they're going to come in here in a minute . . ."

"We don't think it will happen that way," the young officer said. "And besides, you don't have a choice in the matter."

Both men stood up and came very close to the desk. At the same time, the two Soviet bodyguards walked five steps closer to them.

"Now start those executions immediately," the bald officer said. "And not in twos and threes. This is psych warfare—we want to send the enemy a message."

Viceroy Dick was disgusted. He didn't need this after such a long, draining night of partying.

"Just how big a message do you want to send them?" he asked, his voice laced with sarcasm.

"Four hundred prisoners a night," the young officer said. "Every night . . ."

"And, if you fail to make just one quota, we'll be back," the bald officer concluded. "And we'll do it ourselves."

CHAPTER 8

Another day had passed. Another day that Yaz busted his ass digging in The Hole.

But then that night, after the guards secured the large wooden door to the cave and left, Yaz waited until those around him were asleep. Then he crawled over to the spot where the shimmy pipe was hidden. Moving the clump of root camouflage, he crawled through, and was soon inside the pump house again.

Waiting for him on the other side were Elvis and a man named Ace. His talent was explosives.

Elvis pulled out a small map.

"Tonight starts another phase of the overall plan," he told Yaz. "We think it's time for The Circle to know they've got some infiltrators inside the city. Also Hawk is working a particularly delicate mission tonight. So we have to make some noise to cover him."

He indicated two stars on the map, one of them in the center of the city; the other down at the edge of the river, near the docks. Then he pointed at the four boxes lying at Ace's feet.

"These are radio-activated high explosives," Elvis explained. "For tonight, we'll call them HE-one, HE-two, HE-three and HE-four.

"The plan is to plant two bombs at each target. Set the first one off, wait for some Circle chumps to show up, then detonate the second bomb. We have uniforms waiting for us at the jump off point and a line on every manhole cover in the areas that we can use in case we have to get the hell away. OK?"

Yaz nodded as coolly as possible. He knew that Hunter's allies were as adroit in taking the battle to the enemy on the ground as they were in the seat of an airplane. But as for himself, he was just a Navy boy from the country. He wasn't sure how he'd measure up as an urban guerrilla.

Elvis sensed his apprehension right away. "Don't worry Yaz," he said. "Tonight, just watch and take notes. We'll do the heavy lifting . . ."

With that, the three of them set out into the catacombs and toward a specified manhole cover near the center of the city.

CHAPTER 9

Hunter was sweating by the time he had climbed to the top of the Southwestern Bell building. His all-black, camouflage flight suit was made of wool, necessary for where he was going, but a hindrance before he got there.

The Southwestern Bell building was the tallest structure in all of Football City — 41 floors and a flat roof, which was just what he needed. Best of all, because its main electrical system had been damaged in the war against the Family, it was unoccupied by Circle troops.

Just as he had done nearly every night for the past five weeks, he had walked up the 41 stories, negotiating the dark fire emergency stairways with a penlight taped to the rim of his baseball cap. Reaching the top and going out onto the flat roof, he took several welcome gulps of air, then looked out on the lights of Football City.

"There's nowhere like this in the world," he

thought.

St. Louis was transformed into Football City by a good friend of his, a man appropriately named, Louie St. Louie. Actually a Texan, St. Louie turned the post-war city into a midwest mega-Las Vegas. Just about every building in the downtown area was converted into either a casino, a nightclub or a whorehouse. In the center of the city, St. Louie had built an enormous 500,000 seat football stadium, where two teams of 500 continually-substituted players would play in a 24-hour-a-day 365-days-a-year football match. Hence, the city's rechristened name. People could bet on this marathon football match in any increment — by the quarter or up to the whole year.

It was a bold, crazy idea that was just what post-World War III America needed. Just because the Soviets had blasted the center section of the country with a fierce barrage of ICBMs and forced the US into a peace treaty that called for the breaking up of the states into a mish-mash of separate countries, kingdoms and Free Territories, didn't mean that money — or gambling — had gone out of fashion. Hundreds of millions of dollars of gold and silver ran through Football City in its heyday and it attracted both the rich and the poor from all over the continent and all over the world.

Unfortunately, the criminals in New Chicago tried to put the squeeze on St. Louie, an action that led up to the devastating war against the Family. St. Louie had hired Hunter to help protect the city, which he did, but only at the expense of directing a massive B-52 raid which decimated the Family Army but which also laid waste to a full third of St. Louie's dream in the process.

That bombed out area, up near the Football City Stadium, was now a dark and eerie flatland. The center of activity in the city these days was across town, near the old Union Station area of the city. When St. Louie reclaimed his city from the Family, he had rebuilt about a third of the casinos, only to be forced out again by The Circle War. In the months that the city was in the hands of The Circle, its administrators had kept the hundred or so gambling houses open, along with a couple dozen nightclubs and the 10 or so whorehouses. Although at the dangerous edge of the Circle's unstable western border, the city was still a major R&R spot for Circle troops and their allies. It was not uncommon to see Soviet officers breezing through the casinos or walking into one of the cathouses. The same held true for Cubans, Sidra-Benghazi Libyans, South Afrikaners, Chileans, Vietnamese, North Koreans—all the flotsam of the New Order world. The Circle's version of Football City provided a whole new meaning for the word *decadent*.

But Hunter didn't climb to the top of the building just for the view.

It was actually a treacherous rendezvous spot, and his ultra-sensitive ears were just picking up the sound he had been waiting for.

Chopper blades. Coming from the west. Very high, but very quiet.

He strapped his M-16 crosswise around his shoulder and folded his cap into his back pocket. Off in the distance and way up high, he saw the faintest of lights. It was blinking one-two-one. That was the signal—the chopper was ready for the pick-up.

It was a CH-53E Super Stallion which had had its turbojet engine muffled to the point of near silence.

Still, the helicopter—known as the Mean Machine among the Western Forces—had to fly in such a way as to evade the Circle's rudimentary, but still potent early warning radar system. That's why the aircraft was bristling with radar-deflecting electronic gadgets and wearing three coats of radar-absorbing Stealth paint.

It also had a winch-driven hoist basket with no less than a mile of thin, light-weight but super-strength lift cord.

Hunter could now hear the muffled sounds of the chopper drawing closer. He squinted his eyes and concentrated on the night sky to his west. Within a minute he saw the luminous orange spot, still a few miles away but drawing near. The orange dot was the bottom of the hoist basket.

"Bring it steady this time," Hunter whispered as if to send a message to the chopper pilot. The last two times he had done this, the basket was bobbing and weaving so much, it took several flybys before he actually had time to jump in.

The orange dot grew larger now, moving slow and steady. "OK," he thought. "Looks good . . ."

He climbed up on the roof's thin 41-story high ledge and steadied himself against the 15 knot wind. "Nice and slow . . ." he whispered. "Keep it steady . . ."

The orange dot was now only about a quarter mile away and heading right for him. A few seconds later he could see the basket itself.

"Right on the money, guys," he said. "Keep it on line."

The basket was looming up on him very quickly now, its line stretching a full mile practically straight up. He knew from experience that the trick of the mile-long pickup was to leap right into the basket as it flew by.

He went into his crouch when the basket was just 100 feet away. It was moving a little faster than he'd like, but the angle was good. 50 feet. 25. 20 . . .

"I must be nuts doing this," he thought as the basket was suddenly right in front of him.

He took a deep breath and leaped . . .

The basket hit his shoulder first and the impact swept him up inside. He quickly pulled his legs in, then reached up and closed the wire mesh door. He then yanked the red cord dangling over his head. This would let the chopper crew know that he was inside, intact and ready to be lifted. As soon as he hit the red cord, he could feel the basket being drawn in.

Up he went, into the midnight sky over the city. The wind blew harder the higher he got, and now he was thankful for his heavy wool flight suit. Below him the lights of the city started to compress as he was raised high over them.

It's a long way down, he thought. This was not a place for anyone squeamish of heights.

The chopper was across the Mississippi by the time they hauled him in.

The first guy he saw was his old friend, Ben Wa. The Oriental fighter pilot, who had also been in the Thunderbirds demonstration team with him before the Big War, gave him a warm handshake after the basket had been secured and Hunter had climbed out.

"Made it again, eh?" Ben said.

"Well, you guys are getting better at it," Hunter said, rubbing his sore shoulder. "At least we did it on the first try."

They moved up to the flight deck of the big chopper, where another friend and fellow Thunderbird pilot, J.T. "Socket" Toomey, was at the controls.

"Mr. Wingman," J.T. said, giving him a quick handshake. "Nice night for a ride, isn't it?"

CHAPTER 10

Yaz adjusted his South Afrikaner Army uniform and pulled the cap down tighter on his head.

"Does this look OK to you?" he asked Elvis. All three of them were wearing the phony uniforms, left in a manhole by a member of Football City's small but highly-trained underground.

"Sure, you look like a Nazi," Elvis told him.

"I *feel* like a Nazi," Yaz said. The gray-brown two piece field suit did bear some resemblance to a German Army desert dress uniform, circa 1942.

"Well, don't worry," the man named Ace told him. "The Circle and the Afrikaners are tight. No one will bug us while we're wearing these."

They put the radio-controlled bombs, each the size of a paperback book, into a gunny sack, then stuffed their original clothes in around them. Then they set out for the center of the city.

Five minutes later, they were walking down a crowded boulevard, rubbing shoulders with hundreds of Circle troops on liberty. Yaz was fascinated at how lively the place was, despite the fact that just about 30 miles away, an invading army lay in wait. The street was jammed with honking limousines, jeeps and an occasional tank or APC. Hookers of every description, age, color and proclivity lined every street corner, fighting for space with the drug pushers, the gun salesmen, fast-food vendors, insurance hawkers and other types of lowlife. All seemed to be doing burgeoning business.

Yaz saw that just about every building was strewn with marquee-type flashing lights, advertising big jackpots, cheap drinks and *girls-girls-girls*. He hadn't been close to any of the three in quite a while, so he was interested . . .

They walked for several blocks drinking in the atmosphere until they reached a rather subdued-looking casino called The Executive. Unlike most of the other gambling houses, The Executive was a private club, open only to members of the Circle Officer Corps and visiting dignitaries.

It was their first target of the night. . . .

"We'll do the HE-TWO first," Elvis said casually as they walked past the front door of the place, nodding to the two soldiers and an armed doorman on duty. "Let's plant it in that car over there, then stick HE-1 around back."

Ace reached into the gunny sack, retrieved the number two bomb and nonchalantly flipped it into the back seat of an unattended Chrysler New Yorker limo parked next to the place. Then he took HE-ONE and quickly tossed it in the alley at the rear corner of the building.

The bombs in place, they continued walking up to a cafe style restaurant a block and a half away. They took a table outside and boldly ordered three drinks. All the while, Ace was fingering a remote control device in his pocket.

It won't be long now, Yaz thought.

Just then, they heard a racket coming from the end of the street. They turned to see a line of open troop trucks moving toward them, the Circle Army emblem emblazoned on each door.

"Hey, maybe we just got lucky," Ace said. "We could blow both bombs just as that convoy passes by. Take out a lot of those bozos if we do."

"Let's wait and see," Elvis cautioned as the trucks drew nearer.

The lead vehicle stopped right next to them, and for the first time they could see that the men sitting in the back of the truck were not Circle troops, nor soldiers of their allies.

They were POWs . . .

"What the hell is going on here?" Elvis asked under his breath as the lead truck started up again. One by one the trucks passed them, each one carrying 25 bound prisoners in the back. Some of them appeared wounded and sick.

"The Circle moving POWs at night?" Ace said. "I would think that would require too much brain power . . ."

"Well, they're doing it," Elvis said as the last of the 16-truck convoy rumbled by. "And I don't like the looks of it. They usually don't tie prisoners by the hands."

They watched as the trucks took a right turn opposite The Executive and headed east.

"They look like they're going down to the river," Yaz said.

"Yeah, and judging by their direction, I'd say they're headed for the Gateway Park," Elvis said, referring to the location of the battered but still standing St. Louis "Gateway to the West" arch.

"There's nothing down that way," Ace said. "Certainly no construction, not even during the daytime, never mind at night."

"This really smells fishy," Elvis said, estimating that some 400 prisoners were being moved.

He looked around and then said: "OK, let's get this over with. We'll be moving toward that area afterward anyway. Maybe we'll see what's up then."

A Circle Army staff car pulled up in front of The Executive, and two high ranking officers stepped out. They saluted the armed guards out front, tipped the AK-47-toting doorman and went inside.

"Big fish," Elvis said. "That's a good omen . . ."

He did one last check of the streets and sidewalks near the building. Convinced that no innocents were about, he nodded to Ace.

The first thing Yaz saw was the flash—bright, yellow, so intense he instinctively turned away. Before he did he saw the whole rear quarter of the building simply lift off the ground. The sound of the explosion didn't arrive until two seconds later. When it did, it shook the ground so hard, their table collapsed in their laps.

The explosion rocked the landscape for blocks around. When Yaz dared to look back at the building, he saw that it was completely engulfed in flames and already crumbling brick by brick.

He turned to see that Elvis had thrown himself to the pavement, flinging his hat away and intentionally ripping his uniform's collar.

"Act natural," he hissed up to Yaz and Ace. "Look shocked . . ."

The owner and patrons of their cafe came running outside to see the building down the block surrounded by a mass of flames and two Afrikaner officers treating a third who had been knocked over by the explosion.

Soon the streets were filled with soldiers—both Circle and allied. Patrol cars and even a couple cannon-armed APCs screeched up to the site. Circle officers were barking orders to the lower troops, telling them to spread out and look for suspects. Off in the distance, Yaz could hear the sirens of the approaching fire equipment.

Elvis was playing the part of a wounded officer very well. He had rolled his eyes up into his head and held his tongue out, as if he was in a seizure. He had crushed a fake blood capsule between his teeth and was now letting the red liquid drool profusely from his mouth. The act was so convincing, two Circle soldiers ran up to them, took one look at Elvis, and kept right on going.

The saboteurs stayed that way for another minute or so as the pandemonium in the street built up around them. The fire equipment arrived, all of it manned by Circle troops.

They had just started to play the first water hose onto the roaring inferno when Ace detonated the second bomb.

CHAPTER 11

The specially-equipped, high-flying CH-53 Super Stallion leveled off at 21,000 feet and started to circle.

Inside, Hunter, Ben Wa and Twomey were all huddled in heavy arctic gear as the temperature inside the helicopter's cabin plunged to below zero.

"Goddamn, it's cold," Wa said, pulling his collar up around his neck. "You think they would have insulated these birds when they made them a high flyer."

"Hey, at least we know the equipment will work and they can't see us up here," Hunter shrugged, tapping on of the dials in front of him.

He was sitting before a somewhat jury-rigged terrain guidance radar imaging device. By bouncing radar waves off the surface of the earth four miles down they were able to map not only structures on the ground but also those *below* ground. This was how Hunter and the Western Forces came to first learn the layout of the catacombs beneath the streets of Football City.

Now, in their third and hopefully final radar mapping mission, Hunter was intent on solving the final clues of the jigsaw patterns of the catacombs.

"We have a fairly direct route from where the main prisoner holding center is to the flood tunnel," he told Wa as he focused in the radar-imaging screen. "But we have two POW concentrations downtown, plus many exit routes for the civvies that have to be evacuated."

Hunter tried to breathe some warmth onto his bare hands. He had to turn so many knobs and push so many buttons on the radar imager that even his thin and warm flight gloves were a hindrance.

"You are right over the target area right now, Hawk," Twomey yelled over his shoulder to him.

Hunter centered the surface initial signal on the imager and pulled a bank of switches to *On*. Deep in the back of the Sea Stallion, he heard the business end of the radar imager start to hum. Slowly, a more detailed outline of the surface came onto the video screen. Hunter punched in a code into the imager's computer, committing the video read-out to memory. Then he flipped a half dozen more switches and watched as the original image slowly dissolved, to be replaced by a series of thick and slender colored lines, which quickly grew contours. These were the catacombs as depicted by the radar imager. Hunter set the computer's memory to record, then, working through the smoky vapor of their breaths in the sub-zero chopper cabin, he and Wa set about the long task of mapping the tunnels beneath the streets.

An hour passed and finally the task was done.

"OK, J.T.," he finally called out. "Let's get off this dime."

Twomey took the chopper off hover and started moving eastward again.

Hunter was going over some post-mapping data when Wa called his attention to another image which had appeared on the screen.

"What the hell is that?" Wa asked, pointing to a row of perfect rectangular shapes that appeared just below the surface in a relatively abandoned part of the city.

"Very strange," Hunter said, just as another row of the shapes came into view.

"Can you hold it up a little, J.T.?" Hunter called out, feeling the copter slow down almost immediately.

"What the hell you got?" Twomey yelled back to them.

Hunter wasn't sure. The two long rows of rectangles were so exact and thin, he couldn't believe they were part of the catacombs.

"They're boxes of some kind," Wa said. "Big boxes . . ."

"Maybe railroad box*cars?*" Hunter wondered aloud. "The size would match . . ."

"Yeah, same approximate shape," Wa said, trying to focus the image. "But boxcars buried under the ground?"

"Maybe it's an underground garage, or an old railroad service shop . . ." Twomey yelled back.

"That's probably it," Hunter said. "But they're not empty—I'm getting an infrared reading from them. Not strong, but warm enough to indicate they're loaded, with something. There's probably more of them than we're picking up here."

"War material, maybe?" Wa asked.

"Ammo? Weapons?" Twomey pitched in.

Hunter did some quick calculations then punched a swarm of numbers into the imager's computer. The result was an overall view of the city with a thin green line indicating the nearest catacomb tributary.

"We have a tunnel that swings within fifteen feet of that area," Hunter said, once again committing the image to the computer's memory banks and then his own. "If we can, we'll get in there tomorrow night, see what the hell's going on. If that's a weapons supply dump, then it means the Circle has about twice as much firepower as we thought."

CHAPTER 12

Within five minutes, Yaz, Elvis and Ace were five blocks from the area where they had detonated the two radio-controlled bombs.

All three knew they had accomplished their mission—and then some. They had created two separate firestorms of carnage, and they knew the Circle body count would be high.

"There's a thin line between an urban guerrilla and an out and out terrorist," Ace said.

Like a terrorist bombing, the two explosions had also served the psychological purpose: air raid sirens were going off all over the city, adding to the confusion and causing many sections to be blacked out.

"When they find out those bombs were planted," Elvis said, through the sputtering fake blood, "the guys in charge of this burg will really get nervous . . ."

They made their way through the streets away from the downtown area and toward the river, Elvis holding a wet towel given to him by the cafe's owner. The water and fake blood mixed to give his head and throat a particularly realistic, major-sucking-wound look. On two occasions, Circle soldiers stopped to question them, but each time, Ace and Yaz simply shouted down their inquiries by demanding directions to the nearest hospital.

They reached the water's edge within an hour. Their second target was a major pier facility called the Mound City Boat Docks which was just north of two of the reconstructed bridge spans.

Using the darkness as cover, they stole along the river bank until they reached the southern end of the dockworks. There were no Circle guards in evidence. Ace quickly attached the first bomb to the underside of a pier which supported an oil holding tank, then the three scrambled away behind a river jetty.

"Blow it whenever you're ready," Elvis told Ace.

But just as the man was about to push the detonator button, they heard a noise coming from the bridge nearest to them. Yaz looked up to see first one, then two, then a half dozen Circle Army troop trucks pull to a stop right in the middle of the bridge.

"Christ, are those the same trucks we saw downtown?" Elvis asked, trying to focus on the trucks that had stopped beneath the dim lights of the bottom span of the bridge about a quarter mile away.

There were 16 of them, the same as the downtown convoy, and groups of men were riding in their open backs.

"It's them," Yaz said. "I'm sure of it . . ."

"But what the hell are they bring POWs up to that bridge in the middle of the night," Ace asked. "It's certainly not to work . . ."

They watched as Circle troops herded the POWs out of the back of the first truck and up against the railing. Suddenly, one of the POWs fell—or was pushed—off the bridge, falling head first into the river. It was obvious the man's hands and feet were tied.

"What the *fuck* is going on?" Elvis said.

Then another prisoner fell. Then another and another.

"Jesus, they're killing them!" Yaz cried out.

"I can't believe it," Elvis said. Yet as they watched helplessly, the prisoners were being pushed off the bridge, one right after another. It was execution. Those men who somehow survived the long plunge would drown immediately.

"Goddamn, we've got to do something . . ." Yaz said.

Elvis spun around and started shaking Ace. "Blow that fucking thing . . . *now!*"

Ace hit the detonator button and immediately the pier went up in a loud, fiery roar.

The sudden explosion startled the Circle soldiers on the bridge and the executions were halted. Then Elvis retrieved his .45 automatic from the gunny sack and started firing away wildly in the general direction of the bridge. The momentarily stunned Circle troops started returning the fire almost immediately.

"Look, they're backing the trucks off!" Yaz yelled out as they ducked away from the hail of bullets.

"The blast distracted them," Elvis said, pumping off another three shots. "And they'll be firing down here for a while. Maybe they'll call off the executions if they think some saboteurs are running around.

"The important thing is that we get back and tell Hunter about this . . ."

Ace immediately ran to the pier next to the one

77

already engulfed in flame, set up his second explosive device, then scrambled back to the jetty. Without hesitation, he detonated the second bomb, which blew a large section of the pier some 50 feet into the night sky.

The explosion intensified the Circle fusillade coming at them from the bridge.

"OK, let's get the hell out of here!" Elvis told them.

Yaz and Ace needed no prodding. They ran south, right under the bridge where the Circle soldiers were firing from.

Turning back once to look at the two major fires they had caused, Yaz saw by the fire's reflection on the water, about a dozen shapes floating down the river.

They were the prisoners, all bound hand and foot and all floating face down in the dirty water.

None of them were moving . . .

CHAPTER 13

The RF-4 Phantom roared off the bumpy runway and streaked into the early morning sky.

Captain "Crunch" O'Malley banked the jet to the west and climbed to a comfortable 12,500 feet. He passed over University City, over Olivette, then Maryland Heights. Ten minutes later he was no longer over Circle-held territory.

"This is Romeo-Diana-Zebra," O'Malley called into a preset UHF radio frequency. "Come in, Umpire . . ."

His radio crackled once, then he heard a familiar voice. "This is Umpire, Crunch," came the reply. "Had breakfast yet?"

"That's a negative, General," O'Malley called back. "I've got time for some flaps and a cup of joe . . ."

"See you in the mess tent in fifteen minutes . . ." the voice on the other end, that of General Dave Jones, told him.

O'Malley put the RF-4 into a tight turn, overflying a line of SAMs and several troop bivouacs. He lowered his landing gear and came in for a smooth landing on a long stretch of highway just 30 miles outside of Football City.

A ground service crew appeared out of the woods nearby and quickly directed O'Malley into a camouflaged aircraft shelter.

Twelve minutes later, O'Malley was sitting in the camp's mess tent with General Jones.

"What's the news in Circle-land today?" Jones asked him.

"The base was buzzing about the explosions during the night," O'Malley told him. "All of our guys get out OK?"

"Yes, as far as we know," Jones said. "They got a private officers' club and two piers according to the preliminary report."

"Well, it really shook up the people downtown," O'Malley said. "Air raids they can deal with. But putting bombs under their barstools makes them nervous. They're already spreading the word that the explosions were accidents . . ."

"That's the sure sign of success when they start covering up," Jones said. "What other kinds of bullshit stories are they dishing out?"

O'Malley washed down a mouthful of pancakes with a gulp of coffee. "Well, the lead mechanic who services my rig says he heard that a cocaine processing lab was in the back of the private club and that a tank of ether blew up."

"A clever cover story," Jones said, shaking his head in admiration. "Very feasible . . ."

"Well, he did say he heard rumors that saboteurs blew up the dock works," O'Malley added quickly. "Hard to cover up the fact that two major loading piers simply went *blooey*!"

"Well, I hope he decides to spread *that* rumor," Jones said, taking a gulp of his own coffee.

"I'm sure our message was delivered," O'Malley said, lighting an after meal butt. "Between this and our recon misinformation campaign, the Circle will soon be getting very jittery."

"They're still buying our phony photos . . ." Jones shook his head in amazement. "I really thought they'd be smarter than that."

"Me, too," O'Malley confessed. "But for them, the proof is in those photos. They are convinced we're sitting here with almost two hundred thousand troops and plenty of equipment. They have no choice but to believe it. They have no other means of surveillance. And God forbid that they should get an original idea and send out a long range patrol . . ."

"Like any other commander charged with defense of his city would do," Jones said. "They certainly aren't acting like an army that's preparing for an all-out attack."

"Their military guys are worried," O'Malley said. "But old Viceroy Dick acts like he's on vacation. He thinks that just as long as he's holding our POWs, he's sitting pretty."

Jones shook his head once again. "And you know something?" he said. "The bastard is right."

O'Malley finished his meal and he and Jones were met by one of the Western Forces' photo experts. The man handed the pilot two rolls of still picture film and two rolls of movie film.

"What do we show them today?" O'Malley asked.

"More tanks, more SAMs," the photo man said. "We've got a bunch of old Sunoco trucks in there, too, to give the impression that we're bringing our fuel up to the front."

O'Malley had to smile at the simple brilliance of the deception. The Western Forces had a similar RF-4 Phantom recon jet — it, too, was converted for this operation from O'Malley's small Ace Wrecking Company fleet. The Westerners would load up their jet with film and fly it over any number of military staging sites — both active and abandoned — from Missouri back through the Badlands all the way back to the west coast. Whenever the topography was correct, they'd start the cameras whirring. This footage would then be mixed in with actual pictures of the Westerners' strength near Football City, thus creating an impression of a huge army, when less than two-thirds that number was actually in place.

"How much longer do you think they're going to fall for this?" Jones asked O'Malley. "I mean they're dumb, but we don't want to overplay our hand."

O'Malley thought for a moment. "I say give it one more session after this one," he said. "Then I'll just quit. I'll tell them I don't want to be around when the shooting starts."

Just then, Ben Wa and Twomey appeared. They'd been up almost all night flying the mapping mission with Hunter and were just now getting down to their morning chow.

"How's the boy doing?" O'Malley asked them.

"Behaving himself?"

Both Wa and Twomey knew right away who O'Malley was talking about.

"Once again, the famous Wingman had us freezing our twinks off last night," Twomey said. "But he got what he wanted and even more."

"More of what?" Jones asked them.

"We got it in our written report, sir," Wa said. "But in a nutshell, we picked up a very weird image on the radar last night."

He went on to quickly explain to Jones and O'Malley about the underground storage facility containing what were apparently boxcars of some kind.

"It's down near the river," Twomey said. "Hawk is going to try to get down there tonight to check it out."

Jones's face became creased with worry. "God, if it's ammunition, that means The Circle and their allies are stronger than we thought."

O'Malley shook his head. "I'd be real surprised if it was an ammo dump," he said. "These guys are too nervous for someone sitting on top of all that firepower."

"Whatever it is, I hope our boy can get in there tonight," Jones said.

Wa and Twomey went on to chow. Jones and O'Malley walked back out to the RF-4.

O'Malley shook his head in admiration. "I really got to feel for Hunter," he said. "At least Elvis and the others are fairly secure underground in the catacombs. But Hawk . . ."

"He insisted that this was the way he wanted to play it," Jones said. "You know how he is. Sometimes he works best when he's left alone. If he feels that he has to stay topside at all times to keep a constant track of the situation, then I'm not going to argue with him."

"I think he's just antsy," O'Malley said, retrieving his helmet and climbing back into his airplane's cockpit. He routinely checked the extra photo equipment which had been loaded in the now-empty rear seat of the RF-4. "That's what happens when someone loses their rig . . ."

The pilot was referring to the fact that Hunter's beloved F-16—the only fighter of that type known to exist—had been all but destroyed in the hours following the great Suez battle. The remains of the airplane were eventually airlifted back to America and were presently at a former General Dynamics plant near Dallas in the Texas Republic. There, some GD engineers were trying to determine whether or not the famous airplane was a complete loss.

"You're probably right," Jones said. "He misses that airplane. He also misses his lady friend. He misses the way things used to be. Plus just about everyone on the continent thinks he's dead. You never think of a guy like that as being lonely or even bummed-out. But he's definitely in a funk. I think he still feels guilty for leaving us so long to go after Viktor."

"Well, I'd be surprised it was affecting his work habits," O'Malley said. "I know from experience that he can turn these things around. He works harder . . ."

"That's for sure," Jones confirmed. "Somehow he manages to keep in steady contact with us and with Elvis and the others, and he's single-handedly exploring every possible escape route for when D-Day comes, *plus* he's doing the laser-siting work, along with a whole bunch of other things.

"As to where he is living in that city, or how he is disguising himself—who knows?"

"He's probably holed up in some cellar somewhere, living with the rats," O'Malley said. "You know, doing penance for taking off on his Club Med adventure."

85

CHAPTER 14

Hunter woke up to the feeling of someone massaging his back.

"The shoulders, please," he said, still groggy.

The topless woman began concentrating her efforts on the bruised area near his upper left shoulder.

"How did that happen?" she asked, whispering in his ear.

He turned over and finally opened his eyes. She was beautiful . . .

"Occupational hazard," he told her.

Another very attractive woman, also topless, walked into the massive bedroom suite, carrying a tray of hot bread and coffee.

"You came in pretty late last night," the second woman told him. "Running with those bitchsd downtown again?"

Instantly the girl massaging his shoulder stopped. "Were you down in the cathouses again?" she asked him sternly.

Hunter pulled himself up, and fashioned a

backrest of a half dozen silk pillows. "C'mon now, ladies, be nice," he told them, smiling. "Why would I have to go to a cathouse, when I have you two lovely girls right here?"

"What a bullshit artist," the girl with the food said.

Their names were Kara (the massager) and Jackie (the cook). He had met them several weeks before at one of the Football City nightclubs where he had gone on a survelliance mission. They were out of Las Vegas, which was now practically abandoned, where they had been "working girls" before the Big War. It was natural that they would wind up in Football City during its heyday. Somehow they survived the war against the Family and the Circle Army occupation.

They had taken him in to their luxurious penthouse right on the edge of the downtown section, and into their bed, which they shared anyway. The reminded him of Uni and Aki, his two housemates back at his base in Oregon. Like those two girls, Kara and Jackie were smart, beautiful, warm, giving, into being erotic and, when the mood struck them, imaginatively bi-sexual.

They were also the highest-priced call girls in Football City.

"Big doings downtown last night," Kara said, returning to rubbing his shoulder. "The Executive Club was blown up. A lot of Circle big shots went up with it."

Hunter tried to look surprised, but could manage only a satisfied smile. It was apparent that Elvis and the others had gotten Phase Two off on a good start.

"My trick told me there were also some explosions down near the docks," Jackie said, pouring him a cup of coffee. "I suppose you know nothing about any of this?" she asked him.

Hunter shrugged. "What would I know?" he said. "I'm just an innocent bystander. Violence gives me a headache."

"Sure it does," Kara said with no small amount of disbelief. She knew he kept a stash of hand grenades, ammunition, an M-16 and some other crazy electronic contraption under their bed, as well as several boxes filled with different styles of clothing. One night he would go out looking like a vagrant, the next night, he'd be dressed to the nines. He had Circle Army uniforms, from colonels to privates, plus uniforms of some of the Circle allies. She and Jackie knew he was involved in something very mysterious and dangerous every night. But they were much too discreet to ask him exactly what it was. Besides, they really didn't want to know . . .

He finished his breakfast and reached out for Jackie to join them on the bed. She was tall. At 6-1, just an inch shorter than he was. She had blonde hair, cut in the shag style and long, inviting legs. Kara on the other hand was a brunette, somewhat petite, but with a nice figure.

They both cuddled up to his chest. "What should we do today?" Kara asked. "I don't have my first appointment until after sundown."

He kissed them both and drew them closer to him. Despite the presence of the two beauties, he still felt empty. Even melancholy.

Too many things are missing . . . he thought.

"Don't worry," he said, knowing he had a few hours to try to raise his spirits. "We'll think of something . . ."

CHAPTER 15

Viceroy Dick was fuming.

"What in hell happened down on those docks last night, Colonel?" he asked sternly.

They were in the Viceroy's working chamber. There were no teen age girls about; no massive quantity of cocaine. Viceroy Dick was dressed in his standard black Circle Army general's uniform and he looked all business.

Colonel Muss could only shrug at his question. "Someone blew up two piers and a small oil holding tank," he said. "We exchanged fire with them from the bridge, but by the time we got down to the docks, they were gone."

"And this bombing disrupted the prisoner executions?" Viceroy Dick was just about frothing at the mouth.

Muss nodded glumly. "They blew the docks and started firing on us," he said. "We didn't know the extent of their strength, so we withdrew and postponed the executions."

Viceroy Dick pounded his desk top once—hard.

"You have no idea what could happen now, Colonel," he shouted. "If those goddamn Russians get wind of this, they can make big trouble for me. And that means big trouble for you, Muss."

Viceroy Dick took a minute to regain his composure. He wished he was within snorting distance of his cocaine bowl.

"Now who planted those bombs down at the docks? And where the hell did they come from?" he asked Muss sternly.

"It's hard to say, sir," Muss stumbled. "They probably had a boat and came across from the Illinois side. As to who they were, I guess they were saboteurs . . ."

"You *guess* they were saboteurs?" Viceroy Dick asked, his voice rising in anger. "And do you *guess* that they were also responsible for blowing up the Executive Club?"

"I . . . I really don't know, sir," Muss admitted.

"We lost twenty seven officers last night," he told Muss. "Twenty seven men who were very close to the inner-workings of our army. Their knowledge and expertise will be sorely missed when it comes time for us to make our move . . .

"Now you're responsible for the overall defense of this city inside and out, Colonel. That's why when I ask you for answers I'd better get some!"

"I've increased patrols around the city from downtown to the docks," Muss told him. "We'll triple the number of soldiers on-duty in the streets by tonight. And we've increased patrols along our western border. We're also in the process of doubling the buffer zone minefields between us and them and we've increased our NightScope capability up and down our line."

"This is just standard bullshit, Colonel!" Dick screamed. "Just track down those saboteurs . . ."

Muss bowed to the waist. "Sir, believe me," he said.

"We will. And we will also accelerate the executions starting tonight. This part of our plan will not fail . . ."

Viceroy Dick simply stared at him. "It had better not, Muss," he said. "Because if it does, you'll go over that bridge railing right along with the rest of the scum . . ."

CHAPTER 16

It was just past midnight when Hunter found the spot in the catacombs closest to the underground storage area he had spotted on the radar imager the night before.

Using the imager printout as a guide, he was able to determine that the storage area was four feet in from a particular junction of two tunnels on the very northeast section of the network. Confident that he had the correct location, he unstrapped the shovel from his back and started to dig.

It took him less than an hour to break through the clayish soil, but once he did, he came to a thin, metal heating shaft which passed right through a thin concrete wall. Using his jack knife, he was able to chip a hole in the wall large enough for him to put his eye to.

It was completely dark on the other side of the wall, which was just the way he had hoped to find it. Working patiently for another half hour, he was able to cut a hole in the heat shaft wide enough for him to squeeze through. Climbing into the shaft, it wasn't long before he came to a grate, which he quietly kicked out.

Only after he had passed through the grate opening and had his feet on solid ground did he unhook his flashlight and turn it on.

It was a parking garage, an old one that had been recently, and rather amateurishly, reenforced. But the construction of the facility wasn't what interested him. It was what it held. When he had viewed the area through the radar imager he had guessed it contained boxcars. It turned out he was wrong—but not by much.

The garage held more than one hundred tractor trailer trucks. Kenworths, Macks, Ward La France and many others, there were trucks of all shapes and sizes, each one hooked up to a plain, unpainted trailer.

"No way this is all to store ammunition," Hunter said to himself. It was so hot inside the garage, he was perspiring. Knowing that was a relief. Even the dummies who ran The Circle knew better than to store ammo in such a humid space.

Yet what did the trailers contain?

To find out, he climbed up on the back of one rig and tried to open its rear loading door. He yanked, but the door wouldn't budge. He jiggled the lock and handle and gave it another yank. Still, it would not open. He played the flashlight along the sides of the door.

That's when he saw that the door was welded shut.

"Now what the hell does this mean?" he wondered.

He checked several other trucks and found that they too had their doors welded shut.

He moved along the two lines of trucks. There were many more of them down here than had shown up on the imager's narrow beam. Easily 100 rigs or more.

But it was at the front of the garage that he saw the strangest vehicle of all . . .

It was an APC that looked as if it had been stretched out half its size again. It was painted gold, carried no guns or grenade launchers, only several long radio antennas. And although the custom-made vehicle had more than a dozen means of access, all but one of these was also welded shut.

The only hatchway not welded was the one over the driver's position and this was secured by a very sophisticated electronic lock. It defied 10 minutes of his expert lock-picking skills, his conclusion being that the device was laser activated.

He shook his head in frustration. The Circle was obviously hiding something in the trailers, something of such value to them that they welded everything shut. Yet, the treasure trove was mobile. He checked the fuel tanks on several of the trucks and noted that they were all filled to the top. And the fact that the garage was so close to the reconstructed bridges was, he knew, also no coincidence.

It all added up to only one thing: whatever was locked inside the containers, The Circle could move it out of the garage, and presumably out of the city at a moment's notice . . .

CHAPTER 17

Kara was relaxing, dressed only in a bikini, in the rear cabin of the luxurious river yacht when she heard the two jets pass high overhead.

"Goddamn airplanes again," her customer, a Circle Army lieutenant colonel named Hoover, cursed as he opened a bottle of wine.

They both listened as the two jets screamed above the city. The pop-pop of anti-aircraft fire started up at just about the same time as the air raid sirens began wailing.

"Sergeant!" Hoover called out to the man in charge of his personal security squad. "You'd better have that Stinger warmed up."

"It's ready if we need it, sir," the reply came back from above decks.

"Are we in any danger?" Kara asked, the whining of the jets and the booming of the AA guns growing in intensity.

"No, my dear," Hoover said. "Not out here. The

bastards always insist on bombing the center of the city, which is why I'm glad you suggested our little party should take place out here — on a peaceful cruise on the river. If they come anywhere near here, my boys will chase them away."

He sat down beside her, handed her a glass of wine and routinely began fondling her breasts.

"These air raids are getting more frequent," she said, ignoring his groping hands and sipping her wine. "And the bombings downtown. Everyone says the Westerners are going to attack the city soon."

Hoover gulped his wine nervously. "That's bullshit, honey," he said, putting on a brave front. "They're just a bunch of cowboys trying to spook us . . ."

Just then, the yacht shuddered with the sound of two bombs crashing down in the downtown section of the city.

Kara shivered. "Well, they're doing a good job . . ." she said.

The air raid lasted 20 minutes, and finally the whine of the jets disappeared and the steady thumping of the AA guns died down.

"Feel better?" Hoover asked Kara, handing her yet another glass of wine. "I hope this won't affect your . . . performance."

She didn't answer him. Instead she took the glass of wine and drained it in two gulps.

"Colonel?" a voice above decks called down. "We've got a small boat pulling alongside. One guy driving, he's got a girl in back . . ."

Hoover clapped his hands in glee. "Splendid!" he called out. Then turning to Kara he said: "Your partner for the evening is here . . ."

Again, Kara just nodded. Hoover wasn't as fat and ugly as most of the Circle Army officers that made up her clientele. But he was just as depraved . . .

They heard the small boat arrive, drop off its passenger, then depart. Soon the sergeant was leading a young girl down into the cabin, carrying a small suitcase for her.

"Thank you, sergeant," Hoover said. "Now lock that door and don't disturb us for anything short of all-out war."

He turned to the new arrival. "And what is your name, my dear?"

"Angie," was her reply. She was one of Viceroy Dick's teen beauty brigade, lent to Hoover as a reward for his loyalty. Like the rest of Dick's stable, she was young, blonde, used, confused and addicted to cocaine.

"All right, ladies," Hoover said. "Use that cabin over there to get . . . prepared. And please hurry."

Kara got up and took the young girl by the hand, leading her into the small adjacent cabin.

"Don't mind this one," she told her. "He's really not as bad as the rest."

Angie nodded and opened the suitcase. "I went shopping today," she said, nervously. "I tried to get everything he wanted, but what I couldn't get, I borrowed."

Kara put her hand on the girl's shoulder and squeezed it. She was sweet, pretty kid—not the type one would expect to be mixed up in this business. But then again, none of the Viceroy's girls looked that way.

"Really, there's nothing to be nervous about," Kara

97

told her as she kissed her lightly on the cheek. "He won't even hardly touch us . . ."

Angie smiled slightly and emptied out the contents of the suitcase. Then both of them went about the business of getting dressed.

"Hurry, girls!" they heard Hoover call out from the next room. "I can't hold out much longer . . ."

Kara and Angie came out of the small cabin ten minutes later and presented themselves to Hoover.

They were dressed just the way he wanted them to be—their clothes, their hair and make-up were just right.

"Oh, girls," Hoover said, his voice jittery with anticipation. "You are perfect . . ."

Both were wearing identical outfits: a female-version of a black tuxedo, a silk blouse, open to the navel and exposing the bosom, a garter-belt holding up black stockings and short leather boots. Each wore a string of fake diamonds around their neck and a glass tiara to hold back their hair. The overall effect was both regal and trashy at the same time.

Hoover opened a bottle of champagne and poured out three glasses. Then he opened a small snuff box and took a long, strong sniff of cocaine.

"This is heaven, girls . . ." he said.

They drank the champagne as Hoover continually insisted both women turn pirouettes for him. "You look just like her . . ." he moaned over and over.

He leaned back and unfastened his belt buckle.

"Kara, you know what to do," he said.

She smiled at him and then slowly, like an actress in a high-class porn movie, she began removing Angie's clothes and rubbing the young girl's body.

Hoover reached inside his pocket and produced a well-worn photograph. It was of a woman, dressed exactly like the two girls in front of him now.

As Kara stripped Angie naked and proceeded to seduce the young girl, Hoover tried his best to keep one eye on the live action.

But his attention was always drawn back to the photograph.

"She was once ours . . ." he murmured as he prematurely reached his first climax.

CHAPTER 18

The second air raid of the night came in at exactly 1:15 A.M.

Just as with the previous attack, Hunter was stationed on top of the Bell Building, armed with what looked like an oddly shaped rocket launcher. In reality, the device was a PAVE PENNY laser designator. His role in this raid, as in all the previous ones, was to locate targets of opportunity for the attacking jets. He did this by shooting a laser beam from the PAVE PENNY at a target. A pod being carried on each of the attacking jets would detect the laser radiation being bounced from the target. Then, once the raiders' Maverick missiles were released, they would seek out the laser designation track and follow it right down to the target.

The air raid sirens went up not thirty seconds before the two A-4 Skyhawks appeared over the city. They came in low, dropping no bombs on

100

their first pass but making the maximum amount of noise in the process. As the small jets flashed across the well-lit downtown area, their pilots routinely maneuvered away from the scattering of AA fire coming up to meet them.

Hunter checked that all systems were working in the laser designator. Then he leaned over the building's railing and, clicking on the device's low-light scope, started panning the city, looking for a suitable target.

His first was a gasoline storage facility the Circle had foolishly built on a stretch of flat ground near the now-abandoned massive Football City Stadium. It was a perfect target: cutting the enemy's fuel supplies was important to the Western Forces' overall strategy, and the target was isolated and therefore away from any innocent civilians.

Hunter lined up the bottom of the storage tank in his viewfinder and squeezed the PAVE PENNY's trigger. He heard a sizzling sound come from inside the device, as the internal CO_2 laser guidance link went to work. The faintest stream of bluish light shot out of the front and he saw the reassuring red "pop" show on his low-light rangefinder. This meant the laser beam was targeted perfectly on the base of the gasoline tank three miles away.

Both Skyhawks had circled the city and now the lead A-4 was swooping in for its bomb run. Hunter knew the pilot was monitoring the laser target acquisition reading on his cockpit's Head's Up Display. He watched as the A-4 banked toward the target and dropped down to 500 feet above the deck. All around the airplane lights bursts of small AA fire were going off, but nothing deterred the airplane's pilot from making his run.

About a half mile from the target, the A-4 pilot launched his Maverick. Keeping the PAVE PENNY designator steady, Hunter could see the missile's fiery trail out of the corner of his eye. Then, with a brilliant flash, the missile slammed into the gasoline tank. Suddenly, half the city was lit up with the glow the good-sized explosion. The noise from the blast reached him a few seconds later . . .

"That's one," he whispered as he quickly sought out another target.

The sound of the explosion caused Viceroy Dick to wake up in a shot.

He ran to the window of his opulent bedroom and saw the flames from the destroyed gasoline tank leaping into the night sky.

"Jesus Christ!" he cursed, quickly putting on his satin robe. "Those sons-of-bitches . . ."

He picked up the phone and was punching in Major Tomm's headquarters when the woman in his bed woke up.

"Get out of here!" he yelled at her, just a second before he screamed into the phone: "Get me Tomm, now!"

"Can I get paid?" the woman asked, routinely gathering her clothes.

The Viceroy gave her the evil eye. "Hey honey, I heard you were the best lay in town," he said. "What happened?"

"What happened was you did so much coke you couldn't get it up . . ." she snapped back at him.

He got up in an instant, grabbed her and slapped her hard across her face. "That's a very foolish way to talk to me," he said harshly.

The woman played it smart. She fell to her knees and hung her head. "I'm sorry, sir," she said with a convincing sob. "I'm sure if we had . . . more time, I would have been able to please you."

It was exactly what the Viceroy wanted to hear.

"OK, bitch," he said. "Get up and talk to the major of the guard outside. He'll pay you . . ."

She quickly thanked him with a long French kiss and a gentle squeeze between his legs. "Let me try it again some time," she cooed.

"Maybe," he said, returning to the phone.

As she was leaving, she heard him say into the phone: "For Christ's sake, Tomm, can't your anti-aircraft guys hit anything?"

She walked down the long bedroom corridor and met the major of the guard.

"Two bags of gold," she told him. "Or ten bags of real silver."

The major whistled as he reached inside his desk and came up with the silver. "You're an expensive piece of ass," he said.

"You'd have to pay to find out," she told him, slipping the ten bags into her purse. "But, frankly, I don't think you can afford it . . ."

The man's face turned a slight red. "Don't be so sure, honey," he retorted. "Wait until pay day comes around."

She laughed in his face. "OK, big boy," she said. "If you got the money and you the guts to do it, just ask your boss for my number.

"The name is Jackie . . ."

Three minutes later, the major of the guard was dead.

As soon as the woman left, he had heard another elevator rising up to the penthouse. Assuming it was another woman or two for the Viceroy, he settled back behind his desk and waited for the lift to arrive.

But once it did, he was surprised, then shocked, when instead of a pair of teenage girls, a squad of Soviet soldiers trooped off.

He never even made it to his gun. Two bullets from a silencer-equipped AK-47 had caught him in the forehead and in the temple, the muffled shots making a sickening punching sound as they split his skull wide open.

The Soviet soldiers, five gunmen and one officer, marched down the passageway and kicked in Viceroy Dick's bedroom door just as the man was laying out several lines of cocaine.

"What the hell is this?" Dick demanded. He instantly recognized the officer as the younger of the pair that had visited him recently.

"You were told to do something and you failed," the officer said, as the five soldiers instantly surrounded the Viceroy. All six Russians were wearing the same black leather style uniform.

"If you are talking about the POW liquidation, we are taking care of that right now," Viceroy Dick said, his voice shaky.

"Too late," the officer said. "You have devoted far too much time to drugs and fucking little girls. My superior is a very impatient man. He's angry. And that makes me very angry . . ."

"So now what?" the Viceroy asked, a little shakily.

He knew these were not ordinary Soviet soldiers—they were part of the *Spetsnaz*, the Soviet Special Forces, renowned for their brutal tactics.

"Now, you will do exactly what we tell you to do," the officer said. "Then we might allow you to select your way to die . . ."

CHAPTER 19

Kara gave Angie a long, hard French kiss.

"Good night now, sweetie," she said, helping the young girl into the small boat that had pulled alongside the yacht. "Maybe we can play together again sometime . . ."

"OK, maybe . . ." Angie said, settling down into the skiff.

The driver gunned the outboard engine and the boat moved quickly away from the yacht, heading in toward shore.

Kara lit a cigarette and checked her watch. It was 3:00 in the morning, almost time to get her own show on the road. She walked to the back of the deck and looked out toward the city. Four separate fires were burning—the largest being one in the heart of downtown, and the others near the old stadium grounds. She believed these were the result of the air raid they had heard go over about an hour before.

She sat down on a deck chair, intent on relaxing before she had to go back down and jerk Hoover off for the third and final time. She had to admit that she had enjoyed their little dress-up show. There was something very pleasurable in dressing up like this woman the Circle officers called the Queen. All the high-priced girls were being asked to do it. In fact, it was becoming quite the rage among the paying clientele of Football City. Besides, she knew the act would be worth at least six bags of silver for her.

She finished her cigarette and was about to flick the butt off the side of the boat when she saw a floating object moving toward her. She leaned over the railing, trying to focus her eyes to the darkness and figure out what it was. She did this not simply out of curiosity; criminals in Football City had been known to wrap all sorts of things — weapons, cocaine, stolen articles — in floating bales and set them free in the river for pickup by accomplices downstream. Perhaps Kara had found some kind of floating treasure chest.

The object was now about five feet off the bow and gradually moving closer. It was tied with several lengths of rope and was bobbing with an irregular motion. Then she saw another one, about 15 feet off the bow. Then another just slightly further away.

She grabbed one of the yacht's docking hooks and after a few attempts, managed to snag the floating object. Despite some difficulty provided by the river's current, she was able to pull the object right up to the back of the boat, close enough for her to reach down and turn it over.

When she did, she thought she had suddenly been thrown into a nightmare . . .

It was a body. She thought it was a man, but she

couldn't be sure because its throat had been horribly slashed, and this had caused the facial features to scrunch up.

She screamed and immediately three crew members were standing beside her. One of them used the hook to snag another of the objects floating by and this too turned out to be a dead man.

The soldiers turned on the yacht's rear beacon lamp and aimed it out over the river. Even they were horrified to find that the yacht was surrounded by literally hundreds of floating bodies.

Each one, they were sure, with its throat slashed . . .

CHAPTER 20

The big helicopter set down outside the abandoned town of St. Charles just as the sun was beginning to rise.

Waiting nearby, sitting atop an armored personnel carrier, was General Dave Jones and Marine Captain John "Bull" Dozer. They were about 21 miles from Football City, right at the southern junction of the Free Canadian front lines.

"This has got to be serious for him to risk blowing everything to come here and talk to us," Dozer said to Jones.

"So serious he didn't want to send it even in a secure transmission," Jones agreed. "I'm almost afraid to hear what he has to say . . ."

Just then the sliding door on the big Sea Stallion opened and Hawk Hunter climbed out.

The two officers jumped from the APC and met the pilot halfway, vigorously shaking hands with him.

"Jesus, Hawk, you look none the worse for wear," Dozer told him, seeing his friend for the first time in weeks. "We've been taking bets on how many sewer rat bites you'd have by this time."

"I wish I was living in a sewer back there," he told them, his voice fraught with worry. "It would probably be safer."

"What's up, Hawk," Jones asked. As commander-in-chief of all the Western Forces, he knew that Hunter's report would affect everyone from him on down.

"We've got to attack the city at once," Hunter told them. "We can't possibly delay any longer . . ."

Jones was stunned for a moment. "But why?" he asked.

"They've started killing the prisoners," Hunter told them bluntly. "Mass executions. In the middle of the night. Elvis and his guys stumbled upon one two nights ago when they were blowing up the dock works. Without realizing it, their action postponed the killings. But now, last night, a friend of mine saw at least five hundred bodies in the river. All of them wearing prisoners' uniforms. All of them bound hand and foot. All of them with their throats cut . . ."

"Good God . . ." Jones whispered. "Five *hundred*? Is your source reliable, Hawk?"

"Believe me, she has no reason to lie about it," he said. "In fact, she was in a near state of shock when she told me. I checked with a couple of my other sources. They confirmed that a few hours past midnight, Circle guards went into one of the

POW compounds and just randomly selected five hundred prisoners."

Jones shook his head. "We expected something like this when the battle started," he said. "But why in hell are they killing those guys now?"

"I know it doesn't make any sense," Hunter said. "It's almost as if Viceroy Dick suddenly stopped giving the orders. But they're doing it."

"They're dealing away their only trump card," Dozer said. "If they kill the prisoners, they'll be holding nothing to bargain with."

"Damn!" Jones said angrily. "Have we been reading these bastards wrong all along?"

The three of them were silent for a while. Finally Hunter asked: "Can we do it? Do we have enough men and resources right now to risk it?"

"As of this moment, we're more than evenly matched with them," Jones said. However, I think we've done a good job in fooling them that we are actually twice as strong."

"Who are the closest reenforcements now?" Hunter asked.

Jones thought a moment. "Well, a big group of Texans are about six days away," he said. "There's a division of men right there. We got two brigades of Free Canadian Volunteers that are about ten days away, plus a reenforced PAAC division coming right from back home in LA. But they won't be here for two weeks."

Hunter shook his head. "It will be too late if we have to wait for them," he said. "How about our equipment?"

This was Dozer's department.

"They got the edge in armor; we've got the edge in airpower," he said simply. "Luckily, they're not

111

holding many SAMs that we know of . . ."

"That's another thing," Hunter said. "I'm sure Ben and J.T. told you about the strange underground area we found on the imager the other night . . ."

Both men nodded. "You got down there to see what it was?" Dozer asked.

"Not exactly," Hunter replied. He went on to tell them about the hundred or so tractor trailers and the strange elongated APC.

"And their doors were *welded* shut?" Jones asked. "What the hell for?"

Hunter could only shrug. "It's been driving me crazy ever since," he admitted. "What could be so valuable to them that they would not only go to such great lengths hiding it, but would weld it inside of a hundred tractor trailers? And this strange gold APC. It has a laser lock on it. Probably the most sophisticated piece of electronic equipment in the city."

"Just another strange piece of this jigsaw puzzle," Jones said, pulling his chin in thought.

Hunter checked the time.

"It's going to be fully light soon," he said. "I'll have to get going . . ."

"OK," Jones said. "I'll put out the call immediately, to the Texans and everyone from here to the Pacific. We'll have to get some troop airlift going, but even still I can't imagine our getting more than five or six battalions before then.

"But it will have to do . . ."

Hunter shook hands with both of them. "That's what I hoped to hear you say, sir," he told Jones. "I'll alert the underground and Elvis and the boys. We'll have to work quickly, but I'm sure we can have the escape routes plotted by midnight tonight."

"OK," Jones said, checking his watch. "We'll open up with the big guns at oh-four hundred tomorrow, just about twenty-four hours from now. I've got to start passing the words to the others. We'll jump off at oh-five hundred. . . ."

"Well, I've got a lot of work to do before then," Hunter said. "Not the least of which is the prevent them from cutting five hundred more throats tonight."

With that, he turned and ran back to the helicopter, which took off immediately.

"He's got that look in his eye," Dozer said. "I don't know how he does it—taking on all this. He's just a pilot, for God's sake . . ."

Jones nodded in agreement. "Well, if he's so charged up now," the general asked, "what's he going to be like when they get his jet fixed?"

CHAPTER 21

Yaz's back was already sore and he'd only been digging for an hour or so.

The problem with being an urban guerrilla, he told himself, was that if you worked in the day and planted bombs at night, you didn't get very much sleep in between. The only thing keeping him going was the fact that he knew a hundred or so people inside the city—and tens of thousands waiting just outside of it—were working toward freeing him and the others.

That was a cause he could definitely rally behind . . .

Just then, someone poked him in the back. He turned to see a Circle Army guard, one he didn't recognize.

The man didn't say a word. Instead, he held both his hands up, palms out. Then he made two V-for-Victory signs and put them together. The four fingers formed a "W."

Yaz was astounded. The "W" hand signal had originated back in the Med by the Moroccan desert fighters who had helped Hunter and the Brits fight in Suez. The Arab soldiers had come to admire The Wingman and, whenever they saw him, they would make the sign of the "W" and give a deep bow. Now this Circle Army soldier had done the same thing.

At least, he thought he was a Circle soldier . . .

"Follow me," the man said, unlocking Yaz's leg irons.

The other POWs digging nearby were studiously ignoring the encounter. Rumors had been flying around the work site all morning about The Circle staging mass executions of POWs. Therefore, many of them feared the tap on the shoulder or the poke in the ribs, thinking they might turn and see the Grim Reaper standing behind them.

But Yaz followed the guard without question and soon the man led him to the isolated part of the tunnel and the entrance to the pump chamber. He pointed to the crawl pipe, indicated that Yaz should go in, then he quickly walked away, back up to the front of the tunnel.

Yaz squeezed through the pipe and knocked on the door at the other end. It opened and he was surprised to see the chamber was filled with more than 100 fighters—some in POW garb, others in trusty uniforms, still others wearing black guerrilla outfits. There were more than a few people wearing Circle uniforms too.

In the middle of the crowd he saw a familiar face. It belonged to Hawk Hunter . . .

The morning found Colonel Muss meeting with

his front line commanders.

"We sowed two hundred fifty claymores last night, Colonel," one of his officers—the commander of the mine-laying squads—told him. "We will be able to put in another two hundred or so tonight, if you wish . . ."

They were standing on a bluff that looked out to the west. The terrain in this part of the continent was odd—the result, Muss knew, of a major earthquake that had hit the area in the 1800s, a quake so strong it had re-routed the Mississippi by more than a mile. The shake-up had left miles of flat plains, interrupted at irregular intervals by the high bluffs.

By using his high-powered binoculars, Muss could just barely see activity off in the distance. Trucks moving about, a helicopter dipping in flight, the smoke or steam from some unknown engine. It was the advance elements of the Western Forces armies he was watching, and he had the distinct feeling that someone way out there was watching him through their binoculars.

They are getting ready to pounce, he thought.

"You may have other things to do tonight," Muss told the officer in charge of laying mines along the buffer zone. "Make sure your men are well-fed and carrying their full load of ammunition . . ."

The man snapped a salute. "Yes, sir," he said confidently, without reminding Muss that most of his men were engineers and therefore of very little use if it came down to hand-to-hand fighting.

"What is our anti-aircraft capability?" Muss asked another of his officers.

"We have a dozen operating SA-7's, sir," the man in charge of AA told him. "They're shoulder-launched models of course. We have twenty mobile radar-guided guns, plus four stationary SA-2 sites."

"And what do we estimate their air strength to be?" Muss asked.

The AA officer glanced around nervously. "Three squadrons, sir, that we're sure of," he said. "Maybe more."

" 'Maybe more,' or *definitely* more?" Muss asked.

The man was on the spot and he knew it. "Probably 'definitely,' sir . . ." he answered. "But, I'm sure with time, I can convert some of our artillery pieces to do AA duty."

Muss turned and addressed the man directly. "That kind of time we don't have," he said. "Can your fixed SA-2 sites be readily dismantled?"

The officer nodded. "Yes, sir," he said. "But we just put them in place . . ."

"Be ready to break them down again," Muss said. The order surprised all of the eight officers surrounding him, but no one dared ask the reason behind it.

Muss then surveyed the elaborate trenchworks that stretched out before him for a mile and as far as he could see both left and right. He knew they ran along the entire front.

"Our trenches, they hold how many men?"

"About two divisions, sir," the fortifications officer answered.

"Close to twenty thousand men, then?" Muss asked.

The officer nodded. "Shall we dig more, Colonel?"

Muss shook his head slowly. "No," he said. "There'll be no need for that."

He turned and addressed the entire group. "There's been a change in our . . . strategy, let's

117

say," Muss told them. "We will now be working under a plan known as tactical defense. That's all I want you to know at the moment. Please get all of your units ready to move out at a moment's notice."

This order openly shocked the officers. But once again, every one of them decided to keep his mouth shut.

"You will be getting reenforcements around noontime," Muss continued. "Allied troops. Afrikaners, as well as North Koreans and Cubans.

"Pull your men out and let the new arrivals take up their positions in the trenches. When the allies get here, provide them with enough ammunition to keep them supplied for ten to fifteen minutes of fighting, but not a single bullet more."

He took one last look at the enemy lines, nearly 20 miles away. He could almost *feel* activity on the other side, almost hear the hum of their work, like the noise of a beehive. How things had changed, he thought. Once he was convinced that The Circle would rule *both* Americas—north and south, and someday, other continents as well. Now he was telling his officers to count their bullets. Tactical defense indeed . . .

He turned to walk back to his staff car, then remembered one last item. "And gentlemen, when the allies arrive to take the trenches," he said. "Don't bother to feed them, either . . ."

CHAPTER 22

Yaz inflated 248 inner tubes before the small motor on his air compressor ran out of fuel.

He waded his way through the rubber donuts that were now cluttering every square inch of the pump chamber, and out into the catacomb where a barrel of gasoline was available. Filling up a five-gallon can, he returned to his compressor and was soon inflating inner tube number 249.

His reunion with Hunter had been all too brief. The rumors about The Circle's systematic killing of prisoners was true, the pilot had told them all. Now the whole timetable for releasing the POWs and evacuating the citizens from the occupied city had been drastically compacted into 24 hours. And still they had to move fast to prevent further mass executions.

So Yaz was given the job of blowing up 1500 of the inner tubes. Other members of the underground and the Western Forces guerrillas were distributing the life rafts to strategic points around the tunnels. Still others were quietly passing the word all over the city that midnight was the H-Hour for the escape to begin.

Hunter had told him and the others that he had finally completed mapping the catacombs, and at that moment, two squads of guerrillas were spray painting directions in the tunnels all over the city, while others were hastily erecting water barriers which would direct the flow of water correctly when the water lock was opened at H-Hour.

All of the major POW holding points had been located from below, and guerrillas within their ranks were ready to direct prisoners to their escape hatch when the time came.

The same held true for the 500 or so citizens remaining in Football City. Just about everyone of them knew that nearly every restaurant, nightclub and bar in the downtown area had a hatch leading to the catacombs, courtesy of the St. Louis 1930's gangsters. Many of these had been sealed up by the police in the 1940's, but the Football City underground had been working for the past few weeks unsealing the ones that remained, about 100 in all. Those civilians who could be trusted were being told to go out for a drink around midnight — and be prepared to get wet when they did so.

It was three in the afternoon when Yaz finally inflated his 1500th inner tube. Throughout the day, guerrillas and members of the underground had been carrying the tubes away at regular intervals. Now that they'd all been dispersed, Hunter himself climbed into the pump chamber.

"What's next, Hawk?" Yaz asked him.

"Believe it or not," Hunter told him. "Eat, then sleep."

He had a gunny sack with him, which turned out to be holding several loaves of bread and some warm milk.

"God only knows when we'll get our next meal," he said to Yaz.

CHAPTER 23

Colonel Muss had never felt better . . .

He hadn't slept in nearly 24 hours, his throat was dry, and his stomach empty. His nose was also running. But none of this bothered him — just 30 minutes before, he had done four long lines of Viceroy Dick's best cocaine and now he was feeling like he was on top of the world. And the plastic bag of the stuff he had hidden in his shoe insured him that the feeling would continue, at least through the night, possibly even into the next day.

He was riding in the lead car of a long column of troop trucks, 22 vehicles in all that was heading for the river's edge on the eastern fringe of Football City. They were slowly making their way down the crumbling road known as Route 70, and would soon turn off to 1st Street, which would bring them down to the river. Then it would be a right turn onto the entrance ramp to one of the recently-reopened bridges.

Loaded in the back of the troop trucks were 500 more prisoners, selected at random from one of the POW camps inside the city. Just as the night before, they were to be lined up on the bridge railing, 25 at a time, blindfolded and legs and arms tied. Then—and this was the part that Muss promised himself he would not watch—their throats would be slashed and their bodies thrown into the Mississippi. It had gone off like clockwork the night before, due in no small part to the presence of five Soviet *Spetsnaz* troopers, who not only oversaw the whole operation, but wielded the knives when the time came to slit the prisoners' throats.

Muss reached down to his stash of cocaine just as the convoy turned off Route 70 and onto 1st Street. He hadn't seen Viceroy Dick in nearly two days—and didn't even know whether the man was alive or not. He didn't really care. A *Spetsnaz* officer was giving the orders in Football City now. One of his first acts was to make Muss the coordinator of the executions. In return, the Soviets had given Muss the run of Viceroy Dick's former digs, including the drug-stocked "recreation" chamber. This is where Muss had found and used the cocaine and this is where Muss had made arrangements to have four teen age girls waiting for him after the executions were carried out.

The convoy moved along the darkened river road, the lights of the bridge just visible ahead of them. Muss had just snorted two more loads of coke, when he looked up and saw a man standing in the middle of the roadway.

123

"Who the fuck is that?" he asked his driver as the man slowed the car down, caused the convoy trucks behind him to squeal their brakes.

The man was dressed in what looked like a black flight suit and he was wearing a baseball cap over his hooded mask.

He was also armed with what looked to Muss to be a rocket-propelled grenade launcher . . .

"Jesus Christ, run him over!" Muss screamed to his driver.

But it was too late . . .

The man quickly raised the RPG launcher and fired directly at the car. The projectile hit the radiator grating and exploded, lifting the car off the ground a full five feet, and instantly killing the driver with a chunk of shrapnel in his chest.

Muss went out through the windshield and was thrown off to the side of the road. Even while he was in the air, he caught a frightening glimpse of many men, dressed like the one who had fired the RPG, running up from both sides of the road, firing weapons.

Muss landed hard in a clump of grass and sticks, breaking his left arm and leg. His face and chest were covered in blood pouring out of deep cuts he received when he crashed through the windshield. Yet he was still conscious and shock had set in, effectively, if temporarily, blocking out the otherwise excruciating pain of his wounds.

From the clump of grass he watched as the armed men made short work of the Circle guards who had been driving the troop trucks. The sharp firefight lasted all of 30 seconds. Then he was suddenly aware of people running over him—stepping on his face and back, stumbling over his body in the dark. They were the POWs—they were being freed from the trucks and running toward the river. All of the troop trucks were now ablaze and Muss could hear the black-suited men yelling and talking to each other.

Certain they would kill him if he made a sound, the Circle colonel closed his eyes and pretended to be dead . . .

CHAPTER 24

A North Korean regimental commander heard the noise first.

Way off in the distance, a barely perceptible *pop,* followed closely by two more.

It was two in the morning, and up until this time, everything had been quiet in his sector. His troops, along with a mixture of Libyans and Cubans, had taken up positions in the Circle front line trenches shortly after noontime the day before. The Circle troops were marching back toward Football City just as his troops were marching forward. The commander would never forget the look in the eyes of the Circle soldiers as they viewed his troops.

One Circle trooper had even yelled it out: *"Suckers!"* he had said.

Now the North Korean watched as a thin yellow streak crossed the sky. It was high up when he focused his NightScope binoculars on it, the infra-red image revealing a large cylindrical object. As he watched, the tube deployed a parachute, and was now slowly dropping toward his lines.

He immediately barked out an order for all his men to hunker down in their trenches, and when he regained sight of the cylinder, it was only about 200 feet above the ground, about a quarter of a mile from his position.

Was it a camera of some kind? Or gas? Or perhaps a failed long-range rocket launch?

Just as the cylinder was 100 feet above the trenches it suddenly burst open with a deafening *crack!* and a flash of yellow fire . . .

With a strange jingling and hissing sound, the cylinder had exploded and shot out thousands of small sharp projectiles which ripped into the hapless North Korean troops in the trenches, exploding the minefields in front of them at the same time. Suddenly another parachute cylinder burst a half mile away. Then another even further away.

The North Korean commander felt a spray of tiny bullets rip his arm clean off his body. He was knocked backward just as another wave tore his left foot clean off. Lying in an instant pool of his own blood, the commander looked up at the night sky to see it was now criss-crossed with the yellow streaks and the hideous, slowly-descending cluster bombs . . .

One word came back to him as he slowly passed into Hell: *"Suckers . . ."*

The opening shots of yet another Battle for Football City had been fired . . .

Cluster bombs were falling all over the front as the Western Forces prepared to jump off in their invasion of Football City.

The efforts at deceiving the Circle with the phony recon photos were now paying off. The Westerners simply launched their attack from points where The Circle had thought they'd been the weakest, ignoring the Circle's frontline concentrations that had been established across from where they had thought the Westerners were the strongest.

It was a total diversion. From the Free Canadians in the north, down through the combined Pacific American-Football City Army in the middle to the anxious Texans in the south, the democratic troops rolled through the areas obliterated by the cluster bombs, got behind the Circle-sponsored trench troops and began a series of wide encircling pincer movement.

Once the enemy's sides were "rolled up," the Westerners' air corps went to work. Attack airplanes of all types — from PAAC A-7s and F-5s to Texan Phantoms and Free Canadian Skyhawks — bombarded the trapped enemy with barrages of anti-personnel bombs and napalm. There was no anti-aircraft opposition to speak of, and many of the trench troops — hired hands with little loyalty to The Circle — simply hid or fled after the initial air attacks.

From his mobile headquarters which was now following a column of Football City tanks into the outskirts of the city itself, General Jones was on the radio constantly, directing the overall battle. Beside him were Ben Wa and Twomey, who were overseeing the air operations, and "Bull" Dozer, who was coordinating the ground attack.

Within two hours they had breached the Circle lines in a half dozen places, and Western Forces troops were pouring through the gaps and heading for the heart of the city. Yet Jones and the others were far from complacent. Despite the initial successes, they knew the Circle trenches had been manned by the unreliable mercenaries and that was the reason the attack had started so well. Still ahead they knew they faced tough fighting against battle-hardened regulars of the Circle Army.

They had no idea what was happening within the city itself . . .

The Circle demolition squad arrived outside the POW compound and started flailing away at the large wooden door.

Confusion now reigned in the city—they could hear the booming of guns to their west and every man now knew the long-awaited attack on Football City had begun. Overhead, enemy jets streaked unimpeded, and it seemed like explosions were going off all over the city.

In the panic, the demolition team commander realized that no one had brought a key to unlock the massive wooden door. Now, as the troops took axes to the chains and padlock, the commander checked his watch. His orders—like those to the other demo teams now fanning out in the city— were crystal clear: kill all the POWs inside the chamber by detonating a half dozen concussion bombs just inside the entrance. Circle Army engineers had determined that the POWs deep inside the Holes would either die quickly from the concussion itself or from the cave-in which would surely follow. Either way, the commander knew he had to blow this cave and another one two miles away before he could join his main unit, which was already pulling out of the city.

It took five long minutes before his troopers had hacked and weakened the chains enough to finally break them with a fusillade of an AK-47.

"Quickly!" he yelled to his troops, as they pulled back the enormous doors. "First team, set the charges. Second team, go below and make sure none of those prisoners move a muscle . . ."

He watched a pair of F-5s roar overhead, their silhouettes taking on a ghostly glow in the near-dawn darkness. Where the hell were the Circle airplanes? Or the SAM battalions?

Another huge explosion went off just a block away, showering him and his team with pieces of hot rock and metal.

"Jesus Christ! Hurry!" he called out to his men who were setting up the concussion bombs as quickly as they could under the circumstances.

Two more Western Forces jets went over, each one firing a long stream of rockets at some target three blocks away. The commander knew the enemy airplanes were roaming freely, looking for targets of opportunity. Eventually one of them would spot them at the cave entrance . . .

"Bombs set!" his sergeant called out finally.

The commander heaved a sigh of relief and started hustling all of the non-essential troops out of the cave entrance.

Just then, two troopers who had gone down into the prisoners' cavern came running back out.

"Sir?" one of the them said to him. "There's no one down there . . ."

The commander shook his head once, as if to rid himself of the nonsensical statement. "What the hell do you mean, no one's down there?" he shouted at the man. "There better well be twenty-five hundred of those bastards down there!"

The man just numbly shook his head. "There's not . . ." he said. "They must have all escaped somehow . . ."

The commander repressed a desire to slap the man. Instead he grabbed the rest of his soldiers and with them, entered the cave himself.

It took a minute to run down into the huge cavern, but once he got there, he found out his trooper had been right. The cavern's gas lanterns were still lit, casting a dim light around the Hole. And there was evidence of the POWs—clothing, broken bowls, a pile of dirty blankets. But not a single prisoner remained . . .

"Sir, over here!" one of his troopers called out. The commander ran to the spot and found a narrow metal pipe had been wedged into the side of the cavern. At the other end he could see a large room with concrete walls, pipes and various dials and switches.

He was about to send a man through the pipe when he heard a rumbling coming from the entrance way. Suddenly the whole cavern seemed to be shaking, clumps of dirt started to fall. Then the gas-powered arc lights went out and the cavern was plunged into a frightening darkness.

"The bombs!" the commander screamed out. "Something set them off!"

Those were his last words. Three seconds later a massive concussion ripped into the Hole so powerful it violently threw several of the troopers against the cave wall. Others felt their heads split open. Moments later the cavern's roof fell in, burying the commander and his remaining troopers alive . . .

Colonel Muss was still conscious an hour after the POW convoy had been attacked.

He had yet to feel any pain, a fact he attributed to his non-stop ingestion of the cocaine stash which had survived intact in his boot. But the cocaine could not stop the pandemonium that was going on all around him.

The sky was filled with enemy jets. He could hear and sometimes feel the explosions go off in the city a half mile away. The commandos who had attacked his convoy had left the area, moving off toward the river as had the freed POWs. But the sound of nearby gunfire was still very much in the air.

Muss knew he had to get to the river, too. He was covered in the blood from a hundred separate glass cuts and his arm and leg were numb. In his drug-induced state, he felt that if he could make it to the water's edge and wash his wounds, they would heal and he wouldn't feel any pain — ever.

Slowly, he set out. Using his good elbow and his good leg to propel him, he crawled across the rubble-strewn river park and down the embankment to the muddy water of the Mississippi.

A patch of river weeds provided him adequate cover. Once in the water he washed the dirt and caked blood from his eyes, allowing him to see more than 10 feet in front of him. His ears were stinging, so loud were the sounds of explosions and gunfire. Now, looking up from the weeds, he saw why the noise was so intense: he had crawled right into the middle of a battle . . .

No sooner had he poked his head up out of the weeds than he was pulling it back down again. The scene before him was so outlandish, so *crazy*, he was sure that all the cocaine was making him hallucinate.

First of all, he had a clear view of three of the bridges that spanned the river. The two farthest away from him were presently jammed on both levels with fleeing Circle Army vehicles. Even in his shocked state, he knew he was watching Viceroy Dick's vaunted "Tactical Defense" in action. Back in the old days, it was simply called a "bug out." The once great Circle Army was retreating once again, and right behind them was another army—these were the hustlers, the criminals, the human leeches and the leftover mercenaries who were also fleeing in the face of the oncoming Western Forces. Even from this distance, Muss could sense their panic . . .

On the bridge closest to him, there were no marhcing troops, no fleeing human wreckage. Instead it was filled with a strange conglomeration of tractor trailer trucks, all moving at full-speed, their cabs and trailers covered with Soviet soldiers, most hanging on for dear life. In the midst of this parade was an odd-looking white and gold tracked vehicle which bristled with radio antennae. It, too, was carrying a number of Soviet soldiers, all of them wearing uniforms made of black leather.

As this flight went on, advance elements of the Western Forces—soldiers of the Football City Army mostly—had taken possession of various points along the river's edge and were firing nearly point blank at the bridges carrying the retreating Circle Army troops.

But the weirdest thing of all was what was happening *underneath* the bridges. It was so bizarre, Muss shook his head a few times, so sure was he that he was seeing a vision . . .

In the middle of all the confusion on the spans, the explosions coming from the city, the enemy jets streaking overhead in the pre-dawn sky and the gunfire rippling down the water's edge, there were hundreds, possibly thousands, of people, floating down the river. On inner tubes.

CHAPTER 25

The fighting in and around Football City lasted
most of the morning. But by noontime, the main
elements of the advancing Western Forces troops
found they had very few people to shoot at.

General Jones arrived in the city itself at two
that afternoon. By that time, the invading troops
were mopping up against ragtag stragglers and the
few unlucky foreign hired-guns The Circle had
double-crossed in their hasty, but nevertheless successful retreat.

Jones directed his driver to the enormous Football City stadium which was now serving as a ral-
lying point for the commanders of all the
invading units. He wasn't there more than ten
minutes when the large Sea Stallion helicopter appeared in the sky above the stadium and came in
for a landing.

This time, Hunter was at the controls . . .

"It feels like I haven't flown anything in

135

months," the fighter pilot told him as they met outside the big chopper's access door. "J.T. and Ben let me hop over here in this."

Jones shook his hand, long and hard. "Congratulations, Hawk," he said sincerely. "We pulled it off and the lion's share of the credit goes to you . . ."

Hunter immediately held up his hand. "Please, don't heap the praise on me," he said, rather glumly. "It was guys like Elvis and Ace and the rest of them that did the hump work . . ."

Hunter's attitude disturbed Jones. Here they had just recaptured their first major objective and still the pilot was serious and unsmiling.

"I'm assuming that you've just returned from the river," Jones said, as they walked toward his mobile command center, which was actually an armored Winnebago. "What's the situation down there?"

"They're still fishing some of the POWs out of the river," Hunter told the senior officer. "But the break-out went like clockwork. We busted the water gate in the catacombs just after midnight, and by four this morning, every POW and friendly civvie was out.

"The inner tubes worked very well. Guys that would never have made it because of their wounds or whatever were coming out of that culvert like it was an amusement ride. Our barges got to most of them, and they picked up a lot of the healthy guys who were able to swim out to them. Meanwhile, the bridges are filled with Circle troops just bugging the hell out of the city. I'll tell you, it was quite a scene . . ."

A smile spread across Jones's face. "Our casualties were so low, it's almost unbelievable. Those

136

nickel-and-dime soldiers in the Circle trenches were a joke. Then all the way in, my line commanders kept radioing back that they were not encounter-. ing any opposition whatsoever. So, we just figured it was better to put the pedal to the metal and see how far we'd go. Never did I expect to take back the whole city with barely firing a shot."

"They obviously fell for O'Malley's fake recon pictures lock and stock," Hunter said, as they sat down inside the command center. Jones had produced a no-name bottle of whiskey and was pouring out two drinks. "But they also took something very valuable with them."

"What do you mean?" Jones asked, sipping the whiskey.

Hunter ran his hand through his long hair. "In the middle of the retreat, they moved those trailer trucks I told you about, plus that strange APC. We were shooting at them from the river's edge, got some of the guards riding on top, but we didn't have the firepower to get one of those big rigs."

Jones shook his head. "What could be so valuable inside those trucks that they would bother to save it?" he asked.

"It's a real mystery to me," Hunter said, swigging his drink. "But to tell you the truth, I think whatever it was, it was more important to them than hanging on to this city."

By nightfall, the stadium was mobbed with thousands of victorious Western Forces troops.

A bank of searchlights provided the illumination for the hastily-erected stage at the 50 yard line. Among the leaders on the platform were Jones,

137

Hunter, O'Malley, Elvis, Yaz and Louie St. Louie, the founder of Football City. The ceremony, in which Jones officially turned the city back to St. Louie, was filled with emotion, especially for the tough Football City Army troops, who hadn't seen the inside of their city in what must have seemed like ages.

Jones then made a stirring speech in which he outlined the plans for the battles ahead, a campaign which had been appropriately named: Operation Eastern Thunder. This war is just beginning, he told the assembled troops, warning them not to take the relatively easy task of regaining Football City as a false indication of the Circle Army's unwillingness to fight.

Then the general put forth a proposal to those gathered:

"We are all Americans here—our Canadian friends included," he said, his voice booming around the stadium via a loudspeaker system. "And this is a war of Liberation. From the tyranny of the Circle. From the tyranny of the New Order. From the tyranny of the Soviets. Right across that river, our fellow Americans are waiting for us. Waiting for the day when they hear us coming. We can't let them down!

"So I think we should rename our combined army. Our goal is to reunite this country. So, I propose that we should be known from now on as *The United American Army!*"

The proposal was met with a thunderous ovation.

"I'd say the motion has passed," Dozer leaned over and said to Jones.

The ceremony was a case of real-life *deja vu* for Hunter. In what seemed like ages ago to *him,* he recalled another celebration, held right in this very stadium on the occasion of defeating the Family Army from taking over the city. It was the first big battle between the democratic forces and those aligned with the Soviet-backed New Order.

But now, here he was again. The enemy called itself by a different name, yet the cause was the same. By force of habit, he reached to his breast pocket and felt the reassuring bulge of the small American flag he always kept there. This is what they were fighting for. *America.* To his dying breath — all for his country. Yes, he had been here before, but one thing was different: this time, the democratic forces — the men of the United American Army — were on the offensive . . .

Now if only the deep, empty ache inside his heart would stop . . .

PART TWO

PART TWO

CHAPTER 26

Mike Fitzgerald walked out into the clear Texas morning sunshine and beheld the two massive airplanes in front of him.

They were C-5 *Galaxys,* the largest airplane ever built in the Free World. A cargo giant—it could haul 130 tons, more than three times that of the not-at-all diminutive C-141—a Soviet "wanna-be" called the An-124 was now larger by a few inches.

But the C-5 was tougher and smarter than the Russian flying dumptruck. The Galaxy could carry more, fly higher, faster and for longer spans of time. Despite its massive size—its length was only 53 feet shorter than that of a football field—it could operate from unfinished or even cratered runways.

Most importantly, pilots loved it . . .

Up until the outbreak of World War III, the only gun a C-5 had carried was one to shoot off emergency flares. It was strictly a behind-the-lines supply animal.

But Mike Fitzgerald had changed that.

He wasn't exactly sure when the idea had first hit him, but it was a few days after he had arrived in Dallas at the request of General Dave Jones to inspect some aircraft for possible lease. The trip had meant he had missed the surprisingly quick outcome at Football City two weeks before, but even that couldn't dampen the excitement about his idea for the two airplanes.

Everyone on the continent who was familiar with the art of air support for ground troops, knew Puff the Magic Dragon. Born in Viet Nam, Puff was the brainchild of a nameless Air Force officer who first got the idea to stick three machine guns into the side of a C-47, a small, two-prop cargo-only airplane. Then, by flying the airplane into a slight left hand bank, he found out that he could support ground troops below with an accurate, ever-moving, concentrated and manageable field of fire. The idea caught on quickly in Viet Nam, much to the bad luck of the Vietnamese communists.

The idea was made one better when the Air Force installed three 6000-round per minute Gatling guns into the side of the larger, more sophisticated C-130 Hercules cargo carrier. Dubbed "Spookys," a number of these gunships were still in operation in the Pacific American Air Corps, the outfit home of Hunter, Jones, Twomey and Ben Wa.

Now Fitzie had taken the idea to its next logical extreme. He had armed the C-5.

The best part was that the Texans had given him two airplanes at a reasonable price, leaving plenty of money left over for him to work with. And there was no shortage of weapons the Texans could give him to stick inside the cavernous C-5 hold.

In fact he had enough to pack three airplanes. So

Fitzie got another idea: one aircraft—C-5B-23E/R No. 1—would be fitted with one and only kind of weapon: the GE GAU8/A 30mm Avenger cannon. Later on he would admit that he might have gotten carried away with the number of guns he'd installed on Number 1. Some thought the number was excessive—that is, until they saw all *21* Avengers firing as one at an enemy. The critics shut up after that.

Each Avenger was capable of firing 4500 rounds per minute of cannon shells made of depleted uranium, the projectile which spontaneously ignited on striking its target. The effect, especially at night, was so frighteningly breathtaking it was almost otherworldly.

But after he had had the 21 guns—and their literally miles of ammunition belts—installed in Number 1, he still had many weapons left over, including 19 Avengers. But Fitz was a born Irishman and therefore one side of him leaned to the unconventional. So instead of lining up another neat row of deadly Avengers on C-5B-23E/R No. 2, he installed everything but.

He started with six elderly GE Gatling guns—each capable of firing 8000 rounds a minute. Then came the five Mk 19 automatic grenade launchers, complemented by a single Italian-made AP/AV 700, three-barrel multiple grenade-launcher. Only then did he get into the heavy stuff. First there was the Soltam 120-mm mobile field gun, which was capable of firing IMI illuminating rounds, as well as rocket assisted charges. Then there were the two Royal Ordnance 105-mm field artillery pieces and the three German-made Rheinmetal 20-mm converted anti-aircraft guns.

A reasonable man would have stopped there. But Fitz hadn't become a Thunderbird pilot and now a millionaire soldier/businessman by being terminally reasonable. So he installed the 17-ton West German-made LARS II 110-mm Multiple Rocket Launcher, specially-fitted with a "rearend blast" deflector, which piped the backfire down and out of the airplane. The monster was capable of firing 36, six-foot-long, high-explosive-filled rockets in less than 20 seconds.

So if the effect of Number 1 firing all its guns was beautiful but scary, the sight of Number 2 firing all *its* guns was beyond description . . .

Fitzgerald, whose philosophy training came to him from the bottom of tea boxes, was now a firm believer in the school of thought that machines—like people—have personalities. He had proof. The two C-5s in front of him were brothers, yet they were worlds apart. From their crews to the way they flew, they were complete opposites, the *yin* and *yang* of deadly air support.

Inside Number 1, was a portrait of high tech. The 21 guns were lined up like so many soldiers preparing to fire a salute. The automatic ammunition racks ran in almost artistic cylindrical patterns around the inside of the cabin. Batteries of video targeting gear, radar imagers, electronic counter measures devices and a host of other futuristic doo-dads highlighted the starboard side of the aircraft. When the humans on the right side worked with the guns on the left side, the result was a neat, concentration of fire that was spit out at a rate of 94,000 rounds a minute, or 1575 rounds *per second*. The firepower was so intense, that special cowlings had to be installed on the C-5's portside engines, so the jet turbines wouldn't suck up all the smoke and gas resulting from the awesome 21-gun "salute."

Inside Number 2 was a portrait of nightmare. The menagerie of weapons and their various ammunition and venting needs had turned the guts of the ship into a spaghetti bowl of wires, ammo belts, oil lines, gas lines, electrical generators, shell dispensers and everywhere, firing mechanisms. Number 2 also carried a battery of four Sidewinder missiles under its belly, and the controls for these were also jammed into the melee. Added to all this were four flare dispensers and a half dozen chaff dispensers. No wonder the air crews had dubbed the clownish Number 2 "Bozo."

Soon after that, Number 1 was labeled "Nozo."

So now Fitzgerald had all this fire power, plus two KC-135 aerial tankers to keep it flying, what was he to do with it?

He asked General Jones that question two days after the successful reclamation of Football City. The senior officer asked him two questions in return: first, could he get both planes and both tankers first to Football City, then prepare for a risky covert operation? Fitz answered yes, although he couldn't imagine the two flying leviathans going undercover.

Jones's second question was more technical: Could Fitzgerald fit a recently-reconditioned F-16 into the hold of one of the massive airplanes?

CHAPTER 27

It was three weeks to the day after the victory at Football City when C-5 Number 1 — "Nozo" — screeched in for a landing at New Chicago's airport.

Fitzgerald himself was behind the controls of the big plane, which had been given a hasty coat of dull black paint for the occasion. It also had all of its guns dismantled and packed away.

Fitz rolled the C-5 to a stop at the end of the airport's longest runway and found the airplane immediately surrounded by a half dozen tanks and APCs.

"New Chicago Tower, this is C-5 requesting taxi and parking directions . . ." Fitz called into his microphone, ignoring the ring of hostile vehicles.

"C-5, prepare to be boarded by our landing fee collection officers . . ." came the reply.

The Irishman looked over at his friend in the co-pilot's seat and shrugged.

"Can't get away with anything these days," Hunter

said to him.

Fitz switched his radio over to intercom and called out: "OK guys, get ready. The New Order Cosa Nostra are coming aboard . . ."

Next to The Circle, the overlords of New Chicago — known as The Family — were the Westerners' bitterest enemies. Soviet-backed and supplied, the criminals who ran New Chicago and the surrounding territories were still smarting from their defeat at the first Battle of Football City. Hunter himself had led a devastating air raid against the city at the height of that war, a raid which KO'd the city's once vast railroad system and fuel depot facilities.

So when the Circle took over the eastern half of the continent and more, the Family, still licking its wounds, simply sat back, signed a non-aggression treaty with them and let the conquering army pass them by.

Now The Family was working to regain its strength, just as The Circle was losing theirs. Its army — decimated at the first Battle for Football City — was now being rebuilt. Its war chests were again beginning to fill up; its tentacles were again beginning to spread.

When the Circle Army retreated from Football City, they headed north, toward New Chicago. Now the bulk of that force was camped 30 miles south of the center of the city — and paying The Family a fortune in gold for the privilege. Allies like these The Circle could do without. It was only because Moscow was footing the tab that The Circle could afford the high-rent prices.

The moral of the story: Everything was for sale in New Chicago.

There was a sharp knock on the bottom hatch of the C-5, and soon, two Family majors were standing on the flight deck, palms outstretched.

"What's the price, gentlemen?" Fitz asked them after introducing himself and Hunter as "merchants."

The two men looked at Hunter very closely, but the pilot knew he wouldn't be recognized. Although his face was well-known even before the big war, he was an expert at changing his appearance. For this occasion, he had dyed his blond hair to black, cultivated a two-week beard and popped in brown contact lenses to discolor his blue eyes.

"Ten bags of gold for landing," one of the officers finally said to them. "And ten bags of gold per day for parking fees."

"Is this negotiable?" Fitz asked them.

The two officers looked astonished. "Of course not!" one of them said sternly. "Now pay up, Shamrock, or we got to call the Boss."

Fitz paid them twenty bags of gold, a fortune in New Order America.

"Now what are you doing here?" the other officer asked. "Business or just a stop over?"

"Business . . ." Hunter told them, pointing to the plane's cargo hold. "Some of those crates you see are filled with 50-caliber ammunition. We're meeting a guy here tomorrow who's going to buy them."

The Family officers studied the cargo hold for a few moments, then asked: "Why here?"

"Know a better place?" Hunter replied. "We don't need any flag-wavers mucking up our deal."

The officers shook their heads. "Well, you know there's going to be a transit fee," one of them said. "Plus a city tax."

"All of it up front . . ." the other added.

"But we have to get our money from them

first . . ." Fitz started to protest.

"Up front . . ." the Family officer said. "Those are the rules. And people who question them wind up in trouble."

Fitz shook his head in disgust. "How much?" he asked.

"Thirty bags of gold," came the reply.

The Irishman nearly went nuts. *"Thirty* bags!" he shouted. "The whole shipment is only going for sixty bags."

The officers smiled. "That's the price you pay for coming here," one said.

The other turned very serious. "Now pay up or we have our boys break the wing off this monster . . ."

Fitz came up with the gold. The Family officers then inspected the front of the cargo hold, and finally left.

"Whew!" Fitz said, stage-mopping his brow. "Did they fall for it? Was I convincing, do you think?"

Hunter patted his friend on the shoulder. Fitzie was a notorious skinflint. "You acted like they were taking your own personal gold, Mike," he told him.

"Damn they would," Fitz replied. "I'd have shot them both if it were my own money . . ."

Three hours passed. Then, right on schedule, a battered old C-46 cargo plane came in for a landing at New Chicago airport.

The airport security force that had formerly surrounded Nozo now formed a ring around the unmarked cargo carrier. Watching intently from the C-5's portholes, Hunter, Fitz and the 12 crewmembers saw the same two Family officers board the C-46, no doubt to extract the various fees from them too.

"Just as long as they don't snoop around in the back of that rig, we'll be OK," Fitz said to Hunter.

"Don't worry," the Wingman replied. "J.T. will be flashing that gold under their noses before they're even in the doorway . . ."

Hunter's prediction seemed to come true. No sooner had the Family officers climbed aboard the C-46, when they were leaving again, all smiles.

"That looks promising," Hunter said, as they watched the officers and the security tanks and APCs pull away from the old cargo plane. "Ready for part two?" he asked Fitzgerald.

It was just an hour before sundown when the chief of New Chicago's airport security, a colonel named Crabb, received an urgent call from one of his captains.

"Boss, you got to get over to that C-46 that came in today," the captain told him. "I think the deal between them and the C-5 just went bad."

"How bad?" Crabb asked the man. He was busy at the moment with a hooker named Irene.

"*Real* bad," came the reply. "The guys from that C-5 went into that ship about five minutes ago and they were packing the heavy artillery. Now we just heard a lot of shooting . . ."

Crabb shook his head in disgust. "I'll be right there," he told the captain, hanging up the phone.

He turned to the beautiful redhead. She had just finished undoing his buckle and zipper when the call came in. "Got to put you on hold, baby," he told her, redoing his pants and putting on his uniform jacket. "Got some trouble out on the flight line."

Irene looked authentically disappointed. "How long will you be gone?" she asked.

152

"Not long," he said, putting his .357 Magnum into his shoulder holster. He reached inside his desk and retrieved a vial of cocaine and a gigantic dildo that had been left behind by another of his hired girlfriends.

"Here," he said, giving Irene the coke and the obscene modality. "Use these until I get back . . ."

Crabb walked out of his office at the airport's control tower and found his limo waiting for him.

He was upset and in a bad mood. If it were up to him, he wouldn't allow *any* outsiders to land at the airport to do business. The money extorted from the traders was usually substantial, but it never made up for the trouble that always seemed to break out between the buyers and sellers.

But as his limo pulled away and streaked across the tarmac to the C-46, Crabb knew that he couldn't change the rules of order at the airport. They were blessed downtown, at City Hall. And to question the mayor — *whoever* that may be this week — was dangerous.

Crabb arrived at the C-46 and was met by the captain who had summoned him.

"What's the situation?" Crabb asked him.

The captain gave him a shrug and said: "These C-5 guys play rough. They just took out every guy on the C-46 except the pilot."

"Just like that?" Crabb asked, midly shocked upon hearing of the violence.

The captain snapped his fingers and repeated: "Just like that."

Crabb climbed the access steps and walked inside the C-46. He looked in the cargo hold and saw twelve-bullet ridden bodies scattered about.

"Jesus Christ," he said with disgust. "What a mess . . ."

It wasn't like he hadn't seen it all before. The deal goes bad, someone gets shot. But 12 guys machine-gunned to death? His captain was right. The C-5 guys did play rough.

"Where's the pilot now?" he asked his captain.

"Went back to the C-5," the man replied. "I think he was in on the deal from the beginning. He seems to be pretty buddy-buddy with that Mick and his friends."

A few minutes later, Crabb and six of his heavily-armed security guards were walking into the flight deck of the C-5.

"You boys made quite a mess back there," he said to Hunter and Fitzgerald.

Hunter shrugged. "Just a little disagreement," he replied, nonchalantly.

"Well, things like this are bad for our reputation here," Crabb told him. "The mayor doesn't like violence, especially when it's so out in the open."

"We don't like violence either," Fitz told Crabb. "So we have something in common with your mayor, now don't we?"

Crabb looked at Hunter and Fitz and at J.T. who was lounging in the background.

"What was the scam, guys?" he asked them. "You really hauling fifty-caliber ammo? Or did you just tell that to those guys in the C-46?"

Hunter laughed. "Sure we're hauling it," he said. "We've been hauling it around for a year . . ."

Crabb laughed himself now. He could appreciate the simplicity of the double-cross. Entice a buyer for the ammo, agree to make the deal at a neutral spot, get the sucker's money then machinegun him. Crabb knew these guys were real pros—they had even taken the added precaution of planting their own guy as pilot of the sucker's airplane.

"Where you guys work out of?" Crabb asked.

"Been down in Mexico for a while," Fitz told him. "This operation works like a charm down there. It gets hot south of the border though, so we moved up to a more comfortable climate for a while."

Crabb looked around the cabin of the C-5. "This is one motherfucker of an airplane," he said. "What else can you do with it?"

A little bell went off in Hunter's head. *Bingo* . . .

"What do you have in mind?" he asked the man.

Crabb just shrugged. "Nothing in particular," he said. "But the mayor might be interested in hearing about you. If the right person mentioned you to him . . ."

Fitz already had the bag of gold in his hand. "Will you be talking to His Honor soon?" he asked, smoothly passing the bag of gold to Crabb. At the same time, Hunter was distributing a bag of silver to each of the lowly Family guards.

"I'll be talking to him tonight as a matter of fact," Crabb said pocketing the gold like an expert.

"Well, what a coincidence," Hunter smiled. "Be sure to tell him we said hello . . ."

CHAPTER 28

It was midnight before Hunter climbed into his bunk in the nose of the C-5, determined to get some sleep.

But it came hard to him these days. Hundreds of thought were ricocheting around his head like so many billiard balls. The sudden "victory" at Football City. The mysterious cargo in the trailer trucks. The calculated race to the East Coast, using a plan where the slightest glitch could ruin the chances for liberating the eastern half of the country. Also he hadn't flown — *really* flown — in so long, his bones were starting to ache.

But it was this goddamn ache in his heart that bothered him most . . .

He reached inside his pocket and took out the small American flag. Carefully, he unfolded it, then took out the picture he always kept there. It was of his girlfriend, Dominique. This was the same picture The Circle had distributed to its drug-crazy troops during the Circle War when Dominique had been forced to be Viktor's mistress. Hunter had rescued her then, and sent her to a safe haven in Free Canada. And although he knew she was in safe hands these days, it still did nothing to end his longing for her.

He looked at the picture, now dog-eared and faded. She was posing in a black tuxedo jacket, low-cut silk blouse, black nylons and short black boots. Her Bardot-like face, that blond shagged hair. She *looked* like a queen and that was exactly what Viktor had told his troops. Through no fault of her own, men died for her image. And in his twisted perverted plan, Viktor had taken her, both physically and mentally. Now Viktor was dead, and all rational thought would suggest that Hunter should hate the photo, hate how she had been posed by the super-terrorist. But the truth of the matter was that he didn't hate it. Quite the opposite. He felt an erotic charge run though him every time he looked at it. The best of both worlds is when your lady is also your fantasy. He shivered at the thought of it. There were other women, but nothing like Dominique. He loved her. He wanted to be with her. But when would he see her again? He couldn't answer the question and that was partly what the ache inside him was about.

It seemed like it had been this way forever. The two great loves of his life: his country and his girlfriend. He knew he had to fight to protect both—to the death, if necessary. But his country was at peril now, so he knew his place was here, fighting for it. But every minute he spent away from her, he felt that she was slipping that much farther away from him.

He softly kissed the photo, did the same to the flag, then carefully placed them back inside his pocket. He knew he had to think of other things or he'd never get to sleep . . .

CHAPTER 29

The A-37 Dragonfly streaked up the eastern edge of the Illinois River, no more than 50 feet above the ground. Ben Wa was at the controls of the small, yet rugged jet; Yaz was sitting in the right hand side co-pilot/gunner/navigator seat. Usually used as a COIN—for counter-insurgency—aircraft, this Dragonfly was on a different mission. Its two jet engines were quiet, its small size to its benefit, and still, it was able to carry a lot of gear.

In other words, it was easily converted into an armed spy ship.

Ben and Yaz were looking for the Circle's convoy of trailer trucks. United American Army spies in the New Chicago area reported to them shortly after the retaking of Football City that although the bulk of the Circle Army was now camped just inside New Chicago's secure defense perimeter, the mysterious convoy of trucks—and the elongated APC—were not with them. Therefore, they could only assume that for whatever reason, the big semis had fallen behind the main group shortly after passing into Illinois. Thus, the search for them had been launched.

"Scope still clear," Yaz said to Ben as the plane banked around a wide curve in the river. "I'll pump it up to fifteen klick radius."

Yaz had been given a crash course in operating the navigation and search modes of the A-37's newly installed APG-56 radar. The airplane was also carrying a LANTIRN pod, which allowed it to operate on the darkest of nights and in the worst kinds of weather. Shortly before he had left for New Chicago, Hunter had somehow jammed all the gear into the diminutive jet and showed Yaz the ins and outs of its operation.

It was a far cry from working a nuclear sub, a duty that Yaz was more accustomed to.

"OK, let's swing in up here," Ben said, noting they were just south of Peoria. "There's a convergence of several major roads outside the city. Maybe we'll get lucky . . ."

He raised the jet up to 150 feet and turned hard to starboard. "Better arm the missiles," he told Yaz. "Just in case . . ."

They could see a few lights ahead in what was the mostly abandoned city of Peoria. This part of Illinois was a Free Territory these days—meaning there was no government, no police, no army and therefore, practically no people. Yaz knew any infra-red reading he got from the ground below would most likely be coming from weapons used by either one of the several notorious air pirate gangs known to operate in the area, or maybe Circle troops.

"Got nothing . . ." he told Ben as they swept low over the deserted city. The only lights burning were in the top floors of the few skyscrapers.

"How could they hide a hundred or more big

semis?" Ben asked, for what had to be the hundredth time. "If the stuff inside was so valuable, why would they not keep up with the main Circle column? They would have had forty thousand bodyguards if they did."

They were both quiet for a while, streaking through the darkened, moonless night, skimming the treetops.

Then an idea came to Yaz. "Maybe we're just looking in the wrong place . . ." he said, thinking out loud.

"Like how?" Ben asked.

Yaz shifted in his seat and unloosened his oxygen mask a little. "Well, are we just assuming that the semis stuck with the main group?" Yaz asked rhetorically. "If they're not outside of New Chicago, and not on the main roadways in between, maybe they didn't head that way. Maybe they went south or straight east . . ."

"Could be . . ." Ben said. "We've been at this for three nights now and all we've done is burn fuel . . ."

They completed their pre-determined run right up to La Salle. Still finding nothing, Ben turned the jet around and they headed back for Football City.

CHAPTER 30

The next morning, Hunter awoke to the sounds of machinery grinding away outside the C-5's window.

He looked toward the C-46 and saw an ancient garbage truck had pulled up to its rear hatchway. A crew of workers were lifting bodies out of the airplane and throwing them into the back of the garbage truck. "On their way to some cement plant, no doubt," Hunter thought as he shook the sleep from his eyes.

Getting the bodies had been the grisliest aspect of their plan, but one that was needed to lend the correct amount of authenticity. The bodies were actually those of Circle troops or mercenaries killed in the fighting at Football City. In anticipation of the foray to New Chicago, the corpses had been gathered up, frozen, then thawed shortly before the C-46 set down in New Chicago. J.T. drew the short straw and thus was stuck with splattering the twice-dead stiffs with chicken blood to complete the ruse.

"How much for the cleaning crew?" Hunter asked Fitz as he walked up to the flight deck and poured himself a cup of coffee.

"Five bags of silver, it was," Fitzgerald answered. "Cheap for such a job. But I don't feel for them at all—they're former Chicago meat packers, used to the muscle and blood."

"Well, that's breakfast," Hunter said, feeling his stomach do a slight somersault. "What's next?"

"The goons were out here about fifteen minutes ago," Fitz said. "We have a meeting with the mayor at noon. That is, if there isn't a *coup* before then . . ."

Hunter checked his watch. "Jesus, that's four hours from now," he said facetiously. "You think they can keep it together that long?"

They both shared a laugh. Nothing had changed much in Chicago politics—it was still as Byzantine as ever. The only real difference was that the pace by which the leaders of the Chicago Machine rose to power had quickened—as had the rate of their downfalls. In the past year the longest reign of any mayor had been three weeks. The average term in office was now just nine days. The average life expectancy of a deposed leader who wasn't smart enough to get out when he could was considerably less.

The process of selecting the mayor had also not changed much. Party bosses would select a candidate. The candidate would then go out and buy the votes of the people that would sell and shoot the ones who would not. The mayor would be sworn in, his tax collectors would immediately cover the city, and his defense force would get paid. But while all this was happening, other parties were selecting other candidates. Inevitably, someone would pay off the security force or a close associate of the mayor, there would be a *coup d'etat,* and the whole crazy cycle would start over again.

Overseeing it all was the Family. No matter who got elected, The Family knew it would collect its pound of flesh, whether it be in gold, silver, guns, drugs or girls.

"Who *is* the mayor this week?" Hunter asked.

Fitz ruffled through some papers. "Some guy named Bruceland," he said, locating the name of his landing document. "This Crabb fellow apparently knows him well. Says he's a real 'businessman.' "

Hunter gave Fitz a stage wink. "Just what we need," he said.

The Chicago City Hall was a palace.

"No wonder they kill each other to get in here," Fitz said as he and Hunter got out of Crabb's limousine which had pulled up to the front entrance of the place. Appropriately enough, the main entrance way was a revolving door.

"Nice touch," Hunter commented as Crab escorted them into the front lobby.

The City Hall looked more like the Taj Mahal. Everything seemed to either shine gold or silver or sparkle with diamonds. The walls were done in velvet wallpaper, the floor was highly polished marble. No less than six crystal chandeliers hung from the ceiling and one entire wall of the huge lobby featured the longest, best stocked bar Hunter had ever seen.

Everywhere they looked, there was an armed guard.

Crabb led them upstairs and into the mayor's chambers — an opulent room scarred only by a few bullet holes in the walls and in the stained glass windows. The three of them sat down and took a drink from a beautiful servant. Mayor Bruceland walked in

163

two minutes later.

"So these are the guys who shot up my airport," he asked with a wide grin, shaking hands with Hunter and Fitz.

"Just a misunderstanding," Fitz told him. "All cleaned up as of this morning."

The mayor let out a hearty laugh. "OK, just as long as you're clean about it," he said. "The guy before me had a thing about shooting litterers . . ."

Bruceland was about 50 years old, clad in a pre-war business suit, with an unmistakable bulge under his left lapel. Hunter determined the man was packing either an old Colt M1911A1 or a Beretta Model 92F. Whatever it was, it qualified as a hand cannon.

"I hear you guys are quite resourceful," Bruceland said, settling in behind his desk.

"We can be," Hunter told him. "But we don't come cheap."

"Who does these days?" Bruceland asked. "As it turns out, I'm looking for some help with a particularly irritating group of business associates. You guys interested?"

"We'll listen," Fitz said, taking a sip of his drink.

Bruceland lit up an enormous cigar. "As Colonel Crabb here probably told you, I've only been in office several days.

"Now, my predecessor — wherever he is — had made arrangements with a rather large group of visitors concerning their use of quite a bit of our turf about thirty miles from here.

"These people camped out and paid my predecessor the correct amount of . . . well, let's call it 'rent' for use of the land. But since my predecessor moved on, shall we say, to parts unknown, these people have refused to pay me *my* rent."

"How can we help you?" Hunter asked, surrepti-

164

tiously crossing his fingers for luck.

Bruceland leaned back in his leather chair and blew a series of smoke rings. "These people need to be taught a lesson," he said finally. "The problem is, there are a lot of them. And me and my boys just don't do a lot of 'group things,' if you know what I mean . . ."

"How much?" Fitz asked. "And we want only gold . . ."

Bruceland shrugged. "Name your price," he said. "After the job is done, that is . . ."

"Got any reservations about how we handle it?" Hunter asked him.

The mayor just laughed. "Just be neat . . ." he said.

Both Hunter and Fitz rose and shook hands with him. "You got yourself a deal, Mr. Mayor," Fitz said. "Now just point us in the right direction and tell us who the welchers are."

Bruceland did one better. He walked over to his wall and pulled down a map of New Chicago territory. To the south of the city they saw an area that had been shaded red.

"They're camped right here," Bruceland said, pointing to the colored area. "They call themselves the Circle Army. You guys ever hear of them?"

CHAPTER 31

Major Tomm, the former commander of the Circle Army's anti-aircraft battalions, was awakened early the next morning by a strange, high-pitched whine.

No one else in his tent was stirred by the noise, but he could hear it — way off, very high, possibly circling.

He pulled on his boots and threw his uniform jacket around his shoulders. It was just a half hour before sunrise, but he still needed a flashlight to see his way out of the tent and around the darkened camp grounds. Stopping for a moment to concentrate on the sound, he headed out of the woods, down to the flat lands nearby where he could get a better view.

Tomm had been demoted less than two days after being one of the last senior officers to make it out of Football City. He wasn't on duty at the time of the Western Forces' attack — he was in a cathouse called the Two-Ladies-Three. And he got word of the coming invasion only when he saw the lights blinking out downtown, and had called the front desk to see what was up.

The next thing he knew, he was caught up in a maddening crush of gamblers, drug dealers, hookers, retreating soldiers and mercenaries—all of them intent on getting out of the city before the Westerner's juggernaut arrived. It was like rats jumping ship—three hours of panic, confusion and hysteria.

He caught a ride with some retreating Libyans and arrived at the Circle Army's encampment outside of New Chicago a day and a half late. That's when he learned that he was now second-in-command of the housekeeping unit—in charge of the cooking and the cleaning for the camp grounds. As far as he knew, the Circle Army command had yet to name his successor to the anti-aircraft unit.

He walked out onto the plain and looked up into the slowly brightening sky. He could still hear the whining—now louder than ever. This concerned him. He knew it was an airplane. And he knew it certainly wasn't one of theirs.

Ten minutes went by and the sky was getting brighter. Things were starting to take shape in the plain. The square mile meadow was where the encampments' SAM site was located. He walked among the rows of neatly-packed, canvas-covered SA-5s, and SA-2s, still searching the sky for the source of the sound. Suddenly Tomm caught a quick glimpse of black and silver, passing over the eastern horizon. It was a large aircraft, no markings, just circling at about 25,000 feet, leaving behind a corkscrew of vapor. He looked closer and soon enough realized that it was a C-5 Galaxy.

"A cargo plane," he said, with some relief. It was probably circling waiting for clearance to land at New Chicago only 30 miles away.

He started to walk back up the hill to the tree grove where most of the Circle Army tents were pitched when he heard another noise—a different noise.

He looked up at the C-5 and saw long puffs of smoke shooting out of its belly. At the end of each smoke trail he saw a bright flash of fire, dropping slowly.

"They're dropping flares," he said, at the same time wondering why the hell they would do that.

Now his attention was glued to the airplane as it continued to circle and pump out flares. He had been a SAM officer for three years and he knew that the only reason why an airplane would drop so many flares at regular intervals was fear of getting shot down by a missile. The flares' heat would fool the heat-seeking devices in most SAMs.

But why would a cargo airplane have such concerns? Unless . . .

The C-5 was getting lower, and not making any move toward New Chicago. It was circling directly over the sleeping Circle encampments and pumping out flares every five seconds.

He didn't know what was happening, but he knew something was very wrong with how the airplane was acting. He ran back up the hill, into the woods and up to the tent of the officer of the guard.

"Call the commandant's bivouac," Tomm told the young captain, his voice shaky and out of breath. "There is a strange aircraft circling overhead, dispensing flares . . ."

The officer looked at him like he was nuts.

"Do what I say, man!" Tomm shouted at him. "Can't you hear that airplane up there? Have you ever heard an airplane like that before?"

The officer shook his head. "No way am I calling the commandant's bivouac," he said. "We're right on the landing pattern of the Family's airport, mac. Now go back to bed."

Tomm almost blew his stack.

"I'm a *major,* captain," he yelled at the man. "Make the call!"

"I'm the officer in charge, Major," the young man countered. "And I make the decision whether the commandant's phone rings or not. And like I told you, it ain't gonna ring this morning."

Tomm was already running out of the tent, heading back down to the row of tents where he knew the SAM crews were sleeping. He planned to rouse them and get them down to their missiles.

But the whining noise was now so loud, he didn't have to wake anyone up. Men were standing outside the tents in various forms of dress, looking up through the trees to the early morning sky, searching for the airplane.

Tomm spotted a squad of his former charges and ran up to them.

"We've got to get down to the missiles!" he said. "That airplane is dropping flares."

"It looks like a cargo plane to me," one of them said.

"There's only one reason an airplane drops flares and you guys know what it is," Tomm told them sternly. "Now let's go . . ."

Only half the men decided to follow him. Tomm led them back down the hill, yelling back orders to them as he went. But by the time they reached the plain, they saw that the C-5 was now only 1000 feet above them and banking hard to its portside.

Tomm and the others stopped dead in their tracks as they watched 21 separate hatchways open up on the left side of the ship and 21 muzzle snouts appear.

"Jesus Christ," Tomm said, unable to close his jaw.

"It's a gigantic gunship . . ."

No sooner had the words left his lips then all 21 guns opened up.

There was no *rat-a-tat-tat* or fire crackling sound. Only a strange, very mechanical whirring and a sudden rush of blue-gray smoke. The barrage only lasted 4.5 seconds but in that time, 7,481 spontaneously-combusting depleted uranium bullets had been sprayed at the SAM site. In a flash of fire and smoke, it seemed as if the field had suddenly been hit by an earthquake and a volcanic eruption at the same instant. There was a sheet of flame so intense, it instantaneously melted the needles on the pine trees surrounding the SAM field, quickly filling the air with a sickeningly sweet burnt pine smell.

The airplane was gone in 15 seconds, climbing stiffly, the gun hatches closing all at once. Tomm had never seen anything like it. Complete, quick, total destruction. He felt faint and bit his lip in an effort to prevent his body from going numb in near-shock.

When the smoke began to lift only 20 seconds after the attack, he saw all that remained of the Circle Army's neatly lined-up SAMs was a deep hole and a few burning strips of metal.

CHAPTER 32

Hunter and Fitzgerald pulled up to the front of the Chicago City Hall and were met by three security guards.

"The mayor is waiting for you," one of the soldiers said as they were led through the magnificent lobby and up to the mayor's chambers.

But it wasn't Bruceland who sat behind the mayor's desk. It was Colonel Crabb.

"Is the mayor around?" Fitz asked.

"You're talking to him," Crabb said with a mile-wide grin. "We had a quick example of democracy in action about thirty minutes ago."

Only in New Chicago, Hunter thought.

"Well, I hope this doesn't affect our previous agreement?" Fitz asked cautiously.

"Not at all!" Crabb said, motioning for them to sit down. "In fact, a guy from The Circle was just here, paying up, both principal and interest . . ."

"Glad to hear it . . ." Hunter told him. "Can we get

paid now?"

"Absolutely," Crabb said. "What was the price again?"

"It was negotiable with your predecessor," Fitz said. "But ten bags of gold will do."

Crabb pushed an intercom button on his telephone and a few moments later an absolutely gorgeous, blond woman walked in. She was naked except for the barest of bikini panties.

"Pay these gentlemen," Crabb told her. "Fifteen bags of gold, *apiece* . . ."

Both men were surprised at the mayor's generosity. *Fifteen bags of gold for four seconds of work,* thought Hunter. He knew he could be a rich man if he wasn't so damn honest.

But the operation was more important than gold. He and Fitz had accomplished two things: first, getting into favor with the Chicago Machine (although its wheels seemed to be spinning at 8000 RPM), and as gravy, being paid for knocking out The Circle's SAM capability.

"That's quite a flying machine you have there," Crabb said, as the near-naked woman counted out 15 bags of gold for them. "I'm surprised you haven't made a living just hiring out as ground support."

"We pick and choose how we use it very carefully," Hunter told him. "Also we can't hire out to those dogooders out West . . ."

Crabb waved his hand in disgust. "Those people make me sick," he said. "What a bunch of dreamers! They kicked the Circle out of Football City. So what? Everyone knows the Circle jerks were just marking time there anyway.

"Now these flag-wavers are all hopped up I suppose. Thinking they can kick ass on what's left of The Circle. Well, I got news for them, there's plenty more enemies where The Circle came from. And all of them get paid in rubles, if you catch my drift . . ."

Hunter and Fitz did.

"But take you guys," Crabb went on, allowing the blonde to sit on his lap. "No flags. No causes. Just do the job and get paid. I like that kind of work ethic. And how many are there of you? Fourteen in all? That's amazing. You can throw a lot of weight around, just you guys and that big airplane . . ."

Crabb's next thought got caught in his throat. Hunter immediately sensed that the man realized he was talking a little too much, giving them ideas.

He cleared his throat and began fondling the blonde's breast. "Well, anyway," he said after a few moments. "If you stick around, I might have some more work for you. Interested?"

"We're always interested in making this kind of money," Fitz said.

"Glad to hear it," Crabb concluded. "Tonight, we're having a big bash here—right here at City Hall. It's my inauguration. I want you guys to be my guests of honor. Then we can talk about using you—on a retainer basis."

Hunter gave Fitz a quick thumbs-up sign.

"What time does the party start?" he asked.

CHAPTER 33

Yaz had to stare at the infra-red scope for a few moments — it was the first time he had a legitimate target.

"I've got something, Ben," he said finally, adjusting the A-37's infra-red scope power.

They were 40 miles west of what used to be Terre Haute, Indiana, but what was now part of the fiefdom of a notorious air pirate gang named McDeath. They had stopped searching for the "assumed route" of the semis, and instead started looking for the mystery trucks further east.

Now it appeared as if they had struck paydirt.

"Call it out," Ben said, as he steered the Dragonfly through the night, once again at treetop level.

"I got six readings, twenty miles straight ahead," Yaz said. "All uniform, all emitting actively. They're coming back with numbers that could correspond to the tractor-trailers."

"Just six, eh?" Ben said, activating the A-37's ECM pod. "Maybe that's our answer. Maybe the semis split up right after crossing into Illinois . . ."

"Could be," Yaz said, turning back to his scope. "Readings still strong. Fifteen miles now . . . I see no threat activity."

"Roger, we're level at one hundred fifty feet," Ben said. "We'll do one pass quick, see if anyone's awake."

They bore down on the target area, which was set into the side of a mountain. The infra-red readings were telling Yaz that six targets as big as semis were parked around a long, rectangular building. The tractor trailers stuck out like so many sore thumbs—these kinds of trucks were virtually non-existent in New Order America.

"OK, target right ahead," he told Ben as they both dropped their NightScope visors down. Suddenly Yaz felt like he was in another world. A world of ghosts moving through the bluish haze of nightvision.

"I see them!" he called out when they were just three miles from the target.

"OK, hang on," Ben said, switching on the airplane's infra-red nose camera.

They flashed over the building ten seconds later. Yaz heard the A-37's camera whirring away, but it was what his own eyes saw—via the NightScope— that told him they were on the right track. There were six tractor-trailers parked right alongside the building, covered with tree branches as a quick form of camouflage.

"That's got to be them," he called out as they passed by the building. "I'm picking up some heat from defensive weapons. Small rockets, maybe a Stinger or two. Nothing's active though . . ."

175

"No guards on night watch . . ." Ben said, as he pulled the A-37 up and banked to the right. "I guess they weren't expecting company."

"Could they have made a deal with McDeath?" Yaz asked. "You know, pay them a fee to pass through their turf?"

"Maybe," Ben answered. "Although it must have been expensive. Everything I've heard about McDeath leads me to believe they don't play cheap."

He turned the A-37 back west and climbed up to 5000 feet. They settled in for the trip back to Football City.

But Yaz was still shaking his head. "What the hell could those semis be carrying that's so damn important?"

CHAPTER 34

"I've got several theories on what was in those semis," J.T. was saying as he took a drink of a gigantic Scotch and water.

Hunter, Fitz and he were in the lobby of the ornate New Chicago City Hall for the occasion of Colonel Crabb's inauguration party. The place was packed with cretins of all persuasions: out-and-out gun-toting criminals with the obligatory moll on each arm, uniformed officers from the myriad of New Chicago's Family-affiliated militias, several skunky Soviet plainclothesmen, even a few leather-jacket air pirates. Two Circle Army majors cowered over in one corner, trying their best to avoid contact with anyone, for fear someone would threaten to raise their rent.

Hunter and his friends had been at the party for just an hour, eating and drinking and looking at the girls. The mayor had introduced them to a number of big shots as the guys "who put the hurt on the Circle" earlier in the day.

Now they had drifted to a relatively deserted corner of the hall to hold a more private discussion.

"I say they retrieved a bunch of the bigger SAMs from the Badlands," J.T. said, keeping his voice low. "You know, the ones that have to be set in concrete and so on. Some of those babies can go up to ninety-seven thousand feet and range out at two hundred miles. I'd say the Russians would be very anxious to get those kinds of missiles back and that would explain why The Circle never bothered to set up any of them around Football City."

"That's a possibility," Hunter replied. "Although if they've got one hundred semis out there, that would mean a lot of big missiles have fallen into their possession. I'm not sure that many SAMs of any size survived the first Circle War."

"Could be they dug up the launchers and controls too, and they're shipping them alongside," Fitz offered.

"Maybe it's just gold," Hunter said, hoping it was all that simple. "I mean, they welded the stuff inside and kept the hiding place secret within Football City. I'll bet that ninety-five percent of their own people never even knew what was going on inside that underground garage."

Fitz guzzled his drink and in the same motion, took another one off the tray of a passing waitress. "But if they're so rich in gold, why would they welch on the rent money to the Family?" he asked. "They just lost their assembled SAM capability because they didn't pay their rent."

"We'll know more if and when Yaz and Ben find the goddamn things," Hunter said.

Just then Colonel Crabb called for the attention of the guests.

"Welcome, my friends," he said with a true politician's flair. "Thank you for coming. I'm not one for speeches, but just let me say that my administration will be dedicated to keeping New Chicago strong. We will continue to be tough with anyone who doesn't play by the rules . . ."

He eyed the two Circle Army officers with this line. Just about everyone else broke into applause.

"All right, I have a surprise for all you guys out there—maybe some of you ladies, too."

He clapped his hands once, and suddenly the lights in the lobby dimmed. A soft, seductive melody oozed from several speakers around the hall. From a side door, a group of women appeared. "My good friend Madam Meenga has sent over some of her best, ah . . . students," Crabb announced. "These are very generous gals, so guys—and ladies—help yourselves!"

The women began filtering through the crowd, automatically mingling with the guests. Hunter, Fitz, and J.T. were on the opposite side of the room, and with the lights dimmed, they had yet to catch a good glimpse of the women.

"Crabb seems to know how to keep his constituents happy," Fitz remarked.

"Free food, free booze, free chicks," J.T. replied. "That's a platform I can get behind . . ."

But Hunter couldn't say anything. He had just got a good look at one of the "students."

She was a petite blonde who had made her way through the crowd and was now being fondled by an air pirate. It wasn't what she looked like that had startled Hunter. It was what she was wearing . . .

Women's style tuxedo coat. Low cut silk blouse that showed a lot of boob. Black nylons and short black boots. It was the exact ensemble that Dominique was wearing in the photo he kept in his pocket.

"What the hell is going on here?" he said through gritting teeth.

"Hawk? You OK?" J.T. asked, seeing the strange look come across his friend.

Hunter didn't answer him. He walked over to the girl and literally pulled her away from the air pirate.

"What's with that get up?" he asked her, an anger building inside him.

The woman, surprised by his sudden action, was at a loss for words.

But the air pirate wasn't . . .

"Hey, *asshole,*" he hissed at Hunter. "What the fuck you think you're doing?"

Hunter ignored the man.

"You got a hearing problem, jerk-off?" the air pirate said, louder this time.

But still Hunter didn't acknowledge him. Instead, he repeated his question to the girl.

"It's the Queen's outfit, mister," she said, straightening out her jacket. "What's the big deal? All the girls are doing it . . ."

She was right. As more of Madam Meenga's "students" came toward him, Hunter could see they were all dressed in the same, alluring outfit.

"Who's The Queen?" Hunter asked her, once again paying no attention to the air pirate's rebuke, even though the man was drunk and his voice near the 90-decibel range.

"You know, man, '*The* Queen,'" the girl said. "The one that Viktor nabbed? The one that all the Circle guys are in love with. She's the most. The absolute *most!* Everyone is into wearing her style . . ." She then shocked Hunter by pulling out a photograph that was exactly like the one he kept in his pocket.

"You must be new around here, mister," the girl said, showing him the picture. "The Circle gave this snapshot of the Queen to all their guys. They went nuts over her. Fought a big war with some people out west. Of course, no one really knows who she is. But now these photos are like gold, man. I had to turn five tricks in one night just to get the cash to buy this one, and I'm never giving it up. It's the only way I can get my look right . . ."

Hunter couldn't believe it. Could it really be that the X-rated get-up that Viktor had Dominique wear for those infamous photos was now the fashion rage of hookers in New Chicago?

"Not just here either, man," the blonde told him. "All over the east, I hear the women are really getting into it."

Just then, the air pirate came up behind Hunter and screamed in his ear: *"Hey asshole, I'm talking to you!"*

For the first time, Hunter turned around and confronted the man. He was about 6-5, built like a barrel and with a face so scarred it looked as if he'd been ejected out of a canopy without bothering to open it.

"What's your problem," Hunter asked him.

"You're my problem," the man said threateningly, as a small crowd gathered around them. "No one just comes up and takes . . ."

Hunter cut him off. "Take a fucking walk . . ." he said, dismissing him.

The man became so enraged, it seemed as if steam would start pouring out of his ears.

Hunter had partially turned back toward the girl when he just caught sight of the punch coming. Instantly his hand was locked around the man's wrist, using the momentum to toss the pirate head over ass. He even managed to land a punch upside the man's face as he was tumbling by.

A gasp went up around them as the air pirate hit the hard marble floor head-first, echoing a brutal crack. Hunter's boot was on the man's chin in a second. "You were saying?" Hunter asked the man sarcastically.

Suddenly, the mayor himself was standing beside Hunter.

"Jesus Christ, do you know who that is?" Crabb asked him in an urgent whisper. Even the two girls hanging all over him looked nervous.

Hunter just shrugged and pressed his boot harder into the man's face.

"I don't give a damn *who* he is . . ." he said to Crabb. "He's bothering me . . ."

Crabb looked like he would expire on the spot. "He's a group leader for McDeath." the mayor mumbled in Hunter's ear. "They're the guys who we hire for our air protection."

Hunter stared down at the man, who was just coming out of a semi-conscious state. He was so big, Hunter couldn't believe he could fit into the cockpit of a jet fighter.

"So, what do you want me to do with him?" Hunter asked Crabb.

"Jesus! Let him up!" Crabb said shakily.

Hunter complied and two of the air pirate's cohorts helped the man to his feet.

"You're a dead man," the pirate hissed at Hunter, his face no more than an inch from his.

Hunter hit him again. This time square in the jaw. The man once again hit the solid marble floor like a ton of bricks.

Crabb grabbed hold of Hunter's arm. "For Christ's sake will you stop!" he commanded. "These guys will drop an air strike on us in a second."

The man was back up in an instant, his face totally red from the blood and also from embarrassment. His two colleagues made a big deal of holding the man back.

"You're dead meat, mister," he screamed at Hunter.

Hunter cocked his fist back, as if to hit the man again. The air pirate cowered involuntarily, to the laughter of the crowd. He was being made a fool of—and by an expert, no less.

"This is a shootout!" one of the other pirates yelled.

A cheer went up from the crowd.

"Tomorrow," the battered air pirate said. "At high noon. You and me go at it, fly boy."

"How?" Hunter asked him, legitimately curious.

"In fighters, how else?" the man sneered, still pretending to be held back by his buddies.

Both Fitz and J.T. instantly burst out laughing. They actually felt sorry for the man.

"I don't have a fighter," Hunter said honestly.

The injured pirate smiled, displaying a set of cracked and stained teeth. "Don't worry, the mayor will set you up."

With that, he and his seconds stomped out of the hall.

"Is this going to be a duel type of thing?" Hunter asked Crabb.

The mayor nodded. "Yep," he said, almost sadly. "And it's really too bad. I was beginning to really like you guys . . ."

CHAPTER 35

The next day dawned bright and cloudless.

Hunter was up early as usual, finding it nearly impossible to sleep. The sight of the party girls wearing the same provocative clothes as Dominique had proved very unnerving. "Queenies" is what they called themselves, and if the one girl he talked to could be believed, the fashion was even more the rage back east, in the heart of Circle-held territory.

He ate breakfast and took a shower in the C-5's midget lavatory. Then, at ten on the button, he, J.T., Fitz and the rest of the Nozo's crew gathered around the C-5's radio. Within minutes they were in touch with Jones who was broadcasting back in Football City via a high-range band frequency that they knew wasn't compatible within any the Family used.

The most important news was about Ben Wa

and Yaz tracking down six of the mysterious tractor-trailers. Jones told them that the A-37's videotape had been analyzed and segments of it magnified to reveal the weld marks on the semis spotted near Terre Haute.

"Was there any sign of the gold APC?" Hunter asked.

"Negative," was Jones's reply. "Just the half dozen semis. Our thinking now is that the convoy split up right after bugging out of here."

"So what's next?" Hunter asked Jones. "Can you chopper in a strike force to the location, and have them see what's inside those trailers?"

"We're working on it," Jones replied. "The territory is heavy with McDeath pirates, so we're going to have to play it very safe."

Hunter told him about his confrontation with the McDeath air pirate the evening before.

"They're a tough bunch," Jones said. "Be careful."

"You, too," Hunter told him. "Good luck to the guys who are jumping in. And please let us know what you find inside those trucks. The smart money here says it's gold bullion."

"Or big leftover SAMs . . ." J.T. yelled in the background.

"Your guesses are duly noted," Jones said. "Personally I think they're carrying a load of uranium or something radioactive. Those trucks could be lead-lined for all we know. And if someone wanted to start making A-bombs again, you need the ingredients."

"That's a reassuring thought," Hunter answered dryly.

"How is your operation going?" Jones asked them.

186

"On schedule, with no problems," Hunter replied. "We've been real lucky in several respects. It pays well, too."

"Pays well?" Jones asked.

Hunter quickly explained how they'd made more gold than expected for taking out the Circle's SAM capability.

"Quite an enterprise," Jones told them. "Fitz must be tickled green . . ."

"How are things on that end?" Hunter then asked. "Will you be ready with Phase Three when we need you?"

"We're getting the equipment together right now," came the reply. "I'm happy to say that Elvis is adapting quite nicely to his role of military governor here. As you know, all our supplies will transit through this city, so his job is really crucial right now."

"He's a good guy," Hunter said, an opinion seconded by the others. "He can't help but do a good job."

"We've also got to do some more repairs to the airport here," Jones continued. "It's a real mess, especially for the high-performance stuff. *Then,* we have to arm and outfit the former POWs and get them ready for the next phase."

"Well, we both have full dance cards," Fitz said.

They signed off with a promise to talk to each other in 24 hours.

No sooner was the transmission broken when the lookout spotted a small convoy of jeeps heading for the C-5.

Hunter waited for the knock on the C-5's hatch and opened it to find Mayor Crabb, blonde on one arm, a redhead on the other, plus the usual phalanx of security men.

"I hope you can drive a Mirage," he said right away. "It's the only bird I could rustle up on such short notice."

The duel had been in the back of Hunter's mind all morning. Although it was an inconvenience, he knew there was a way to fit the aerial fight perfectly into their plans.

"What's it packing?" he asked Crabb.

"It's got a bolt for a single Sidewinder and that's it," the mayor replied, almost embarrassed by the answer.

"That's the best you could do?" Fitz said, coming to the hatchway. "A shitty French plane with one missile?"

"Hey, what do you think this is?" Crabb snapped. "We lost all of our own airplanes to the cowboys a long time ago. That's why we have to order out for our air support."

"And what's the McDeath boy flying?" Hunter asked.

Crabb didn't say anything, he simply pointed to a spot across the tarmac, near a rundown terminal building.

"He's right over there," Crabb said.

Sure enough, Hunter could see the checkerboard pattern on the side of the pirate's fighter. He was fairly surprised to see the pirate would be driving a hot-shit Soviet-built Su-27 Flanker. There weren't many of the Soviet-built airplanes left in the world, never mind in the inventories of the air pirates.

"I count four missiles under his wing," Fitz said. "This is grossly unfair . . ."

Crabb just shook his head. "Look, guys," he said. "I like you. But we're in New Chicago now. These air duels happen about two times a week, and that's in a *slow* week. It's the biggest bet in town; there's more action on these things than half the stuff down in Football City . . ."

"So?" Hunter asked, wondering what Crabb's point was.

"So, someone has to be the underdog, you see," he answered. "You know: point spread, odds betting, over-under?"

"He's got four missiles, I got one," Hunter surmised. "So let me guess—I'm the underdog."

Crabb slapped him on the back. "Now you're catching on," he said, squeezing his girls for good luck. He started to leave, turned and said: "Good luck, pal. And, really, I appreciate what you guys did for me. Nice knowing you . . ."

Hunter took more more look at the Flanker then turned to Fitz and said: "Let's go, we've only got an hour before I have to suit up . . ."

"Go where?" Fitz asked.

Hunter looked at him for a moment. He assumed Fitz knew what he had in mind.

"Where else?" he said to the Irishman. "To bet that gold we got yesterday . . ."

"Will there be any rules of engagement?" Fitz was asking the second for the air pirates.

"What do you think, Potato-head?" the man answered gruffly. "We consider the fight on as soon as they start their engines. You'd better watch it: our man might just toss a grenade up your friend's ass before he even takes off!"

The crowd at the airport was enormous. They lined the terminal walkways and had spilled out onto the runway itself. TV cameras were everywhere—they would beam the duel back to New

189

Chicago's many barrooms, where even more people were betting on its outcome.

Those lucky enough to get close were filled with "oohs" and "ahs" looking at the pirate's Flanker. The jet was top of the line for the Soviets when the balloon went up in Europe. In looks, it resembled a cross between an Air Force F-15 Eagle and a Navy F-14 Tomcat, two airplanes thought to be non-existent in the New Order world. It carried four AA-10 heat-seeking missiles, plus a large gun the pirates had jury-rigged under its nose.

For Hunter's part, he was sitting in one of the crappiest airplanes he thought he'd ever seen. It was a Mirage in name only. More than half the avionics were gone—there was no engagement radar, no fuel gauge, no afterburner, no gun and one, rusty Sidewinder that was carrying half the normal load of explosive in its warhead.

A siren went off at exactly noon, signalling both pilots to begin taxiing to the runway. To say the air pirate was the overwhelming favorite would have been an understatement. Even as the two combatants were moving toward the take-off point, the air pirates were moving through the crowd, taking bets on their boy.

The match was delayed ten minutes as a small storm front moved through the area. No rain, but plenty of wind and low clouds, which would obscure the battle. So the jets waited at the end of the runway, their engines warming, waiting for the go-signal from the New Chicago tower.

Hunter took the time to catch a cat nap, and was aroused only after the tower controller had whistled into his microphone. "Wind down to fifteen knots," the controller told him. "You can begin your take-off roll as soon as your opponent lifts off."

Hunter looked over to his left at the air pirate who was doing his last minute check before taking off. The man laughed at him, gave him the finger then streaked away.

"Real class . . ." Hunter said, disgusted.

He knew the odds against him were at XX-to-1, but he was sitting on the horns of another dilemma: he couldn't let the pirate get him into a long, protracted dog fight, not because he was afraid he'd lose, but because he didn't want everyone in New Chicago to find out who he was. And to beat the pirate's sleek Flanker with his rickety Mirage would take a number of his best air combat maneuvers, moves that he had to admit, in all modesty, that no one but The Wingman could perform.

So the solution called for a short match. This, and that fact that Hunter loathed every second he spent sitting in the Mirage, had convinced him it should be very, *very* short.

He watched the Flanker reach its take-off point, and as soon as its wheels left the runway, he gunned the Mirage and lifted off cleanly.

The Flanker was bigger than his French flying shitbox, and, were it to be an even fight, the only obvious advantage Hunter had with his quicker take-off speed. But now the Flanker had done a quick twist and was heading back toward him even before he could pop the Mirage's throttles. The pirate was intent on shooting Hunter even before the Mirage could lift off.

"OK, jerk," Hunter said, legitimately smiling for the first time in what seemed like years. "You've just solved my problem for me . . ."

Hunter wasn't even airborne when he launched

191

the missile—he had simply raised the nose of the Mirage and fired the damn thing. It came off his wing with surprising smoothness, rose up quickly and impacted on the Flanker's nose cone.

The Flanker's forward section exploded immediately; the air pirate hadn't even had a chance to pull his trigger. An instant later, the Soviet jet's filled-to-capacity fuel load ignited and completely obliterated the airplane.

End of duel . . .

CHAPTER 36

The recon strike force left Football City shortly after sundown and headed east.

The CH-53 Sea Stallion was loaded with two squads from the Football City Special Forces Rangers, an elite unit that was made up almost entirely of ex-professional football players who once earned their living playing the never-ending matches that made their home city so famous and successful. Escorting the chopper were two A-7D Strikefighters, whose home base was the Pacific American Air Corps air station near Coos Bay, in the old state of Oregon. These unique duo-role airplanes would be able to provide ground support for the troopers and also fend off any intervening enemy fighters.

Also accompanying the strike force was the A-37 Dragonfly, with Ben at the controls and a pilot from the Texas Air Force riding in the right hand seat. The A-37 would function as the small group's air warning platform and radio link, a job which required someone on the ground with the troops to maintain the contact.

That job fell to Yaz . . .

The target was the warehouse where the mysterious tractor trailers were spotted. A high-flying reconnaissance flight early that day, courtesy of Crunch O'Malley, had confirmed the mystery trucks were still hidden at the remote location. O'Malley's RF-4 cameras also spotted a half dozen guards surrounding the warehouse.

The plan this night was to land near the target area, overtake the guards and gain access to both the mystery trucks and the warehouse. Two of the troopers were carrying photographic and video equipment. The opposition was hoped to be either McDeath ground troops or mercenaries in their employ. The worst case scenario would be that the guards were regular Circle Army troops, though this was unlikely.

The 200-mile trip across Illinois took nearly three hours as each aircraft had to refuel in mid-air before approaching the target, and the chopper was inherently slow. Once they were in the area, the Strikefighters went up to 23,000 feet, and started to orbit the target. Meanwhile, Ben and his co-pilot used the A-37's hardware to scan the target for any heavy weapons indications. Finding none, the chopper moved in.

There was a small clearing a quarter mile from the warehouse, large enough to allow the Sea Stallion to land. Quickly and professionally, the Football City troops disembarked from the copter and moved into the nearby woods, Yaz sticking to the rear of the 24-man group with the radio operator and the medics.

They walked through the pitch black forest for 10 minutes until the target was spotted. The strike force leader, an Oklahoman major named Shane, told the bulk of the group to stay hidden, as he and five advance men moved closer to the target to assess the opposition. Should it turn out to be stronger than believed, Shane had standing orders from Jones to abort the mission and get out of the area quickly.

Five minutes went by. Then Yaz heard the first shots.

Suddenly it seemed like the air was filled with streaking bullets and rocket-propelled grenades. The trees themselves were exploding, raining thousands of sharp, burning splinters onto the Strike Force. The group's two radios were crackling with commands and excited conversation. All that Yaz could make out of it was the scouting party ran into a changing of the guard at the warehouse and that the guards were not McDeath hirelings as was previously thought. Nor were they regular Circle Army troops.

Most of the Strike Force had moved up to the forward battle line, leaving Yaz, two medics and one of the radiomen behind. The sparky jabbed a microphone into Yaz's face.

"It's the major," the man said.

Yaz had barely acknowledged when he heard Shane say: "Call in those airplanes . . . Now!"

"What are the target coordinates?" Yaz asked, getting his own ground-to-air radio set up.

"Have them lay down something heavy at coordinates three-five-zero by six-seven. Tell them to hurry. We just walked in on about one hundred fifty bad guys and we need some cover so we can get the hell out of here . . . Just make damn sure they don't hit the trucks or that warehouse . . ."

Yaz was talking to Ben Wa inside of ten seconds. He relayed Shane's message, and even before he signed off he could hear the screech of the approaching A-7s.

There was an odd kind of controlled confusion all around Yaz as the Football City Rangers began falling back. Major Shane was no fool—he was outnumbered nearly eight-to-one, and there was no better reason to cut the visit short.

The A-7s came in and each one laid down a wash of napalm. The exploding jellied gasoline lit up the forest as if it were daytime. Shane called back to Yaz immediately after the jets' first pass. "Good shooting!" he yelled over the squawkbox. "Keep it coming!"

Yaz relayed the message and repeated the coordinates. By this time, the wounded were being rushed back toward the choppers. Once again the Strikefighters roared in and dropped a napalm cannister apiece. Once again the nearby woods were splashed with two flaming waves of liquid fire.

Shane and his advance men moved back to Yaz's position next, carrying the body of one of the enemy. The major was surprised to see Yaz still at his position.

"Shit, boy, you should have been the first one back on the chopper," he said, managing a grin.

Shane took ten seconds to go through the dead man's pockets, trying to get some identity on him. To Yaz, the dead soldier didn't look like an American. It turned out he was right.

"Jesus Christ . . ." Shane whispered as he finally located the man's ID chain. "This guy is *Spetsnaz* . . ."

Being an old US Navy boy, Yaz knew *Spetsnaz*. "God, we just walked into a hornet's nest of them," he thought.

But not for long.

Shane ripped the ID chain from the man, then jumped up and yelled "C'mon, boys . . . *Let's go!*"

They double-timed it back to the chopper as the A-7s came in a third time, laying down another napalm blanket to dissuade any pursuers.

After that, there were none.

"Spetsnaz?" Hunter was astonished. "I'm having trouble believing that."

It was the next morning and Hunter & Co. were huddled around the C-5 radio, talking to Jones. They had quickly filled him in on the last 24 hours in New Chicago—the duel and the celebration Crabb had put together for them that night. Now the crew of the Nozo was getting its first report on the abbreviated raid on Terre Haute.

"Shane did a great job getting his guys the hell out of there," Jones told them. "He estimates there were at least one hundred fifty *Spets* hanging around that warehouse."

"Well, this certainly changes things a bit," Hunter said with understatement. "The Kremlin gang doesn't just send in its best troops to guard something so trivial as gold or even big SAMs . . ."

Both sides were silent for a while. Then Hunter spoke up.

"I think that we should try again to locate and open up one of those trailers," he said. "But, also, we should agree that the gold APC may be the key here. Those mystery trucks were welded shut. But that tank had a laser lock on it that was more sophisticated than anything I've ever seen.

"So whatever is in those trucks may be important, but it could very well be small potatoes compared to what they are hauling in the gold armored car. And God knows how many *Spets* they have guarding it . . ."

"OK, let's get in agreement," Jones radioed. "We'll see if we can locate more trailers, and determine the ones most vulnerable to attack. Plus, we'll intensify efforts to locate the gold APC."

"Sounds good from this end," Fitz said into the microphone.

"Time to sign off," Jones said. "Just wanted to let you know also that all our reserves have arrived here, plus we've armed the POWs. We also have six squadrons of aircraft. Sounds impressive, but I don't have to remind you that our intelligence tell us that The Circle and The Family could field a combined army of one hundred ten thousand just in your neighborhood alone."

Hunter took the mike. "That's all the incentive we need to complete our mission here," he said. "If you can launch the next phase within forty eight hours, I guarantee those enemy troop numbers will drop . . ."

"I'll take that as a matter of faith," Jones kidded him. "After all, it is coming from a thirty-to-one long shot . . ."

Hunter turned and looked at the ten large piles of coins on the table next to the radio—the contents of 300 bags of gold, their winnings on the duel the day before.

"And I'll take that as a compliment, General," he concluded. "Everyone knows that Americans love the underdog."

CHAPTER 37

For Hunter and the crew of the Nozo, the next 36 hours were devoted to eating, drinking and gambling—especially gambling. Each of the 15 agents were given five bags of gold and were told to go forth and multiply it. The tactics ranged from trying their luck at one of New Chicago's dozen casinos, to bribing officials at the city's harness track.

Everyone agreed that intuition and innovation would be the keys. Thus, J.T. went out and bought himself the contract to a club fighter from the city's still-uproarious South Side. All in one afternoon, he arranged a fight for the man, bribed the referee and judges, and artificially pumped the odds up on his guy, so that an hour before fight time, his fighter's opponent was a rock-bottom 75-1 shot. J.T. then paid his fighter the equivalent of twice the winner's purse for taking a dive. Hunter and Fitz had 100 bags of gold riding on the underdog; at fight's end, they needed a truck to collect their 7500 bags of gold.

The rest of the crew was just as successful although on a smaller scale. The fact that they were from the Nozo—coupled by the fact that they were friends with the pilot who had so shrewdly beaten the air pirate on the shortest air duel in the city's history—made them all instant celebrities. Celebrity status was essential in fixing the city's myriad of gambling opportunities, and the Nozo crew soaked up every last drop of their instant fame.

By the end of the 36 hours, they had amassed a staggering fortune in gold totaling 18,553 bags.

It was in a mansion on the city's east side that Hunter and Fitz met the man they called "The Kiss."

It had cost them 100 bags of gold just to arrange the meeting, but money couldn't really buy the advice only The Kiss could give.

The man—approaching his seventies, small, frail, and ailing—was still one of the most powerful men in New Chicago. He had more tentacles than a school of octupi, and ties into every last facet of the roaring city. He was a senior member of the board of The Family's ruling committee, the overseers of all that went on in New Chicago. He alone controlled the finances of The Family's army, who, for obvious reasons, stayed mostly to their barracks in a huge camp in the city of Aurora, right outside the old Chicago city limits. And he alone could bless who the next mayor would be to walk through the revolving door at City Hall.

The man's nickname was derived from "Kiss of Death." While his profession was a high-paid "consultant" and fix-it man, many a hood had met a painful end after being fingered for one reason or the other by The Kiss. In the pre-war days, he would have been called a "don" or a godfather. The word around the town was pay him in advance, follow his advice and don't get him upset, or figuratively, he'd plant a big, wet one on you.

Word of the meeting had spread around town, so much so that a crowd of on-lookers and minor city officials just happened to be in the neighborhood when Hunter and Fitz arrived at the grand mansion.

The place looked old — almost antique — from the outside, but once past the front door, it was decorated in regal, if dark excellence. Hunter and Fitz were ushered into a large drawing room, where they found The Kiss sitting on a throne-like chair. They sat in plush seats before him, fully aware of the dozen bodyguards standing in the recesses of the room.

"So you are the new heroes in town," the man said, his voice raspy. "We've never had airmen as the upstarts here before."

"Maybe that's why we're so . . . well, popular these days," Fitz told him. "People just can't seem to have a good time without us."

"It passes the time," The Kiss said. "We're not what we used to be here — before the first big battles started after the New Order came in. But we've still got a big army and we're learning that it's better and easier and more profitable to make friends than it is to make enemies."

"That's my kind of philosophy," Hunter said. "There's a lot of cash to be made on legit angles. And it primes the pump for the other business . . ."

"We are in total agreement on that," The Kiss said. "And I compliment you. You are very smart for a pilot . . ."

The Kiss poured them each a glass of wine, taking his own glass in his bony hands and sipping it.

"So, gentlemen," he said after a while. "This is a courtesy call, I understand. But tell me, is there anything I can do for you?"

"Advise us," Hunter said. "We're new here, we've only been down a few days and things happen very fast, as you know.

Tell us what our next move should be . . ."

The Kiss took another long sip of wine, then said: "You must strive to reach your potential just as fast as you can. Don't let a moment pass you by. Use the resources at your disposal. Any obstacles in your way you must destroy—quickly. Because always—*always*—someone will be at your heels.

"Now I understand you have a lot of money. Spend it. Buy the things you will need to achieve your goals. This is what makes our city turn. You have power in that airplane of yours. You have popularity because you so cleverly defeated the air pirate. Now you have money to get the things you want."

He took another sip of wine before continuing. For their part, Hunter and Fitz had no intention

202

of interrupting him.

"I'll tell you a story," he went on. "A while ago, back when the city was a little more, shall we say, 'expansionist,' we went into a small town near Football City, in preparation for our battle against Louie St. Louie. The people in the town were obviously aligned with the so-called democratic forces, therefore they were our enemies. So we routinely eliminated all the men of fighting age and the elderly. We sold the young kids to the Mid-Aks, and took all the attractive, fuckable women back here with us. It was all business, you see. And we made a tidy profit on the operation, where some bunglers like the Russians or The Circle would have just leveled the town and killed everyone in it.

"We've repeated this pattern over and over again ever since; in fact, we conduct these raids into Indiana frequently, and occasionally even up into the border towns of Free Canada. It's become a money-maker, simply because we are doing what we do best. That's why there are so many party girls in this city, and also, it is a major reason why we have so much money floating around.

"And by liquidating the men of fighting age, we reduce the number of enemies in the area and the likelihood of armed uprisings and things of this nature. It's a winning business philosophy.

"The point I'm trying to make is that we use our resources wisely. We're not wasteful and we turn a profit, simply because we were the conquerors."

Both Hunter and Fitz—hard-nosed veterans though they were—were shocked at the ease and self-removal with which The Kiss talked about the corporate massacres.

"This is revealing advice, sir," Fitz said. "And not surprising coming from you. Your reputation truly does you justice."

The Kiss did a slight head bow. "Thank you for your kind words," he said a bit wistfully. "It is the advice of an old man, true. But sound advice nevertheless . . ."

"Thank you for your time, sir," Hunter said. "We will take your counsel to heart."

"One more thing," the man said, his mood now lighter than at first, no doubt due to the wine and the compliments. "If you want to make a move—then make a big splash. Do something that will make the people in this town take notice. The bigger, the better. Get the respect of the people, so you won't be just another flash in the pan.

"Do you understand what I mean?"

Hunter and Fitz both nodded.

"Perfectly," Hunter told him.

CHAPTER 38

It was two hours after Hunter and Fitz left their meeting with The Kiss when those who lived near the mansion heard the strange, whining noise and saw the vapor trail crisscross the sky above them.

Bodyguards for The Kiss disregarded the noise—they weren't too far from the airport, and big planes flew in and out on a routine basis.

Even when the speck at the end of the vapor trail began to descend, turning the whine into a growing roar, they ignored it. Their boss was safely ensconced in his castle, so why sweat a little noise?

It was only when the huge C-5 passed no more than 1000 feet overhead that the bodyguards began to worry. And by that time, it was too late . . .

The C-5 turned once again and came in at an altitude of 600 feet. Those in the neighborhood fortunate—or smart enough—to take cover, saw the airplane go into a sharp bank, its port wing dropping noticeably.

Then they heard the mechanical whirring, saw the long terrifying stream of smoke and fire pour out of the side of the ship and engulf the mansion. It lasted no more than five seconds—still long enough for more than 8,000 uranium incendiary shells to perforate the building and incinerate all those inside.

After the airplane had departed and the smoke and noise and fire cleared away, there was nothing left of The Kiss or his grand house . . .

Mayor Crabb woke up to the sound of an air raid siren, blaring right outside his City Hall chamber window.

"Up, girls!" he said, shooing the three naked women from his bed. "Who ever called this drill will be shot . . ."

It was two in the afternoon, but Crabb was still recovering from another marathon night of drinking and debauchery, courtesy of Madame Meenga's girls.

He wrapped a bathrobe around his ample frame and opened the nearest window. Not fifteen feet away, the klaxon set up on a telephone pole was blowing so hard, the glass in the window was shaking.

He reached for his phone, punched a button and was soon talking to his chief of City Security, a colonel named Roy Boy.

"What the fuck is going on?" Crabb screamed at the man. "It sounds like these sirens are going up all over the city."

"They are!" Colonel Boy shouted back. "We're under air attack!"

Crabb was stunned by the news. New Chicago hadn't been attacked by air since the democratic forces bombed the railroad yards and the oil dumps during the first Battle for Football City.

Besides, Crabb knew there was a good chance that Roy Boy was drinking.

"Who's attacking us?" he demanded of the man.

"The *fucking Circle!*" came the reply. "There's four MiGs bombing the airport right now. I can see them from my window. We also have a report that two more

206

are attacking our main power station at Evanston . . ."

As if to confirm the report, the lights in Crabb's chamber started to blink. Then he could hear the sounds of explosions coming from the direction of the airport.

"Jesus, what the *hell* are you doing about this?" he shouted, pulling on his pants.

"What do you want me to do?" Roy Boy asked defiantly. "We don't have any interceptors and not many SAMs. The AA guns are going like crazy at the airport, but they haven't hit anything yet . . ."

Crabb blew his stack at this point. "You sniveling little bastard!" he shouted into the phone. "Your ass is fried after this is over . . ."

He hung up on the man, and quickly dialed a special number only the mayor of the city was privy to. It went to a secure line that led to the mansion owned by The Kiss. Crabb knew it was his duty to inform the Family member of the air raid.

Oddly, he couldn't get a ring on the other end of the line. He dialed the number once again, but still got only an earful of dead air . . .

He slammed the receiver down and hastily put on his uniform jacket. "Those Circle bastards will pay for this . . ." he vowed.

Once dressed, he burst out of the living chamber and into his office. He was surprised to see there was a crowd of people already there.

"What the hell is this?" he asked no one in particular in the crowd of 40 or so soldiers.

The small man with a heavy Irish accent stepped from the crowd.

"It's a coup, Colonel Crabb . . ." Fitzgerald told him. "We've taken over . . ."

CHAPTER 39

It was dusk when the A-37 Dragonfly touched down at New Chicago airport.

Ben Wa and Yaz could see several fires still burning around the periphery of the air field, and the smoldering remains of two transport aircraft littered one of the maim runways.

Off toward the main terminal they saw the huge C-5 called Nozo, parked snugly beside the C-46 decoy. Neither airplane had received so much as a scratch from the air raid.

Ben taxied the Dragonfly up to the C-5 where they were greeted by J.T. Twomey.

"It seems like years . . ." the ever-cool J.T. told them.

"Never thought I'd be landing here unopposed," Ben said.

"Things change," J.T. said simply with a grin. "Now secure your aircraft and come with me.

There's someone who's been waiting for you."

The ride to the City Hall was quick, thanks to the squad of Family motorcycle cops leading the way.

A doorman let them out of the big white limousine, for which J.T. rewarded him with a handful of gold. They walked into the lobby and he waited a few moments for Wa and Yaz to gawk at the palatial setting.

"I've never seen anything like this," Yaz said. He was particularly impressed with the bevy of semi-naked women who were lounging around the lobby, relaxing and drinking.

"You get used to it," J.T. told them, as they walked up the magnificent staircase to the set of huge doors marked *Mayor's Chambers*.

J.T. routinely saluted the Family guards outside and one of them courteously opened the door for them.

"Your guests are here, Mr. Mayor . . ." J.T. boomed in mock seriousness.

The big leather chair behind the desk slowly turned around.

"Good to see you guys," said Hunter, leaning back in the chair. "Welcome to New Chicago . . ."

A sumptuous meal followed, interrupted only by Family bureaucrats shuttling in and out asking Hunter to authorize this, sign that. All in all, Yaz thought his friend was handling the rigors of the office very well.

Whenever they were alone, Ben and Yaz updated Hunter and J.T. on the situation in Football City — the gathering of the ground forces and supplies, the readying of the air squadrons, the launching of spying activities in the east.

But most important was the videotape the A-37 crew had brought with them. Hunter had a large video playback machine brought into his office and left orders with the captain of the security force that he was not to be disturbed. Then, between glasses of beer, they watched the footage that Ben and Yaz had shot the night before.

"You can see we located another six semis," Ben said narrating the video. "We found them inside Indianapolis, near the Colts' football stadium. The same situation as the warehouse—half dozen trucks, a few APCs and jeeps. We've got to assume these rigs are being protected by *Spetsnaz*, too, although the general feels that it's a much lighter force, maybe twenty to thirty guys . . ."

Hunter watched as the infra-red videotape showed the domed Colts stadium with the six semis parked as if they were covered wagons ready for an Indian attack. The unmarked black military vehicles were lined up nearby. The infra-red device was able to shoot right through the fabric that made up the dome. Inside figures could be seen moving through the stadium stands, almost as if they were gathering something.

"What are those guys up to?" Hunter asked. "It looks like they're piling something on the field."

"We can't figure it out," Yaz told him. "Maybe they're looting the place for blankets, or bandages or something along those lines."

The videotape, which consisted of one, quick, high-altitude sweep, came to an end.

"So what's the next step?" J.T. asked. "Those guys won't be hanging out in Indianapolis forever."

"We've got to find a way to get to them without running into another bee's nest like the last time," Hunter said. "Trying to take them in that stadium might prove disastrous."

"That's how Jones feels," Ben said. "In fact, for all we know, they may have moved on already.

"He suggested that we keep an eye on this group of trucks and hit them at a spot where they are most vulnerable . . ."

They watched the brief videotape once again, before shutting down the VCR. "And there was no sign of the gold APC?" Hunter asked.

Yaz shook his head. "No, not on this run," he said. "And, if I'm not mistaken, we're soon to reach a bingo point with how far we can fly the A-37. We just barely made the round-trip from Football City to Indianapolis and back."

There was a knock on the door and Fitzgerald was let in. He quickly greeted Ben and Yaz, then turned to Hunter.

"You've got to make a statement to your new constituents," the Irishman said. "We got a gang of people down in the lobby. They want to meet the guy who erased The Kiss, and they want to know what the hell gives with The Circle . . ."

All five of them laughed. "I wish St. Louie were here right now," Hunter said. "He's the politician . . ."

The Circle attack on the airport and the power station had been a ruse. Texans, flying captured MiGs with Circle markings, had carried out the raid. The inherent unpreparedness of the city's air defenses, coupled with the big splash of taking out The Kiss and their fortune in gold, had propelled Hunter into the mayor's seat faster than any candi-

211

date before him.

Now, as the group walked out of the chamber to the balcony that overlooked the luxurious lobby, Hunter tried to put his thoughts in perspective. He knew he was at the most critical junction of the operation.

The crowd gave him a spontaneous round of applause as he walked out on the balcony.

He looked down on the sea of faces—mostly middle aged men wearing dark uniforms and handfuls of "fruit salad" on their hats and their chests. How many times have they been through this? he wondered.

He cleared his throat and began: "As of one hour ago, we are at war . . ." he said, to a collective gasp of the crowd. "Our enemy is the army that sits no more than thirty miles from here. The Circle . . . And I don't have to remind you that my predecessors allowed these misfits to camp so close to the city. Now, they are obviously trying to take us over. It's our job to stop them . . .

"We found out that The Kiss as well as many others in the New Chicago city government were in the employ of the Circle. Well, we don't have to worry about these people any more, do we?"

The crowd erupted into a long, sustained cheer.

"But the time for celebrating is still far off," Hunter continued. "As of this moment I am mobilizing the army. I will send orders to the line commanders to move out and attack The Circle encampments immediately. I also hereby order every able-bodied man in this city to report to the airport for mustering into irregular units.

"The time for talk is over. The time for doing is at hand . . ."

212

With that, Hunter dramatically saluted the crowd and walked back to the mayor's chambers. The crowd once again exploded in applause.

"That was quite a stirring talk," Fitz told him. "You had me convinced . . ."

Hunter was gulping down a glass of beer. "Don't bullshit me, Mike," he said. "I had to bribe my professor in college to pass me in Public Speaking . . ."

J.T. helped himself to a beer also. "Is that right, Hawk?" he said facetiously. "What was her name?"

CHAPTER 40

The small Family armed patrol boat had just passed from Lake Michigan into Lake Huron when the captain spotted the first barge.

It was a big one—bigger than the coal boats he was used to seeing at this end of Lake Michigan. It sailed out of the thick lake fog silently. Ominously . . .

The captain radioed down to his communications officer, telling the man to get the barge on the wireless. Then he ordered general quarters on the 150-foot ship. Within a minute, all eight of the ship's guns were manned.

"They're Canadians, sir," the radio officer reported. "Heading for New Chicago . . ."

The captain had maneuvered his ship to a course parallel to the barge. It sat low in the water—but not quite low enough for a coal scow.

"What's he carrying?" the captain wanted to know.

"Lumber and cement," came the reply.

Something didn't smell right. The captain was the

Family's eyes and ears way up on this part of the lake, the first line of warning for any mischief makers who would be sailing the 250 miles down to New Chicago.

"Tell him to prepare for boarding," the captain barked.

The armed Family sailors climbed over to the barge and immediately went to the bridge. There they were met by the scow's captain and his first officer.

"What's the problem, boys?" the friendly skipper asked.

At that moment, the patrol boat commander came up to the bridge, surrounded by another complement of armed sailors.

"You're not riding very low to be carrying lumber and cement," he told the skipper right out. "I demand to check your cargo hold and bilge."

The Family captain thought the scow skipper looked just a little uneasy.

"Can we discuss this privately, Captain?" the skipper asked.

Both men retired to the skipper's quarters which was a two-room cabin just behind the barge's bridge.

"A drink, captain?" the skipper asked.

"I'd much rather have an explanation," the man answered. "If you are in violation of the Family's rules of commerce, you'll be sunk before you get within one hundred miles of New Chicago."

"I realize that, Captain," the skipper, a man about 40, said. "Can you and I come to an . . . agreement?"

The Family officer knew right away what the man was talking about. He'd been offered bribes before . . .

"Talk," he said to the man.

"Ten bags of gold for free passage," the skipper

said, getting right to the point.

Ten bags was about twice the size of the normal boodle offered in these parts.

"A lot of money," the Family captain said. "Are you aware that New Chicago is at war?"

The scow skipper shook his head. "When? With who?"

"As of this morning," the captain said, "against The Circle . . ."

"But I thought you were allies," the skipper said.

The Family officer nodded. "We were, until today," he said. "So you see, this can not be an agreement as normally conducted out here. I must see what you are actually carrying. If it is war supplies, I cannot possibly let you pass. Even for one hundred bags of gold . . ."

The skipper nodded. "I'm aware of your situation," he said. "Come with me, I'll show you our cargo . . ."

They left the private cabin and walked down two flights to the barge's hold. The skipper opened one fire door and let the Family officer peek inside. Even for a veteran like himself, the Family officer found his jaw dropping.

The first cargo hold was filled with 100 or more young women. All of them were chained to mattresses; most looked heavily drugged.

"This is a special order by the new mayor of your city," the skipper said. "We were told to make New Chicago as fast as possible . . ."

"Slavers?" the Family officer asked incredulously. "On a coal barge?"

"These are dangerous times, Captain," the skipper told him. "And we both sail in dangerous waters . . . I couldn't very well sail a cruise ship down to New Chicago. I'd be attacked by the lake pirates or seaplanes in a minute."

The Family officer knew he was right. "How many are you carrying?" he asked, fascinated. This kind of human cargo usually flew on airliners and under heavy guard.

"We have ten holds full," the skipper said. "And I have two mates just a few hours behind. Nearly ten thousand of the wenches in all . . ."

The Family officer whistled. *"Ten thousand?"* he said. "The new mayor must be quite an operator . . ."

"He's an enterprising sort," the skipper said. "Few things can turn such a profit these days as a nice young virgin. I believe me and my mates have the last ten thousand virgins left on the continent."

"Twenty bags of gold," the Family officer said. "From you. Twenty bags for every barge that goes by me. No more discussion . . ."

The Canadian looked at him and smiled.

"Done," he said.

CHAPTER 41

Ex-Major Tomm reached the top of the high bluff just as the first wave of Family soldiers reached the Circle Army's front lines.

"This is madness . . ." he said, as the air quickly began to fill with the sounds of gunfire and smoke. "How could this have happened, so suddenly?"

He was deserting. He wanted no part of The Circle or the Russians or anything having to do with this insane, never-ending civil war. He had decided this even before the camp learned that a large Family army was marching their way and would attack soon.

He had stood by and watched as his superiors fell into lock-step and without question set up their defense lines, certain to throw more lives to the slaughter. No reasons were given as to why the erstwhile ally was about to attack; the aerial destruction of their SAM contingent had been just a slap on the wrist, or so they thought. Now the New Chicagoans were bent on all-out war. So sudden was the action—more than 55,000 Family troops had left the city just hours before—that The Circle commanders set no plan of defense. They simply regressed back to the days of medieval warfare when war was won by the numbers: whoever had the most soldiers left standing was the winner.

Now Tomm watched from his safe vantage point as the carnage began. It was hand-to-hand fighting; some of The Circle soldiers hadn't even had time to put on their boots, the battle was joined so swiftly. At some points along the two mile front he could see Family soldiers had instantly breached The Circle line. At other points, the attackers simply disappeared into a cloud of smoke and fire. Missiles flew from both sides, grenades were launched, mortars fired, artillery brought to bear.

It was all so senseless, he thought.

That's when he heard the frighteningly familiar sound of the whining jet engines . . .

Fitz handed Hunter a fistful of cotton and suggested that he get it into his ears, pronto.

The big C-5 was now only ten miles from the battlefield, and already Hunter could see the clouds of smoke rising from the mountain valley where The Circle Army had camped. He routinely activated the flare dispensing system. Although he knew that The Circle had practically no good-sized SAMs left, there was always the possibility that they had a few shoulder-launched missiles operating.

"Crew to posts," he called through the Nozo intercom, as he turned the large airplane into a slight leftward bank. In back, he could hear the 21 shutters—nine forward of the wing, 12 behind it—snap open and the Avenger cannons deploy out. "Check in . . ."

Fitzgerald was in the co-pilot's seat and he patiently went down the pre-firing list with each of the 10 gunners and the four ammunition control men. Hunter could hear him call out the essential equipment checks: "Forward firing generator to on . . ." and he heard ten separate affirmative responses come back.

"Video screen anti-interference mode secured . . ."

"Check!"

"Power drift stabilizers to on . . ."

"Check!"

"Ammunition engage light lit . . ."

"Check!"

On it went as Hunter drew the C-5 closer to the battle. He throttled back and checked his fuel capacity. It was down to one half; he had taken off intentionally with a light load, all the better to maneuver the big ship at low altitudes.

"We are *go,* Hawk . . ." Fitz finally told him. "Ready when you are . . ."

Hunter nodded and slowly brought the C-5 down to 500 feet. It was if everything was going in slow motion, a sensation he rarely experienced in his fighter.

J.T. was manning the fuselage-mounted TV camera monitor which gave them a wide angle, color view of the battle below.

"Doesn't appear that any one side is in advantage," J.T. called up to Hunter and Fitz.

"Just the way we like it," Fitz responded.

Hunter did a final check of his instruments, then told the crew to get ready. They were going in for the first run.

Hunter had just got the cotton in his ears when he put the big plane into the sudden plunge and dipped to the left. Suddenly his body was vibrating. A tremendous sound wave passed right through his feet, ran up his spine to his brain. Hunter and Fitz felt the same thing. It was the combined electricity of the 21 Avengers firing at once.

He turned and looked out the window to see the tremendous wave of smoke and flame fire out of the 21 openings. His earphones filled with the gunners chattering back and forth, calling out coordinates, matching them with their video targeting systems, confirming hits.

He brought the C-5 across the Circle's rear area in one long sweep, the Avengers firing more or less as one for a span of ten seconds. Once again, nothing but a smoldering hole in the ground was left in the airplane's wake.

Hunter put the Nozo into a sharp 180-degree bank and once again crossed the Circle's lines.

"Fire!" he heard Fitz yell as soon as their coordinates matched up. Once again, the airplane shuddered as the rapid-firing cannons erupted. Once again, a massive tongue of fiery destruction rained down on the hapless soldiers below. Once again, bodies were instantly reduced to only bits of marrow and tissue . . .

"Mechanical death," were the words that came to Hunter. "Clinical, electric, *mechanical* death . . ."

The airplane made ten more passes—marking a dozen in all before Hunter turned it back toward the airport.

The battle continued, but at a vast advantage for the Family troops. However, as soon as the C-5 cleared the area, six MiGs appeared and began a methodical strafing of the Family troops.

On it went, bitter hand-to-hand fighting in the dense woods of the Circle encampment, neither side willing to give ground, each side's commanders ordering more and more troops into the fray.

Into the dusk, the battle dragged on. Hunter brought the C-5 back over the area and completed eleven additional runs, the furious fire from the 21 Avengers lighting up the night sky like some enormous monster from outer space. Once again, as soon as he cleared the area, the Circle-marked MiGs appeared and provided air support for the Circle commanders even though not one officer on the ground had any idea where the MiGs had come from and who was behind their deployment.

Night fell and the fighting tapered off, at least temporarily. The sides fell back and were content to batter each other with long-range artillery. Neither side had won anything in the long day of brutal fighting. As the moon came up and the streaks of artillery passed overhead, the dead lay rotting and unburied and the wounded screamed in pain, unattended.

The sounds of the battle could be heard in the city the next morning. And all available men of fighting age were either at the front or heading toward it.

So it was only the hookers and the barmaids who noticed the three enormous lake barges that had appeared out of the morning mist to anchor just off the old Navy pier near the place they called Ogden Slip.

Quickly, small boats were launched from the rear of the barges, and soon a precision-type operation was going full tilt. Loaded boats would drop their passengers ashore, then return to the barges for more. On it went for two hours, practically unnoticed, never mind unopposed.

By nine that morning, 10,000 members of the Free Canadian Volunteer division were moving through the deserted streets of New Chicago.

From his perch in the mayor's chambers, Hunter watched as the Canadians moved through the city, taking over key installations without firing a shot.

It was quick, efficient and easy.

CHAPTER 42

The A-37 was at 21,000 feet, just south of Muncie, Indiana, when Yaz's infra-red terrain scope started buzzing.

"We may have our target," he told Ben as he tuned the device for clarity.

"Mark it," Ben said, as he checked his coordinates.

"That's them," Yaz confirmed. Six trailers moving fast along the open highway. "They're emitting a lot of heat," he reported. "Been traveling for a while . . ."

"That's a good sign," Ben said, calling back to Football City to immediately report their find. "If we're real lucky, they'll pull over in a couple hours."

They continued to pace the convoy, up too high for anyone on the ground to notice. An hour passed . . . The mystery trucks continued to barrel eastward, their accompanying military vehicles straining to keep up with them.

Suddenly the A-37's intercom was buzzing.

"Dragonfly? Fastball here. Come in," both of them heard coming from their helmet speakers. Yaz recognized the voice as that of Major Shane, the Football City Special Forces commander.

"Fastball, we read you," Yaz answered. "What's your location?"

"We are about twenty minutes behind you," came the reply. "You'll be picking us up on your scope soon."

Yaz knew the Strike Force had been waiting on stand-by for two days. The revised plan was for he and Ben to locate the convoy after it had left Indianapolis, track it and call for the chopper troops.

Ben brought the A-37 down to 9000 feet and, within the half hour, the strike force chopper was off their left wing. They would maintain radio silence from then on, so their greetings were confined to waves and hand signals. Ben put the Dragonfly into a wide-out circle as the chopper sped ahead to a pre-determined spot 50 miles up the highway.

Now they would try a more unorthodox means of determining just what the mystery trucks were carrying.

Team Leader Lieutenant Yuri Sudoplatov was getting hungry . . .

The convoy of six tractor trailers and four jeeps had been on the road for more than six hours without a stop for food or rest. Yet they were still three and a half hours away from their rendezvous with the fuel trucks, and their orders were not to stop for anything until then.

He settled back into his seat in the lead tractor trailer, lighting a cigarette to help quell his rumbling stomach. *Everything is so flat,* he thought, looking out at the Indiana countryside. And the roads so wide and well-paved. It was a far cry from Soviet Georgia, where he had been raised, and where the main road was nothing but a worn down trail of packed dirt and oil.

He knew they had to be careful. They were just at the beginning of their long journey. Another group of trucks was attacked a few days before while they were awaiting orders. It was only by chance that a new detachment of *Spetsnaz* was also at the location waiting for deployment that the attackers were driven off. But the attackers were not just bandits or a small air pirate raiding party. They had had coordinated air support, a fairly modern helicopter and sophisticated communications. The thinking around his camp was that the raiders were actually part of the democratic forces who had recently taken over Football City.

But all this made no difference to him. As a member of *Spetsnaz,* his job was to deliver the trucks to their ultimate location, stopping at the assigned points along the way. It was not for him to question his orders or even wonder why his commanders thought the cargo in the semis was so important. Just do it, quickly. Efficiently. And kill anyone who gets in the way.

He routinely radioed back to each of this trucks, checking on the two-man crews. Other than the expected complaints about not eating, everything was going well. When they had started out from Football City, he and his men had many problems figuring out how to handle the big American rigs. Now, with several hundred miles under their belts, they were cruising along like experts, even managing to master the CB radios found in each cab.

He finished his cigarette and leaned back further in the cab of the big Kenworth. If he could sleep for a hour or so, then the refueling point would be that much nearer and his stomach that much closer to being filled.

He had drifted off for only a few moments when he was suddenly awakened by his driver applying the brakes of the truck.

His head hit the windshield and opened up a slight cut. Somewhat dazed, he was about to turn to his driver and chastise him when he saw why the man had stopped so suddenly in the first place: there was a large helicopter hovering in the middle of the highway, no more than a quarter mile up ahead.

Lieutenant Sudoplatov immediately got on the CB and screamed orders out to his team. "Prepare for action," he told them. "And protect the trailers at all costs!"

He brought up his own AK-47 and quickly checked that its magazine was full. The truck was now crawling along at 20 mph, its driver not quite sure what to do.

Suddenly a missile flashed out of the side of the chopper and exploded in the pavement just in front of them. His driver was able to veer to the left to avoid the gaping hole left by the explosion, but the truck began to fish-tail. Just then, a large caliber machine gun opened up on them, puncturing the truck's radiator and breaking its headlights.

"Go!" Sudoplatov screamed at his driver and into the CB microphone simultaneously. "Don't stop! *Keep going!*"

The convoy drivers obeyed and floored their rigs. The chopper meanwhile had lifted off and was moving backward, keeping pace ahead of the rigs, firing at least three machine guns at them.

Another missile—the Soviet officer recognized it as a TOW anti-tank weapon—flashed over his cab and struck the jeep right behind him, instantly killing all five of his men inside. Still he was screaming into his CB: "Go! Don't stop!"

The chopper turned and hop-scotched ahead by about a quarter mile, its machine guns never once pausing.

"They are aiming for our military vehicles!" the lieutenant shouted to his driver. "They are trying not to damage the trucks!"

Suddenly he heard a screech behind him, and, by chance, caught a glimpse in his side view mirror of an aircraft bearing down on them. It was not a fighter—more like an armed recon jet.

He saw four puffs of smoke spit out of its wings, with long trails of fire behind. The four rockets struck the jeep at the end of the convoy, the resulting explosions lifting it up off the highway and throwing it into a ditch.

"Bastards!" he swore, scouting the road ahead. It was nothing but flat, open highway. There were no underpasses or tunnels in which they could hope to hide. The attackers had picked their spot well . . .

The big helicopter fired two more TOWs at his remaining jeeps, missing both, but just barely. Now it suddenly banked to its left and headed back toward the convoy. As Sudoplatov watched in amazement, the copter pulled right alongside his rig, and kept pace no more than 20 feet away from him.

"These are crazy people," he yelled to his driver, who was doing all he could just to keep the truck on the roadway.

The lieutenant had his AK-47 out the window in an instant and began firing at the chopper. It was so close to him that he could see the faces of the men inside, firing back at him. He knew they were aiming for the tires on his rig—if they had wanted to destroy him, another TOW missile at this distance would have done the job.

"Faster!" he commanded his driver, all the while firing at the helicopter. "Do not slow down!"

The copter pulled back and began peppering the third truck in line, its driver nearly losing control when the highway came to a slight curve. The attack jet once again roared overhead, spitting out four more rockets which hit one of his jeeps head on, destroying it instantly.

Still the convoy rolled on at its desperate pace. Lieutenant Sudoplatov saw it as an intractable situation. The helicopter would keep up the high-speed chase until it disabled one of the tractor trailers. He and his troops could fire at the aircraft all they wanted, but he knew it would take a one-in-a-million shot to bring it down.

In all his years of training for *Spetsnaz*—infiltration, sabotage, silent killing, psych-ops and behind-the-lines reconnaissance—nothing had prepared him for this insane confrontation.

Just then he heard a cry from the radio by one of his drivers. Hanging out the cab window he saw the last truck in the convoy wheeling out of control, its right side rear tires shot out and in shreds. The truck yawed to its right and started to spin violently. The helicopter stayed right next to it, like a hawk waiting for its prey, thus allowing the other five trucks to pull ahead and escape.

Lieutenant Sudoplatov knew he had failed. The attackers — no doubt members of the democratic forces — had snagged their prize. It would be child's play for them to cut through the trailer's welds and discover what was hidden inside. Then the secret would be known.

Suddenly, Lieutenant Sudoplatov wasn't hungry any more . . .

CHAPTER 43

It was windy on top of the building, the stiff breeze coming off the lake chilling the Wingman, and causing him to pull his coat collar up around his neck.

The sun was down and lights began popping on all over the city. *His* city. He could still see smoke rising to the south where the Circle and Family armies had clashed in 36 hours of bloody fratricide. Neither side had won—only the death was constant. They had succeeded in reducing their strengths to half, meaning 40,000 bodies lay twisted in the woods and the valley where the battle had been fought.

Meanwhile the diversion had worked; the backdoor had been left open. Even now, retreating Family troops were still streaming back to New Chicago, only to be astonished to find Free Canadians were now in control and disarming anyone carrying a weapon.

Yet, now, as he beheld the city before him, the huge metropolis of which he was the head of state, he felt yet another wave of melancholy wash over him.

For the second time in only a few weeks, the United American Army had succeeded in taking over a key city without incurring any casualties.

Yet he felt lost. It was like he had been moving on auto-pilot for the past few weeks, two large parts of him missing, doing things by rote. It really came down to one question: Did he want his airplane or his woman most? A frightening thought—that he may someday have to choose between them—ran him through like a sword. He shook his head as if to knock out the disturbing thoughts. He turned and faced the north, 300 miles away was Free Canada . . . and Dominique.

It was because of her that his heart ached. He missed her that much. He suddenly felt an insane desire to get ripping drunk, acquire one of the many Dominique look-alikes that were still roaming the city and bed her immediately. Wouldn't it be the next best thing?

"Hawk?"

He turned, the voice behind him liberating him from the disturbing thoughts. It was J.T.

"What are you doing, pal?" J.T. asked him.

Hunter turned back to look out on the city. "Just thinking, partner," he said. "Thinking about where it's all going to end . . ."

J.T. joined him at the railing.

"I hope it ends back on the east coast in a few weeks," J.T. told him. "That *is* the plan. It's been going like clockwork so far . . ."

"We've been lucky . . ." Hunter said. "The Circle is so disorganized, they can't shoot straight, at least in this part of the country. As for The Family . . . I mean, look out there. You would never know that a major battle was fought just thirty miles from here.

"The lights are all on. Look at those cars and trucks in the streets. The casinos are open. Bars are open. It's just another day for them. They've become used to even the most insane conditions . . ."

"And you're their mayor . . ." J.T. said, smiling, trying to cheer him up.

"Yes," Hunter said. "And that's the most insane notion of all . . ."

J.T. had known Hunter for years. It didn't take a shrink to know what was bothering him.

"You're operating under a double-whammy, Hawk," J.T. said. "You can't be with your lady and you can't fly your airplane. But the world doesn't stop turning . . ."

Hunter just shrugged. He wasn't surprised that J.T. had guessed his plight. But this hero stuff was suddenly getting very old.

"Now, you can do two things, Mr. Wingman," J.T. continued. "You can sit up here like Hamlet, pissed off and feeling sorry for yourself, or you can do something about it.

"Put a goddamn call into Jones and have him tell those cowpokes in Texas to get your goddamn airplane flying. If it's a question of money, shit, send them some of the gold we got. There's still a pile of it left—and we haven't even collected our first taxes yet."

Hunter remained silent. He knew his friend was right. Self-flagellation was not the solution.

"As for that beautiful lady of yours," J.T. continued. "Well, at least you know she's safe . . ."

Hunter nodded slowly in agreement.

"You know, our old buddy General *Seth* Jones would kick your ass if he saw you moping like this," J.T. said, putting his hand on his friend's shoulder. "I know a lot of the heavy stuff gets left to you, Hawk. But that's the price you have to pay for being a super-duper kind of hero. You made the name for yourself, now you have to uphold it. You're like the power hitter on a baseball team. People have just come to expect it from you. So, until you decide to quit the business, you'll have to keep the old lip stiff and upper."

"Yeah, yeah," Hunter said, in a tone of voice like he had heard it all before.

J.T. slapped him on the back. "That's the spirit!" he said. "Now, let's go get something to eat, something to drink and something to poke . . ."

Hunter turned toward him for the first time. "You go ahead, I'll catch up," he said.

J.T. smiled and nodded. "Sure, Hawk," he said, walking away "We're partying right over at that Palmer House. I'll save you a seat . . ."

Hunter thanked him and he left.

He took several deep breaths of the night air, hoping it would help clear his head. Almost unconsciously, he put his hand over his breast pocket and felt the reassuring folds of the flag he always kept there, wrapped around the photo of Dominique. When he got like this he always seemed to be able to draw strength from it.

This time was no different.

Hunter fully intended to take J.T.'s advice and

was descending the stairs to his chambers when he saw Yaz and Ben Wa rushing up to meet him.

"We hit the jackpot!" Yaz told him as they quickly walked into his office. "We stopped one of the semis, just around Muncie."

Hunter immediately brightened up. Time to get back to work, he told himself.

"What happened?" he asked.

Ben quickly told him about the high speed interception of the convoy of mystery trucks.

"Everyone OK?" Hunter asked.

"No casualties on our side," Ben told him. "We do have a bunch of dead *Spetsnaz* though . . ."

"So they *are* in charge of running those trucks east," he said. "The Strike Force meeting them in the woods that night wasn't a fluke . . ."

"That's an affirmative," Yaz said. "There wasn't a Circle guy around. It was strictly a *Spets* operation . . ."

Ben continued. "When we left, the Football City guys were just breaking into the trailer. In fact, we heard the chopper landed at the airport just after we did."

"Any idea what they found inside?" Hunter asked.

Both Yaz and Ben shook their heads. "We had agreed not to discuss it even on the secure channels," Ben said. "But whatever it is, those Soviet Special Forces guys sure busted ass trying to protect it."

Then, as if on cue, Major Shane of the Football City Special Forces was let into the room.

But the normally smiling cowboy was wearing a very perplexed look.

"Shane, good to see you, man," Hunter said, rising to greet him with a handshake. He got right

235

to the point. "Did you bust into the truck?"

Shane nodded, his face still a mask of puzzlement.

"Yeah, we got into it," he said, removing his beret and running his fingers through his hair. "But, I'll tell you, I almost wish we hadn't."

"What do you mean?" Hunter asked him, his curiosity getting the best of him. "What the hell was in the goddamn truck?"

Shane looked him straight in the eye and said just one word: "Books."

CHAPTER 44

"Books?" Jones exclaimed over the radio. "What the hell are they doing hauling 'books' around?"

"Beats me," Hunter told him, adjusting the radio's tuning knob to get rid of some pesky static. "But that's what they were carrying. A trailer full of books. About eight thousand in all . . ."

It was about an hour after Shane had reported the find. He, Hunter, Ben and Yaz beat their brains out trying to come up with a logical reason as to why the Soviets would assign their top special teams to escort convoys of tractor trailers carrying books. But it was a fruitless session—there seemed to be no logical answer.

"Did Shane say what kind of books they were?" Jones asked.

"All kinds," Hunter told him. "Hard covers. Paperbacks. Large print, small print. Everything from the Bible to some skin books. Even had a bunch of cookbooks . . ."

Hunter could just imagine seeing Jones, brow furrowed, fingers twirling, trying as he had to figure out what it all meant.

"And should we assume that these trucks, the same

ones hidden under Football City, are *all* filled with books?" he asked Hunter through a field of static.

"At this point, who knows?" Hunter answered. "We'll just have to hook another one and find out . . ."

There was a short pause, then Jones asked him: "Is this the craziest thing we've run up against yet, Hawk?"

Hunter didn't answer right away; they'd seen some pretty crazy things since the New Order came into force.

"It's certainly in the running for Number One," he finally replied.

Nearly 800 miles away, in the old nation's capital of Washington, DC, a massive traffic jam was in the making.

There were soldiers on every corner—Circle Army troops mostly—trying their best to direct traffic. But it was proving to be an impossible task. Even the man responsible for control of the city, a *Spetsnaz* General named Andrei Yetimov, had spent the last two days tearing around the streets in his staff car, trying to unsnarl the city's gridlock, but all to no avail.

It was just an oversight, though now one of potentially serious, if not frustrating, ramifications. No one in the planning stages—no Soviet or Circle officer—had realized what a problem the traffic would become.

And so it went on for days, as the thousands of trucks from all of the eastern half of the continent converged on Washington, pulling trailers loaded with books . . .

PART THREE

CHAPTER 45

It had started to rain again.

Hunter pulled his coat tighter around him, though it did no good, as it was already soaked through. His hair was wet, and the last drops of black hair dye were running out onto his forehead and dripping down his cheek, like strange black tears.

The air base was deserted. From the looks of it, no airplane of any importance had landed there in years. Yet now his sixth sense told him an airplane was approaching. He looked back at the Sea Stallion helicopter that had carried him to this place, and saw J.T. and Wa, their faces lit by the green glow of the cockpit instrument panel, talking about something and paying no attention to him.

For this, he was glad. It was going to get very personal in a few moments . . .

The air field was somewhere near the undefined border of the Free Territory of New York and Free Canada. They had passed over Niagara Falls in getting here, and had seen the lights of Toronto briefly before that.

It had been four weeks since the takeover of Chicago. The newly liberated army of POWs had moved in and were now helping the Free Canadians run the city. Hunter and his allies had stayed on only for ten days before the next phase of the operation had to begin. The remnants of The Circle Army that survived the battle against the Family had retreated eastward, first to old South Bend, Indiana, then to Detroit, where they were forced to move again after incessant air strikes from the United American Air Corps and from the Free Canadian Air Force.

Those enemy soldiers straggling out of Detroit—still some 22,000 strong—had invaded the nearly deserted city of Cleveland and set up camp there temporarily before continuing their retreat. Just at the New York border, the Circle forces split up. Some headed for Pittsburgh, now the enemy's most western outpost. But a much larger contingent headed for the Syracuse Aerodrome, the sprawling, former "truck stop of the sky" that was created by Mike Fitzgerald shortly after the New Order went down. As it would happen, The Aerodrome—whose territory actually encompassed the old city of Syracuse as well as its airport—was the next major target in the leap frog campaign of the United American Army.

The enigma of the mystery trucks had continued and deepened. A unit of PAAC paratroopers, operating out of huge C-141 Starlifters and complemented by Cobra helicopter gunships, had

242

found and attacked a concentration of tractor trailers outside the old city of Cincinnati two weeks before. The *Spetsnaz* troops protecting the trucks had literally fought to the last man, finally succumbing to the much larger United American Force. When the victors pried open the ten trailers they had seized, they found these too were loaded with books.

However, the most disturbing news of all came from a report by a long-range Free Canadian P-3 Orion radar ship, that had ventured out nearly to Iceland just five days before. They had found the lead elements of the Soviet-sponsored invasion fleet that was heading for the east coast of America. Judging by its direction and its operational, but very slow speed, the Canadians estimated the entire fleet could arrive off the east coast of the American continent within two weeks, three at the latest.

So now the race against time had really begun . . .

Yet all this was strangely of little concern to Hunter at the moment. He could hear the airplane getting closer and wondered if the fog surrounding the base would affect its landing.

He felt himself shivering—not so much from the cold but from anxiety. He had arranged to meet this flight, thinking it would bring him some peace of mind. But in the three weeks he had waited—not knowing, but thinking of little else—the apprehension of what would be said this night had proved almost unbearable.

Finally he could see the airplane's landing lights cutting through the thick fog. He felt the lump in his throat grow to over-sized proportions. His stomach was creaking—he hadn't eaten in days—and he was embarrassed to feel his legs go a little wobbly as he shifted around in an effort to get warm.

The airplane—an ancient C-47—rumbled in to a relatively smooth, if not pretty, landing and taxied toward the beacon on the chopper's tail rotor, just as the pilot had been instructed to do. Hunter took a deep breath as the airplane stopped about 25 feet from him, the pilot immediately fluttering the propellers, but not shutting them completely. The aircraft wouldn't be staying that long.

The rear door finally opened after what seemed like an hour. He swallowed hard again as the dim cabin light caught the reflection of the fog, lighting up the otherwise gloomy setting.

Here goes, he thought as he slowly approached the airplane. *However it goes, this was all of your own doing . . .*

A single figure stepped out onto the tiny access ladder that automatically pushed out from the airplane. Slowly the figure walked toward Hunter. He wiped the mist from his eyes and tried to focus on the person. It took a few seconds as they drew closer, but finally his eyes saw the face that made his brain flash, his stomach leap and his heart start pounding—all at the same instant.

They finally came face to face and all of a sudden he wasn't cold any more.

It was Dominique.

"Hi, honey . . ." he said, awkwardly stumbling on the words. "How are you?"

"I'm fine," she said, nervous and formal. "I suppose it is foolish for me to ask you the same question?"

"I'm the same, I guess," was all he could come up with.

Right away he knew it was going badly. He expected an embrace, a kiss. She looked beautiful as always. Even the dark trenchcoat and the kerchief she wore couldn't hide her lovely features. Yet they stood three feet apart, and it seemed like three miles.

"I . . . I had to see you," he said. "I've missed you very much . . ."

She didn't answer him; she just looked at the ground.

He hadn't seen her in so long—since he'd rescued her from Viktor in New York City. Some allied commandos had taken her with them and escaped to the relative safety of Free Canada. Now, after Hunter had made a special request to Major Frost, his good friend in the Free Canadian Air Force to fly her here, she was before him. And he was almost speechless.

"You've become very popular down here," he said finally, his throat dry, his voice cracking.

"I know . . ." she said. "People keep telling me about it. I can't leave where I live without a crowd following me. It was even very difficult for me to come here."

How could this turn into such a disaster? he asked himself, his emotions verging on panic. The only underlying positive point was that he knew no woman could ever make him feel like he did at the moment. He loved her and he knew it . . .

"Dominique," he said, finally deciding to let it all hang out. "I can't tell you how much I want to be with you. How much I think of you. But . . ."

He couldn't get the rest of the sentence out.

She was looking right at him. Through his eyes, into his soul. Her Bardot-like features were quivering only slightly. But those eyes . . .

"It's a very difficult time for me right now, Hawker," she said in a voice not much louder than a whisper. "I am having so many conflicting feelings . . ."

"About what?" he asked.

She lowered her eyes again. "About myself," she answered, a touch of defiance in her voice. "About how I will live the rest of my life . . ."

He felt another shiver run up and down his spine. "You know I want us to be together," he said. "When this is over, I will be able to . . ."

"When *what* is over?" she asked him suddenly. "This war? That war? Whatever war you're fighting at the moment? Do you really think it will be the last?"

He couldn't answer her.

"I think you assume too much, Hawk," she said. "You just assume that I will always be there, waiting for you. But you have to realize that every day I wait, I wonder when it will end. If ever . . .

"I just don't know if I can wait any more."

He was stunned, although he knew he shouldn't have been.

"Is . . . is there someone else?" he asked her, not really wanting to know the answer.

"Does that really concern you?" she asked him softly. "What would you answer if I asked you the same question?"

Suddenly the rain started falling harder. A wind swept up and tossed her hair around. Why couldn't he just reach out and hold her?

"I have to go," she said, giving him one last,

long look. Then she turned and walked back to the airplane.

He stood there as if frozen to the spot. She was leaving, walking away, and he couldn't move. He couldn't stop her. She was right. He had assumed too much. Taken too much for granted. Now as she climbed back into the airplane without a wave good-bye or a look back, he knew he was on the verge of losing her forever. He was crushed. And he knew it would never be the same again.

Before she disappeared into the airplane, he thought he saw a tear running down her cheek. But he knew it might have been the rain . . .

CHAPTER 46

Viceroy Dick wished he had just one line of cocaine . . .

He was trembling and sweating and his head felt like it would burst open at any moment. He had no sense of taste, or smell, and his nose bled every morning when he woke up.

It had been like this ever since the Soviets spirited him out of Football City, just ahead of the advancing United American Forces. At the time, he was certain that he would be hanged or shot by the Soviet Special Forces, and considering the coke withdrawals he'd been going through, he often wished they *had* executed him.

But he was alive, though miserable, and, at the moment, sitting in a makeshift office on the perimeter of the Syracuse Aerodrome, waiting for a cartel of arms dealers to arrive. He was certain that the Circle leadership—its main HQ now located in Washington DC—had gone completely insane. One moment he had been a near-prisoner of the Soviet *Spetsnaz*. The next he was in charge of purchasing weapons for the defense of the Aerodrome. It was a demotion in rank, to be sure, but that he could live with. If only he could get some white lady, it might even be bearable.

His being plucked from the noose only underlined the desperation that was creeping into The Circle Army. The United American Forces had swept into Football City without hardly firing a shot, managing at the same time to save their POWs. That victory was a testament to The Circle's scheme of Tactical Defense, which, when properly translated, meant: hold out then get out. Dick knew The Circle never really intended on making a fight of it for Football City, so the United Americans' triumph there wasn't as fluky as it might have seemed.

But The Circle High Command was absolutely astonished when they learned that it was United American undercover agents operating in New Chicago that had engineered the devastating battle between the Circle Army and the Family. Now the reconditioned POW soldiers from Football City were in control of the strategic city, with some help from the Free Canadians.

The Circle soldiers that survived the battle outside New Chicago had been straggling eastward ever since. Some were being diverted to DC, while others were directed to Syracuse, where everyone knew the next battle would take place. And this would be no cakewalk like in Football City or an inside job as in New Chicago. No, for this looming battle The Circle would need every able-bodied man it could muster, the more experienced, the better. And through these improbabilities of military incompetence, Viceroy Dick had been named the man in charge of buying weapons for that battle.

The weapons cartel, a shady group of dealers known as The Party, arrived outside the concrete bunker that served as Viceroy Dick's headquarters. The four men walked in and immediately began sniffing around — literally. It was obvious from the smell of the place that the Viceroy's concrete office building was once used as an ammunition bunker for aircraft operating out of the Aerodrome itself.

Viceroy Dick greeted the men quickly and formally. They all sat around a large wooden table and, declining an offer of a drink, got down to business.

The blond man named Frankel made it known quickly that he was the spokesman for the group.

"Each of us represents a weapons' specialty," he said. "You tell us what you want and how much you have to spend and we'll see what can be done to accommodate you."

Viceroy Dick pulled out his shopping list.

"I don't have to bore you gentlemen with the details of what we are up against here," he told them. "We're expecting a combined land and air attack by the United Americans sometime within the next two weeks. We are in an obvious defensive posture here. And although I hesitate to use the term 'Tactical Defense,' our orders are to hold out against them until . . ."

"Until your invasion fleet arrives from Europe," Frankel finished for him.

Viceroy Dick eyed the man suspiciously. The news of the Soviet-sponsored fleet was supposed to be secret. "That's correct," he said. "Though I was under the impression that the fleet's arrival was not common knowledge."

"That's an incorrect impression," Frankel told him, his voice oozing arrogance.

Viceroy Dick didn't like Frankel, or the other three Party members. They were all dressed in the same jet black, yet nondescript uniform, with riding pants and knee-high patent leather boots. They all carried non-functional riding crops and Lugers. And they all seemed to look alike, as if they were close first cousins.

"In any case," Dick went on. "We'll need tanks, rocket launchers and heavy artillery for the defense of the airport and the city itself.

"Also SAMs and radar-guided AA guns, if you have them. Plus any interceptor aircraft. We've got the pilots, we just need something for them to drive."

Frankel nodded and, as one, each man dove into his briefcase.

"We can sell you forty M-1s and M-60 tanks," one of the other three said. "We've also got some leftover APCs and about a hundred converted half tracks . . ."

"Converted to what?" Viceroy Dick asked.

"To whatever you want," the tank man said. "SAMs, movable artillery, even flame-throwing capability."

"Sounds good," Viceroy Dick said, making a note in his orders book. "What about rocket launchers, TOW missiles, mines . . ."

A second Party member spoke up. "We can deliver one thousand Claymore mines to you within the week," he said. "TOWs will take longer. Maybe ten days."

"Again, sounds good," Dick confirmed. "How

about SAMs?"

The surface-to-air salesman handed him a ten-page typewritten document, with Polaroid photos attached. "Take your pick," he said. "We've got Stingers, Blowpipes, Rolands and SA-7s. All portable. All excellent for close-in fighting."

Viceroy Dick had to admit he was impressed. "You guys have quite the inventory," he said, looking over the document.

"It's our job," Frankel told him.

Dick made several more notes, then asked: "How about aircraft?"

"That's my line," Frankel said. He, too, whipped out a catalog and handed it to Viceroy Dick.

"Our standard package begins three squadrons of MiG-29 Fulcrum counter-air fighters," Frankel said. "They come complete with Doppler lookdown/shootdown radar, and day/night, all-weather capability. They have a five hundred-mile combat radius, which should serve you nicely, and can go Mach two-point-two at altitude. They are fitted to carry up to eight AA-ten air-to-air missiles, plus an overhauled Vulcan gun in the nose. Also, in a pinch, you can convert them to a ground attack role.

"Along with this, we can offer you one squadron of MiG-27 Flogger Swing-Wings and Sukhoi SU-7 Fitters each, for the important ground attack role. Both airplane types carry two large guns in the nose and just about any bomb under the wings. Both have a combat radius of two hundred forty miles or so.

"Of course, each squadron comes complete with two service aircraft, an inflight-refueler, and a small shuttle craft for parts and repair."

Viceroy Dick's head was spinning with the descriptions. The Party was offering five squadrons—nearly 60 aircraft. He doubted the United American forces had very much more.

"All this sounds great," he said. "But, what's it going to cost?"

For the first time a smile came to Frankel. "That depends . . ." he said.

Viceroy Dick prepared himself. Here comes the whammy, he thought.

"Depends on what?"

"It depends on whether you are interested in purchasing our Supreme Command package," Frankel answered. "If you do, then everything we've just described to you is free . . ."

Viceroy Dick resisted a temptation to clean out his ears.

"Did you say: 'free?' " he asked. "As in *free of charge?'* "

All four men nodded. "That's correct," Frankel said. "Absolutely free and guaranteed delivery with two weeks."

It sounded like the deal of the century—Viceroy Dick was immediately suspicious.

"OK, I'll bite," he said. "What's in the Supreme Command package?"

Frankel took a deep breath and lowered his voice. "Twenty-two battlefield nuclear weapons . . ." he said. "Small-end range. One-point-two kiloton. For a surface blast you would get a crater two hundred fifty feet deep, twelve-fifty across. Total blast radius is two-point-one miles for anything and everything: three-point-two for buildings. Double those numbers for an airburst. Radiation is low and cleared completely within twelve hours, except at absolute ground

253

zero . . ."

Viceroy Dick found that his jaw had dropped involuntarily. "You guys are selling *nukes . . . ?*" he asked, incredulously.

"Yes, we are," Frankel answered. "They are *guaranteed* nukes, I might add . . ."

"You guys are nuts . . ." Dick told them. "No one does nukes here . . ."

"No one does nukes, sir, because they are not so readily available," Frankel said, a hard edge returning to his voice. "Certainly you wouldn't expect your Soviet patrons to provide you with them . . ."

"And I'm glad of it!" Dick exclaimed. "There'd be nothing left . . ."

Frankel shook his head. "You are missing the point," he said. "With the Supreme Command package, your victory in the upcoming battle is virtually assured . . ."

Dick was shaking his head. "No, no . . ." he said. "Believe me, the top New Order guys in Moscow wouldn't allow it. If one guy starts dropping nukes, there'll be a race to out-nuke everyone else and the place will look like the moon in a matter of weeks."

"More appropriately, it will look like the Badlands," Frankel said. "And that, sir, was courtesy of the 'top guys' in Moscow . . ."

Viceroy Dick was adamant. "No way am I buying nukes," he said. "Just give me a price on all the other stuff and we'll talk business. But no big ones."

"You are making a serious error, sir," Frankel said, as the other three men started totalling up the charges for the conventional weapons. "Because, someone, somewhere, some day will buy

254

one of our Supreme Command packages. And when that day comes, you'll wish you got in first. I can assure you, that our Supreme Command *Deterrent* packages will be much more expensive, and they will not be offered with the free-of-charge conventional packages."

They handed him a price list that totalled 263,000 bags of gold or 1,315,000 bags of real silver. It broke down to roughly 2000 bags of gold per airplane—just a tad higher than the going price—plus 63,000 bags for the rest of the equipment.

"The price is high," Dick said. "Call it two hundred sixty thousand and you got a deal."

"Done," said Frankel. "Though you are not getting the best deal . . ."

Viceroy Dick ignored the comment. "You'll get half in two days, half when the stuff is all delivered," he said.

The Party members closed their briefcases and got up to leave. There were no handshakes, no small talk.

"Just out of curiosity," Dick asked them. "What was the price on the nukes?"

"Twelve thousand bags of gold each," Frankel said. "Or the entire package is irresistible at two hundred ten thousand."

Dick was amazed at the low price. "Jesus, are you saying you'd sell a nuke to any scum bum who can come up with a lousy twelve grand of gold?"

Frankel nodded.

"But that's incredibly cheap," Dick said. "It's almost like you want us to go at it with the heavy stuff . . ."

"Not at all," Frankel said. "It's just business.

Strictly business."

The Party cartel left and Viceroy Dick sat down at his desk and went about the procedure to request funds for the weapons.

Yet, he couldn't get the men or their offerings out of his mind. There was something very odd about them, especially Frankel.

Viceroy Dick thought he had detected a slight German accent in the man's voice . . .

CHAPTER 47

There's a fire that burns in a man's soul when something absolutely irreplaceable has been suddenly lost. The aching never really goes away, it is simply transformed into other means of action or reaction. The yearning turns to anger. The wanting turns to rage. The power of love can turn to pure hate. Rarely at what has been lost—the positive memories still remain; they can't be changed or transmuted.

So grief can make the human creature lash out, like the wounded animal. Channel the feeling to another internal plane. Regardless of the consequences; regardless of the toll. Reverse the energies and hope for the best. And try to be cognizant of the fact that if only a spark remains, it can ignite the largest of conflagrations.

Hunter had burned with the fire for two days straight. No sleep, nothing to eat or drink. Sitting alone in his quarters, a mobile home similar to that

257

of General Jones, that was being towed by a deuce and half belonging to the Texan Army, The Wingman smoldered.

For every loss, there is a gain . . . he told himself over and over. Dominique was gone. Lost not to some twisted, power-mad ego-maniac like Viktor, but to the callings of her own heart. Freaks like Viktor, Hunter could handle. But he was powerless over what was in Dominique's heart . . .

For every loss, there is a gain . . .

He never thought he could hurt this much, but he was numb. He had been selfish, even greedy with the assumption that she would always want him, always *love* him. But to expect devotion like that required a return of absolute devotion. And he hadn't come close to evening out the bargain. He was guilty. Of negligence. Of neglect. Of taking the most important person in his life for granted. It seemed like such a foolish thing to do, yet he had done it rather easily. *Never assume anything,* Seth Jones used to tell him. Good advice in life and love—advice that Hunter had chosen to ignore . . .

For every loss, there is a gain . . .

What was she doing right now? he wondered with an ache in his heart. Was she in the arms of some new lover? Was she warm and safe and happy and in love with someone who had recognized her needs and rushed forward to fill the vacuum? Were they making love right now? Was she laughing? Was she moaning in delight, the music he had heard when they had been together?

He couldn't bear to put his hand inside his breast pocket and feel for the flag-wrapped photograph of her. There was a limit even for an extraordinary person like himself. It would take him a long time just to touch the flag again. Whether he would ever look at the photo, was another story . . .

For every loss, there is a gain. If this was true, he thought angrily, then where is it? Where is *my* gain? He wanted it and he wanted it now.

The cosmos owed him one . . .

Their new forward base was located in the old city of Erie, Pennsylvania.

The site suited the United American Forces well. There was a workable airfield in the mostly-abandoned city, and with its access to Lake Erie—and therefore Lake Michigan—the bulk of their equipment and troops could be moved over water from New Chicago and Milwaukee, both of which were now in friendly Free Canadian hands.

Erie also put them within 220 miles of the Syracuse Aerodrome, an acceptable distance for most of the American Forces aircraft, even without their substantial mid-air refueling capabilities. And, by using the Niagara River, they could move large forces of men from Lake Erie up into Lake Ontario and float them over to Oswego, which was only 40 miles north of Syracuse. The roads leading from Erie to the Syracuse area were fairly passable, and most important, the civilians between Erie and the Aerodrome were, to a man, loyal to the United American cause.

The United American convoy—including the trailers used by Jones and Hunter—arrived at the former Erie International Airport just after midnight. Looking out on the tarmac, Hunter could see that most of their fighter aircraft had already arrived, as well as the C-5 called Nozo.

No sooner had he arrived than Hunter was driving a jeep up and down the flight line. As commander of the UA air corps, it was his duty to make a status check on the airplanes at hand. But even Jones had told him it could wait until morning.

Trouble was, Hunter was in no mood to wait for anything . . .

The Football City Air Force was already deployed to Erie—14 rare, high-tech F-20 Tigersharks, among the hottest fighters on the continent. Hunter felt a personal affinity for the aircraft (which were actually souped up F-5Es) because he had engineered their confiscation from a band of air pirates just before the first Battle of Football City.

Next to the Football City contingent were two squadrons from his own unit—the Pacific American Air Corps. Of these 32 PAAC airplanes, 24 were dedicated to ground support. Specifically 14 A-7E Strikefighters and eight A-10 Thunderbolts, the squat, rugged airplane known to its enemies as "The Tankbuster," because of the powerful Avenger cannon it carried in its snout. Two A-4E Skyhawks—the same ones that had performed so well over Football City—rounded out the air attack arm.

The remaining ten PAAC aircraft were fighters—five F-5E Tigers, two aging F-106 Delta Darts, two F-101 Voodoos and a single F-104 Starfighter.

Next to the PAAC deployment area were the 12 F-4E Phantoms of the Texas Air Force. The Texans were incredible pilots, with a seeming disregard for life or limb. They flew the elderly Phantoms as if they were just pups, something helped along by a radical re-engining of the Vietnam-era warplanes.

Also attached to the Texans, not just for convenience but for camaraderie, were the two F-4X "Super Phantoms" flown by Captain "Crunch" O'Malley's famed Ace Wrecking Company. These F-

4s had a longer range, and could carry more bombs and ammo than the Texan F-4s.

Hunter went way back with O'Malley—he and Elvis (who was now running the military side of things back in Football City) were the pilots dispatched by Jones to track Hunter to the Middle East on his search for Viktor. The Aces and their support had arrived just in time during the Battle for the Suez Canal, and saved a lot of good guys from dying in the process.

Using the same facilities of the F-4s were Mike Fitzgerald's Shamrock Squadron of F-105X Thunderchiefs. These 18 re-engined fighter-bombers were originally based at the Syracuse Aerodrome when Fitz ran the place, but they had been orphans ever since The Circle conquered the eastern half of the country. Officially "neutral" in the war against the first Battle for Football City, the "Potato Heads" served with distinction during The Circle War. Operating out of secret bases just over the line in Free Canada, the F-105s continually bombed and harassed the Circle northern forces, causing them to finally stall, and thereby not play a major role in the ultimate battle at the Platte River.

Hunter moved down the line, passed the four PAAC C-130 gunships and the berth where Nozo was being serviced. A squadron of PAAC Huey attack helicopters were just coming in, having leapfrogged over from Toledo. With them were the Cobra Brothers, the four-man, two-chopper attack team that had also served bravely in New Order America's all-too-frequent wars. Also on hand was the big CH-53 Sea Stallion chopper known as The Mean Machine, which usually served as the lift for the United American Strike Teams.

At the end of the flight line was the real Bastard

Squadron, a mix and match dozen of airplanes that PAAC and the Texans had picked up along the way. One of these was the valuable A-37 Dragonfly. There were also two ancient F-94, 1950s-era fighters, a creaking F-100 Super Sabre, three T-38 Talons, which were actually trainers converted for attack duty, two F-8 Crusaders, originally a Navy interceptor, and the granddaddy of them all, an A-1E prop-driven Skyraider.

Hunter had been taking notes as he drove along and now, his inspection tour complete, he returned to his trailer to spend the time until sunrise filling out the status report.

Two hours went by. Hunter had just lit a stick of incense when he felt an almost imperceptible vibration run through him.

He looked up from his paperwork and focused on the sensation.

Far off. Getting closer . . .

He closed his eyes and concentrated.

Coming from the west. Up high now, but starting to descend . . .

He stood up and let it all come to him clearer.

There's a lot of them . . .

Five out front, maybe eight or nine more close behind. In the center, a really big one . . .

"There's something inside the big one," he said out loud.

For every loss, there is a gain . . .

His breathing became rapid, his pulse began to race. Suddenly electricity was running through him from head to feet and back again. It had been so long, he thought he'd never experience it again.

It was *the feeling* . . .

There was no way to describe it. It was one thing and it was a million things. It was ESP and it was *deja vu*. It was pure intuition. It was synergy. It was the feeling that came to him when aircraft were approaching, although they were still too far away to be seen on any radar screen. It was the feeling that he got when he took off in an aircraft and not so much flew it as became part of it. It was the feeling that let him know that all things ethereal could be real. All things were not causal. Synchronicity was a fact.

It was *the feeling* that made him the best fighter pilot that had ever lived . . .

For every loss, there is a gain . . .

He ran outside, jumped into the jeep and drove like hell to the end of the runway. The sunrise was still a half hour away and a slight fog was hanging low over the airfield. The synchronized landing lights gave the place the eerie look of a gigantic video game. There was no wind, no noise . . .

He waited . . .

Twenty minutes went by before he saw the first lights. Two reds and a white, blinking out of sync. He heard them next — first a whine coming from way off, but now getting louder by the second. Then he saw more lights and the whine turned into a dull roar. The lights were circling, high up, slowly descending . . .

Here they come, he thought.

The first of the 12 B-52 Stratofortresses came in low and smooth, its tail-chute deployed, its engines spewing clouds of brown smoke. Right down over him, down the center of the beckoning landing lights, its eight jet engines screaming now in un-

263

abashed power. It was a sight that never failed to move him. Wings, fuselage, bombs and jet engines — the 'Fort was one tough motherfucker . . .

A second one appeared in the ever-brightening sky, then a third and a fourth. One by one, the twelve of them landed, not a rough touchdown in the bunch.

But he knew the show was just beginning . . .

Once the B-52s were in, he turned to see a white airplane making its approach. Smaller but sleeker than the 'Forts, this first airplane — like the four behind it — was a B-1B, swing-wing intercontinental bomber. But these five airplanes were not ordinary B-1s, if there was such an animal.

These were the *Ghost Riders* . . .

Five intricately interconnected B-1s that, when working together, the *Ghost Rider* pilots could simply wipe their radar signature off any screen. By using a combination of five ECM-crammed black boxes — one in each airplane — the Ghost Riders could make themselves invisible on radar and therefore invulnerable to the enemy's radar-guided SAMs and AA fire. The five B-1s had turned the tide in the last battle of The Circle War, demolishing a miles-long Soviet-led column before it even reached the Democratic Forces' front lines.

The *Ghost Riders* came in as smoothly as the old B-52s, their newer, high-tech engines emitting little smoke and even less noise.

But as impressed as he was about the arrival of the 16 heavy bombers, it was the last aircraft in line — the huge C-5 they called Bozo — which was the major cause of the vibrations that were sweeping through his body.

There's something inside. For every loss, there is a gain . . .

The C-5 roared in right over him and touched down to a screeching, smoky landing. He was back in the jeep and racing down the access road as it taxied toward its parking area. The sun was now up—a very important day had begun.

Hunter pulled up to the front of Bozo just as the pilots began shutting down its massive engines. He felt an authentic spiritual sensation wash over him as the front of the Galaxy lifted up, almost magically, like a whale ready to swallow a present-day Jonah. The insides of the monstrous cargo hold were dark for the moment, but Hunter needed no illumination at this point. His heart was beating faster than he could ever remember. His feet felt like they were floating—unwilling to touch the ground.

Suddenly the bright cargo hold lights switched on and he was staring inside the belly of the airplane. One great wave of electricity washed over him as he focussed his eyes on the object inside the jet.

For every loss, there is a gain . . .

Inside the hold of the C-5 was his refurbished, his reconditioned, his *reborn,* F-16 . . .

CHAPTER 48

Yaz's eyes were stinging from the camouflage grease paint he had just smeared all over his face.

His uniform felt like it weighed a ton, due to the forest of bushes and twigs he had attached to his arms, legs and chest. Somewhere on his back, covered with realistic moss netting, was the small high-frequency radio set that had become his constant companion since the United American campaign began.

He was sitting in a large clump of bushes alongside Otsego Lake, smackdab in the middle of Circle-held territory in central Free State of New York. Not 50 feet from his concealed position, two dozen *Spetsnaz* were eating their noontime meal. Another two dozen were scattered about at various positions in the immediate area. And hidden amongst the bullrushes and scrub along the lake were 35 of Major Shane's Football City Special Forces, most of them veterans of the abbreviated raid on the first mystery truck camp and the more successful truck hijacking on the Indiana freeway.

The bizarreness of the notion that for whatever reason the *Spetsnaz* were hauling books in their tractor-trailers had started to fade by now. The mission had switched from "what" to "why." Shane's Rangers—as they had come to be known—had been put on the case, and Yaz had been "recruited" once again to be their air support controller.

After the Indiana highway battle and hijacking, the Rangers had picked up the trail of the five other mystery trucks just outside of Cleveland. The city was practically deserted by the time the *Spetsnaz* came through, its few citizens had fled in order to avoid the retreating Circle Armies. The Rangers had kept a safe distance, using the A-37 to spot the trucks, then landing the chopper a mile or so away and hoofing it to a better vantage point from which to observe the Soviet Special Troops.

It was in Cleveland that the Rangers started noting another strange pattern of behavior being displayed by the *Spets*. Just as in Indianapolis, the Soviets had camped out near a sports stadium—in this case the ancient ballpark known as Municipal Stadium, home of the Cleveland Indians baseball team as well as the Cleveland Browns football club.

The Rangers, with Yaz in tow, had managed to hide out at the edge of a rail yard located near the stadium and watch the Russians through Nightscopes as they hauled a couple dozen boxes out of the ballpark and loaded them into one of their trucks just before departing. No one in the Rangers' team—nor back at United American headquarters—even had a guess as to what was in the boxes. But from that point on, it was clear that the Soviets—or least some of them—were hauling more than books in the back of the Mystery Trucks.

The Rangers stayed close to the *Spets* convoy as it rumbled out of Cleveland. The smart money figured the convoy would head southeast to the safety to the main Circle lines which at the time were collapsing back through Pennsylvania and for a while this prediction looked good. The Rangers were waiting for them when they pulled into The Pitt, just two days after a large contingent of Circle troops pulled out.

Once again, the *Spetsnaz* made camp near a ballfield—in this case Three Rivers Stadium—and once again, they were seen carrying boxes out of the facility and loading them onto the trucks.

But then the plot thickened when the convoy took a sharp left and headed north, then east, skirting Erie, and apparently heading for the massive Circle enclave at Syracuse. Then the Soviets pulled another surprise: instead of taking refuge within the occupied territory of the Aerodrome, they diverted south again, past Syracuse, stopping only when they reached the shore of Lake Otsego, the waters of which were now soaking through Yaz's boots.

A contingent of Circle troops were waiting for them when they arrived. The Soviets immediately dismissed their allies and took over guarding a small building near the edge of the lake. And there they now sat, eating beets and casually sunning themselves, completely unaware that the Rangers were part of the scrub brush nearby.

Yaz was over his initial nervousness about traveling with the Football City Special Forces. He believed the Rangers were tough enough to take on the 50 or so elite Russian troopers and win. No, now he was simply fascinated by what the hell the Soviets were doing. Only a moron would miss the pattern that had formed—a moron or someone who didn't know sports. First, the *Spets* stopped at the Indianapolis Hoosier Dome. Then they moved to Cleveland's Municipal Stadium. Then to Three Rivers. And now they were camped on the edge of Lake Otsego, which was right next to a small New York village named Cooperstown, which happened to be the location of the Baseball Hall of Fame.

So Yaz and the others sat silently and watched as the Russians ate, and came in and out of the small building they were guarding and tinkered with their big Kenworth and Mack trucks, which were parked right next to the ballfield that was located right next to the Hall of Fame itself.

Yaz had to wonder what The Babe would have thought of all this . . .

CHAPTER 49

"There he goes!" several people cried out at once as they watched the reconditioned F-16 take-off, turn on its tail and roar straight up into the heavens.

Inside the cockpit, Hunter feared that he would have an involuntary bodily function. Back in the old days, flying his F-16 felt so close to having sex that he sometimes worried about whether or not his libido was pointing in exactly the right direction.

And that was the "old" F-16 . . .

Now, he was approaching Mach 1 in this . . . *this new* airplane and the sensation running through him was identical to the feeling he would get by having sex with a completely new, absolutely beautiful, exciting, intelligent, versatile, *uninhibited* woman.

For every loss, there is a gain. The cosmos had just paid him back.

It was true that the engineers at the GD plant in Dallas didn't have the parts to restore the F-16 to its original condition. The jet had been battered, shot full of holes and had crashed in the Saudi Arabian desert during his relentless pursuit of Viktor. When it finally arrived back in the States inside the hold of a C-5, it was so beat-up, the GD engineers knew it was hopeless to try to rebuild it in its original condition starting from square one.

So what they did was modify it — a lot. What he got back was a radically different airplane, technically known as an F-16XL . . .

To the casual observer the biggest difference was in the fighter's outward appearance. The F-16 was now "cranked" — its tail wings were gone and its front wings were now shaped in a delta pattern and extended all way back to the rear of the aircraft. In the business, it was called SCAMP — for Supersonic Cruise And Maneuvering Prototype. But with the overall effect looking like an arrowhead, it was no surprise that the few previous pre-war models of the F-16XL led to its nickname, "The Cranked Arrow."

But there was more that was new about his beloved ship than just the shape of its wings. The engineers had slapped a number of flight technologies onto the airplane. It was now an official "CCV" meaning control-configured vehicle. Canard surfaces — actually small stubby wings — were added beneath the air intakes on each side of the nose wheel housing. The fuel system was modified to allow better control over the airplane's center of gravity. The flight control system was rewired and reprogrammed.

All this changed the way the aircraft could maneuver. Normal aircraft flight was simply a case of cause and effect. One movement was often related to another movement. To go left, the pilot would bank, twisting the airplane to go in the desired direction. To climb, the pilot had to put the airplane's nose up. To dive, he had to put its nose down.

But with the new modifications, all that twisting and turning was now obsolete. Now, the F-16 could raise or lower its nose while still staying level. No longer would the up-or-down maneuver affect its flight path. It was called "pitched axis pointing"—the airplane would simply rise in a "vertical translation." It could now move side to side without banking—a "lateral translation." The new abilities would allow the airplane to move cleaner, faster, with less effort and stress.

But the weirdest talent of them all was its new talent to perform "yaw axis pointing." This allowed the nose to be moved side-to-side *without* changing the direction of flight. Like a controlled skid of an automobile, no longer would the nose of the aircraft have to be pointing in the direction it was traveling. He could sway the snout of the airplane about 20-degrees to either side while still traveling in a straight line. It was hard to explain, but even stranger—almost spooky—to try.

The GD engineers had also thrown in an alphabet soup of new dogfighting technologies. The F-16XL CCV, was also fully AFTO—meaning it had Advanced Fighter Technology Integration to control its new CCV systems. It was also christened with an AMAS—Automatic Maneuvering Attack System, whose main components were a sensor pod containing a FLIR (Forward Looking Infra-Red) system, a new, more powerful laser range finder, a switch-on helmet-mounted sight which would display all necessary dogfighting information to him right on the visor of this strange other-wordly headgear. It also now had a digital fire-control system, a radar altimeter, and an extra computer which would allow data from FLIR to automatically steer the ship toward the target, if he wanted it to.

The GD engineers had left the original engine intact—they couldn't have improved on his redesigned GE F110-FC turbo-fan turbine which he had reworked just before The Circle War to carry him past 2000 mph and close to Mach 3. They also didn't tamper with his Vulcan "Six Pack"—the half dozen Gatling guns that stuck out of the airplane's nose, three on each side. The increased wing area of the delta shape would allow him to carry more under wing munitions though, and for that he was grateful.

They did repaint the airplane however, as just one night in the wind-blown Arabian desert had so ruined the finish it looked like someone had taken an electric sander to it. They retained his original red-white-and-blue Thunderbird colors. But now the entire delta wing surface was red, the trim along the top of the fuselage was blue and everything else was white. It looked sharp—*very* sharp. It also looked bad—very *bad,* as in bad-ass. But the best touch of all was what the GD engineers had painted on its underwing. The outline of the Thunderbird logo was still there. But surrounding it, in a slightly luminous enamel, they had painted a large *"W."*

He roared through the cumulus, passed 35,000 feet, passed 40,000 . . . The airplane was incredible to fly. It *felt* like his old airplane, but it was very different just the same. He knew that its spiritual alignment was proper—the wave of *the feeling* that was pumping through his body was more intense than anything he'd experienced in the old design.

For every loss there is a gain. He had lost Dominique, he had gained a new part of himself.

Past 55,000 feet he was singing. Sweet streams of vapor flew by him. He looped at 61,000 and dove to

18,000, letting the five-g bathe him in a familiar excitement. *Goddamn . . . he was flying a real airplane again.*

He experimented with the new maneuvering systems and attained new heights of pure aerodynamic ecstasy. He dropped down—in a "vertical translation"—to just 1500 feet, low enough for him to show off in front of the whole base. He put on a show for the next ten minutes. Looping, rolling, performing double-eights and six-point turns. Then he got into the exotic yaw axis pitching. The seemingly-impossible maneuver had them dropping their jaws back on the ground. He did a number of extreme "vertical translations" giving the impression that the F-16 was lifting almost vertical like a VTOL Harrier. He crisscrossed the base twice via a "lateral translation"—to the people on the ground it appeared that he was actually moving sideways.

Finally, he brought it down to 250 feet and booted in the powerful afterburner, rocking the airfield with an explosive shock-wave as he roared by doing close to 2000 mph.

Those that were there that day would later swear they had never seen such a display of flying, *ever.*

Now even he believed it: The Wingman was back . . .

CHAPTER 50

It was an hour later and the mid-morning briefing had just begun.

Crowded around the table in Jones's trailer was the general himself, Hunter, J.T., Ben Wa, Fitz, Captain Dozer, Crunch O'Malley, the Cobra Brothers plus representatives from the Football City Armed Forces and the Texas Army.

"First of all," Jones began. "We are now fully deployed to this base. I'm sure everyone saw the PAAC Heavy Bombardment Squadron come in, along with the other C-5. With their arrival, all of our forward air elements are here. As you know, we do have several squadrons in reserve, and the Free Canadians have taken over our long range air recon out on the west coast.

"Our infantry and armored forces have also all arrived and have taken up positions in and around the city. We are awaiting a number of water transports that are coming from the various lakes, and when they arrive, we will quickly get some of the ground troops on board and get them up in Lake Ontario for the assault on Oswego."

Everyone took the pause in Jones's report to take a swig of coffee or light a cigarette.

Jones himself sipped his cup of java, then continued: "As for The Circle, we believe his southern forward line is now somewhere near Altoona, in the center of old Pennsylvania. It's rough country down there, so I'm sure the going is slow and tough for them."

"Me heart is breaking . . ." Fitz yelled out in his thick brogue.

"Well, their northern line had an easier time of it," Jones went on. "They split their forces and the half that's going through Old Penn will, I would guess, head straight for DC. Their northern line is already entrenched in and around the Aerodrome. And they're just waiting for us.

"We received a rather disturbing report that a large airlift is in progress at the Aerodrome. Fitzie's spies tell us that unmarked Antonovs—from small An-72s right up to the big boy An-one 24s—have been coming in around the clock, off-loading and leaving again . . ."

"They must have made a large arms purchase," Hunter said. "I'm sure they have no shortage of weapons peddlers knocking at their door . . ."

"The jackals never sleep," Jones said. "They're bringing in everything from M-1s and M-60s to small SAM batteries. It must have cost them a fortune . . ."

"Ah, but money has never been a problem for them," Fitz said.

Everyone at the table nodded in agreement. The Circle spent money like a drunken sailor—funds no doubt supplied from Moscow. It seemed that the New

Order Soviets had acquired a bad habit from the prewar democracies. If a problem persisted, try throwing money at it.

"They're well under way in deploying this new material around the Aerodrome and the city itself," Jones went on, his voice taking on a grim tone. "They're going to be armed to the whatzits and time is on their side. They're making this stand at Syracuse because all they have to do is hold us up long enough for the mercenary fleet to reach the east coast. If that happens, well . . . we'll be drinking vodka only for then on."

"Well, it's *not* going to happen," Hunter said sternly, his tone serious and decisive.

"Well, then, right after this meeting, we should start laying out our timetables," Jones said. "Strategic bombing. Tactical stuff. Invasion routes. The whole nine yards. Every minute we delay, that's to The Circle's advantage . . ."

There was another murmur of agreement, this one subdued and somber.

Jones shuffled some papers and went on.

"Now, we've been getting some very odd reports about these damn tractor trailers, these 'mystery trucks,' " he said. "Shane's Rangers are right on the tail of the same bunch that we snatched the one rig from in Indiana. We just got a message from them through Yaz about an hour ago.

"Now get this: They followed these guys to Cooperstown. Anyone here *not* know what Cooperstown is famous for?"

No one raised his hand—they were all sports fans.

Jones went on, shaking his head as if he couldn't quite believe what he was saying. "Well, they've got the Hall of Fame itself surrounded as well as a number of other buildings. They are particularly concerned with a smaller building at the edge of the town and Shane's guys saw them bringing in bottles of water and packs of food into this building."

"Maybe they have a bunch of honeys in there," J.T. offered. "I'm sure even the *Spets* have to get a little scooty now and then . . ."

"I wouldn't be so sure," Jones said. "Those guys make robots look human."

"Maybe they have some prisoners inside," Hunter said. "Like hostages or something . . ."

"Could be," Jones said, with a few others nodding in agreement. "But why would they start taking prisoners now? They didn't back in Football City."

Hunter shrugged. "Maybe they're special prisoners, someone they can ransom, or someone who is . . . well, irreplacable."

"Well, if they are holding prisoners," Jones said. "They're really watching over them."

"There's got to be a way to find out what's going on," Dozer said.

"There's really only one way, that I can think of," Hunter said. "Capture one of the Spets and beat the crap out of him until he talks."

Jones smiled for the first time. "I just sent an order to that effect to Yaz," he said. "My guess is that they're planning just how to do that right now."

CHAPTER 51

Spetsnaz Lieutenant Yuri Sudoplatov had an hour to kill before he took over as officer of the watch.

He had contemplated walking through this Hall of Fame again—he had become fascinated in a way by who the Americans had chosen to call their sports heroes: Babe Ruth, a drunken, oversexed, repressed adolescent; Ty Cobb, a mean-spirited man who left his cleat imprints on many an opponent's head; Jackie Robinson, a bitter man who was spat on by the white fans who didn't want their *bourgeois* game of baseball sullied by the presence of a black man. Most of these worshipped players were hooligans—where was their discipline? Where was their dedication? What was the big deal about hitting a horsehide covered ball with a piece of wood?

No, he had already walked through the Hall a half dozen times and it was affecting him. So today he decided instead to walk along the lake.

Relaxation was not in his personal vocabulary, but

he came as close as his *Spetsnaz* training would allow him as he walked along the water's edge, feeling the sun's warmth and the lake's cool breeze at the same time. Flocks of singing birds flew over him. The sound of insects chirping and the water noises added to the symphony of natural sounds. Now *this* landscape reminded him of his home in Soviet Georgia.

He saw a fish jump out on the lake and immediately thought it would be a good idea to fashion a fishing line. Or better yet, many fishing lines. Fresh fish — a meal he had yet to enjoy in the service — would be such a welcome change from the beets and dried eggs he and his troopers had been gagging on lately. They could leave that slop to the prisoners . . .

He was intent on jogging back to the camp site to order his troops to start making fishing poles. But when he turned around, he saw there was a half-man, half-bush standing behind him, a twelve-inch long knife in one hand, a wet rag in the other . . .

Hunter was in the Erie base's communications room when the message from Yaz came in.

One of the Texan communications specialists typed it out, deciphering the scrambled transmission that Yaz had bounced off the A-37 which was orbiting high over central New York.

Hunter read the message, shook his head, read it again then *ran* to Jones's office.

The general's reaction was identical to his own. "This is the craziest thing I've ever heard," he said. "I think . . ."

"They're sinister bastards," Hunter said, his insides burning with anger. "They're as bad as the Huns . . ."

"We'll have to tell the others, quickly," Jones said, pushing a nearby radio button in order to summon the other principals at the base. "Now we've got two problems to deal with . . ."

The group was assembled inside Jones's mobile office within ten minutes.

"We've just got a very unusual report from Shane's boys in Cooperstown," the general began. "They were successful in capturing a prisoner and, after using some interrogation techniques that we don't have to get into right now, they were able to get this rather startling piece of information out of him.

"Hawk, why don't you fill them in?"

Hunter stood up and faced the others. "Believe me, this is going to sound very strange," he said. "After I first heard it, it took a while to sink in, but, boy when it did . . .

"In addition to backing up the Circle and arranging for that goddamn invasion fleet, the Soviets have apparently embarked on a campaign of, for want of a better word, *iconoclasm.*"

Most of the men in the room had heard the term before, but some were shaky on exactly what it meant. Hunter had already anticipated the problem, so he had dug up a dictionary.

"*Iconoclasm,*" he read. "*The doctrine or strategy of the iconoclast, i.e. one who attacks and destroys cherished beliefs or institutions.*"

Hunter slammed the book shut.

"Simply put," he said in an angry tone, "They have their *Spetsnaz* guys running around the country, gathering up those things which stand for what made our country great.

"Those trucks full of books? They are on their way to Washington DC where they will be burned."

"What?" several of the members asked at once.

"It's true," Hunter said, his teeth gritting in anger. "The Circle is force-marching as many citizens as it can find to Washington where they are going have a massive book burning. It's an ultimate act of Psych-Ops. The total demoralization of a people through the destruction of their culture."

It did take a few moments for the news to sink in. Then to a man, those gathered felt a rage well up inside.

"And why are the *Spets* stopping at sports stadiums?" Hunter asked. "Because among the other things they aim to destroy is our national pastime. They are gathering gloves, baseball bats, bases, uniforms — you name it. They're also robbing museums, libraries, closed-down TV stations. They're gathering the *icons* of American life and they're going to destroy them!"

"They want to wipe the slate clean," Dozer said, his voice also rising in anger. "They want to destroy our *goddamn* heritage . . ."

"Exactly!" Hunter said. "But I know no one here misses the importance of this threat. We've got to stop this. It's almost more important than beating them on the battlefield. We can lose to them in Syracuse or wherever, but we're replaceable. A lot of the stuff they want to destroy is not!"

He was getting emotional and he knew it. But he also saw that every one of the others was also feeling the same way he did.

"What were the specifics of Yaz's message?" Ben Wa asked. "Obviously those guys in Cooperstown are part of a bigger plan . . ."

"That's definitely the case," Jones said. "These *Spetsnaz* gangs are roaming the eastern part of the country, following the Circle line of retreat. As far as the unit at Cooperstown, they're looting the Hall of

Fame but they're also holding hostages there, with orders to kill them should anything go wrong."

"And now that this *Spetsnaz* officer is gone—Shane's boys got him on ice—they might carry out those orders."

"What can we do about it?" one of the Texans asked. "Can Shane's boys handle all those guys?"

Jones shook his head. "Probably not now," he said. "The element of surprise will be gone when they realize one of their guys is missing. They'll be looking for him and expecting something at the same time."

"That means we've got to hit them quick," J.T. said. "Fly in some reinforcements to Shane and nail them. Free the people they're holding . . ."

"We really don't have any other choice," Jones said in agreement. "Hawk? Can you put a plan together?"

Hunter looked at all of them, his facial features were like granite. "I already have," he said.

CHAPTER 52

Sergeant Misha Borsuk had just dispatched the third search party of the day when the big tractor-trailer truck rolled into the village square.

He was about a quarter mile away, supervising the troops that were dragging the shallows of the lake for Lieutenant Sudoplatov's body, when the big rig pulled in. He saw two Circle soldiers jump out and wave to him. He waved back. It was just another rig, moving through to Washington.

The lieutenant had been gone for nearly 24 hours now and an extensive search of the nearby woods had proved fruitless. Sergeant Borsuk had ordered the dragging operation after the lieutenant's hat had been found floating about 20 feet off the shore. Already, rumors were spreading through his troops that Sudoplatov had drowned himself.

"We have something!" one of his corporals yelled. The man was standing in a small boat—one of two dozen the *Spetsnaz* troops had found at a tourist house nearby and had pressed into use. He was some 50 feet offshore.

Borsuk climbed into his own boat and was rowed to the spot. Sure enough, the man's line had snagged a leather boot. Pulling it aboard, they opened the top flap and saw Sudoplatov's name and uniform number printed inside.

The sergeant yelled for all the boats dispersed on the lake to gather in on the area. Slowly the ten additional skiffs closed in, their lines dragging behind them.

"Here!" another man on another boat cried. Borsuk's boat was moved to the spot just as the men were pulling in Sudoplatov's uniform jacket. Its pockets were filled with rocks.

Borsuk examined the coat. It wasn't ripped or soiled in any way. "Maybe it *was* suicide . . ." he thought.

He briefly considered ordering the rest of his men on shore to get more boats and join them in the search. Right now 30 men were out on the lake, 16 were guarding the prisoners. If three or four more boats could be launched, the task of finding the lieutenant's body would be accomplished that much quicker.

Once Sudoplatov's body was found, Borsuk would have to assume command. His first orders would be to kill the prisoners. Then, once the Hall of Fame was completely looted, they would set fire to the entire town, poison the lake then move on.

"Another boot!" the man in the boat next to him announced.

"Here is his holster!" he heard from a boat further away.

That was enough for Sergeant Borsuk — he told his rowers to move him to shore where he would dispatch three more boats and once and for all, find the lieutenant's body. Perhaps he could even enlist the aid of the Circle troops who had just arrived.

But the sergeant never made it to the shoreline. A tracer bullet from an M-16 hit him square in the jaw and exited out his left ear. He fell back into the boat hard—capsizing it and throwing his two rowers into the water.

One by one the men out in the boats were quickly picked off by gunmen hiding in the scrub bushes on the shore. Two boats went over, then a third and a fourth. Confusion reigned as the surviving unarmed men furiously tried to paddle their way out of range. But it was futile—RPGs were now being launched at them. One hit a boat carrying three *Spetsnaz* straight on—the explosion killed all three instantly and disintegrated the skiff. Other boats were being sunk in quick succession by near or direct hits from the rocket-propelled grenades.

Those troopers who were the last to meet their fate thought they saw entire bushes moving along the shoreline, so complete was the camouflage of their attackers.

Most of the soldiers guarding the prisoners immediately withdrew into the small brick building at the sound of the first gunshots. Six of them were cut down in the crossfire though. Now, as the 10 survivors watched from the front door, they saw United American troops pouring out of the back of the tractor trailer that had so innocently pulled into town a short time ago. The Soviets quickly began firing on the Americans as they ducked into doorways and behind walls for cover.

The corporal in charge of the guard knew it was time to kill the prisoners. He chose three of his men and told them to follow him up to the second floor hallway where the 26 men were being held.

"We will use pistols," he told his men. "One shot, one man. We will save our rifle ammunition for the battle."

All four *Spetsnaz* troopers checked the clips on their 9-mm Makarov PM handguns, then moved up the stairs, fully aware that the intensifying gunfire they heard outside indicated that the Americans were slowly moving toward the building.

The corporal was the first to reach the hallway. He looked down the two lines of men. Each one was gagged, tied hand and foot and propped up against the wall. He nodded to two of his charges to pick up the first prisoner and hold him against the wall. As the other prisoners watched in horror, the corporal cocked his pistol and placed the barrel against the back of the man's neck.

He slowly pulled the trigger . . .

Suddenly there was a great explosion of glass at the near end of the corridor. The four *Spetsnaz* troopers whirled around in amazement to see a man wearing a pilot's helmet had come crashing through the hallway window. The corporal's pistol went off, but he was distracted enough at the last moment for the bullet to go into the prisoner's shoulder, only wounding him.

A bullet from the interloper caught the corporal in the eye a second later; another burst blew out one of the other troopers' chest.

Two more men leaped through the window, screaming at the prisoners: "Get down! Get down! We are *Americans* . . ."

The prisoners did as told the best they could. The two remaining Russians had taken cover at the far end of the hall. Two more *Spetsnaz* soldiers were climbing the stairway, having heard the commotion from below.

This stand-off didn't last long. The man in the pilot's helmet tossed a concussion grenade down into the stairwell, then threw a flash grenade at the two Russians hiding at the end of the hallway. The near-simultaneous explosions rocked the second story with a brilliant flash and an ear-splitting *boom!* that left Soviets and prisoners dazed alike.

Suddenly the three Americans charged down the hallway and shot the blinded Soviets point blank. Two more American soldiers crashed through the splintered window and shot the wounded Russians who were sprawled on the stairs.

The action on the second story was over as quickly as it began. The battle down on the first floor was still going strong. The five Americans gathered at the top of the stairs after first indicating that the prisoners should lie still and quiet.

One Soviet soldier poked his head into the stairwell and was immediately gunned down. The pilot flipped two more gredades down the stairs in such a way they bounced into the main room where the rest of the *Spetsnaz* troops were positioned. The two unexpected blasts killed three more Soviets.

By that time, the Americans outside the building had concentrated enough firepower to blow away one entire side of the structure. The UA troops flooded in and made quick work of the remaining half dozen Soviet Special Forces soldiers.

It was all over inside of three minutes.

Most of the prisoners were just getting their vision back when the American soldiers started untying them. One of the first to be freed — an older black man — hugged the man wearing the pilot's helmet.

"Who the hell are you guys, anyway?" he asked him, laughing with relief.

Hunter removed his helmet.

"We're from the United American Army," he said, staring closly at the man. "But I know who you are, don't I?"

The man shrugged. "You might . . ."

Hunter felt the name of the tip of his tongue. "You're Lamarr Johnson. Of the Cleveland Indians."

"Been a long time since someone put those two names together," the man said. "That is until these creeps came along . . ."

Other prisoners were being untied and helped to their feet.

"Jesus," Hunter exclaimed, looking at two close by. "That's Ken Dowling of the Orioles. And Greg Masto of the Mets!"

Johnson laughed again. "Yep, and that's Mickey Ruggeri of the Cardinals," he said pointing to another prisoner being untied. "There's Keith Sullivan of the Red Sox, Jason Kelleher of the Cubs over there. Scooter Vogel and Fred Haas of the Reds . . ."

"You guys are *all* professional baseball players?" Hunter asked, somewhat astonished.

"Former professional ball players," Johnson told him. "Most of us were captured like a lot of people when the Circle took over. We were scattered all over in work camps, prisons and such. Then the Ruskies started looking through someone's files and started gathering us together. And here, in Cooperstown, of all places . . ."

"What were they planning on doing with you?" Hunter asked, secretly vowing to get each man's autograph later.

Johnson shook his head. "They were going to line us up and shoot us," he said angrily. "They're planning this big demonstration in Washington DC."

"We've heard about that," Hunter said.

"Yeah, well we were going to be one of the star

attractions," Johnson continued. "They were going to execute us, as kind of a symbol. Killing the national pastime. *It's sick . . .*"

"That it is," Hunter said, bitterly.

CHAPTER 53

It wasn't until two days later that word of the Cooperstown Raid reached the Circle headquarters in Syracuse.

Viceroy Dick heard the news from his superior, a major general of the Circle Air Corps named Herr.

"Christ, those Russians are *fucking* thick!" Herr said upon repeating the news to Dick. "They're supposed to be these elite shitheads and they fall for the oldest trick in the book . . ."

"I'm glad it doesn't affect us too much here," Dick said. "That party going down in DC, I'd just as soon avoid."

"Me, too," Herr admitted. "That's the Russians' show, not ours. We can't argue with them if they think they're going to accomplish something. But, in my opinion, if you gather a bunch of civvies together, force march them to DC, show 'em the country's books burnings and all the sports celebs getting shot, I think they'll have a riot on their hands."

Dick nodded in agreement, dabbing his perpetually runny nose with a hankie. "They're making a big mistake thinking the people left in this country are like Russians. You know, sheep who will do what they're told and when they're told. There's a lot of hotheads still running around this part of the continent. And God knows what the Cowboy Army will do."

"That's just my point," Herr said. "Frigging Russians expect us to duke it out with the Cowboys while they have their little weenie roast down in DC. That way when that invasion fleet gets here, they figure all the citizens will be bummed out and pacified."

"And most of us up here will be dead . . ." Viceroy Dick finished for him.

Herr nodded dejectedly. "Exactly . . ."

Just then, one of their radar officers burst into Herr's office.

"We got bogies coming our way, sir!" he just about screamed. "Big ones and there's a lot of them!"

Herr and Viceroy Dick were in the Aerodrome's Combat Control Center within a minute. On a large radar screen before them they could clearly see the large airborne force moving in their direction.

"Jesus, heavy bombers," Herr said. "They look

292

like B-52s."

"And fighter escorts," Dick said, pointing out a series of smaller blips surrounding the bomber points.

Herr reached for a nearby microphone. "Sound the attack alert!" he shouted. "Get the scramble jets up now! Get the mobile SAMs and Triple-A guns hot. We're going to be under attack in fifteen minutes!"

The CIC was instantly engulfed in a swirl of confusion, ringing phones, blinking lights, warning buzzers and fear. The United Americans weren't wasting any time, Dick thought, wondering where the hell the Weapons Requisition Officer was supposed to hide during an air raid.

"Boy, I could sure use a few lines of blow right now," he thought, wiping his nose again.

General Dave Jones was leading "Buick Flight," the first wave of three B-52s that would cross over the enemy target. Behind him was J.T.'s "Chevy Flight"—the second trio to go in. Finally would come Ben Wa's "Dodge Flight."

The nine B-52s were cruising at 33,000 feet, high enough to avoid most of the low-level SAMs in the Circle's arsenal. But even at this height, they would be vulnerable to the SA-2 and SA-3 SAMs that they knew were set up at various points around the city and the Syracuse Aerodrome.

This was to be a strategic bombing strike. The United American Command had decided they had two priorities: destroy as many Circle Army troops as possible before the inevitable land invasion of the Syracuse area, and destroy as much of the enemy's air power as possible. In line with the first aim, Jones had directed that this initial B-52 strike be concentrated on the city itself, where most of the Circle infantry troops were billeted and where their supplies were stored. A secondary strike on the Circle air base at the Aerodrome would be carried out simultaneously by the PAAC A-7 Strikefighters.

"Five minutes to target," Jones called out to all the aircraft involved.

Ahead of him, he saw the two F-106 Delta Darts get into positions. They were carrying dispensers that would, on his command, release a cloud of chaff—the radar reflective tin foil which would serve to confuse the enemy's SAM and AA radar beams. It was quite possible that these F-106 pilots were in the most dangerous position of the mission. The drag of the chaff dispensers attached to their underbellies slowed down the normally quick, if aging, fighters. Also the cloud of chaff blossoming behind each airplane marked its location like a red flag for the AA operators.

Jones looked to his left and saw five Football City F-20s move up into position ahead of the bombers. The Tigersharks—these five and six more behind—were riding fighter escort for the B-52s. This meant these fighters would stick close to the bombers throughout their bombing runs.

Farther out on the flight's perimeter he saw four Texas Air Force F-4s riding a little higher than the

294

rest of the group. The Texans would be providing the CAP—or "combat air patrol." This meant they would roam the skies above and below the bomber flights pursuing any enemy fighters that rose to meet them. Those Circle aircraft getting through the CAP would be dealt with by the Football City Tigersharks.

Assuming all nine B-52s reached the target area, they would unleash a total of 270 tons of heavy bombs on the Circle supply and troop concentrations. Jones knew it would also wipe out a large portion of downtown Syracuse in the process. But, in war, some things just couldn't be helped.

"Three minutes to target . . ." he radioed, and once again checked the position of the escort and CAP fighters. They were the B-52s' bodyguards and, as such, lent a good amount of security and confidence to the bomber crews.

But Jones knew the flights had an additional weapon. He scanned the skies above him and off to his sides.

Somewhere, out there, he knew Hunter and his new F-16XL were waiting to pounce . . .

The Circle's Fulcrum MiGs had been lifting off from the Aerodrome's main runway two at a time for the past ten minutes. The newly reconditioned fighters—purchased from the Party arms cartel—were loaded with AA-10 air-to-air missiles as well as nose cannons for close-in fighting. Their pilots—some of them Circle regulars, others mercenaries and allied air pirates—were beaming with the knowledge that every confirmed kill they registered meant 100 bags of gold.

As each Fulcrum rose, the Circle's Combat Center air controllers vectored them toward the nine heavy bombers approaching Syracuse. On their present course, the B-52s would have to pass close to the Aerodrome on their way to their bombing runs over the city of Syracuse itself. The Circle's fairly sophisticated radar net was providing up to the second information on the bombers as well as the escorting fighters. Thirty enemy interceptors had already launched—they alone outnumbered the 28 escorting United American aircraft—and two dozen more were warmed up and waiting in reserve.

So with all of the Circle's radar screens and operators concentrating on the heavy bombers, those at the Aerodrome were caught completely by surprise when the lead wave of A-7 Strikefighters roared in on the occupied airbase at treetop level.

The first three of the stubby attack jets came in, dropped their bombs loads and escaped without a shot being fired at them. Their munitions were placed perfectly on two SAM sites and a radar station at the edge of the base. Three more A-7s screamed in, again using laser guided bombs to take out a pair of SAM sites. The follow-up trio of airplanes were carrying two 500-pound "Ironman" bombs apiece. These heavy-duty explosives were used for runway busting. They performed as advertised as two of the Strikefighters dashed through the increasing cloud of AA fire to blast moon-crater sized holes in the Circle's main runway. The third A-7 had to divert from its bombing run due to heavy groundfire. It dropped its load on the likeliest target of opportunity and quickly departed the battle area.

Within a minute of the A-7's sneak attack, pandemonium had broken out at the enemy air base. The rogue A-7 had hit the airfield's main communication station with its Ironmans, knocking the primary communication link between the Circle Combat Control center and the Circle interceptors. So, although few of them realized it at the time, the Circle aircraft rising to meet the United American bombers now had to rely on staticky secondary radio links, then they would return to their base to find its main runway was mortally cratered.

"Two minutes to target . . ." Jones called out.

No sooner had the words left his mouth when he heard his rear gunner yell: "Here they come! MiGs at five o'clock!"

Suddenly the sky was filled with Texan F-4s diving through the bomber ranks to meet the climbing MiGs.

"I count more than two dozen," J.T. radioed ahead to Jones. "I suggest the escort engage also . . ."

Jones had no time to mince words. "Do it, Tigershark leader," he radioed. Immediately half the F-20s were rolling off toward the swarm of Fulcrums.

The air battle was soon joined. The B-52s were

now at 29,500 for their bombing runs and just 5000 feet below them a swirling knife-fight between the Circle and UA fighters had ensued. Glancing downward, Jones could see thick trails of brown jet exhaust criss-crossing with thinner white trails from air-to-air missiles. He saw a least three Circle MiGs get it in the span of ten seconds. Also one F-4 was smoking heavily and all this just in the small confined area he could see. His headphones were a racket of dogfight chatter: "Watch your ass!" "I got 'em!" "Missile lock!" "Smoke confirmed!" "Tango away!"

In the middle of it all, Jones tried his best to concentrate on the bomb run, now just 90 seconds away.

That's when the SAMs started coming

up . . .

Both UA and Circle pilots alike saw the strange F-16XL roar into the swirl of battle below the B-52s. Under its wings it carried no less than 12 Sidewinders—only eight more than a normal F-16 might carry.

But this airplane was far from normal . . .

One Fulcrum pilot—an air pirate named Worm—was working on chasing an F-4 who in turn was blasting away at another Fulcrum with its nose cannon. Suddenly Worm was aware of the F-16 coming toward him at approximately the same altitude. He immediately laid off the F-4 and started to bank toward the exotic F-16. All of the Circle pilots had been warned that the legendary Hawk Hunter—The Wingman himself—might be flying with the United Americans. But Worm didn't believe in legends. Besides he had it on good authority that Hunter had been killed months ago over in the Middle East somewhere.

The pilot flying this F-16 therefore had to be an imposter.

Worm leveled his MiG so it would sweep past the F-16 first, thus allowing him to roll into the UA jet and get on its tail. They were about a half mile apart when he started punching in arming instructions to his AA-10 air-to-air missiles, all the while keeping the approaching F-16 in sight via his cockpit Head's Up Display.

Suddenly, the F-16's nose started to turn toward him. The strange jet didn't alter its course—but, incredibly, it was turning on its axis . . .

"What the fuck is this?" Worm cursed as he watched the airplane perform the bizarre gyration. "He can't do that!"

As they passed by each other at a combined speed of more than 1000 mph, the nose of the F-16 appeared as if it had suddenly burst into flames. Actually, all six of its snout cannons were firing at once. In an instant, the first four feet of the Fulcrum were gone—disintegrated in the combined fusillade of the six guns.

It happened so quickly that Worm had barely breathed. The F-16 shot by him in a nano-second and was soon out of sight. With his nose gone, Worm felt the MiG start to drop—and fast! He yanked the ejection lever once and nothing happened. He hit it again as the cockpit started to fill with fuel fumes. Still nothing. A third as the ejector blast went off—but the canopy fly-away mechanism had been destroyed by the F-16's awesome barrage.

Worm ejected right through the hard canopy glass, severing his aorta in the process. His chute opened properly enough, carrying the air pirate's limp and bleeding body down through the raging air battle.

The F-16 quickly engaged two more Fulcrums, staying level yet rising straight up to meet them head-on. Two buttons were pushed. Two Sidewinders leaped from the aircraft's cranked arrow wings. Two more Fulcrums were soon plummeting to the ground.

One F-4 pilot was in deep trouble. He had spotted four MiGs going after the chaff dispensing F-106s and had sped to the rescue. Now two of the MiGs had turned on him and were squeezing him from both sides. He twisted and turned in his aging Phantom, his radar control officer in the back seat yelling out "Missile lock!" until he was hoarse.

Suddenly the F-16XL was beside him. The F-4 pilot looked up and saw the man inside the exotic fighter wave, then point up. The Phantom driver got the message. He suddenly yanked back on his stick and put the F-4 into a straining, gut-wrenching climb. No sooner had he moved when the F-16 did an near-impossible sideways maneuver, taking his place in the line of the Fulcrums' fire.

As the F-4 pilot watched, the F-16 suddenly dropped straight down, then, all in one motion, pointed its nose in the vertical and fired off two

Sidewinders. The Fulcrum pilots had had no time to react whatsoever. Both of the 'Winders ran true, destroying the MiGs within two seconds of each other.

The F-4 pilot couldn't quite believe his eyes.

"How the hell did he do that?" he yelled back to his radar officer.

"I'm dizzy just watching him," came the reply.

For the next 45 seconds, the F-16XL twisted, turned, yawed, rolled, climbed, dove and generally "translated" through the enemy fighters. Fulcrums were falling out of the skies in two and threes. Finally they pulled back.

Not one had reached the B-52s . . .

But the heavies were already in enough trouble.

The chaff airplanes were doing their best, but a stiff wind was scattering the tin foil strips, thereby cutting down on their effectiveness. Jones's aircraft's ECM was cranking so hard it was getting hot, but still it was all he could do to keep the Stratofortress level in the barrage of SAMs coming up toward them.

"Thirty seconds to go!" he called out, remembering that prior to this mission, the heaviest action he'd seen was a strike against a Circle nuclear plant in the Badlands. But that had been a cakewalk compared to this . . .

Suddenly he saw a speck of light climbing up to meet him in amongst the streams of SAM smoke.

It was Hunter.

"Hey, Hawk!" Jones called out to him, dodging

301

a pair of SA-5s on his starboard side. "It's getting very hairy up here."

"Just follow me," Hunter radioed back.

With that, Hunter put the F-16 a quarter mile out and 500 feet below Jones's lead airplane. Then, to the astonishment of all, he started shooting. At SAMs . . .

Turning the F-16XL in its yaw-axis mode, Hunter swayed back and forth, shooting at all the approaching SAMs with his Vulcan Six Pack. He looked like a farmer clearing a row of wheat through a field. The nine bombers simply tightened up their formation and followed him through.

They were soon roaring directly over the downtown section of the city.

"Ten seconds . . ." Jones yelled out. "Five. Four. Three. Two . . . One . . . *Bombs away!*"

On his call, each B-52 bombardier pushed his release button. Instantly, more than a half million pounds of bombs were falling toward the city.

"Climb! Climb!" Jones shouted into his microphone, but the Strat pilots needed no further encouragement. As one, they put their huge jets into a steep climb. Then they banked away from the city, which was now just feeling the impact of the first of 270 tons of bombs . . .

CHAPTER 54

Yaz's infrared scope was flashing like crazy . . .

"Jesus, there's something hot down there," he said to Ben Wa who was next to him, piloting the A-37 Dragonfly spy ship.

Wa noted the heading and banked toward it. They were some 100 miles east of Syracuse, patrolling the highways for evidence of Circle troop movements, more mystery trucks or any other enemy activity. After his first taste of behind-the-lines combat, Yaz had to admit he felt more comfortable riding along at 10,000 feet.

"Signal getting stronger," he said, fine-tuning the infrared scope. "This one is burning. Sun's been down for three hours and it's glowing. Pushing out a lot of internal heat . . ."

"Let's go down and take a closer look," Wa said, putting the A-37 into a dive.

They were over what used to be known as the New York State Thruway. Now the highway—which at one time stretched up and across the entire state—was little more than a collection of long strips of concrete separated by fallen bridges. Air pirates had been known to set up shop where the roadway was straight and flat and boasting tree cover on each side. These the long spans of highway proved ideal for landings and take-offs. Hunter and his cohorts had once fought a brief war in this area against a notorious air pirate gang known as The Cherry Busters. But now it appeared that most of the road was abandoned and little used by either surface vehicles or aircraft.

Except for those right below them.

"I read ten vehicles in all," Yaz said, as the A-37 passed directly overhead. "The hot one is right in the middle. They are not semis. Much smaller readings. And they're not barreling along like the semis did. They're only going about 35 mph, tops."

"Something's slowing them up," Ben replied. "They already know we're here, might as well go down for a real close look . . ."

With that, he put the A-37 into a tight 180 and brought it down to just 250 feet. Yaz automatically turned on the small jet's ECM pod, and he armed its ten small, air-to-surface missiles—just in case. He also switched on the AGM-65 radar's threat warning indicator.

"No threat indications," he reported, meaning that no one on the roadway below was warming up a weapon—such as shoulder-launched SAM—to launch at them.

Ben headed straight for the convoy, the A-37's bright nose light switched to on. The glare illuminated the ten vehicles enough for the airplane's belly cameras to get a good photo of them.

"Smile guys," Wa said as the A-37 streaked over the convoy, which had now stopped.

Yaz felt several *pings!* hit the underwings of the Dragonfly; someone below had taken a few shots at them with a rifle or an automatic weapon.

"No damage done," he reported ten seconds after they made their photo sweep.

"Did you see anything really unusual?" Wa asked him. The pilot had been so busy during the low pass just controlling the jet that he had barely caught a glimpse of the vehicles in the convoy.

Yaz had had a better, albeit brief view. "Armored jeeps I think," he said. "It looks like they're escorting a tank of some kind . . ."

"Only one way to find out for sure," Ben said, turning the Dragonfly westward. "Let's get the hell back and look at what the camera saw . . ."

Three hours later, Hunter, Jones, Ben and Yaz were gathered around a small video monitor, waiting to see the footage the A-37 had shot for the first time.

"Here we go," Ben said as he started the VCR.

The screen flickered to life. At first it was simply dark. Then gradually, outlines of the roadway, the center island and the trees on either side came into view. Suddenly a bright flash sent a wave of static across the screen, the result of Ben turning on the A-37's nose beacon.

"Here's where we get illumination," Yaz said.

Now the footage clearly showed the ten vehicles lined up on the side of the roadway, stopped at the first sound of the airplane. A few figures were seen scurrying about as the camera drew nearer.

"The vehicle in the middle of them was the one giving off all the heat," Yaz said as the camera passed right over the front end of the convoy. "Here it comes . . . right now!"

The airplane was moving so fast, it was hard to discern just what kind of vehicle it was. But that was what slow motion and freeze-frame were for.

"Let's back it up," Jones said.

Yaz did so and within a few seconds they were watching the fast sweep in slo-mo and reverse.

"Freeze it right there . . ." Hunter said.

Yaz complied and when the static cleared, all four of them were looking at a relatively clean image of the vehicle that had been glowing on the infrared scope.

It was the gold APC . . .

Viceroy Dick gobbled up the handful of painkillers and washed them down with a swig of champagne.

"Is your head better, baby?" the young girl beside him cooed, softly stroking the bandage over his left eye.

"It's getting there," he said, taking another gulp

of bubbles.

He had been knocked out cold during the A-7 air strike—while he was watching the scope showing the heavy bombers approaching Syracuse, the attack planes had caught those at the Aerodrome completely by surprise. When they pulled him out of the rubble of the base's communications center, he was covered with bumps and scrapes, the most serious needing twenty stitches over his left eye.

But Dick made the best of the situation. His wound relieved him from the hideous duty of pulling the 150 corpses from the demolished communications center. The Circle doctors had patched him up, gave him a bottle of codeine pills and sent him on his way. He had gone straight to one of the Aerodrome's still-functioning bars, and although it was about three in the morning, was able to pick up the young hooker and bring her back to his quarters to start his recuperation.

Like some many of the girls who had chosen to stay at the Aerodrome, she was dressed in this latest "Queenie" fashion—woman's tux, silk low-cut blouse, dark nylons and short boots. Her hair was cut in the perfect blond shag style that completed the look.

Dick had her remove the blouse and as he fondled her pert breasts, he evaluated his situation.

The United American air strikes—both the raid on the Aerodrome and the carpet bombing of downtown Syracuse—had been devastatingly accurate. Not only had the A-7s creamed the base's communications center, they had so cratered its main runway, that the surviving Fulcrums had had a bitch of a time returning to base and landing on the shorter secondary runways. Two of the valuable airplanes had wound up in ditches because of the abbreviated landing space.

"Sixteen airplanes shot down," he murmured. "Two in the goddamn ditch, two take off for parts unknown. And we didn't get a single shot on those bombers . . ."

"What are you talking about, baby," the girl asked as she rubbed him softly between his legs. "Those guys who bombed us yesterday?"

"Yeah, that's it," Dick said, at first not even realizing he was talking aloud. The codeine was starting to take effect. "What would you know about it?"

She shrugged and pushed her hair back, preparing to perform oral sex on him. "I just know that guy they call the Wingman was involved," she said. "Everyone was talking about it right afterward . . ."

That's all he needed to hear. Even the lowliest bargirl knew that the great Hawk Hunter—he being the person whose bones were supposedly rotting over in the Arabian desert—was very much alive and working with the United American air forces. Dick had believed all along that Hunter was alive. Even Viktor couldn't take out the famous flag-waving pilot.

"Yeah, what do you know about this guy?" he asked her.

She reached for the champagne bottle and gargled down a mouthful.

"We hear all kinds of things," she said. "He's

the best in the air. He's the best in bed. He has ESP. You know, they say the Queen is his girlfriend and . . ."

"Enough!" Dick scolded her. "I'm sick of hearing about this guy. Just get on what you've been paid for . . ."

She took another gargle of champagne and then went down on him.

He lay back and tried to figure his next move. Damn these United Americans! he thought. It's time they got a taste of their own medicine . . .

CHAPTER 55

The sun was just coming up when Hunter spotted the ten-vehicle convoy. They were 60 miles east of the position where Ben and Yaz had first spotted them and were now close to the old state capital of Albany.

He had loaded up his F-16XL with an even dozen air-to-surface missiles and had set his radar on the search and destroy mode. He was intent on taking out the convoy, quickly, thus allowing him to get back to the more pressing duties of the battle for Syracuse.

Once they were certain the gold APC was part of the convoy Wa and Yaz had found, he and Jones engaged in yet another round of speculation as to what the armored vehicle was carrying. They had estimated more than 100 troops—probably *Spetsnaz*—were accompanying the vehicle, a heavy guard which indicated whatever was inside the

APC was more important in the enemy's eyes than the cargo being hauled in the Mystery Trucks.

It was also something small, so Jones's guesses included the so-called "key" mechanisms used to launch ICBMs. With proper adjustment, the keys could fire the remaining mid-west-*cum*-Badlands ICBMs—assuming there were some left—to just about any spot in the world. Hunter leaned more toward something having to do with the SDI systems in space. Perhaps the Russians were stealing the essential elements to the old SDS system in an attempt to reprogram their own bargain-basement orbiting stations. Rumors to that effect had been floating around the continent since the New Order was installed. And Hunter knew that it was more in the Soviet way of doing things to steal the technology than bother to develop it on their own.

But no matter what was inside the gold tracked vehicle, he had taken off from Erie determined to blast it to smithereens. Because whatever it was, he was sure that the whole United American cause would be better off without it.

He rolled in on the convoy and fired off his first two-missile barrage. Both AGM-65 Mavericks ran true and found the first two armed jeeps in the convoy to their liking. The pair of enemy vehicles disappeared in a flash of fire and smoke.

Hunter looped quickly, watching over his shoulder as the vehicles in the convoys scattered to either side of the road. His "threat warning" buzzer started humming, indicating that someone on the ground was preparing to launch a SAM at him. He took note of the alarm, and set his ECM package to "on."

Once again he swooped down on the convoy, once again launching two missiles, and once again finding two targets. He was certain that most of the vehicles were empty now—their passengers having taken refuge in the nearby woods. All except the APC, that is. He could see it trying to maneuver its way through the snarled wreckage on the thruway.

He went in for a third, equally successful run, blasting away the convoy's rear pair of jeeps.

Now he knew it was time to go after the gold APC itself.

It was easy to lock the Maverick onto the APC—the gold-painted vehicle was emitting every kind of "signature" that he could think of. He brought the cranked-arrow fighter down to 125 feet, did a quick vertical translation to avoid the pesky SA-7 shoulder-launched SAM that had had his cockpit threat warning abuzzing, and lined up the APC through his special video-visor helmet.

His finger cradled the missile-launch system trigger. The electronic image of the APC now filled his field of vision. He was about to blow it apart.

"Get ready," he whispered to himself. "Three . . . two . . . one . . ."

But then a voice inside him said: *Don't do it . . ."*

He suddenly yanked back on the stick and put the F-16XL into a screaming climb, flipping a switch that would temporarily disarm the Maverick.

What was this? he thought. He had been blasted with a sudden flash of intuition *not* to destroy the APC. He closed his eyes and let *the feeling* soak through him.

It was as if every nerve ending in his body was telling him to go in and take out the APC, while this small, but persistent buzz in his brain told him not to . . .

He immediately turned back and flew over the area, watching as the APC—its drivers no doubt confused but thankful—found a side road and quickly scampered into the woods. He climbed and set a course back to Erie, disarming his remaining missiles for good.

He didn't know why his sixth sense warned him off. But after all this time, he knew better than to distrust his perceptive instincts . . .

CHAPTER 56

It was a Free Canadian AWACs plane that saw them first.

Secretly patrolling the skies above the Erie base, the E-2A—a military version of the Boeing 707—had detected the incoming force as soon as the first enemy aircraft lifted off from the airfield in Syracuse.

The word was immediately flashed to the United American Combat Communications Center in the Erie control tower. Seconds later the base's air raid klaxons were going full-throat. The anti-aircraft weapons were turned on and manned, and ground mechanics quickly started working on their respective jets. Within two minutes, the first of the UA scramble jets were taking off.

J.T. was the flight leader of the first intercept group, piloting one of four Football City F-20s.

"We got twelve blips in the first wave," he called out to his three partners as they rushed toward the enemy airplanes. "They look to me like Floggers. Twelve more two minutes behind them, and a third dozen lingering out on the periphery. This last group might be Fitters. No escorting fighters, so far . . ."

General Jones, monitoring the radio transmissions on the ground, broke in on J.T.'s line. "That third group will probably hang back or they might disperse and come in from a different direction," he said. "We'll keep an eye on them and the second group here. You guys try to cut off that first wave."

J.T. was already doing that. He let go with a long-range Phoenix missile while the enemy was still 46 miles away. Each of his three counterparts did the same thing — firing their single Phoenix missiles at the still over-the-horizon targets.

Upon releasing their missiles, J.T.'s flight streaked up to 21,000 feet, 5000 feet above the altitude of the approaching enemy. Each pilot watched his radar screen as their Phoenix missiles homed in on the first dozen Soviet-built Floggers.

"Go baby, go . . ." J.T. urged his particular rocket.

Suddenly, one of the blips disappeared from his screen. Then another vanished. Then another and another.

"Yee-hah!" J.T. yelled out, mixing in with similar exclamations from his partners. "Four bye-byes . . ."

But their celebration was brief. There were still eight Floggers heading right for them. And 12 more behind them. And 12 Fitters somewhere behind *them*.

J.T. knew the easy part was over . . .

He was in visual range of the first wave of on-coming Floggers when his APG radar starting clanging. He pumped up the visual on the screen and saw a whole new series of blips rising up to meet his flight.

"Jesus, they *did* bring some interceptors with them . . ." he whispered as he watched as many as two dozen indications appear on his display. Instantly he knew The Circle had pulled a fast one. They had

315

flown their slower attack force—the Floggers and the Fitters—at a normal altitude. But they had sent their Fulcrum interceptors at about 250 feet, under the Free Canadian radar screen.

He quickly got his radio. "These guys have babysitters," he said. "They flew their interceptors below the radar line-of-sight . . ."

Now he knew they would have to tangle with the Fulcrums, and while doing so, the first two waves of Floggers would get through. The second flight of F-20s had by this time caught up with him, as did an eight-flight of the Texas F-4s.

The odds were now 16 United American fighters against 24 Fulcrums . . .

Jones was quickly on the line. "We're launching everything we can to stop the first two waves of Floggers that get through," he told J.T. "You guys have to take on those Fulcrums. Good luck . . ."

Less than a minute later the skies about 25 miles from Erie were a swirl of F-4s and F-20 Tigersharks and MiG-29 Fulcrums. Sidewinders flashed, nose guns spit flaming lead. AA-10 air-to-airs returned the fire, the Fulcrum's formidable cannon adding to the fray. Two Fulcrums went down. Then another. But then a valuable F-20 got it, caught between two MiG-29s.

J.T. himself blasted one Fulcrum to bits even as he was launching a Sidewinder at another one further away. He saw two F-4s buy it within a second of each other, another—its entire fuselage bathed in flames—purposely collided with a MiG-29, causing both to explode in a tremendous flash of fire and smoke. He felt a lump gather in his throat as he watched for friendly parachutes.

There were none . . .

Meanwhile the attack force of 20 Floggers—the first and second wave—aircraft were passing right over the dogfight and heading for the Erie base.

To counter the approaching force, Jones had taken the unusual step of sending up *his* attack planes—the A-10 Tankbusters and the A-7 Strikefighters—to intercept the enemy. Neither airplane was well-suited to air-to-air combat, but then again, neither were the oncoming Floggers.

He also radioed around the base to check on the SAM and AA teams. All sixteen of his Hawk and Roland SAM sites were hot and tracking the approaching force, as were their three dozen radar-guided AA guns. Five roving teams of three men apiece were dispatched to the edge of the airfield, armed with shoulder-launched Stinger and Blowpipe anti-aircraft missiles. Several of these teams were made up of the baseball players liberated during the Cooperstown Raid. To a man, they had volunteered for service. So Jones had assigned them to SAM duties as well as to the base's rescue squads.

In the meantime, the heavy bombers at Erie were also in the process of taking off. The luxury of the Free Canadian AWACS warning allowed Jones the time to order them to get off the ground and avoid being targets during the air raid.

The B-52s went first, followed quickly by the B-1s and then the heavy C-5 gunships and the various other cargo ships. Each airplane immediately struck out to the north and into friendly Canadian air space, each pilot knowing the Circle attackers wouldn't have the equipment nor the intestinal fortitude to chase them.

All the while, Jones was hovering over the base's huge radar screens watching the approaching enemy.

"Ten miles to go," the radar operator told him. "Our A-10s and A-7s will meet them head-on in about a minute."

Jones shook his head at the absurdity of the situation. It was like sending out two sumo wrestlers to fight a boxing match.

Ben Wa opened the throttle on the A-10 to full and leveled off at 15,000 feet. Rarely did this kind of airplane even venture up to this height, never mind fight at it. Altitudes of 5000 feet and below was much more to its liking. But the situation was desperate, and therefore required desperate measures.

He was the flight leader for the entire attack airplane force. He knew that none of the A-10s or A-7s were carrying air-to-air missiles, nor were they equipped with any hot-shot radar systems. But neither were the Floggers. No, this battle would be fought with the nose cannons—in his case, the GE GAU-8/A Avenger sticking out of his snout. The Strikefighters, who were a little more adept at interception, but not much more, were armed with twin Vulcan cannons.

He was the first to spot the lead line of Floggers. They had come down to 12,000 feet and were descending fast in order to get to their attack altitude of 500 feet. They were flying in four groups of three, the Fitters somewhere behind them.

Ben ordered his guys to go in attack formation. He knew they would have to make this quick. They were only eight miles from the base and he didn't want to be in the line of fire when the UA anti-aircraft forces started doing their thing.

"OK, guys," Ben radioed. "We each get one pass. Make it a good one."

He nosed his A-10 into a steep dive and released his nose gun safety switch. Without benefit of an intercept radar system, the Floggers had no idea that the A-10s and A-7s were about to pounce . . .

He actually saw the expression on the face of the pilot of the first Flogger when he looked up, his mouth open in amazement as the A-10 bore down on him. He tried to bank away, but it was too late to move the large MiG-27 Flogger, which was actually an over-loaded version of a MiG-23 fighter. Ben opened up at just under 150 feet. He felt the kick of the Avenger as he fired off a three second burst. Two hundred and thirty seven armor-piercing incendiary shells immediately impacted on the cockpit of the Soviet-built attack plane, ripping through the pilot's head and chest. The airplane went into an instant nose dive, its bullet-riddled pilot slumped over the controls.

Ben pulled up and away, firing off a glancing burst at the trailing two Floggers. He twisted in his seat to see that his guys were mimicking his maneuver perfectly. Three of them had passed through the formation behind him before the Circle pilots got the message and started to disperse their closed-in rank. Two Floggers flipped over and headed downward, with another smoking heavily.

Then the second wave of A-10s dove through the confusion of Floggers, each one with his Avenger blazing. Two more MiGs went down.

Now the A-7s came on. Each pilot selected a Flogger and went after it, guns blazing mercilessly. The lighter, if not faster, A-7s were able to imitate every twist and turn the Soviet planes made. The big Vulcan bullets ate through the MiG-23's tail sections as if they were flesh.

It was all over in 45 seconds, still quite long in dogfight terms. Eight Floggers had been hit in the surprise intercept, three badly damaged enough to turn back.

Not a single A-10 or A7 was lost.

Trouble was, nine Floggers made it through the gauntlet and were now just a minute away from attacking the Erie base . . .

J.T. had exhausted all his Sidewinders and was now taking on the Fulcrums with his nose gun.

The dogfight, which had swirled around for an eternity of pure savagery, was now winding down in intensity. It was as if the very jets themselves had run out of breath and were looking for their second wind.

More than twelve Fulcrums had been shot down at a loss of five F-4s and three F-20s. Four enemy fighters had been damaged enough for their pilots to turn back and three more had simply departed the fight, either for lack of ammunition or nerve to continue.

The five surviving MiGs were still out there, battling to get closer to the Erie base and cover the Floggers during their attack.

CHAPTER 57

"Here they come!" someone on the eastern fringe of the Erie base called out.

The first Floggers to reach the edge of the base were met with a stream of SAMs and AA fire.

Still the Circle pilots brought their aircraft down to 500 feet and began arming the large air-to-surface Kerry missiles.

"We've got six coming in from the south . . ." the officer in charge of base air defense radioed Jones. "Three more from due east . . ."

"Stay on them!" Jones shouted back, even as he heard the popping of the AA guns going off.

He ran outside, Captain Dozer at his side. Neither of them could stand to watch the attack on the passive electronic radar screens although the CIC was heavily fortified and therefore was a safer place to be.

The base was in a state of barely-controlled confusion. The AA guns were going off with deafening frequency, a sound broken only by the occasional *whoosh!* of a Hawk or Roland SAM lighting off.

"Jesus, General, here comes two of them!" Dozer yelled to Jones, pointing to the east.

Sure enough, two Floggers, flying side-by-side, roared in, nearly on top of them, and let go their Kerry missiles. Both men watched in horror as the air-to-surface bombs screamed down and impacted on two hangars no more than 200 feet away. The resulting blasts knocked both of them off their feet.

"Christ, they've got those missiles loaded with high explosive!" Jones yelled out, quickly getting up.

Both hangars — one a housing for three departed B-52s and the other a maintenance facility — had been reduced to piles of smoking rubble.

Just then two more Floggers came in. They too released their Kerrys, but just as the trailing attack craft launched his missile, his tail was hit by a direct shot of a Hawk anti-aircraft missile. The powerful weapon blew the rear third of the Flogger to bits. The Soviet plane immediately flipped over and plowed into the space between two hangars, exploding on impact.

"What a shot!" Dozer yelled, his tone mirroring the excitement of the air raid.

"Here comes another one!" Jones shouted, as a single Flogger dropped a Kerry on a fuel depot at the far edge of the base. The Soviet missile impacted right on the side of a nearly empty storage tank. Still the resulting explosion shook the ground like an earthquake.

"Christ! Imagine if it were full!" Dozer shouted above the noise.

There was another huge *boom!* and accompanying explosion off to their right. Someone in the AA teams had hit a Flogger square on its fuel supply, obliterating it in mid-air.

Two more MiGs flashed in, hastily launched the Kerrys then quickly departed. One of the air-to-surface missiles fell into the already burning hangars, the other plopped harmlessly into nearby Lake Erie.

Then, suddenly, everything got quiet . . .

The scream of jet engines faded and the AA fire quickly died down. The base air raid sirens which had been blasting throughout the attack were finally switched off. Within a minute the only sounds were of the crackling fires raging throughout the base.

But the worst was far from over.

In the confusion of the two aerial engagements and the air raid, the third wave of Circle attack planes—they being 12 Sukhoi Su-17 Fitters—had swung out over the lake and were now bearing down on the Erie base from the north.

Their commander—an East German mercenary named Mausser—could barely stop chuckling to himself. Their deception had worked perfectly. They had flown under strict radio silence and just barely 25 feet from the top of the water's surface. And they had timed their arrival to coincide with the conclusion of the first Circle attack—plus three minutes. Now he was certain he'd catch the United Americans off-guard and licking their wounds from the initial air raid by the Floggers.

Mausser pushed his microphone button twice, causing the other 11 pilots in his flight to hear a pair of static clicks—the pre-determined signal to arm their Kerry air-to-surface missiles. Each man did so and clicked three times in return. Just then the shoreline of Erie came into view.

"Voon-da-ba!" Mausser called out. They would soon be rich. He and his pilots were getting paid in gold for every target they could confirm as knocked out.

But suddenly, Mausser knew something was wrong. *Deadly wrong . . .*

Where there was once clear sky between him and the Erie coastline, now there was a new object. It was an airplane—a jet fighter, so he thought. But it was so strange-looking. And the way it had instantly appeared! It was as if it materialized out of the lake mist . . .

A seconed later, he had no throat left.

He had seen a quick flash of light spitting from the odd plane's nose a split-second before, and now realized that his canopy had shattered away and uniform from his neck down was soaked with blood.

Mausser never got a chance to counter-maneuver. He blacked-out immediately and his Fitter smashed into the lake, the armed Kerry missile exploding in the crash. The last thing the East German pilot saw was the red-white-and-blue fuselage of the arrowhead-shaped jet.

The F-16XL disappeared as quickly as it had materialized, the rest of the pilots in Mausser's flight watching as the airplane performed the seemingly impossible maneuver of staying level yet shooting straight up and disappearing high above.

At this point the Fitter pilots broke radio silence. Their leader gone, a South African pilot named Jooge took over command.

"Stay level!" he instructed the others, knowing that a successful air raid meant he'd get the departed Mausser's share of gold. "Continue in on the target . . ."

But suddenly the strange airplane was back again. It streaked through their formation from the east, traveling at terrific speed. Its nose was firing so many cannons it appeared as if it were on fire. First one, then two Fitters simply vaporized in the furious fusillade from the F-16XL. Once again, the jet roared off—this time disappearing over the western horizon.

The remaining Fitters were now just 90 seconds from landfall and under two minutes from their target. Yet a hot debate had erupted among the pilots.

"Did you see the speed of that plane!" one pilot asked, his voice filled with panic.

"It is not like anything I have ever seen . . ." another said.

"We must turn back!" a third cried. "It is this American Hunter in that airplane . . ."

"No . . ." Jooge said. "The man you refer to—this American Wingman—is dead. I know that for a fact. This is not him. We must continue the mission."

Two of the pilots didn't agree with Jooge; they simply dropped out of the formation and headed eastward.

"He was spotted during the air raid on Syracuse," one of the remaining pilots. "This Wingman lives . . ."

"No!" Jooge shouted. "You have been listening to rumors and it is now affecting your performance as pilots. Keep in formation. We are going in . . ."

No sooner had the words left his lips when Jooge was suddenly aware of a dark shadow filling up his cockpit. He looked up and nearly vomited at the sight of the large arrowhead-shaped aircraft underbelly that was screeching along with him, no more than 10 feet above. There was a large *W* painted on it . . .

Suddenly he felt something hit the rear of his airplane with a sharp bang. An instant later his Fitter was spinning out of control. He twisted around and saw that his starboard rear stabilizer and most of his tail wing were gone.

He couldn't turn the airplane left or right, nor could he dive out from under the frightening airplane above him. He reached for the ejection button, but knew that if he yanked it, it would be blown upward and smashed into the plane's underbelly.

He was helpless . . .

The others in the flight who were watching the incredible aerial encounter were shocked to see the arrowhead fighter force the Fitter right into the lake. As before, the fully-armed Kerry missile exploded, destroying the Soviet-built airplane and its pilot.

That was enough for the six remaining Fitters. As one, they jettisoned their missiles and banked eastward in an attempt to get away from the F-16XL. But five of them would not be so lucky. The Cranked Arrow pursued them, getting position on each of the slower airplanes' tail and blasting it to kingdom come with the awesome Vulcan Six-Pack.

Soon there was only one left. The F-16XL rode right up the pilot's ass, and closed to within firing range . . .

But he didn't fire.

Instead, the fleeing pilot heard the F-16XL pilot come on his radio frequency.

"Do you speak English?" the voice demanded.

"Yes," the pilot, an Austrian fascist, answered nervously. "Some . . ."

"Then return to your base and tell your comrades what happened here," the almost unearthly voice said. "Tell them what you saw. Tell them they will meet the same fate if they keep flying for The Circle . . ."

The enemy pilot was trembling so much, he could hardly push his radio button to transmit. "But who should I say was responsible?" he finally managed to ask the voice.

There was a burst of static. Then the voice said: "Tell them it was The Wingman . . ."

With that, the flying arrowhead suddenly rose, streaked right over his head, then turned and disappeared off to the west. The Austrian pilot wiped the sweat from his brow, vowed to give up flying altogether then quickly steered a course back to the Syracuse Aerodrome.

CHAPTER 58

Three days later the ground attack on the Circle forces at Syracuse began . . .

It started in the early morning hours when a fleet of lake barges and ferries commenced landing United American troops at the port of Oswego, just 40 miles north of Syracuse. The Americans crushed what little resistance the Circle-aligned troops guarding the city offered, and within two hours, 20,000 men were ashore and moving toward the enemy lines.

Meanwhile, another 8,000 men—most of them from units of the Pacific American Air Corps ground forces—had been moved through the night to a point just 22 miles west of the Syracuse Aerodrome. Their deployment was masked by another daring midnight air raid carried out by the UA A-7s on the Aerodrome itself. Once again, 500-pound "Ironman" runway busting bombs had been used with great effectiveness. By the time the 20-minute air strike was over, three of the Aerodrome's five working runways had been knocked out.

The rest of the UA force, 2500 elite PAAC paratroopers, were waiting inside a variety of aircraft—

from Texas C-141s Starlifters to PAAC C-130s — back in Erie.

The Circle Command Staff had been anticipating attacks from several directions and had deployed units around the city as well as the air base. Circle fighter jets were warmed and waiting alongside the Aerodrome's runways, waiting to launch and intercept any United American aircraft spotted on the Circle's still-operating radar net. Its few attack jets were also standing by, waiting to give ground support when the Circle troops went into action.

The first clash between the UA and Circle troops happened just outside of the small village of Skaneateles, just 17 miles from Syracuse. A Circle artillery base was suddenly overrun by the advance unit of the PAAC 1st Infantry. The Americans, under the direct command of Captain "Bull" Dozer, kept right on going. Using a squadron of large PAAC Chinook helicopters — known as the "Crazy Eights" — the democratic troops leap-frogged up through Marcellus, through Navarino and across the Onondaga Indian Reservation. The Circle troops in their way collapsed under the weight of the attack. By the time the Americans stopped just before noon, they were sitting atop Howlett Hill, a 600-foot cliff that overlooked the southwest side of Syracuse.

The Circle command dispatched six Fitter attack planes to bomb the Americans on the hill, but a combination of shoulder-launched SAMs and two prowling F-4 Phantoms chased away the Fitters. Within an hour, the Americans were raining artillery shells and rocket fire onto the city itself.

High above it all was Hunter . . .

He'hadn't slept or eaten in days, standard working conditions when he was on a combat buzz such as

328

this. But, like never before, he was taking out his misery—his deep-down hurt—on the enemy. He loved the F-16XL—the way it flew, the way it performed, the way it *felt*. And he had shared nothing but success with it since it arrived from the GD factory, the strange incident with the gold APC notwithstanding.

But although the airplane had filled a certain need within him—and a selfish one at that—it still couldn't dissipate the emptiness inside him resulting from his meeting with Dominique. He knew that he could go anywhere, win any war, bed any woman—and he still would never forget what he had lost in her.

His friends knew it, too. He was almost unapproachable around the Erie base most of the time. All business the rest. He wasn't mean and brusque—that would have been too out of character. He was just quiet, and giving out a lot of "please-leave-me-alone" vibrations. Jones, Dozer, Fitzgerald and the others knew better than to go against his wishes.

Besides, there was a war to be fought . . .

So Hunter had loaded down his F-16XL with a gaggle of munitions and weapons and joined the fray. He carried six Sidewinders—two on each wing tip and two more close in under his fuselage. He carried two Paveway laser-guided bombs, one on each wing next to the fuel tanks, plus a Mk 117 750-pound bomb under his portside. To balance this out, he had installed a LAU rocket launcher under his starboard wing, and a AGM-45A Shrike anti-radar missile next to it. To top it all off, he was lugging a AGM-109 MRASM cruise missile that was packing 2000 lbs of high explosive, plus six Mk 82 500-pound general purpose bombs.

It all added up to 17,890 lbs. of ordnance fixed to the 18 hard points on his arrowhead wing frame, not counting the six Avenger cannons in his snout.

The 750 bomb went first. American troops moving down from Oswego ran into a roadblock some 11 miles outside of the town. Some Circle troops had blocked the main highway, Route 481, with a movable iron pillbox being hauled on the back of a flatbed trailer, that was in turn being pulled by two souped up tractors.

The pillbox had effectively slowed down the Americans' advance as its controllers had placed it in a narrow pass on Route 481 around which there was no alternate route. The pillbox contained three Bofors 88-mm artillery pieces, plus a number of .50 caliber machine guns. Already it had chopped up the Americans' advance units and now, several Fitters were napalming the stalled force.

Enter the Wingman . . .

He blasted both Fitters from the sky without warning, using his Six Pack and a quick vertical translation to give the illusion that he appeared out of nowhere. Then he flipped the XL over and came straight down the pike. Twisting and turning to avoid the pillbox's .50 caliber ground fire, he laid the 750-pounder right at the base of the flatbed. There was an earth-shaking explosion and when the smoke cleared, all that was left was a crater and a few pieces of burning scrap metal.

The next obstacle was a line of Stalin Organs—mobile units which carried multiple rocket launchers—that the Circle had placed on one side of Route 481. Hunter came in low and hard and emptied the LAU rocket launcher into the eight vehicles, destroying five of them and damaging another. Mortar fire from the advancing Americans took out the remaining two launchers.

A line of captured M-1 tanks provided Hunter's next target. Strategically placed on top of six rolling hills just three miles from North Syracuse, Hunter made short work of the armor via his half dozen Mk 82 500-pound bombs.

Another 40 minutes of strafing followed and by two that afternoon, the American amphibious troops were within shelling range of the Aerodrome itself. Only then did Hunter take a break and rendezvous with a KC-135 tanker to fill up with gas.

The second round of fighting started around three-thirty that afternoon.

United American sappers had blown a number of bridges around the city, thus preventing the Circle troops from half their means of easy escape. A combined A-7 and A-10 attack was launched against the Aerodrome around four, with the Football City F-20s shooting down three Fulcrums which had risen to challenge the slower attack planes. A single A-7 was lost in the raid.

At 4:30, Dozer's troops left Howlett Hill and began fighting their way into the Syracuse city limits. Enemy troops began retreating back toward the former Syracuse University grounds and bitter house to house fighting ensued.

Hunter had teamed up with two Texas F-4 Phantoms and provided air cover for the advancing United American troops. When Dozer's scouts reported that the Circle was using a tower on the campus as an observation post, Hunter laid his Paveway laser-guided bomb at the base of the steeple, destroying its foundation and toppling it altogether.

Hunter was moving in a controlled frenzy, providing a kind of "flying artillery" for the advancing American troops. Every Circle fighter that dared to fight him was quickly dispatched. Any SAM crew that chose to fire at him was instantly perforated with

Vulcan cannon shells. When he got a call from the commander of the troops advancing into North Syracuse that a large concentration of howitzers were pounding his troops from the edge of the Aerodrome, he programmed his AGM-109 MRASM cruise missile to the coordinates and let the "fire-and-forget" rocket fly. It was more than ten minutes later when he heard from the commander that the missile had found its target and destroyed more than a dozen big guns in the one, long-range, shot.

By the time night had fallen, the Americans had forced the enemy troops into two large pockets—the northside of the university campus and the perimeter of the Aerodrome itself. A day of bitter fighting had finally come to an end. Casualties on both sides had been heavy; close to 6000 dead and wounded for the Americans, more than twice that for The Circle.

Now as a large orange full moon rose in the sky, both sides hunkered down to contemplate their next move.

CHAPTER 59

That night back in Erie, a council of war was held in Jones's trailer. Hunter, Fitz, Ben Wa, J.T. and Dozer were in attendance as well as the various unit and air corps commanders. Each person had a glass of whiskey before them.

The topic of the meeting was simple: How best to knock out the enemy troops before they were were able to break out of their encirclements. It was a grim discussion, because it centered on the most efficient way to kill some 30,000 humans.

"We can't let them escape wholesale," Jones said, not at all relishing his role as head executioner. "Between the problems we still have to face in Washington and with the mercenary fleet, I'm afraid this is no time to be magnanimous . . ."

The five others solemnly nodded in agreement. Unlike their continental enemies, these men detested war, detested the taking of a single human life. But they also shared the near-religious belief and devotion to the preservation of what used to be the great country of America. Blood had been shed to bring this idea into being, blood had been shed to maintain it. Now more blood would be shed to preserve it.

"I don't think we have any choice but to launch major air strikes on both targets," Jones said. "The priority being the Aerodrome where the largest concentration of their forces are now gathered."

He turned to Fitzgerald. "I'm sorry about this, Mike," he continued. "I feel I have to send in the heavy stuff over your place . . ."

Hunter thought he could see tears well up in his friend's eyes. The Aerodrome was Fitzie's life. He had built it up from a one garage airplane repair shop to one of the most profitable enterprises in the post-New Order world. Now he would have to not just witness, but actually participate in its destruction.

He accepted his fate well. "Won't be the first time that something has to be destroyed in order to preserve it," he said. "We can always build again, if not there, then somewhere . . ."

Jones took a strong belt of his drink—they all did.

Dozer spoke next. He was still dressed in his battle fatigues, having been shuttled back to Erie by one of the Crazy Eights. "I think our first priority is to knock out their Central Command Center. They run everything from there, and I wouldn't be surprised if there were a bunch of Soviet techs doing the brainwork. If we put the *kibosh* on it, then, the chicken will be without its head. Our northern units can sweep into the Aerodrome and our southern guys can move on the encirclement at the university."

"Do we even know where this CIC is?" JT asked.

"We just have to look where they've got all their SAMs stacked," Ben Wa said. "I'd guess it's somewhere in the main terminal building at the air base."

"It's probably under the control tower itself," Fitz said. "There's a bunker we put in underground to keep our state secrets, codes, important stuff like that. I'm sure that's where they set up shop. And I have to agree with Ben, they've probably got the SAMs three deep around it right now."

Jones rubbed his chin in thought. "Well, we all know there's only one way to take it out then," he said. He turned to J.T. and Ben. "Will you guys handle that, please?"

They both nodded.

"And how about the university?" Dozer asked. "They've got a lot of guys packed in there, and frankly, we're very thin around the lines. They could concentrate on one side and break out with not much problem. If they do, we'll lose them again."

"Then we won't give them the chance," Jones said firmly. He turned to Fitz. "Mike, you know what to do . . ."

Fitz nodded and took another good stiff belt from his drink.

All during the meeting Hunter had kept silent. He was simply listening, watching, preparing himself for the next day's battle. And wondering what Dominique was doing at that moment . . .

The next morning dawned crystal clear and warm.

The Circle troops that had spent the night within the university grounds were now preparing to break out to the east and retreat from the city. Each infantryman was issued a full ration of ammunition, and given a small breakfast. By 0700, the breakout would begin, led by the two dozen tanks that had withdrawn to the campus the afternoon before.

But it was just 0630, as the Circle troopers were finishing their morning meal when they heard a strange whining noise coming from the west. Most of them had no idea what the racket was. But the troopers who had retreated to Syracuse from New Chicago knew the sound represented a flying death . . .

They saw the vapor trails a few moments later. Two thick ones, cutting across the deep blue morning sky, trailed by a half dozen thinner ones. Someone, somewhere on the campus fired a SA-7 shoulder launched SAM at the aircraft, but they were much too high for the missile to be effective. Several larger, longer-range SA-2s were then launched, their flight being controlled by the mobile radar station the Circle commander had placed out on a playing field at the university. But these missiles too fell short, stopped no doubt by intensive ECM being put out by the airplanes.

Suddenly one of the thinner vapor trails disappeared, indicating that the airplane was diving out of the cooler air that caused the icy crystals to form in the first place, to the warmer air below. Suddenly another streak was seen crossing the sky. Its tail was spitting fire—the tell-tale sign of an incoming air-to-surface missile.

Those Circle soldiers who had been watching the aircraft pass over now rushed for cover. The missile—an AGM-45A Shrike, launched from the F-16XL—flew right over their heads and impacted square on the mobile radar station, destroying it. The Circle AA teams on the campus were now effectively blinded.

The two thick vapor trails had now separated and they too disappeared from view, indicating the airplanes were dropping in altitude.

At the campus encirclement, the Circle soldiers were forming up their lines, waiting patiently as the tanks were started up and loaded. The fire resulting from the Shrike missile strike was still crackling in the background, but the commanders had ordered the mobile SAMs to pack up and get in line directly behind the tanks.

Suddenly the ethereal whining heard earlier returned. This time louder and stronger. Veterans of the New Chicago debacle now began to worry anew. With good reason . . .

Then they saw them. Not one but two huge C-5s, starting a lazy circle around the university, like hands of a clock at opposite ends of the dial. Flying slightly above each of the gigantic airplanes were three smaller jet fighters.

And in amongst all these was the strange, arrowhead-shaped red-white-and-blue jet fighter.

The first C-5, the one with the name Nozo emblazoned on its tailfin, opened up without warning. The whining of the C-5's big engines was suddenly drowned out by a sinister whirring noise. The airplane was down to about 450 feet and it looked like a solid sheet of flame was shooting out of its side. Suddenly the ground directly below it erupted into fire and a gas-like vapor. When this smoke cleared, the head of the tank column and several hundred soldiers huddled nearby were simply gone . . .

Panic immediately ensued among the soldiers who had witnessed the action. Those who had been lined up at the head of the column were now falling back toward the buildings of the university. Soldiers at the end of the line had heard the racket but had no idea what had happened.

They would soon find out . . .

The second C-5, the one with the name Bozo painted on its rear, dipped to its port side toward a thick concentration of troops located near the school's dome-covered sports stadium. At once, six Gatling guns, five Mk 19 automatic grenade launchers and two Rheinmetal 120-mm converted anti-aircraft guns opened fire. The massive aircraft shuddered from the recoil—a long thick stream of fire

337

flashing to the ground. There was nowhere to run for the hapless Circle soldiers. More than 200 of them were massacred on the spot.

Those lucky enough to escape the first fusillade ran in every direction. The guns on the airplane were silenced for a moment. Then the AP/AV 700 triple-barrel multi-grenade launcher opened up, followed by the 120-mm Soltan mobile field gun firing illuminated rounds. A second later, the pair of Royal Ordnance 105-mm field artillery pieces also started firing.

Once again, it was a massacre—more than 700 soldiers fell to the awesome, terrible scythe of fire.

Still the airplane continued on its lazy circle. It dipped toward an administration building where some of the fleeing troops had sought refuge. The latest weapons were silenced only to be followed by the incredible blast of the LARS II 110-mm multiple rocket launcher, its prominent backfire spouting straight down and out of the C-5's tail. More than 500 rockets were fired in a ten-second span, reducing the building to its crumbling foundation.

For the next ten awful minutes, the two aerial leviathans continued to circle the university, firing at ten second intervals. No missiles were shot at them, no one challenged them with an AA gun. There was no resistance—only the blood-curdling screams of those about to die. There was nowhere to hide, all of the buildings had been reduced to rubble. Those Circle soldiers not yet killed in the onslaught were reduced to non-functioning, instantaneous cases of shell shock.

For many, it was as if the end of the world had finally arrived . . .

CHAPTER 60

By contrast, things were quiet at the Aerodrome, the only disturbing noise being the screams of the Circle commanders coming through the radio speakers from the bloodbath at the university. Grim-faced officers listened helplessly as they heard their brothers in arms decimated by the UA flying battle forts.

In amongst the officers sat Viceroy Dick, his head wounds still wrapped by healing, his bloodstream pounding with the force of the painkillers. He never imagined things would go so badly for the Circle, but the rout of their forces the day before probably had few parallels in military history.

"Should have bought those nukes," he whispered to himself.

Just then the overall commander of the Circle forces at the Aerodrome called an emergency general staff meeting in the CIC. The officer, a Soviet five-star general named Chestopalov, told those assembled that he had received orders from his superiors that the Aerodrome had to be held at all costs. An audible groan went up from the officers; many wanted to bug out now, get beyond the perimeter of the air base and strike out for the swampy, and therefore hard-to-track terrain to their east. It wouldn't be an orderly retreat—more like every man for himself.

"We must stay!" Chestoplatov said sternly after detecting the officers' negativity. "There is something bigger than our petty lives here at stake. Our comrades in Washington are counting on us . . ."

"Fuck them!" someone yelled out.

All eyes turned to Viceroy Dick. He sat with his mouth open and wearing an expression that said: *Did I say that?*

"What was that comment?" Chestoplatov demanded of them.

Suddenly Dick found himself standing up and beginning to speak. It was like someone else had taken over his body. He swore right there that he would stop taking all kinds of drugs.

"I said fuck those guys in Washington!" he heard himself scream. "Our asses are on the line here—not theirs. We got a bunch of chicken-ass soldiers here, who will be lucky to get one shot off when the Americans roll in. And the pilots are even worse. They're too chicken-shit to take off, for Christ's sake, because they believe that ghost called The Wingman is up there flying around. Face it, the situation is hopeless. Dying just so they can have their party down in DC is ridiculous . . ."

The Russian general's face turned bright crimson. "This is out-and-out subversion!" he screamed in heavily-accented English.

"Well, fuck you too then!" Dick screamed back at him. His mind was gone, he kept telling himself. He had finally cracked from using too many drugs. Someone else *had* taken over his body and that someone was about to get both of them shot.

Suddenly his handgun was out of his holster and he was firing it at the general. Three bullets hit the man square on the forehead, pitching him back over his chair and slamming him against the wall. He was dead before he hit the floor.

"OK, I'm in charge here now!" Viceroy Dick's other being shouted. "Any problems with that?"

One man started to raise his hand, so Dick shot him in the head too.

Then Dick heard his strange voice call out: "Any other questions?"

CHAPTER 61

The five B-1s had taken off shortly after dawn and formed up out over Lake Erie.

They positioned themselves into a diamond formation—*Ghost Rider 1* rode out on the point, while *Ghost Rider 2* and *3* took the sides and *Ghost Rider 4* brought up the rear. In the middle of the formation was *Ghost Rider 5*.

Once in place, the five airplanes climbed to 20,000 feet and turned as one toward the east . . .

J.T. was in *Ghost Rider 1*, riding lead on the formation. Once he had leveled off, he, like the other pilots in *2*, *3*, and *4*, began throwing a number of switches on a side control board in the cockpit. The signals were instantly transmitted to *Ghost 5*, the jet bomber that was carrying most of the electronic gear. Ben Wa sat behind the controls of this aircraft, splitting his time between flying the plane and making sure all the required signals were coming in from his four counterparts.

The computer aboard *Ghost 5* instantly began

processing these signals, coughing out computations in airspeed, altitude, engine exhaust heat and fuel loads. Within two minutes every aspect of the five airplanes' radar "signatures" was identified by *Ghost 5*'s super-computer. Then, one by one, those signatures were masked electronically.

On the control board before J.T., there were five red lights. Suddenly one of them started to blink.

"Ghost 1, on lock," he radioed back to Ben Wa, tightening up the formation in order to give the electronics in Ghost 5 every advantage.

Several moments later, another red light on the panel started blinking, followed by the call: "Ghost 2, locked on." Ten seconds later a third red light popped on. "Ghost 3, locked on . . ." Then a fourth: "Ghost 4, locked on . . ."

Thirty seconds later, the fifth and last red light started blinking. He heard Ben's voice say: "Ghost 5 locked on. System locked on . . ."

"Verify system lock, Ghost 5," J.T. quickly called back to Ben.

A few seconds passed, then came the reply: "System lock verified. . . . We are now 'in system.' "

J.T. clapped his hands once in triumph—the way-out hardware had worked again.

The five B-1s were now "invisible."

Viceroy Dick was hustling from one command post to another, his entourage of bodyguards in tow, informing the officers on station that he was now running the show at the Aerodrome. No one argued with him, especially after he told them to get ready to break out of the perimeter.

Some would be left behind however. The coordination needed to successfully move the remaining 11,000 men and their equipment would have to come

343

from the all-important Command Center. Therefore, he ordered the operators to stay at their posts until they received further orders from him.

He ordered all but the shoulder-launch SAM teams to stay behind also. Should an air raid come, the bigger the fight between his AA crews and the attacking American aircraft the better. All the more confusion that would help to cover his withdrawal.

His final order was to the five remaining Circle-hired pilots. He told them *not* to take off until the first attacking jets were spotted on radar. Then he promised them no less than 200 bags of gold for every kill they could confirm. They responded anxiously and told him they would do their best. But both he and the pilots knew they were bullshitting each other. As soon as they could, Dick knew the pilots would take off and be gone. His reasoning was that they would shoot down a few UA jets just out of self-preservation. That would mean fewer UA jets harassing him during his bug-out.

His troops formed up on the tarmac, nervously waiting in four-deep ranks. He intended on leading them eastward, through the Cicero Swamp, then up around Oneida Lake and finally into the wilderness of the former Adirondack Park. He planned to loot anything and everything in his path and once settled in the forests, lay low and figure out how best to use his 11,000-man army.

He did one last quick check in the Command Center, totally ignoring the dirty looks from those who would be left behind. He counted on the radiomen to continue to update him on the advancing American columns, both the one that was approaching the airbase from the due north and the one that he was sure had already taken possession of the bloody grounds around the university. He also needed a constant reading on how many UA airplanes were in the area and exactly where they were, as his only air defense would be the squads of shoulder-launched SAMs.

It seemed like everything was set. That's when he heard a distant rumbling . . .

He was about to order his troops to start marching when he looked skyward and saw five glinting shapes of white coming toward the base from the west.

"Jesus Christ! UA bombers!" he screamed. "Why didn't we pick them up on the radar . . ."

He immediately ran down the steps to the Command Center, his nine-man bodyguard squad doing its best to keep up with him. Once there he was shocked to find his radar operators grudgingly staring at blank screens.

"They are five bombers heading our way," he shouted to the officer in charge. "Order the SAMs to start tracking them!"

The officer looked at the "non-active" screen and then back at Viceroy Dick. "There are no read-outs on the scope, sir," he said. "Perhaps you were mistaken . . ."

Dick grabbed the man by the scruff of his neck and with the help of his guards, hauled him up the three flights of stairs.

By the time they reached the surface, the five specks were nearly over them.

"Look up there, shithead!" Dick screamed at the man. "What do those look like to you?"

The man never answered him. The first bomb landed just ten feet away . . .

Dick felt the strangest sensation run through his body as he was blown up and away from the Command Center building. Even in his last conscious moment, he felt his nose was running . . .

"Right on target!" J.T. heard his navigator call out.

He took a glance at his ground radar TV screen and saw the video projection of the explosions that were rocking the central terminal of the Aerodrome.

"One of those would have to have hit that Command Center," he called back to Ben Wa in *Ghost Rider 5*.

"I'm not worried about it," Wa replied. "That whole terminal is ancient history already."

J.T. banked his B-1 to the left and caught a look at the results of the bombing himself. Ben was right, the main terminal building was consumed in one massive fiery cloud. He could see large secondary explosions going off within the larger plume, adding further to the destruction.

Satisfied, he called back to Erie control tower. "Mission accomplished," he reported. "There's nothing left standing down there . . ."

He turned the five radar-proof bombers back to the west and headed home.

"Sorry, Fitz . . ." he added.

CHAPTER 62

Hunter brought the F-16XL down for a bumpy but successful landing at the Aerodrome.

PAAC paratroopers were still floating down as he taxied his plane up to what was left of the main terminal building. He could see a pitched battle was raging out on the southside runways between the American Airborne soldiers and the remaining Circle troops. But he knew the enemy would soon be taken care of. Very few had survived the massive B-1 strike or the two hours of smaller fighter-bomber strikes that followed. Maybe 1500 or so had escaped, but no more.

Nearby were the remains of an A-7, still burning after being shot down by a Circle SAM. Farther off was the charred wreckage of a Texan F-4, also a victim to a SAM. But aside from those two airplanes, there were no further losses to the United American air arm.

He surveyed the whole base. Everywhere there seemed to be fires, wrecked equipment, broken glass and bodies. Mostly bodies. Some were twisted and gnarled and burnt to the bone. Others were lying peacefully, as if they were just sleeping.

"What a waste," he whispered to himself.

A C-130 rumbled in right behind Hunter, it too finding the landing bumpy on the cratered, bomb-scarred runway. The big Hercules pulled up beside his airplane and Jones was the first to jump out. Behind him was a solemn-looking Mike Fitzgerald.

"Well, we did it," Jones said, looking around at the practically demolished Aerodrome. "Not a whole lot left to claim though, is there?"

Hunter pointed toward the southside runway. "They're still mopping up over there," he said. "Any prisoners they can bring back, we should get them hoofing on burial details."

Dozer was already on the ground, having jumped in with the paratroopers. He soon appeared, escorting three young women who were obviously call girls.

To Hunter's dismay, they were also all wearing the fashionable Dominique-look "Queenie" outfits.

"Found them in the rubble," Dozer told Hunter and Jones. "They say that most of the civvies got out before the big battles began . . ."

Jones thumbed them back to the C-130. "We'll take care of them," he said, turning back to Dozer. "What's the latest from the university?"

"Just clearing out a few last pockets of resistance," Dozer replied. "Just got off the phone with them. There's not much left over there either. They're burning the bodies now."

Hunter excused himself and walked over to Fitz who was standing at the edge of the runway, looking out at his blasted, burning dream.

"It's all gone, Hawker, me friend," he said sadly. "Lot of work went into this. Lot of memories . . ."

Hunter put his hand on his friend's shoulder. It seems like everyone was losing something these days.

"Mike, as soon as this is over," he said. "I'll be the first one back here with you. Just give me a shovel and a wheelbarrow . . ."

Fitz's eyes misted over. "We'll see, Hawker," he said, walking away. "We'll see . . ."

348

PART FOUR

CHAPTER 63

The Free Canadian Sea King helicopter touched down to a shaky landing on the rolling deck of the troop transport.

The weather was terrible—the seas were nearly at 12 feet and it had been a bumpy journey out from Newfoundland. But as Major Frost alighted from the chopper, he knew the trip had to be made. It was, in fact, critical.

Several unsmiling guards were waiting for him just off the helipad. They frisked him, then escorted him down to the captain's quarters. Once there he met a man introduced to him only as Karl. They didn't shake hands, he was offered no coffee or liquor. The man simply stared at him for a moment and said: "Talk . . ."

Frost took a deep breath.

"This attack on the American East Coast that you are planning is complete insanity," he told him, his voice stern and strong. "You'll be cut down on the beaches . . ."

The man laughed. "Come now, Major Frost," he said in an English that was tinged with some kind of Eastern European accent. "I didn't agree to this meeting just to have you spout your friends' propaganda at me."

"It's not propaganda," Frost shot back at him. "These are facts. You are a fool if you expect to link up with any allies—the Circle or anybody—once you land."

Karl's face became compressed with anger. "Very few men have dared to call me a fool, Major," he snarled.

"They will have reason to if you carry out this operation," Frost countered. "The United American Army has just defeated The Circle at Syracuse. Within the last few weeks they have also beat them at Football City and at New Chicago . . ."

Karl held up his hand. "Stop right there, Major Frost," he said. "I am aware of these battles. I am also aware just how your friends were able to trick the Circle into withdrawing from each of those first two campaigns. In fact, can you deny that troops from your own country now occupy New Chicago?"

"I'll be honest with you," Frost said. "There is too much at stake here to be otherwise. You're right to say that clever diversions helped the victories at Football City and New Chicago. And yes, our volunteers are helping as part of a 'peacekeeping' force in New Chicago.

"But let me assure you sir, that the battle at Syracuse involved no gimmicks. An entire Circle Army Group and their air attachment were wiped out by the United Americans."

Karl thought for a moment, then said: "All right, let us assume this is true. There is still a very large contingent of Circle troops in Washington, no? And I understand that a demonstration of The Circle's actual power will take place there very soon.

"I am also aware of the fact that the patriotic mood among the citizens living under The Circle's rule is now very low. They are coming to accept the New Order—finally! They no longer crave these things that were available to them before the Big War started. There are no more addictions for 'Moms and Apple Pies,' so to speak. And very soon, these citizens will start to realize that the United Americans are simply troublemakers, people who cannot accept the reality of the situation."

"Which is?" Frost asked sternly.

"Which is that the New Order means stability for the citizens' otherwise unstable lives, Major," Karl said, with a sinister smile. "People become complacent toward an occupying army much sooner than your patriotic friends might think. And while it may be true that these United Americans have taken over a few cities, to what end is it? As I understand it, most people live out in the rural areas these days. What can your friends do for them?"

"They can give them freedom," Frost said quietly. "And believe me, they will battle you to the last bullet if you land your troops . . ."

Karl leaned back in his chair and was silent for several long minutes. Frost studied the man. He was big, broad-shouldered; obviously East European in origin. And he was simply a commander-in-chief for hire. The men on the dozens of ships bobbing in the rough seas around him were his employees. They fought wherever they could get paid for it. No loyalty to any one flag. No cause except for the pursuit of lucre.

But Frost knew that, as a businessman, Karl had to choose his wars carefully. Being on a losing side—or even winning but at a high cost—was considered very bad for business.

"This is what you can tell your friends," he finally said to Frost. "Convince me that the people—the remaining Americans that they are fighting so valiantly to free—would just as soon accept the United American flag as opposed to The Circle, and I'll consider bargaining with them."

"Bargaining?" Frost asked. "On what terms?"

"Convince me first," Karl said. "Then we'll talk terms."

Frost shook his head. "These United Americans will not let you dictate a peace to them . . ."

Karl let out a hearty laugh. "I'm not talking about *peace* terms, Captain," he said. "I mean *financial* terms. Have them convince me that some aspects of the old sentimental American way of life exists, then I will talk business with them, just as I would talk business with the Soviets, or the New Order or the Circle. It's really that simple . . ."

Frost nodded in sudden agreement. "Maybe it is at that," he thought.

CHAPTER 64

The line of civilians stretched for miles.

It was hot and many of the old and the weak had fallen by the wayside. Their near-lifeless bodies were pushed or kicked into the highway's ditch and left there to die by their brutal Circle guards.

This was the scene on Route 95, the main thoroughfare that led into Washington DC from the north. But it was a tragedy that was being repeated on just about every major highway leading to the nation's capital. Tens of thousands of civilians, having been rounded up from the countryside by the Circle, were being force-marched to Washington.

And Yaz was one of them . . .

Just before the Battle of Syracuse, he and 25 of Shane's Rangers had been air-dropped near Annapolis, dressed and given the identities of civilians. They were swept up in a Circle round-up just outside Baltimore and thrown into the parade of human misery that had just now reached the former nation's capital.

His job, along with the others, was to observe. Take in everything that was happening in DC. Shane, who Yaz had stuck close to, was carrying a miniature radio/receiver in his special hollowed out boot. At least once a day, usually during the single toilet stop, they were able to get off a short, coded burst message back to the United American base at Syracuse.

Now that they were actually within the capital city, there was a lot to report. The question was, would the officers back in Syracuse believe it . . .

It was past midnight when their group of about 5000 first reached Washington. Their handlers ordered them to bed down out in the open in the Constitution Gardens, next to the once-famous, but now bone-dry Reflecting Pool. Exhausted, Yaz had fallen right off to sleep. But now, with the early morning light filling the red skies, he was roused by the guards and given a small tin can full of some slop they called breakfast.

But as soon as he rubbed the sleep from his eyes, Yaz realized it would be impossible for him to eat — and it wasn't just because of the bad smell of the food. He was simply too amazed from looking at all the books . . .

It wasn't until the full light of day that he found they were camped so close to the Washington Monument. And now, beside that once proud sentinel, he saw one of the most astounding and perverse accomplishments ever.

Right next to the Monument there was a tower rivaling it in height and built entirely of books. Tens of millions of books . . .

"How the hell did they do that?" Yaz asked Shane, who, like everyone else, was staring at the strange column. It was surrounded by an elaborate network of staging of the type used in building construction.

"They must have packed them very tight or glued them together," Shane said, still not quite believing what he was seeing. "The staging keeps it together . . ."

Parked right next to the tower of books were a dozen gasoline trucks, their faded logos still betraying hints of names like Exxon, Sunoco and Gulf.

"So the ball players were right," Yaz whispered. "They're going to burn all the books they can find. All at once . . ."

"Destroy the culture, destroy the race . . ." Shane said angrily. "And they drag every civvie they can find to this place to watch the heart be cut out — or really *burned out* of the country . . ."

Just then the guards ordered everyone to their feet and soon they were marching again. They walked right past the tower of books, many people nearly gagging on the strong gasoline fumes that permeated the area. The books were being washed down with the gas via an elaborate system of pumps and hoses. This told Yaz and Shane that the massive book burning would take place soon.

They walked across Constitution Avenue, past the hundreds of empty tractor-trailer trucks and alongside the White House. They could see Circle troops moving in and out of the former Executive Mansion and they were chilled to see a gasoline truck parked nearby.

They were herded over to Lafayette Park, which was located directly across from the White House and told to sit. Here they saw Circle troops constructing more towers. But they weren't made of books.

"Jesus, are those baseball bats?" Yaz asked, studying a large, squat pile of interlocking pieces of wood. It looked like an elaborate child's construction of matchsticks.

"They've really got it in for the national pastime," Shane said with disgust. "There must be fifty thousand bats in that pile."

Next to the bats were several piles of baseball mitts, some old, some new. They were stacked at least twenty-five feet high and gave the impression of gigantic, leather-sided igloos.

Beyond the gloves were piles of tennis rackets and golf clubs. Piles of hockey sticks and skates, football uniforms and helmets, partially-deflated basketballs, sneakers, tenspeeds, snow skis, water skis, even a pile of bocci balls.

"Jesus, these guys are as efficient as the Nazis," Yaz said. "All they need is baby hair and gold teeth . . ."

Shane nodded. "I think they take more than a few cues from *Mein Kampf* . . ." he said.

For the next two hours, Yaz and Shane and the other 25 members of the undercover team took mental notes of what they saw going on around them.

It would make for an astonishing report back to Syracuse.

CHAPTER 65

The F-16XL banked over the old city of Schenectady and descended through the early morning clouds.

Inside, Hunter spotted the three-runway airfield below him and flipped his radio to the transmit mode. "Schenectady base, this is an aircraft of the United American Air Corps. I am requesting landing clearance . . ."

There was no answer.

"Schenectady, request landing clearance, over . . ."

Still nothing.

"Schenectady this is Major Hawk Hunter, formerly of the 16th Tactical Fighter Squadron, US Air Force, requesting landing clearance."

Suddenly his radio crackled. "Unidentified fighter, you can get in a lot of trouble using that handle," a voice on the other end said. "Everyone knows Hawk Hunter is dead."

Hunter refused to quote Mark Twain one more time. "I can assure you, Schenectady, that I am very much alive," he said. "If you grant me landing clearance, you can see for yourself."

While he was transmitting that message, Hunter lowered the F-16XL down to 1000 feet, and after first ascertaining that there were no hostile SAMs locked on to him, he did a slow, noisy turn over the base.

The long silence at the other end was suddenly broken.

"What the hell kind of airplane is that?" the voice asked, its owner getting a look at the 'XL for the first time.

"It's a long story," Hunter replied. "But I'd be glad to tell you if you clear me to land."

There was another silence, and finally the voice came back on: "You're cleared for runway one-three. And you'd better have a good reason for dropping in on us."

Hunter nodded. "I hope I do . . ." he said to himself.

Ten minutes later he was down and taxiing up to the base's main hangar. His airplane was immediately surrounded by no less than 100 troops, all of them heavily armed. He pulled the jet to a stop, slowly popped the canopy and stood up.

"Peace . . ." he said, holding his hand up, as if in an American Indian greeting. "Just here to talk . . ."

The place was an Air National Guard base before the Big War, home to a squadron of specially-adapted C-130 Hercules cargo planes. Since then, the base personnel had gone into business at the New York Hercules Heavy Air Lift Corporation. They were moving vans of the sky, renting out the big C-130s for heavy lift jobs.

They were in the right location to do so. Right nearby there was a factory that built electric turbines and generators. Now it functioned as a new and used parts exchange for those territories around the country that needed their turbines tuned-up every once in a while. The factory, which employed many of the people in the surrounding area, was the best customer for the "New York Hercs."

But Hunter was here to ask the Hercs a favor and it didn't involve lifting turbines.

A man dressed in a dark blue uniform appeared and told the soldiers to stand at ease. Hunter climbed down out of the F-16 and introduced himself. The officer did likewise—he was Colonel Stagg, the top man at the base. Luckily he recognized Hunter right away.

"So Hawk Hunter *is* alive . . ." Stagg said, shaking hands with him.

"That's what I've been trying to tell people," Hunter said, with no small amount of exasperation. "I guess no one wants to believe me."

Stagg took one look at his F-16XL and nodded. "Well, only one person could fly a jet like this," he said. "God, it's a beauty . . ."

Hunter had to agree. "It flies as good as it looks," he said.

They walked to Stagg's office and Hunter accepted his offer of a drink.

"Heard you guys made quite a racket out Syracuse way," Stagg said, pouring out two whiskeys. "Congratulations . . ."

Hunter hit his glass in a toast and took a swig of the no-name liquor. "Thanks," he said. "But the party is far from over. In fact, I'm here to ask for help. We can pay you. But I'll level with you, it's a dangerous job."

Stagg sipped his drink and lit a cigar. "We're open to any offer," he said. "And it isn't every day that the famous Wingman drops in on us. Back from the dead, no less. So, let's talk. What's your problem?"

361

Hunter gave him a quick update on the recent campaigns of the United American Army, the victories at Football City, New Chicago and Syracuse. He also told him about the approaching mercenary fleet and the huge demonstration being planned by The Circle down in Washington.

"We've heard rumors of that," Stagg said. "But we're just a small outfit up here. Too small to mix it up with anyone, never mind The Circle. They've been around here a few times. Not lately though. When they are, they leave us pretty much alone. Just as long as we pay our taxes, that is. We thought the IRS was bad!"

Hunter nodded. "Well, if things work out, you won't have to bother with any of them any more," he said. "We dusted most of their guys over in Syracuse. Hurt them bad. So bad they won't have any presence up here for a long time. If ever."

Stagg was genuinely happy. "I'm damn glad to hear that," he said, pouring out another drink for both of them.

"But we still have this problem of the mercenaries," Hunter said seriously. "If they land and get a foothold on the east coast, the New Order will pay them overtime just to stay here and bail out the Circle jerks."

"What can we do?" Stagg asked.

It was the question Hunter was waiting for.

"I understand that before the Big War started, you used to fly cargo runs up to the Early Warning stations in the arctic? Is that right?"

Stagg nodded. "Sure is," he replied. "That's why we got skis on our Hercs. We were the only unit that was adapted for snow landings. They still come in handy these days too. Makes deliveries a cinch in the winter . . ."

"OK, I'm glad to hear that," Hunter said. "Now, for

362

the big question: could you land one of those babies on sand?"

"*Sand?*" Stagg asked, surprised by the question. "Boy, let me think about that for a moment . . ."

He did, then said: "It really depends, Major. How rough is the sand? Is it wet? Is it level?"

"It's not wet," Hunter answered. "And it's level. But it isn't fine stuff. In fact, it's fairly rocky."

Stagg thought it over a little more. "Well, it would probably tear up the birds' undercarriage," he said. "But it could be done, I suppose . . ."

"OK," Hunter said. "Then tell me what you think of this plan . . ."

CHAPTER 66

Captain "Crunch" O'Malley's RF-4 Phantom recon jet landed at the battered Aerodrome just after the F-16XL and the three modified C-130s of the New York Hercs.

"Good timing," Hunter yelled over to O'Malley as he climbed out of their venerable Phantom. "You've got some 'game high-lights,' I assume?"

"Low-lights is more like it," O'Malley said. "There isn't a street or a park or a building within ten miles of DC that isn't covered with people. You know that when your infra red monitor starts flashing in the high end just picking up combined body heat that you got one hell of a crowd.

"It's like Woodstock, for all the wrong reasons . . ."

Ten minutes later they were sitting in a makeshift video viewing room, reviewing the tapes just made by O'Malley's spy cameras. Along with the crew of the RF-4 and Hunter, Stagg and two of his officers from the New York Hercs were in attendance.

"We were way up there as you'll see," O'Malley said, switching on the battery operated VCR. "We topped out sixty-nine thousand at one point . . ."

The video started playing with a long-range overall shot of Washington. O'Malley had been correct when he told them the place was one massive people- and traffic-jam.

"God, there must be more than a half million people

down there," Stagg said.

"At least," O'Malley agreed. "Now right here, near the Washington Monument, you can see the towers that Yaz and Shane reported. This big one has to be the books. These smaller, thicker ones the sports equipment and so on . . ."

Hunter shook his head in disgust. "Some shithead sitting in the Kremlin must be real proud of this," he said bitterly. "I'm sure it's documented somewhere in their greasy little psych-op books: 'How to destroy a culture . . .' "

"With an audience of a half million . . ." Stagg added.

The video continued with a series of zooms in and out of the center of the city. Then, it moved slowly toward the southwest.

"OK, here we are coming up on National Airport," O'Malley continued. "You can see the line of MiGs right there. I count eighteen of them in the first row. Floggers, a few moldy MiG-twenty ones, too.

"Now get a load of this, beside that big hangar there. What kind of planes are those Hawk?"

Hunter strained his eyes to look at the bare outlines of the airplanes O'Malley was referring to. They were too big to be fighters.

"Christ, are they Backfires?" he asked with no small amount of astonishment.

"That's what we think," O'Malley said. "What other airplane fits that profile?"

The Tupolev Tu-26 Backfire was similar in some ways to the B-1. It was an intercontinental bomber, with swing-wings and powerful engines and capable of dropping conventional bombs and launching cruise missiles. Considered one of the best machines the Russians ever managed to get off the ground, Hunter was surprised that the Soviets allowed such valuable aircraft to deploy to America.

"I count six of them," he said. "That's a good indication of the importance the Soviets are putting on this wing-ding."

"There's more," O'Malley said. He pointed to a large hangar at the end of the former commercial airport. Though no whole aircraft could be seen, two tail sections were plainly visible sticking out of the rear of the building.

"How good are you at IDing airplanes by their tail sections?" O'Malley asked Hunter. "Because I got a bag of silver that says those are the ass-ends of two Bears . . ."

Once again, Hunter squinted to make out the shapes on the videotape. He immediately recognized the unmistakable sharp edges of the rear stabilizers, the thickness of the tail fins, the protruding twin cannons in the rear turret.

"You win," he said. "Those are definitely Big Bears . . ."

The Bear was the nickname for the Tupolev Tu-95 heavy bomber—the B-52 of the Soviet Air Force.

"They've really trotted out the hardware," O'Malley said. "But what the hell are heavy bombers doing here, in the country now? They didn't even bring in this stuff during The Circle War . . ."

"Beats me," Hunter said, worried now about this new threat. "They could be using them simply to ferry in Soviet bigshots for the party. Or maybe they're planning to carpet bomb a couple of cities, as an encore to burning everything."

The videotape continued, moving past the runways of National Airport, across the Potomac and eventually centering on yet another airport.

"OK, this is what we want," O'Malley said. "Bolling Air Force Base . . ."

Compared to National, this air base was practically deserted. Only three airplanes were in evidence, each one an Antonov An-12 "Cub-B," a Soviet-built cargo carrier which was frequently used as a Signals-Intelligence or Signet airplane. A few Circle Army trucks were meandering about, and there were a few SAM readings, but that was it.

Just to the south of the air base there was a strip of barren terrain. Stagg was the first to notice the long sandy stretch just off the end of the runways, leading down to the Potomac River.

"I've got a feeling this is where we come in," he said.

Hunter nodded. "That's it," he said, "All of nineteen hundred and thirty four feet of sand. Slightly moist, but firm enough to handle your bird."

Stagg looked plainly skeptical, O'Malley froze the frame so they could better study the area.

"It's not the length that bothers me," Stagg said. "It's the width. We'll be dropping from such a high altitude, so quickly, then negotiating the river edge. And at night — Jesus, it's frankly going to be a very tight jink to set down on that straight and narrow. Especially with no option for a go-around . . ."

Hunter could sympathize with the man. They were asking him to commit his men and his airplane — his very livelihood — to helping them. But everyone in the room knew it was probably the only way . . .

"I have no doubt that you can do it," Hunter said. "The question is: Will you do it?"

Stagg looked at them, then back at the screen. "What the hell," he said finally. "Why not? If The Circle survivors and those mercenaries land, we'll probably be out of business anyway."

Hunter breathed a sigh of relief. Now at least one piece of his crucial plan was in place . . .

CHAPTER 67

Yaz's elbows and knees were cut raw and bleeding by the time he returned to his spot in Lafayette Park.

He, like many of the other Rangers, had spent the first few hours of darkness crawling around the area, trying to gather as much intelligence as possible. He had perfected a method of moving about undetected. He had simply wrapped a blanket around himself and moved, knees and elbows, several feet at a time through the crowd of otherwise sleeping civilians. To the Circle guards standing watch, he was just another sleeper, trying to get comfortable. As soon as they turned away, he would quickly move another few feet. The ruse was aided greatly by the fact that there were so many civilians lying about and so few Circle guards on night duty. The civilians brought to DC were almost entirely too tired, hungry and dejected to pose any kind of crowd control problems for their handlers.

Shane had stayed behind, expertly sending off brief messages back to Syracuse every half hour, despite the presence of a trio of Circle guards nearby. He broadcast his most important message earlier that evening: they had learned that the iconoclastic demonstration

368

would take place the next day, starting sometime in the afternoon. This had made the Rangers' "crawling" intelligence patrols even more crucial.

Now, as Yaz made his way up to him, Shane had just received a new piece of information transmitted from Syracuse.

"Our troops are coming in tonight," he said to Yaz.

"What?" Yaz couldn't believe it.

"It's true," Shane whispered. "They're going to try and head this thing off with a smaller force, while a bigger one fights its way down from Syracuse. I couldn't get any details. Hunter just told us to keep our eyes open and be ready for anything."

"Well, I've got some important news for them," Yaz said. "Can we get off one more message to them tonight before they jump off?"

"We can try," Shane said. "But only if the info is essential."

Yaz nodded. "It is," he said. "I found the gold APC . . ."

Shane hesitated for a moment, then asked: "Are you sure?"

"*Damn* sure, sir," Yaz said. "I just saw it ten minutes ago. It's parked right beside the Treasury Building. And it's covered with *Spetsnaz*."

"Well, Hawk will definitely want to know about this," Shane said, fingering the small radio and playing out the flexible antenna. "Any idea what it's doing here or what they are planning to do with it?"

"I'm not sure," Yaz said, grimly. "But tell him there's a gasoline truck parked right next to it."

It was three A.M. when the first of the New York Hercs appeared just outside of the Circle's Washington radar net.

Stagg himself was at the controls of this ship—designated Yankee One. Strapped down in the back were Hunter, Dozer and a squad of his famous 7th Cavalry Marines, plus 40 members of a PAAC Rapid Deployment Unit. Each man was wearing a black uniform and had a blackened face. They were armed with concussion grenades, flash grenades and a variety of side arms, the largest being a RPG launcher.

A red light began flashing in the otherwise darkened cargo hold of the C-130. "Ten minutes to go . . ." Hunter said to Dozer, who in turn called it out loud enough for everyone on board to hear.

"Let's start our final mental preparation, people," the Marine Corps officer added.

One hundred miles behind them were two more New York Hercs. One of them was carrying twenty more members of the PAAC RDU, plus some heavier weapons such as recoilless rifles and a few heavy mortars. Inside the other were more of Dozer's men, two squads of Football City Rangers and 15 of the baseball players rescued during the Cooperstown Raid.

Everyone was wearing the same black military coveralls except the ball players. They were being brought along not to fight but for another very important purpose—one that might prove even more crucial than anything else the United Americans would do that day.

For this special mission, they were wearing baseball uniforms . . .

Back in the hold of the lead ship, a green light began flashing.

"OK . . . one minute to drop down," Hunter said to Dozer. "Get your pathfinders ready . . ."

Hunter then unstrapped himself and walked up to the cockpit.

"Any problems?" he asked Stagg.

"Not yet, Hawk," the officer answered. "Not so far

370

anyway. We've been flying dark for the past hour . . . Haven't heard anyone talking about us on the Circle frequencies . . ."

Through the cockpit window Hunter could see the faint lights of Washington off in the distance. Below them was the dark shimmering of the Potomac River.

"No threat signals as yet," the Herc's co-pilot reported. He had his eyes glued to the APG radar Hughes had hastily installed in the cargo plane's cockpit. If they were spotted on an enemy SAM radar screen, the set would start buzzing and they would have to take evasive measures. This in turn would effectively end their plan. But as for now, the buzzer was silent.

"OK, there's the Wilson Memorial bridge," Stagg said, pointing to the faint line of gray crossing the Potomac. The pilot put on a special NightScope flight helmet which would allow him to see in the dark. "Starting the descent in ten seconds. You'd better strap down, Hawk. This is going to feel like a runaway elevator ride."

Hunter quickly buckled in beside the Herc's navigator. No sooner had he fastened the safety belt than Stagg put the C-130 into a screaming plunge.

Down they went, the Hercules wings shaking in defiance against the unorthodox maneuver.

"C'mon, baby," Stagg urged. "Stay together just a while longer . . ."

Hunter was being thrown around in his cramped space; he was instantly glad he was wearing his trusty flight helmet. He couldn't imagine what it was like back in the cargo hold.

"Down to seven hundred feet," Stagg reported. "OK, we're at six hundred . . . five hundred feet . . . four fifty . . ."

Hunter was wondering if his stomach would ever

371

catch up with them. He'd been in perilous dives before, but usually only when he was behind the control stick. It was a completely different experience when someone else was driving.

"Down to two hundred . . . one fifty . . ." Stagg was ticking off the numbers coolly. ". . . seventy five feet . . . down to fifty . . . I'm pulling up and holding at twenty five . . . hang on!"

Hunter took his advice and for good reason. Stagg yanked back on his control yoke and the airplane felt as if it had stopped in mid-air. Hunter was thrown against the navigator's weather table, then whiplashed back against the radio set.

By the time he stopped bouncing around, they were at the prescribed height of 12 feet above the waters of the Potomac.

"Looks good so far," Stagg said, adjusting his NightScope helmet. "I see the landing spot . . . we have about twenty five seconds to go."

Hunter managed to catch a peek of the landing strip over the co-pilot's shoulder. It was a long and sandy strip of land, almost like a sandbar. But it was very thin and had more than a few puddles freckling it.

"Jesus, where'd that water come from?" the co-pilot asked as Stagg put full flaps down on the big Herc.

"Too late to worry about that now," Stagg said. He pushed a button on his control panel which started a yellow warning light blinking back in the cargo hold. "You still strapped in back there, Hawk?"

"You better believe it," Hunter replied, assuming the crash position.

"OK," Stagg said, cutting his engines back. *We're going in . . .*"

They hit the sandy strip three seconds later, the Herc's special ski-type landing gear plowing up two large furrows as Stagg fought with the controls to keep the airplane from pitching into the Potomac.

"Reverse engines!" Stagg yelled to the co-pilot, as they careened along. "Full air brakes . . . flaps on lock!"

They screeched and scraped and skidded along the sand, the C-130's engines howling in protest. Finally, they began to slow down.

"C'mon baby," Stagg whispered urgently. "Be nice to me . . ."

Somehow he was able to stop the big bird before it reached the dense overgrowth at the very end of the Bolling runways. Now it was suddenly quiet inside the Herc . . .

"Everyone OK back there?" Hunter yelled back to the cargo hold while unstrapping himself.

"Few bumps and bruises," Dozer yelled back. "Nothing serious . . ."

Hunter was up and standing in two seconds. He patted Stagg on the back. "You did it, sir," he said. "Thanks for keeping us in one piece . . ."

He was back into the cargo hold in an instant, helping some of the more battered troopers get unhooked and up on their feet.

"Ready, Hawk?" Dozer asked him as he made his way to the back of the airplane. Already the Herc's big rear door was lowering.

"I'm as ready as I'll ever be," he said just as he and Dozer ran down the ramp. "The big question is: did anyone hear us?"

Their hope all along was that with the two air fields less than a half mile apart, the people at National would think any racket was coming from Bolling and vice versa.

He and Dozer scrambled to the top of the under-growth and peeked over.

The airbase looked deserted. The three Soviet airplanes were sitting in the same position as on O'Malley's video tape and there didn't seem to be any undue activity taking place at the base.

"Dare I say 'so far, so good'?" Dozer asked.

"Just cross your fingers when you do," Hunter replied. "I say let's get the rest of the gang up here . . ."

Dozer ran back down to the airplane and passed the word. Within a half minute the elite troopers were silently scurrying up to the edge of the runway. Stagg appeared with his NightVision helmet and a long extension cord. He scanned the far off hangars.

"No one around, that I can see . . ." he said. "Maybe they're all asleep."

Hunter unstrapped his M-16 and checked the magazine. It was full, as always, with tracer rounds.

"Well, let's get this show on the road," he said, scrambling over the top. "Everyone stay together and keep an eye on your brother . . ."

"And stay in the shadows . . ." Dozer urged them, checking the clip on his own Uzi. "Remember how we planned it. Just like Entebbe."

With that, the soldiers followed the two officers over the brush and out onto the runway.

Quickly, *silently,* they headed for the base's control tower.

CHAPTER 68

There were six Circle officers and ten enlisted men inside the Bolling base tower, having just come on duty at 3 A.M.

Four of the officers were already drunk when they reported for their shift. The two others were under the influence of the cocaine that was so readily available to all of the Circle's commanders. Even the enlisted men were drinking beer on duty.

The men assigned to the moribund Bolling air base were from the bottom of the Circle's rather cruddy barrel. Anyone with a half a brain and some airport experience was based over at National. The occupation at Bolling was merely an afterthought for the Circle commanders, a place to station a few dozen malcontents, criminals and substance abusers where they would be out of the way.

The shift had been on duty only thirty minutes when the girls were brought in. They had been bought, of course, right in downtown Washington, near the old "J" street intersection, with a bag of money pooled from the officers and men. It had been a weekly activity with this particularly repulsive graveyard shift of Circle soldiers. Two girls, sixteen men, a case of booze and a lot of drugs.

The senior officer, a captain named Lutt, picked over the girls like a man buying livestock. Both of them were barely 17, if that, and they had been dressed up in the faddish "Queenie" clothes of the day. Lutt fondled their breasts, grabbed their rear ends, felt between their legs.

"OK, they'll do . . ." he finally declared. "Get them ready . . ."

The girls were led to the large table that had been placed in the middle of the control tower's main office. It had been covered with three dilapidated mattresses and a mish-mash of army blankets. The girls were hoisted onto the table and made to guzzle from a bottle of no-name whiskey. Then, with a barely-operating video camera turned on, the soldiers drew lots. The first winner could then order the girls to do anything of his bidding. Once he was through, the next man would step up and demand the same and on down through the line.

On this night, the first man to win demanded the girls start off by fondling each other, a favorite of the nightshift. Then he decided they would perform oral sex on him at the same time, much to the whooping delight of his comrades. He finished up by attempting to have regular sex with both of them, a near-impossible task for a man who was a regular cocaine abuser. His less-than-sterling performance lasted all of three minutes, then it was time for the next soldier in line to make his demands.

They were on the fifth trooper when the group heard, but ignored, a quick but fairly loud scraping noise coming from the river's edge.

"Those assholes over at National, screwing something up," was how Captain Lutt decided to dismiss the commotion. "Lay out some more lines and let's get on with it . . ."

His underlings did so, but as they watched the fifth soldier of the night take measure of the young girls, Lutt suddenly found himself looking up a strange face on the other side of the control room door.

"Who the *fuck* is that?" he asked, but before anyone could respond, the door had opened and something was thrown inside.

The next thing he knew, he was blinded by a tremendous white light, so intense, it actually stung his eyes.

"Flash grenade!" someone yelled, but those were the last words Lutt ever heard. Through painfully stinging eyes he could just barely see the black-suited men pouring into the room and making short work of his contingent of soldiers.

Pop! Pop! Pop!

One man, one shot. Lutt could tell the invaders were highly-trained, efficient. He made a vain attempt to reach his gun, but he heard one last *pop!* and then everything turned to black . . .

It took only sixteen bullets to capture the air base control tower, two fairly quiet concussion grenades to neutralize the remaining enemy soldiers in the base's only occupied barracks.

Within a minute of the first gunplay, Hunter and the United American team were in control of Bolling Air Force Base.

"These guys perverted enough for you?" Dozer asked Hunter as the team members disposed of The Circle soldiers' bodies.

"They give perversion a bad name," Hunter said, watching the two rescued girls climb back into their *Dominique* get-ups. "Let's get Stagg up here and contact the other two Hercs. At least we know they'll have a smoother landing than we did . . ."

Twenty minutes later, the two trailing Hercs came in to perfect lights-off landings. Quickly, some of the troopers inside dispersed their heavy equipment to strategic points around the air base, while others went in search of Circle weapons and uniforms that the strike team would be able to use.

Ninety minutes after the first C-130 plowed in to the messy sand landing, a force of 35 UA troopers was driving out of the base in three captured Circle trucks. The first part of their bold mission was accomplished; now phase two had begun.

Hunter was in the lead truck with Dozer and Stagg. Two officers from Dozer's famed 7th Cavalry were commanding trucks number two and number three. The tiny convoy split up as soon as it reached the Suitland Parkway. Hunter's truck and number two crossed the bridge over the Potomac, while the third vehicle continued northward.

Each truck had a target: one of the trio of radar stations that made up the Circle's DC radar net. Truck 3 would be responsible for taking over the large tracking facility up on Mt. Ranier, northeast of the city. The group in Truck 2 would divert to the south and capture the radar station at Fort McNair, which was adjacent to the old Washington Navy Yard.

Hunter's team was assigned to the toughest nut of all—the mobile three-array system the Circle had installed on top of the old Watergate Building.

They boldly drove right through the heart of downtown DC, the few guards they saw routinely waving them along. The reports they'd received from Yaz and Shane had been correct, even understated. The entire District area seemed to be a jumble of Circle military vehicles, abandoned tractor trailers and clumps of

378

civilians—sleeping everywhere.

"This is the POW syndrome," Hunter said to Dozer and Stagg as he steered them along the streets of the capital. "There are probably ten or twenty civvies for every Circle guard, yet no one has the will to resist, the morale is so low."

Dozer shook his head. "It's amazing what happens when you imagine someone has a gun to your head, twenty-four hours a day. You resign yourself to your fate. Your life is in someone else's hands . . ."

"All it takes is a spark . . ." Hunter said.

They drove down Constitution Avenue and saw for the first time the incredible tower of books The Circle had constructed. The smell of gasoline was everywhere. They pretended not to notice and kept driving. Past the Elipse, past the OAS Building and past the Federal Reserve.

But it was near the old Viet Nam Memorial that Hunter saw a sight that really made his blood start to boil.

Out on the field near the black sunken wall, there was a large pile, similar to the books and other items they'd seen stacked along the way. But this pile was different: It was about 25 feet high and square. To the normal eye the colors looked all jumbled together in the early morning light. But Hunter saw right through the dark haze like a laser beam. The colors were reds, whites and blues. It was an enormous pile of flags—*American* flags.

His breath caught in his throat. The Stars and Stripes had been banned from America by the New Order—in fact, it was the first edict to come down after the war. Being caught carrying the flag meant that the person could be shot on sight with a huge reward going to the killer. With no shortage of bounty hunters roaming the country these days, it was no surprise that hardly anyone carried an American flag anymore.

Except Hunter . . .

He reached up and touched his pocket and felt the reassuring folds of the flag he *always* carried with him. Wrapped inside was the dog-eared photograph of his lovely and lost Dominique—but he managed to shake away that thought for the time being. Instead he concentrated on the pile of flags.

"They're going to have a flag-burning," he said almost to himself but quite aloud. "The bastards are going to burn all of those flags over there . . ."

"Son of a bitch," Dozer said. "That's as bad as torching the books."

Stagg strained his eyes to look closer at the pile as they drove by. "Look at the big one next to the pile," he said. "Isn't that the one that used to hang off the Iwo Jima Monument?"

"Yes it is," Hunter said, his voice betraying quiet rage. "It's one of the largest in Washington and these bastards are going to desecrate it."

Hunter felt an urge to stop the truck and gather up as many of the flags as possible, but he knew it would be suicide, even if he could bluff his way through anyone who might see them.

Stick to the plan, he kept telling himself. *Just stick to the plan . . .*

His anger somewhat in check, he took a right onto 23rd Avenue and was soon pulling up in front of the infamous Watergate complex.

"Such an ugly building," Stagg said, looking at the wavy construction that seemed to have no beginning, no end, no structure, and little function. "Wonder what the rental rates are these days?"

"Cheap, I would guess," Dozer said.

Hunter could see the three large radar dishes spinning on the south side of the building's roof. There were also several anti-aircraft batteries installed nearby.

"They look like they're prepared for company," Hunter said, noting the twin Bofors AA guns. "They've probably got a couple SAMs up there, too."

There were two guards at the main entrance and several more inside. Dozer whispered a command back through the window of the captured deuce and a half troop truck to the 15 soldiers in the rear. They quietly got ready.

"Here goes nothing," Hunter said, slowly getting out of the cab of the truck. He was dressed in a standard Circle Army captain uniform. In his pocket was a squirt gun . . .

Both guards saluted him as he approached. "My guys are here to rewire one of the arrays," he said, trying to keep a straight face. "Can you help us carry our equipment up to the roof?"

Both guards unquestioningly nodded and moved to the back of the truck. They were instantly taken up inside and disposed of.

By this time, Dozer and Stagg were standing next to him, each one wearing a Circle Army officer's uniform.

"So far, so good," Dozer said.

The three of them brazenly walked into the building's lobby where they were met by three junior officers of the guard.

"Can I help you, sirs?" one of the men asked them, a suspicious look written across his face.

"Yeah, we're lost," Hunter told him. "We're on our way to the Capitol Building. Which way is it?"

The officer turned to his two comrades for help. "The streets in this town are really crazy," one of them said. "Let me see now, if you take New Hampshire

Avenue over to Pennsylvania . . ."

The man was surprised to see Hunter take the squirt gun out of his pocket. "What is this, a gag?"

"Good guess," Hunter said squirting all three of them in the face.

The trio was unconscious before they hit the ground, silent victims of Hunter's homemade knock-out potion of chlorine and etherized ammonia.

"Boy that stuff really works," Dozer said as the three men crumpled like marionettes without strings. "But it sure does stink . . ."

"Oh God, is that the truth . . ." Hunter said, coughing from the fumes. "I think I made it a little too strong . . ."

All three of them were gagging as they signaled the rest of the troopers to get into the lobby. Soon they had commandeered three elevators and were quickly rising to the top of the building.

Hunter stopped his lift at the floor just under the penthouse, and the troopers in the other elevators did the same. Using hand signals, they quietly moved toward the stairs, taping the access doors behind them, so as not to set off any alarms.

Hunter was the first to reach the top floor, and he quietly opened the access door a crack and peeked in. There was a pair of penthouse suites on the top level. A tangle of wires ran in through two large glass doors, these no doubt leading up to the roof and to the radar dishes. He scanned the inside of the penthouse itself and finally saw the three control boards for the radar sets were installed right next to a large bar and couch pit.

Reclined inside this pit were six Circle soldiers—radar operators who were doing anything but watching their scopes. Instead, just like their compadres back at Bolling, they were passing around two young girls.

"These guys are unbelievable," he whispered to Dozer and Stagg as they joined in looking out of the crack in the door. "Did any of them have normal upbringings?"

Two flash grenades and six shots later, the Circle soldiers were dead, and two more young girls were liberated.

The troopers accompanying them quickly went into action. Some took up guard positions while others started fiddling around with the radar sets. The controls were Soviet in manufacture, but the PAAC guys could operate them nevertheless.

"Typical Russian set-up," Hunter said studying the hardware. "Three main radar set-ups, set for triangulation. The main bases coordinate data and send it to their AA and SAM teams, as well as their air traffic controllers at National."

"Well, if the other units were as successful as this," Stagg said, "then we'll be controlling all the main radar sets in the city."

Hunter nodded. "That's the idea . . ." he said.

CHAPTER 69

By the time Hunter, Dozer and Stagg arrived back at Bolling, the sun was coming up.

Already two United American C-141 transports had arrived, they being routinely cleared to land by "other voices" in the Bolling control tower and guided unhindered through the air space by the UA troops now manning the Circle radar sets.

But although things had gone smoothly so far, Hunter knew they would have to work very quickly. According to the latest information from Yaz and Shane, the Circle demonstration was scheduled to start just after noon. This was when a high-level Circle official was to light the match to set fire to the towering spiral of books and thereby begin the holocaust which would destroy a large piece of America.

Two more C-141s came in as Hunter was taking the stairs two at a time up to the control tower, Dozer and Stagg on his heels. He was glad to see General Jones sitting at the main control panel, personally directing the big planes in for landings.

"I guess we have to assume that the other two trucks reached their objectives," Hunter said to Jones.

"Affirmative, Hawk," the man replied. "But I just hope they can carry out the ruse long enough for us to get set. I mean, eventually, someone's going to come to relieve those radar teams and boom! the game is up."

"We'll be ready before then," Hunter assured him. "We'll send out some choppers once they get here to pull those guys out if need be."

Their attention was turned back to the large radar screen in front of them.

"Five more blips," he said. "The rest of the C-141s, I hope."

Jones did a double-check and nodded. "It's them," he said. "Once they're down we'll have close to a battalion of the paratroopers here . . ."

Stagg whistled. "Nine hundred guys against, what? twenty—thirty thousand Circle troops? You guys do like to bet long-shots, don't you?"

"It's like a second nature to us now," Hunter replied.

Three more blips appeared and then the screen was clear.

"Those will be the last of our supply C-130s," Jones said. "Once they come in, just about the whole party will be here, at least for the opening bell."

Their plan was an involved and complicated one. First of all they intended to move on Washington with the 900 paratroopers and at least disrupt the demonstration for as long as possible. It was simply a time-delaying tactic: the main bulk of the United American force was barreling down Route 81 from Syracuse at the moment, all of the UA's available aircraft—fighters and fighter-bombers, the attack planes, even one of the two C-5s—clearing away any opposition in front of them. It was a 400-mile trip, moving upwards of 30,000 men in a convoy made up of everything and anything that could move. Hunter and Jones knew it would take at least 20 hours for the first elements to reach the DC area under the best of circumstances. But they also knew they couldn't wait that long. The priceless icons of American culture would just be cinders when the troops arrived. So this pre-emptive action was necessary in an effort — although a slim one — to buy some time.

"How long do you estimate it will take to walk the paratroopers over to DC?" Jones asked Dozer.

The Marine captain thought for a moment. "Assuming those MiGs over at National leave us alone, I think they could double-time it in less than two hours," he said. "But they won't be ready to move out for at least another ninety minutes."

Jones checked his watch. "It's eight now," he said. "That puts us in DC at eleven thirty. That will still be cutting it close."

"Do you think we have to make some noise before that?" Hunter asked Jones. "A *pre-* pre-emptive action?"

Jones nodded slowly. "I think we do," he said somberly. "We have to distract them. Get them riled up, let 'em know we're in the area."

"But they're smart enough to know we're not going to launch an air strike against them," Dozer said. "Then we'd be doing their bloody work for them, torching everything in sight . . ."

Hunter was looking down on the runway, watching a Blackhawk helicopter being pulled out of the back of one of the recently arrived C-130s. The sun was fully up now, and he could see some movement at the enemy base at National, just across the river. Amazingly enough, no one over there had paid any attention to what was going on just across the river from them.

"I have an idea," Hunter said suddenly. "If we just want to shake them a little. But I'll need that chopper down there. And two volunteers . . ."

CHAPTER 70

Yaz and Shane were huddled together at the edge of Lafayette Park. Most of the rest of the 25 undercover Rangers were close by, as were a newly arrived contingent of Circle Army guards.

It was 10:30 A.M., just 90 minutes before "The Cleansing" was about to start.

"Maybe they were caught," Yaz was saying. "Maybe they were just plain found out when the first airplane came in and that was it."

Shane shook his head, as much as to shake away his own concerns as anything else. "You know these guys," he said. "Hunter. Jones. Dozer. They won't stop at anything. None of them will . . . Believe me, even if those three are lying in a ditch dead somewhere, they made back-up plans, you can be sure of that. We just have to sit tight and see what happens."

Yaz looked around him. There was a tension in the air so thick, he could feel it in his bones. About ten minutes earlier some Circle guards got trigger happy and shot down two elderly men and a woman. For little reason. The brutal deaths had swept a wave of fear through the tired, battered and beaten civilians.

Despite Shane's brave words, Yaz felt a cloud of despair forming over them all at that moment.

Suddenly, they heard an unusual sound . . .

"Is that a chopper?" Yaz asked Shane, scanning the sky directly above them.

"Can't be," the Ranger leader replied. "I ain't seen a Circle chopper since the battle out in Nebraska . . ."

Yet the noise was getting closer and it sounded like the unmistakable *whup-whup-whup* of chopper blades.

Then Yaz saw an amazing sight. Just beyond them, over near the White House, there was another large group of civilians. They could see something he, Shane and the others could not.

And they were cheering . . .

"Look at those people!" Yaz said to Shane.

The crowd was up and jumping and pointing up to the sky. The Circle guards surrounding them waded through the crowd, battering anyone standing back to their knees with the butts of their rifles. Yet, try as they might, they could not stop the people from jumping up and cheering.

"What the hell is going on?" Shane asked.

Now more people nearer to them were doing the same thing. Jumping up, pointing to the sky and cheering—full-lunged wailing . . .

All the while the chopper noise was getting nearer. Even more people were screaming, yelling, crying for joy. The cheers turned into a roar, even drowning out the noise of the helicopter.

"This is weird . . ." Shane said. Because of their location it seemed like everyone but them could see something approaching in the air. Whatever it was, it had suddenly rejuvenated the listless, defeated, demoralized crowd. A spark of life was now running through them . . .

Then Yaz saw it.

It was still a way off, but it was unmistakable. Shane and the other Rangers finally saw it too.

"Five bags of gold says that's Hunter up there!" Shane yelled above the ever-increasing roar.

They all watched—Yaz feeling a dozen emotions ripping through him. He was joyful to the point of tears, angry at The Circle to the point of murder . . .

Within ten seconds the helicopter was right over them. The Circle guards started shooting at it, but they knew it was no use. Nothing short of a SAM could bring it down. Yaz found himself cheering and laughing with the hundreds—now thousands—of other captured civilians.

They were proud citizens all who saw the Blackhawk helicopter fly over—towing the huge American flag behind it . . .

CHAPTER 71

As frequently was the case, the overall Circle Army Commander for Washington — five star General Zolly Budd — was the last to learn that an enemy aircraft was flying through his airspace.

"He's pulling a *what?*" Budd screamed into radio microphone.

Riding beside him in his staff car was the Soviet general in charge of Psych-Ops for America, and a lieutenant general of the *Spetsnaz*. They had been on their way for an inspection tour of the book tower when Budd received the report of the strange helicopter buzzing the capital.

"We have no idea where he came from," the major on the other end of the line was telling him. "Some of our troops reported seeing the helicopter land over near the Viet Nam Memorial about thirty minutes ago and pick up the large Iwo Jima flag. The helicopter carried no marking, but they just assumed that it was one of ours . . ."

"One of *ours!*" General Budd shouted. "We haven't had a helicopter in this army in over a year!"

The major at the other end was almost too frightened to reply.

"What should we do, General?" he finally raised the gumption to ask.

"What the hell do you think?" Budd roared back. "Shoot the damn thing down! Scramble jets if you have to!"

He hung up the phone and stared into the faces of the two Soviets. Neither could understand English — at least that's what he had been told. But their interpreter, a *Spetsnaz* lieutenant, was all ready with a question.

"My officers want to know what the problem is . . ." he said. Having already eavesdropped on the conversation, the interpreter already had a pretty good idea what had happened.

"A slight security matter," Budd lied, wondering at the same time how anyone within 200 miles of Washington could have gotten hold of a Blackhawk and had the out-and-out balls to steal the flag and brazenly fly it over the capital.

The interpreter translated the remark, along with what he had heard in the radio conversation.

The Soviet general rattled off a long spiel of Russian, which the interpreter translated for Budd: "The general wants to know if this 'slight security matter' will affect the timing of the Cleansing . . ."

Budd quickly shook his head. "No," he said. "Not by more than a few minutes anyway . . ."

The two Soviet officers looked at him sternly after hearing the translation. Then they conversed between themselves, occasionally asking the translator a question. The conversation ended with the three Soviets giving out a loud, somewhat sinister laugh, before fixing their gaze on Budd.

That's when *they* spotted the chopper . . .

It was flying back over the White House now, the gigantic flag fluttering behind it. A huge roar went up from the crowds in the immediate area, followed by several bursts of gunfire.

The Soviets in the back of the open staff car were astonished to see the helicopter, flying somewhat wildly, racing through the sky no more than 250 feet off the ground. At that moment a small SAM went up some blocks away, missing the chopper by a quarter of a mile. The helicopter had already taken evasive measures and now had disappeared from their view.

There was another long discussion among the Soviets, and this one didn't end with a laugh.

"My general suggests that you proceed with the Cleansing as quickly as possible," the translator told Budd. "He sees this helicopter as a bad omen for things to come."

Budd was not a follower of astrology—although he had heard it had once been the rage in Washington. But it didn't take a soothsayer to figure out what the bad omen the Soviets foresaw for him should the Cleansing not go off as planned.

The scene at Lafayette Park was getting ugly.

The revived citizens, their internal fires of pride and patriotism rekindled by the sight of the American flag flying by, now began to get restless. Two Circle guards, sensing the crowd's sudden turn in mood, panicked. When a small group of citizens refused to obey the guard's orders to sit down and stop cheering, the soldiers opened fire. They sprayed the rebellious knot of people with machine-gun bullets, killing at least a dozen of them and wounding many more.

Suddenly all the cheering *did* stop. A strange silence fell upon the crowd even as the echoing of the gunshots was fading away. Would the citizens obey now that they had seen twelve of their number brutally cut down? Or would they decide, *en masse,* what many Americans

392

before them had decided: that death before dishonor is the code of all freedom-loving people everywhere. No matter who the oppressor may be—communist, fascist, bigot, those who would impose one religion on another or those who would disallow one from worshipping at all—there was a time to rise up, to draw the line and *shout,* "No more!"

The time of the turning had come.

Two men jumped the pair of Circle soldiers from behind and started pummeling them with their fists. More soldiers appeared and more shots were fired. More civilians died. But then more rose up and attacked those soldiers. And then there was more gunplay.

Sitting some distance away from all this, Shane, Yaz and the rest of the undercover Rangers were alarmed at the sudden turn of events.

"Jesus, these people will get themselves killed before the cavalry arrives," Shane said in an urgent whisper.

"But what the hell can we do?" Yaz said. "They're fighting for their lives. We can't stand up and *stop* them . . ."

Shane lay face down and started unraveling his radio's antenna. "This is going to spread," he said to Yaz as more soldiers and more citizens entered the fray. "I've got to get word to Jones . . ."

Yaz stood up and watched the brawl which was now going full tilt about 25 feet away. It was now much too congested for the Circle troops to start shooting for fear of hitting each other, so the fracas had now evolved into a large fist fight, with only an occasional gun going off. Still, the experienced Circle troops were getting the better of the civilians.

Yaz felt helpless—as did all the Rangers. If they jumped in now, their superior combat skills would be a dead giveaway and their cover would be blown.

More Circle troops arrived and for the moment they were able to quell the uprising. Now, as the other Rangers formed a protective circle around Shane, the officer expertly sent a quick message to the UA base at Bolling.

He received an even briefer reply.

"They're telling us to sit tight unless absolutely necessary," he told Yaz and the others.

"Then what?" Yaz asked.

"Then, we do whatever is possible to help the civvies," Shane said, adding ominously: "For as long as possible . . ."

A Circle command car arrived on the scene and now an officer was gathering together the civilian instigators. Then the officer waded through the on-looking civilians and started selecting people at random.

One old man, he being too frail to walk without aid, never mind punch a Circle goon, was dragged to a nearby tree and brutally shot in the head by the officer. Another elderly woman was pulled out of the crowd and she too was murdered, shot in the temple by the Circle officer.

"This is what will happen to all of you!" the officer shouted to the crowd.

With that, his soldiers herded the original instigators over to a park wall. Then, one by one, they were lined up against the concrete and shot.

With each *pop!* of the gun, Yaz, Shane and the others found their nerves causing them to jump up — quite involuntarily. They all were frustrated. They were trained soldiers. They could put an end to these brutal executions. True, it would be a temporary end and the retributions that followed would be even harsher. But it was hard to sit with that logic as one brave civilian after another was summarily shot in the head.

It was the fifth man who really got to them. Just a

second before the gun was put to his temple, he cried out: "God bless America!" Then the trigger was pulled and he crumpled to the ground, a long stream of blood spurting from his head.

"That does it for me . . ." Shane said suddenly. He was instantly back on the radio, sending another urgent message to Bolling. He talked directly to Hunter, who had just returned from his wild chopper ride. The Wingman coolly listened to Shane's predicament, got his exact location, then signed off by saying: "Help is on the way."

Shane quickly told the others.

"This is the choice," he whispered. "We step in now. Stop this bloodshed. But we all know they'll eventually get us and we know what they'll do to us."

Another shot rang out, muffling the cries of another civilian victim.

"I'm in . . ." one of the Rangers said.

"Me, too . . ." came two more replies. Then two more, and two more.

Soon, all of the Rangers were committed. Shane turned to Yaz. "You back out," he told him. "This is our job, not yours. You'll be more valuable here, when we're . . . gone and when the reinforcements arrive."

"No way," Yaz said firmly. "I'm with you whether you like it or not."

Shane smiled and clasped his hand. "Way to go, Navy," he said.

Two more civilians were shot while they quickly devised a plan. Then they went into action . . .

The Circle officer had turned over the grisly duty of shooting the innocent people to his subordinates and now he was standing calmly by a tree as the tenth victim of the 45 condemned men was about to die.

Suddenly the officer felt an odd, cool feeling in his

stomach. He looking down to see a small knife was sticking into his mid-section just above his belt buckle.

"What the fuck . . ." he muttered in astonishment. But that was all he could say. The knife was treated with an instant-acting poison. He felt a swell of fluid travel up his windpipe and into his mouth. He coughed out a spew of blood then keeled over and died.

Three more Circle onlookers quickly met the same fate, victims of dartguns carried as standard equipment by the Rangers. Seeing their comrades falling around them, the other Circle soldiers stopped the executions and looked around in panic, searching for an explanation.

Suddenly, one of the soldiers went wild and began spraying the crowd with gunfire. Shane was nearest to the man and he hit him hard with a running block. In an instant, the Rangers materialized out of the crowd and began disposing of the Circle soldiers in the immediate area, taking up their guns and shooting those that were too far away to be dispatched by a knife.

"Get down!" Shane was yelling at the civilians. "We're friends! Get down!"

Many people scrambled for safety or just lay unmoving on the ground. Some cheered. Some were crying.

Within a half minute a full fledged firefight had erupted. All of the Rangers now had guns and they were firing at Circle soldiers hurrying to the scene. The American soldiers formed a loose circle of protective fire and shot at any black Circle uniform they saw. The Circle soldiers unleashed a fusillade of machinegun fire back at the ring of Americans, cutting down two or three with each volley.

Yaz was right in the thick of it, firing a captured M-16 with all the intensity of a man who knew he was soon to be killed.

This is it, he thought to himself. *This is what it's like to die for your country . . .*

Suddenly, it was over. All the shooting stopped. It was as if the 22 surviving Rangers had all run out of ammunition at once.

The Circle soldiers, now some 200 strong, tightened the ring around the UA undercover men. The Circle officer now in charge walked up to Shane.

"You are spies!" he screamed at him.

Shane looked the man directly in the eye and said: "We are Americans."

The officer turned red with anger. "Shoot them!" he commanded his troops. "Shoot all of them, then shoot everyone in this park. This will be a lesson to everyone else."

Like the civilians before them, the 22 Rangers were herded over to the nearby wall. Yaz could see the splats of blood against the concrete from the first set of executions.

"You are all fools," the officer said to them as they were prodded into a long grim line. "Your country is dead."

What happened next went by so quickly, Yaz thought he was dreaming.

A man — ordinary-looking, in his early fifties — suddenly appeared next to the officer. And with one mighty swing, he caved in the Circle commander's face with a baseball bat.

In a matter of seconds, the area was swarming with men — ordinary citizens — wielding baseball bats and slugging every Circle soldier in sight.

Yaz was astonished. He quickly turned back toward the fire piles and saw that there was a rush of people near the huge tower of baseball bats. Ordinary citizens were grabbing the sluggers and heading for the nearest Circle soldier.

"I can't believe this . . ." Yaz said.

"I can . . ." Shane replied. "Now let's help them . . . Rangers! Let's go!"

The next thing Yaz knew he was running. Running through the crowd of citizens, hopping over the clumped battered and bleeding bodies of the Circle guards. It was a full scale riot in a matter of 30 seconds — as if all the pent-up frustrations of all the citizens had suddenly burst forth in a volcano of defiance.

Yaz picked up an AK-47 and drilled two Circle guards who were attempting to flee the park area. Then he was running again, heading for a M-60 tank nearby. Already it was swarming with civilians, some being shot off, but others managing to club and subdue the crew members.

"We're soldiers!" Shane was yelling. "Let us take the tank . . ."

The civilians allowed Shane and three of the Rangers to get inside the tank. Yaz found himself on top, manning the M-60's machine-gun.

"Jesus Christ!" he thought as he saw more civilians arming themselves with the bats — hundreds of them.

But even as he felt the jolts of pride run through him he saw not hundreds but thousands of Circle troops closing in on them from all directions.

Suddenly, Yaz knew how Custer must have felt . . .

Shane himself was working the tank's big gun and his first shot hit an on-rushing Circle APC head-on. Gunfire crackled all around Yaz as he tried to pick out Circle targets — soldiers, officers, vehicles — and open up with the tank's big 50-caliber MG.

But the more he fired, the more Circle soldiers seemed to appear. They were coming at them from all directions. Some stayed back and simply fired their weapons into the park, others were ordered to wade in and do battle with the raging bat-wielding civilians. They were out-numbered, *outgunned* and they knew it — but that didn't stop them from fighting.

Just then, Yaz heard two sounds. One was a high-pitched scream, the other a dull, thunderous roar. He looked up and saw first one, then two, then a half dozen large airplanes flying overhead. White puffs were flying out of their rear ends.

"Good God," he whispered. "Paratroopers . . ."

He reached down and literally dragged Shane up through the turret. Unable to speak in the excitement, he simply pointed up. Shane shaded his eyes, and then he too saw the descending chutists.

"Jesus, they're dropping the PAAC Airborne right on top of all this!" he said, as both of them ducked a stream of bullets that went whizzing by. "This has got to be Hunter's idea . . ."

His thought was confirmed when the high-pitched sound grew louder and louder.

"Look!" one of the other Rangers cried out over the cacophony of shouting and gunfire. He was pointing to the southeast. Yaz twirled around just in time to see the arrowhead shaped airplane screech overhead just behind him . . .

"It's him!" Yaz heard himself yelling.

Shane slipped back down into the tank and prepared to fire the next shot.

"The party's just beginning!" he yelled back up to Yaz.

CHAPTER 72

Few people had seen the massive C-5 streak high over the city just 30 minutes before. But in the hold of the big cargo plane turned gunship was Hunter's Cranked Arrow F-16. No sooner had he landed from his helicopter flag display and talked to Shane about the deteriorating situation, than he was strapped into the already-armed up F-16XL and streaking off toward the growing battle over in DC.

But Hunter had arrived over a very confusing situation . . .

The civilian uprising was spreading out from Lafayette Park, past the White House grounds and into the Elipse. The flow of the crowds were punctuated by the flash of the Circle's heavy weapons being used against the brave citizens. Everywhere he could see explosions going off. Fires, smoke, muzzle flashes . . .

Descending into the midst of this was the PAAC Airborne Battalion, many of them firing their weapons even before they hit the ground. The original plans to march the paratroopers over to the scene had been quickly scrapped following the second call from Shane. Both Hunter and Jones knew the civilians would be massacred by the Circle troops if something was not done. The flames of the civilian uprising had been lit by Hunter's fly-by with the flag. Now the men of the United American Army had to support the civilians no matter what the costs. So after a quick conference with Dozer and the other paratroop commanders, a vote was taken on whether to drop the chutists right into the fray.

It was unanimous . . .

Now Hunter was prowling the skies right above the ever-widening battle, looking for two things: first of all, targets of opportunity that he could blast away with the dozen Maverick laser-guided bombs under his cranked wings.

But secondly, he was on the look-out for the mysterious gold APC . . .

Dozer led the first contingent of paratroopers to land. He immediately set up a radio and command post right in the center of Lafayette Park.

"Hey Hawk, this looks like one big barroom brawl!" Dozer yelled up to him over the radio link. There were hundreds of small fights going on all around him. Civilians battering Circle soldiers with bats and fists, the soldiers firing back wildly at anything that moved.

"Well, I'm glad you're in your element," Hunter replied, flying directly over the park. "Let's see if I can do some street-sweeping."

That's when he went to work.

The uprising had now spilled out onto the blocks adjacent to Lafayette Park. Alerted to the trouble, a large column of Circle armored vehicles was making its way down Pennsylvania Avenue toward the site of the fighting. If they were successful in reaching the park, the citizens' uprising—and the paratrooper‚s support for it—would be over before it started.

"Looks like someone wants to crash this party," Dozer radioed Hunter as he spotted the advancing column through the smoke and gunpowder haze.

"I see them," Hunter replied, flipping the F-16XL over and going into a vertical translation.

Within seconds, he had the F-16XL down to tree-top level and racing dead center above Pennsylvania. He quickly flipped a series of switches, then took a deep breath and fired his first Maverick weapon. He felt the corresponding jolt as the missile, guided by a special-dual sighting laser device in the jet's nose, ran its course unerringly to the lead tank. It impacted on the M-60's turret with a tremendous booming explosion. The tank's gun came twisting off as the tracked vehicle was lifted some six feet in the air. When the wreckage came down, it formed an immediate roadblock in the already-litter-strewn street.

"Just as advertised . . ." Hunter mused as he looped the jet over and lined up on the now stalled column. As the terrified Circle soldiers dove for cover, Hunter opened up with his Vulcan Six-Pack, riddling two APCs and another tank with the heavy caliber, armor piercing shells. Another loop and another strafing run racked up two more tanks and an armored truck. He put the jet into another 360 and came back for a third time, blasting an additional APC and two troop trucks. By his fourth pass, the surviving enemy commanders had had enough, quickly jamming their vehicles into reverse and beating a hasty retreat.

Hunter yanked back on the control stick and punched into his mike button.

"I think we've rained sufficiently on that parade,"

he told Dozer.

Just then he got a call from the flight commander of the last three paratroop-laden C-141s heading toward the battle area.

"We're getting a threat warning near our drop zone," the pilot told Hunter. "Could you do us the favor?"

Hunter acknowledged the call and immediately did a shallow loop which leveled him off just above the Elipse. He saw a few squads of Circle soldiers attempting to set up a SAM unit just off Constitution Avenue, their intended targets being the approaching C-141s that had just taken off and were flying very low. Two Mavericks later, the SAM site was reduced to a heap of smoldering metal and all its operators blasted into cinders.

Now, as he streaked low over the Washington Monument, he recognized a new threat—a large contingent of Circle troops was withdrawing in toward the tower of books. He saw several gasoline trucks also moving in that direction.

He immediately punched in his radio microphone button. "Ground commander, this is F-16, come in . . ." he called to Dozer, somewhere on the ground.

"I read you, Hawk," Dozer called back.

Hunter adjusted his radio tuner slightly. "What's your position now, Bull?"

There was a nasty burst of static, then Dozer came back on the line. "We're moving out of the park," the Marine captain reported, his transmission punctuated by the sound of gunfire in the background. "We've linked up with Shane and Yaz and the boys. They've even got a couple of tanks waiting for us. We've covered them with white shirts and things so you'll know who the good guys are . . ."

Hunter came in low right over the park. "I see your

vehicles," he reported. "But it looks pretty wild down there. What's your situation?"

Another burst of static jumped from the radio. "Things are getting *very* crazy here," Dozer shouted back. "We're trying to get the civvies organized, but a lot of them are taking off at anything that faintly resembles a Circle soldier."

"Well, we've got a problem over at the Monument," Hunter told him. "It looks like we might have a bunch of firebugs heading for the book tower . . ."

"I'm not surprised to hear that," Dozer yelled back, his voice almost drowned out by the sounds of the ground combat. "Some Circle bastards already lit the piles of stuff closest to us. We've stopped some of the fires, but not all of them. That black smoke you see down here is about ten thousand tennis rackets going up!"

Hunter shrugged off that report. He hated tennis.

"Do you think they're going to torch the books now?" Dozer asked him.

Hunter came in low over the book tower, temporarily scattering the Circle troops in the area. "I would say that's affirmative," he told Dozer. "They're moving up their gasoline trucks . . ."

"Well, we'd better break out of here and get the hell over there," Dozer called back. "Can you run some interference?"

"Follow me . . ." Hunter replied.

By this time, the fighting had spread all throughout the parks near the long reflecting pool up to the Lincoln Memorial. The civilian bands, some of them taking on the recently arrived paratroopers as their leaders, were locked in vicious hand-to-hand combat with the startled, disorganized Circle defenders. Some of the civilians had liberated the pile of hockey sticks that were ready to be burned and were swinging them with even more wild abandon than their bat-wielding compadres. Some golf clubs too were being used as weapons—the putters and short irons proved most effective—but a Circle Army squad had managed to torch the largest piles of clubs and they were now raging away.

Some of the civilians had taken to putting on jerseys from the pile of sports uniforms. Others were utilizing the headgear found in the unburned piles of football and baseball helmets. Still many of the civilians were being ruthlessly gunned down by the Circle soldiers. But when they caught a disproportionate number of the enemy, the civilians were in turn killing their former captors, picking up their weapons and moving on.

Hunter flew low over one such civilian group—some 200 strong—who had commandeered several Circle trucks and were now moving on several enemy machine gun nests located in the old Executive Office Building right next to the White House. This group was paving the way for Dozer's larger force which was trying to battle its way toward the book tower. Hunter sighted the target, switched one of his Mavericks to "hot" and let the missile fly. The resulting explosion took out the enemy gun—along with half the front of the old building.

"Goddamn, those Mavs are powerful," Hunter said, shaking his head in amazement.

Just then, he received an urgent call from Jones back at Bolling.

"Hawk, we've just intercepted a message from the Circle high command," the general told him.

"Let's have it," Hunter replied.

"They're up to their old tricks, Hawk," Jones told him. "Tactical Defense, again. They've ordered the bulk of their forces to withdraw up toward Silver

Springs in Maryland. They're heading toward Baltimore, I would guess . . ."

"That's good news," Hunter said. "I think . . ."

"It is in some ways," Jones said. "The advance contingent of our ground troops are a few hours away now. If The Circle keeps pulling back, they'll run smack dab into them somewhere just south of Baltimore."

"Plus this way, we can blast them from the air without worrying about destroying all of DC . . ." Hunter told him.

"Right, but there *is* a problem," Jones said. "They are leaving behind four battalions of specialists, plus a whole gang of *Spetsnaz*. As we read it, these soldiers are to withdraw to the designated zones and carry out their so-called 'termination orders' . . ."

"Damn!" Hunter cursed. He didn't have to be a mind-reader to figure out what that meant. "They're going to blow up everything anyway."

"I'm afraid so," Jones replied. "These guys are probably the Circle's suicide squads. Or if they weren't before, they are now. They'll put up a hell of a fight and then torch everything they can."

"We've got to stop them!" Hunter shouted in exasperation. "Especially the ones that are planning to torch the books . . ."

"Wait, there's more," Jones said. "We've had to lift out all the radar teams, so the Circle is back in control of the radar net. They've also figured out that we're over here at Bolling, of course. We've been shelling the runways over at National, but they're ready to launch some aircraft. You might have company up there very soon . . ."

"That's all we need," Hunter said. "And I can't leave this situation here to get over there and do some damage."

"Well, I've ordered a flight of A-tens accompanying our columns to divert here, *toot sweet*," Jones told him. "They'll go right in after the runways at National. But they won't be here for another ten minutes or so . . ."

"OK," Hunter radioed back. "It won't be the first time we've juggled more than three balls in the air at once . . ."

He did a wide loop over the city. Already he could see the Circle's new orders being put into action. A large contingent of vehicles were leaving the city, heading northeast. Hunter resisted a temptation to fire at least some parting shots at them. He knew he'd need all the ammo he had for battling the enemy troops left behind.

It was these enemy suicide troops that were simultaneously withdrawing in strength to positions around or near the piles of American objects that were slated to be destroyed. Besides the contingent of troops surrounding the Washington Monument and the tower of books, there were large pockets of enemy soldiers holed up at the Capitol Building and around the Lincoln Memorial where the large pile of American flags were to be burned.

Hunter quickly called Dozer and informed him of the Circle's tactic.

The Marine captain had organized a couple hundred paratroopers with the original band of 200 civvies. This force was now moving down a side street, past the Pan-Am building.

"We'll be within sight of the Monument in a few minutes," Dozer told Hunter. "I'll also radio the other units and let them know where the hot spots are . . ."

Within a minute another large force made up of paratroopers and armed civilians was moving toward the Lincoln Memorial. Dozer also dispatched a smaller group to fight its way toward the Capitol Building.

"We're right at the corner of 17th and Constitution," Dozer called up to Hunter. "I can see them putting up barricades at the top of the Monument's hill . . ."

"What's your plan?" the pilot asked him, knowing there weren't many options.

"Frontal attack," Dozer replied quickly. "There's no other way . . ."

The words still stung Hunter's ears. He knew that such an attack would be costly in both human lives and the very object they were fighting to protect. He knew the Circle troops would start preparing to set fire to the books as soon as Dozer's men began their assault.

He needed a counterbalance. They probably wouldn't be able to save all the books. *But* if they were lucky, they could prevent many of them from being destroyed.

Suddenly an idea came to him.

He quickly radioed Dozer. "How long to jump off?" he asked.

"I'd say ten minutes," the officer replied. "We're just getting the civilians sorted out and making sure everyone has some kind of a weapon . . ."

"OK," Hunter called back. "I'll be back to you in seven minutes."

He then put the F-16 down to treetop level and started scouring the city. He wasn't looking for SAMs or even the gold APC, although that was still high on his list.

He was looking for a fire station . . .

CHAPTER 73

Yaz loaded the captured M-16—his third gun of the day—with the last of his ammunition, then took his place in line.

He was right on the curbstone at 17th and Constitution, part of a second line of troops being set up for the assault on Monument Hill. On the top of the bluff he could see Circle soldiers scurrying around, overturning vehicles and other objects to make barricades. He could also see they were giving the huge tower of books another wash of gasoline in preparation for its imminent torching.

In front of Yaz was the first line of the assault force. It was made up almost entirely of PAAC paratroopers and the surviving members of Shane's Rangers. His own second line was led by several paratrooper squad leaders and made up of civilians who Dozer had quickly determined had had prior military service—reservists, militia men and so on. Behind him were two more lines. These were made up of anyone with balls enough to join the attack.

Dozer was now standing in the middle of the street, preparing to address his troops. The noise of the fighting had died down around them for the moment as both sides prepared for the second round. Occasionally some dazed citizens would wander by — they being freed by the civilian uprising, but each time Dozer would have a couple troops escort them to the rear.

They had three tanks at their disposal, plus two APCs. The tanks would lead the first wave, the APCs the second. Most of the men were armed with M-16s and AK-47s taken from the dead Circle troops, although there were a few grenade launchers being carried by the paratroopers in the first line.

"All right men, listen up!" Dozer's voice boomed. "We jump off in two minutes. Stay close in ranks, especially you men behind the first line. Use your ammunition wisely — don't go shooting it all off while you're climbing up the hill. Believe me, you'll need it once you get up there.

"Try to stay low to the ground, but don't bunch up behind the tanks or the APCs. The Circle have anti-tank missiles and if they hit one of our vehicles, then I don't want a bunch of foot soldiers going up with it.

"Good luck and see you at the top!"

Yaz could hear the sounds of heavy guns going off in the distance but he didn't know exactly where. He did know that two other assault teams were preparing to attack the enemy suicide squads at the Lincoln Memorial and at the Capitol Building. He wondered if they would fare any better or worse than this impending attack.

"One minute!" Dozer yelled, himself checking the ammo clip in his Uzi.

The four lines stiffened up — Yaz estimated there were close to 400 men in all. He knew there were at

410

least twice that many on top of the hill.

"OK, Ready!" Dozer shouted. "First line, let's go . . ."

Suddenly the three M-60 tanks started moving, with the first line of the 50 paratroopers and Rangers right behind it.

They had moved about 20 feet ahead when the man in charge of the second line ordered them to move forward.

Yaz took a deep gulp of air and started walking. Across Constitution, across the small level center island and finally up on the mall which led to the bottom of the Monument's hill. He could see the Circle soldiers had stopped moving around and were now taking up positions behind their barricades.

"God help us . . ." Yaz thought, as the first fusillade of gunfire erupted from behind the enemy fortifications.

The tanks immediately returned the fire, blowing small holes in the barricades. Suddenly a pair of anti-tank rockets flashed out from behind the Circle fortifications, both of them impacting at the same time on the lead tank, enveloping it in a huge fiery explosion. When the smoke cleared away, there was nothing left but a large hulking wreck.

Still they kept marching up the hill. Men in the first line were dropping with bullets to their heads or stomachs and Yaz did his best not to walk on top of their bodies. Another concentrated fusillade erupted from the enemy lines, only to be answered by two direct hits from the pair of remaining tanks.

His line was about halfway up the hill when the APC rolled up alongside him. Despite what Dozer had told them, Yaz moved closer to the machine, figuring he'd take his chances should it be hit by an anti-tank rocket.

"First line, double time!" Dozer screamed from his position at the front of the entire force and quickly the paratroopers broke into a run up the hill.

The next thing he knew, Yaz was running too. The air was thick with bullets and hot flaming shrapnel. Men were falling all around him and yet he continued. He was more than halfway up the hill and he had yet to fire his weapon.

Within a few seconds of running, he was out of breath. But he kept going simply on adrenaline. For the first time he could actually see the faces of the enemy soldiers firing down on them—the whites of their eyes!—and it was then he realized exactly what the odds were. There were at least four times as many Circle soldiers behind the barricades than he had previously thought. In an instant a devastating thought came to him. Was this really an attempt to take this hill and save the hundreds of thousands of books in the tower? Or was it more a valiant yet doomed effort—a kind of symbolic gesture that would result in their decimation?

Just as suddenly, he realized he didn't care. For the second time that day he thought: "This is what it's like to die for your country . . ."

They were running full tilt now and he couldn't believe he hadn't been hit, the air was so filled with flying lead. He remembered reading something about how the American Indians prepared to go into battle. They thought if they dwelled on being invisible, they would *become* invisible, and thereby escape injury during the fight.

From that moment on, Yaz tried to concentrate on being invisible. But he knew it would take more than mind power to save them all.

They needed a miracle . . .

Suddenly there was a tremendous screech directly

above them. Then there was a series of tremendous explosions all along the Circle barricades. Then Yaz felt himself running at top speed. It happened so fast, he didn't know at first what was going on. Then he looked up and directly above him—no more than 50 feet high—was the F-16XL.

One miracle coming up . . .

Somehow, the F-16XL made two more devastating strafing runs before Yaz's line reached the top of the hill. Later he would learn that Hunter had already provided similar support to the other UA attacks at the Capitol and at the Lincoln Memorial all within the matter of a few minutes. Yaz would later realize that the Wingman had picked his targets at the top of Monument Hill so carefully, not a single spark had reached the gasoline soaked tower of books.

In the midst of the confusion of battle Yaz had thought he had heard sirens. Now, just as he was about to go over the top of the smoking Circle fortifications, out of the corner of his eye he could see three fire trucks tearing up the hill behind them, several paratroopers and a load of civvies hanging off them.

But now Yaz could realize that Hunter had other problems. There was another screech in the air. He looked up and saw two MiG-23s bearing in from the south. Hunter put the F-16XL into a freakish, near-impossible turn and immediately engaged the enemy aircraft. Yaz felt his stomach flip. It was obvious that Hunter, their guardian angel, would be busy for a while.

Suddenly Yaz was up and over the barricades. The paratroopers who had reached the battlements before him were engaging the Circle soldiers in vicious hand-to-hand fighting. Yaz was instantly firing at Circle troops in every direction. He ran forward, making

413

room for the APC to break through the battered enemy line. The air was filled with not only bullets now, but hand grenades, shrapnel and thick heavy smoke. There was an awful symphony of sounds going on around him. Men screaming, gasping, groaning, shouting, crying. Men dying . . .

A Circle soldier lunged at him with a bayonet. Yaz shot him square in the heart. Another leveled his rifle at him. Yaz put three bullets into his head. A third enemy soldier was about to stab a trooper in front of him in the back. Yaz shot the man first on the ass, then in the groin and chest. A small explosion — probably a grenade — went off beside him, knocking him to his knees. He regained his footing just in time to shoot another enemy soldier who was drawing a bead on him.

He happened to look up to see one of the MiGs, its wings aflame, roar overhead, the F-16XL right on its tail, blasting away with all six Vulcan cannons. The Soviet jet hit the ground some 200 feet down the slope, cartwheeling into cherry blossom trees.

A few seconds later, the third and fourth waves broke through the barricades as did the second APC. Shane himself was manning the big .50-caliber machine gun on the vehicle's small turret and his stream of fire was cutting through enemy troops with wild abandon.

Just then Yaz saw a group of Circle soldiers moving away from the fighting around the Monument and toward the book tower. One of them was carrying a flamethrower . . .

Suddenly Captain Dozer himself was beside Yaz. He too had seen the squad of Circle troopers making their way to the tower of books.

"They're going to torch it!" Yaz yelled.

A second later, he and the Marine captain were

running after the enemy soldiers. The F-16 roared overhead, using its cannons to strafe a clump of Circle soldiers who were still holding the far end of the barricade. But Yaz knew that Hunter could not risk a shot at the soldiers he and Dozer were pursuing. One spark and the books would be gone in a matter of seconds. At the same time, the second MiG came crashing to the ground not 100 feet away. Hunter had riddled the Soviet airplane with his cannon, then had to literally shoot the plane away from the book tower as the pilot was making a kamikaze-like dive into the high stack of volumes.

Dozer stopped about 25 feet from the book tower and shot one of the Circle fire team dead. But it was too little, too late. The man carrying the flame thrower immediately lit it and started spraying the gasoline-soaked books with a stream of fire.

"Jesus Christ, they're burning it!" Yaz screamed.

Both he and Dozer opened up with their weapons, instantly cutting down the fire team. But the damage had been done: a long tongue of flame was quickly working its way up the side of the tower of books. The flamethrower strapped to the dead man's back then exploded, adding to the mounting conflagration.

Both he and Dozer were stunned, unable to move for the moment, watching the flames grow higher up the tall stack of books.

"No! We can't let this happen!" Yaz yelled out.

Dozer looked around desperately. Then he shouted: "We've got to knock it over!"

With that he was off and running back into the thick of the battle at the barricades. As Yaz watched, the Marine jumped up onto the nearest APC and quickly ordered the crew out. Then, jumping behind the controls himself, he gunned the engine and in a cough of smoke, was rumbling right toward the flaming section of the book tower.

"Jesus, he'll kill himself!" Yaz yelled out.

Then Yaz spotted three Circle soldiers, who, having seen Dozer's actions, were preparing to fire an anti-tank weapon at him. Yaz raised his rifle and fired, hitting two of the men just as they were firing the missile. His action distracted their aim enough so that the rocket hit the rear portion of the APC.

However it wasn't enough to stop Dozer. The vehicle roared right by Yaz and hit the bottom of the book tower full force. The impact managed to tip the book tower substantially.

"It worked!" Yaz yelled.

But before he could reach the crippled APC, it exploded, once, then twice, the force knocking Yaz right on his ass and dazing him.

When he finally looked up and his vision cleared, the book tower was still standing, though barely.

He also knew with one look at the burning APC, that Dozer was dead . . .

At the same instant, high above, something went off in Hunter's brain. He heard a scream tear through the fabric of his psyche. His body shuddered once, then was overtaken by a strange calmness.

He knew instantly what it meant: Something had just been lost. A spirit had passed on. A friend was dead . . .

He swooped low over the battle on Monument Hill and saw the teetering book tower and the blazing APC. He immediately pieced it together: Only one man would have dared to ram the tower. He knew Dozer was gone . . .

He could see the fighting around the Monument was now tapering off, the United Americans finally gaining the upper hand. But flames were still roaring up one side of the leaning pillar of books. That's when Hunter felt another sensation run through him.

More enemy airplanes, coming out of the south . . .

Just then his radio crackled on. "Hawk!" he heard Jones call out. "You're going to have more company . . . The big Soviet stuff is taking off now, along with a bunch of MiGs for cover . . ."

"OK, I copy," he radioed back. "The MiGs will probably head this way, while the bombers try to escape . . ."

"That's *exactly* what they're doing," Jones confirmed. "But listen, Hawk. We shot down one of the MiGs when it was taking off. It went up like a box of matches. I'd bet it's carrying napalm . . ."

That was just what Hunter *didn't* want to hear.

"If they're carrying 'palm, it's for one reason only," he called back to Jones. "They're going to finish off these books . . ."

"Our A-tens are only a minute away," Jones said. "We'll gut the runways so nothing will be able to land . . . But you'll still have to deal with the ones that are already up there . . ."

Hunter signed off just as the three-ship flight of MiGs appeared over the Capitol Building.

He felt a jolt of anger rip through him with an intensity that rivaled anything he'd experienced before. "You bastards!" he screamed. "My country. My friends. Is there no end to it!"

But he knew before he faced the MiGs he would have to deal with the burning book tower. Putting the F-16 down low, he swung out, then lined the pillar up in his HUD sighting cross. Then with a push of the throttle, he kicked in the airplane's afterburner . . .

Those on the ground were startled by the tremendous boom as the gallons of raw fuel were pumped

417

into the rear section of the Fulcrums engine. The aircraft shot across the sky like a bullet, heading straight for the smoking, flaming tower of books. Not a second before it would have hit the tower, the airplane lifted straight up—almost magically—its underbelly just nicking the very pinnacle of the stack.

The tower continued to teeter for a moment. But then the full rush of the sonic wave, combined with the incredible jet wash from the powerful afterburning engine, hit the tower of books like a giant mighty fist.

Suddenly the books looked as if they were caught up in a tornado. The intricate stacking pattern instantly came unraveled—books were suddenly flying everywhere, wildly scattering in the man-made maelstrom. What was left of the tower came crashing down. Most of the fire went out instantly, adding billions of sparks to the whirlwind. The three fire engines were on hand to extinguish any smoldering volumes.

Hunter turned toward the MiGs, not once letting up on his afterburner.

The lead Soviet airplane, its wings loaded down with the weight of four napalm bombs, was the first victim. After spotting the F-16XL, the enemy pilot tried to turn away, but it was too late. One of Hunter's two Sidewinders caught the mid-section of the Flogger as it attempted a bank to the right. The resulting explosion broke the airplane in two separate flaming pieces, both of which crashed to the ground near the West Potomac Park.

With this, the two other Floggers suddenly climbed in an effort to get away.

Hunter put the F-16XL into a gut-wrenching vertical translation, and tore straight up toward the fleeing Soviet jets. He leveled a quarter mile behind them and lit his afterburner a second time. Within seconds he was on their tails.

He had only one air-to-air remaining. With a flick of the wrist, he commanded the airplane into a yaw-axis maneuver, meaning while the F-16 continued in a straight line, its nose swung out at an angle. He let his last Sidewinder fly and watched as it was immediately sucked up into the Soviet's tailpipe.

He counted to three and suddenly the MIG was blown to smithereens by the powerful AIM-9 missile.

This left only one son-of-a-bitch to go . . .

The Soviet climbed and turned northeast hoping to put enough distance between himself and the crazy man in the strange American jet. But this was not his lucky day. Before he knew it, the red-white-and-blue jet was right behind him, and 100 yards below his tail. Suddenly its nose rose up, even though the airplane itself didn't. It was called pitch-axis pointing. But the Soviet pilot would never know that. Hunter squeezed off his Six Pack trigger and the powerful shells found their way into the two large napalm bombs the Soviet was carrying.

There was no explosion—at least, not right away. The Flogger evaporated with a loud sizzle and a cloud of green-yellow flame. *Then* came the tremendous explosion . . .

"That's for Bull . . ." Hunter said, steering the F-16XL through the burning MiG remnants and turning back toward Bolling.

CHAPTER 74

Night fell over the peaceful, yet smoky skies above Washington, DC.

The Free Canadian P-3 Orion maritime patrol plane arrived just after sunset, its flight delayed due to a detour around the stormy skies near Baltimore.

Twenty miles south of that city, the retreating Circle forces had collided head-on with the United American Army near the old Fort Meade and a full-scale battle had been in progress for the past 12 hours.

Back in DC, another event, similar in importance, was underway.

The game was in the fifth inning when the P-3 flew over the battered, but well-lit RFK stadium. The stands were filled to capacity — with the civilians who had survived Circle captivity and soldiers who had finally wrested control of the city from the enemy.

The two teams on the field were made up mostly of the former professional players rescued during the Cooperstown Raid who had been waiting back at Bolling. A number of Football City Rangers, a few of which were actually pro football players in the pre-war days, were also in the game.

It was this spectacle that the mercenary leader named Karl stared out at through the window of the P-3, his jaw open in disbelief. Beside him was Hunter's Free Canadian ally, Major Frost.

"They fight for the city during the day and play baseball the same night?" Karl said as the P-3 went into a slow orbit around the stadium.

"They *won* back their capital during the day," Frost corrected him. "This is how they celebrate . . ."

"Amazing . . ." Karl said quite candidly. "Simply amazing . . ."

The Orion then swung out and headed south, flying low over Bolling air base, now bustling with United American jet fighters and attack planes. A turn east brought it over National airport, where the five Ghost Rider B-1s had returned from a bombing raid against the retreating Circle Army. As the P-3 orbited the base, a flight of B-52s took off and headed northeast to continue pounding the remaining enemy troops.

After the Stratofortresses had launched, four F-20s came up to meet the P-3. They would serve as its escort for the ride back up to Newfoundland.

"It's incredible," Karl the mercenary muttered. "I heard nothing but bragging from the Russians, from the Circle about how they controlled this territory.

"Now, all I see are your troopers. In control. Playing games . . ."

"You are convinced, then?" Frost asked him.

Karl slowly nodded, as he looked out into the night only to see the heavily armed F-20s flying close by. The fact that all four were carrying Penguin Mk 3 anti-shipping missiles under their wings was not lost on the leader of the seaborne mercenaries.

"Somehow they have done it," Karl replied. "Your friends the Yanks have taken back their country. It will cost me money, but obviously I cannot proceed with our plan. It would be very bad for business . . ."

For the first time in what seemed like years, Frost relaxed. "I'm glad you see it that way," he said.

The airplane returned for one last circle around RFK Stadium just as one of the players for the Gold Team had hit a three-run homer. The crowd erupted in delight at the first round-tripper to be hit in the game.

High above, Karl the mercenary thought he could actually hear the cheering . . .

CHAPTER 75

It was a half hour before sunrise.

The sounds of the booming guns could be heard from the battle between the United American Army and The Circle that was still raging just ten miles away. Rumbling down the abandoned roadway just outside of Annapolis was the gold APC. Its crew was intent on crossing the Chesapeake Bay before first light. Then they would turn north, head into New Jersey and finally into the wilds of New York City.

The APC commander, a *Spetsnaz* major named Kruszilinski, knew that the no-law, no-order city was probably the only place left on the continent where the APC crew could hide from the United American Army, now that the entire Circle Army was collapsing. He would wait there for further orders from Moscow.

The sun was just peeking over the bay when the APC reached the shore town of Cape St. Claire. Here the mile-long, straight as an arrow four lane bridge over the bay began. Turning in his position atop the APC, Major Kruszilinski looked back to the west to see the dark sky still lighting up from the intense fighting outside Baltimore. The Circle was finished—he knew it, and everyone in his crew knew it. The United Americans had been pounding the remains of the once-great army all night with everything from heavy bombers to attack aircraft to massive ground-based artillery. Now the UA ground troops would soon assault The Circle positions and no doubt would overwhelm them. With that, the bizarre reign of The Circle in America would be over.

The Russian officer had to shake his head and laugh. So much for the highly-touted theory of Tactical Defense. It had lost the Circle four cities in less than two months. And the brainstorm to wage a war of iconoclasm had also gone bust. He had seen what happened in DC, just getting out in time. Instead of demoralizing the American citizens brought to the capital to witness the destruction of their culture, the strategy actually galvanized them. The passive sheep had suddenly turned into a raving pack of wolves and The Circle had paid the price, in men and material, not a small amount of which was owned by the Soviet Army.

Major Kruszilinski tipped his hat in grudging respect for the Americans. It was that crazy man who chose to risk his life flying over the city towing the American flag who had started it all. Once the fuse was lit, there had been no way to put it out.

But all that was ancient history now, as far as the Soviet officer was concerned. His priority was getting to New York City with the valuable case he'd been carrying around inside the APC since the retreat from Football City. Books and baseball bats may be important to the Americans, but they didn't amount to much compared to what he carried in the armored vehicle.

In his hands were the ultimate objects of American culture. He knew he might turn out to be the hero in this war after all . . .

The gold APC rolled onto the bay bridge just as the first rays of sunlight began to appear. They had adhered to their timetable. At this rate, Kruszilinski hoped they could reach the outskirts of New York by nightfall.

But suddenly he knew that was not going to happen . . .

A thick morning mist had enveloped the bridge and at first the Soviet officer welcomed the fog as cover for his escape. But now, up ahead on the straight, narrow bridge he saw first two red blinking lights, then a frighteningly familiar shape.

"Sir!" the APC driver yelled up to him in the turret. "Do you see it!"

"Yes, I do," Kruszilinski said. "Just don't stop, whatever you do . . ."

How the pilot had ever managed to land the strange, arrow-shaped, red-white-and-blue jet on the bridge the Russian would never know. But there it sat, blocking their way. Its nose cannons and God knows what else, armed and ready to fire. It was a showdown. Krusziliniski knew only one of them could survive.

The APC drew closer and the Soviet saw the pilot was standing straight up in the open cockpit, M-16 up and ready. Suddenly a stream of tracers came right toward him. The Russian ducked just in time to avoid the phosphorous shells bouncing off the turret.

"Keep going!" he screamed to his driver. But then he saw the pilot push something with the tip of his boot. Now just twenty yards away, the nose of the jet fighter suddenly erupted in a flash of fire and smoke. It was only a short burst—no more than a second and a half. But in that instant, the APC's driver and gunner were dead, and the front end of the vehicle blown off.

That left only Kruszilinski and the remaining gunner. It was obvious to the Soviet officer that the pilot—this legendary madman who was famous for flying the strange jet—was determined to stop them regardless of the damage it might cause to the contents of the sealed iron box just below the APC's control column. With this in mind, the officer and his gunner quickly abandoned the vehicle and jumped over the side of the bridge, plunging to the safety of the cold waters below.

Hunter didn't bother to shoot the two Russians as they swam away from the bridge.

There had already been enough killing—on both sides. The loss of Dozer was still imbedded in him. It was still hard to believe the man who had led his famous 7th Cavalry through the wild post-war days and established them as the premier democratic fighting force of the land was really gone.

The only small comfort Hunter could take was that the man died fighting for his country. A quote from somebody—maybe Emerson—came to him the night before and he just couldn't get it out of his head: *"Heroism feels and never reasons and therefore is always right . . ."*

"Good-bye Bull," he had already said a thousand times. "We won't forget . . ."

Hunter leaped up into the smoldering wreckage of the APC and climbed down inside. He found the strongbox easily enough—it had been the very key to locating the APC in the first place. After the battle in DC, and in between flying air strikes against The Circle that night, Hunter had been able to rewire the F-16's terrain search radar to pick up the faint, yet discernible signal being emitted by the laser lock on the APC and the strongbox itself. Like a beacon in the night, he had followed the signal to this area and had guessed correctly that the APC crew was trying to make it to New York. The bridge was their only route and Hunter had used his expertise to set the 'XL down on the narrow span.

Now at last he had secured the strongbox and the mystery of what The Circle and *Spetsnaz* thought was so precious was about to be revealed.

He hauled the box out of the vehicle and using a small pocket mirror, quickly disarmed the laser lock. Then he took a deep breath and opened it . . .

All at once he realized why his intuition told him—*ordered* him—not to shoot at the APC that night up on the Thruway. Had he done that, this precious American treasure that lay before him most likely would have been destroyed.

The pieces all fell into place now. The looting of the American culture had begun long before the battle for Football City. And this had been The Circle's major theft. He supposed they would have burned it sometime after all the books had been destroyed. Or perhaps they might have waited and shipped it to Moscow, for a more ceremonious burning there.

Whatever, it was in his hands now, and just like

the flag in his pocket, nothing short of death would allow him to give it up.

He lifted its case and fingered the slightly yellowed document.

"Where would we have been without this?" he wondered.

Then he began to read it, feeling an especially strong jolt of pride as he whispered the first three words:

"We, The People . . ."

EPILOGUE

The Wingman returned to Bolling later that day, carrying the strongbox with the document safely inside. He turned it over to Jones in exchange for a promise that it would be guarded around the clock from now on and forever. It was a fitting price to pay for the tenuous, but nevertheless real reunification of the country.

There was still much to be done. The United Americans held only a handful of key cities. The countryside was as wild and treacherous as ever, and nothing could be done about that for a long time. And Jones and the others knew that the defeat of the Circle Army would in no way deter the enemies of America in their goal of ultimately destroying the fabric of the country. In many respects they knew the biggest battles were yet to come.

After passing the strongbox to Jones, Hunter disappeared. Refueled the airplane and just took off, not telling a soul about where he was going or when he'd be back. Several hours later Jones had received a report from a radar station up in Syracuse that a strange-looking aircraft had been spotted high overhead, steering north, toward Canada, but Jones never could confirm that it was the F-16XL . . .

In the meantime, the revival of Washington DC had begun. The last of the Circle Army north of the city had been destroyed and only mopping up operations remained. Over the next few weeks, the United American troops, with the help of the civilians, worked day and night to restore some normalcy to the city. Everyone breathed easier when reports from the Free Canadian Air Force confirmed that the mercenary fleet had indeed turned back and was heading east toward Europe.

The biggest task facing those inside the city was cleaning up and saving all the objects the enemy had gathered in its efforts to destroy the artifacts of American culture. The bats and balls, and gloves and uniforms were all cleaned and separated and packed into boxes for shipment to the major cities where they would be dispersed to the population.

And for years to come, fathers would tell their children of Hunter and Dozer and Jones and the battle for Washington DC and explain why all the books left in the country smelled of gasoline.

THE WARLORD SERIES
by Jason Frost

THE WARLORD   (1189, $3.50)
A series of natural disasters, starting with an earthquake and
leading to nuclear power plant explosions, isolates California.
Now, cut off from any help, the survivors face a world in which
law is a memory and violence is the rule.

Only one man is fit to lead the people, a man raised among Indians and trained by the Marines. He is Erik Ravensmith, The Warlord—a deadly adversary and a hero for our times.

#3: BADLAND   (1437, $2.50)

#5: TERMINAL ISLAND   (1697, $2.50)

#6: KILLER'S KEEP   (2214, $2.50)

*Available wherever paperbacks are sold, or order direct from the
Publisher. Send cover price plus 50¢ per copy for mailing and
handling to Zebra Books, Dept. 2453, 475 Park Avenue South,
New York, N.Y. 10016. Residents of New York, New Jersey and
Pennsylvania must include sales tax. DO NOT SEND CASH.*